GIRLS I KNOW

GIRLS I KNOW

A NOVEL

Douglas Trevor

(six one seven) BOOKS

Boston, Massachusetts

ISBN: 978-0-9831505-3-4

GIRLS I KNOW

WALT STEADMAN

Outside the open window

The morning air is all awash with angels.

Richard Wilbur, "Love Calls Us to the Things of This World"

CHAPTER 1

As he did every morning, Walt Steadman stepped through the door of the Early Bird Café just before nine: a *Boston Globe* pinched under his arm, his black hair uncombed, his cheeks flushed from the cold. Walt loved arriving at the Early Bird, then chatting a little with Natalie Bittles—who, along with her husband, John, owned the café—and finally joking around with Flora Martinez, the restaurant's only waitress. And he loved having breakfast; it was the one meal he couldn't go without.

The Early Bird—with its tidy yellow awning and its distinct blue door—sat on the corner of Centre and Green Streets in Jamaica Plain. Walt lived on the other side of Boston, in the Back Bay, so he had to take two separate T lines, and walk a fair bit as well, just to make it over here. But the commute and all the walking were worth it to him, even in the dead of winter, which it was then: January of 2001. Walt had trudged through blizzards and rainstorms and combinations of the two for years, just to have breakfast at the Early Bird. His daily routine mattered to him; it added rhythm and logic to a life that might otherwise have seemed a little mundane and a little illogical. Having breakfast at his favorite restaurant was the lynchpin of this routine. Without it, nothing else fell into place.

Walt felt possessive of the Early Bird too. Over the years, he had never brought anyone here. He had never recommended the café either. This was all a little odd because Walt Steadman was otherwise a generous, non-possessive person. He would loan a book to anyone who asked. He had let distant acquaintances sleep on his floor dozens of times: guys who, like him, had moved down from Vermont and were looking for some way to make a life in Boston work. And his relationships with women had usually been open ones, not because he was interested in sleeping around—he had been, for a time, but that time had passed—but just because exclusive relationships seemed stifling and he didn't see any point in being stifled.

Although he had fallen out of touch with a lot of people, Walt still considered himself an attentive friend. If someone he cared about was sick, he'd check in on him, maybe even bring along some soup. But he was also inattentive. He forgot birthdays, the names of friends' girlfriends, where so-and-so had gone to college, what exactly his old roommate from his days in Porter Square did (something having to do with science, he remembered that much). If he found himself in a political conversation, Walt would always nod his head furiously in agreement with whichever person seemed the most outraged and indignant. But he had never registered to vote. He had never filed a tax return. Walt saw himself as a moral person, but he liked being able to wiggle out of entanglements and he thought that telling small lies to facilitate such wiggling was just fine. For him, one way of measuring happiness was to ask himself just how quickly he thought he could leave his apartment for good in the event of needing to evacuate Boston, say because the Pilgrim Station Reactor out in Plymouth was melting down, or because a meteor was hurtling toward the city. Walt thought it would take him about two minutes to grab his favorite books and his absolute best music. Two minutes, in his mind—that was pretty good.

Every once in a while, one of Walt's friends would offer an explanation as to why he was so attached to the Early Bird. It was always the same explanation. For Walt, who grew up in Burlington, in a small family, in a tiny, barely middle-class household, the Early Bird must have functioned as his home away from home. But Walt wasn't convinced by this logic. After all, Natalie was nothing like his mother. She wasn't afflicted with multiple sclerosis; she wasn't confined to a wheelchair. He didn't know if John was anything like his father because Walt had never known his father. He supposed Flora should feel a little like a younger sister but she didn't, maybe because Walt didn't have any siblings and therefore had no clue what having a little sister was supposed to feel like. He didn't have any cousins or aunts or uncles. His grandparents had more or less raised him, but his grandfather had died four years ago. It didn't seem fair to call his friends at the Early Bird family. *Family,* in Walt's mind, was more of a burden than anything, and the Early Bird didn't feel like a burden at all. If anything, he assumed that he liked the café as much as he did precisely because it *didn't* feel like a home away from home. He didn't know for sure, and he didn't care to overanalyze it. He just knew that he loved being at the Early Bird, and living in Boston. He loved his life, and growing up, he hadn't had a whole lot to get excited about, so he didn't take his happiness for granted.

He was twenty-nine years old.

Later, months after the shootings at the Early Bird Café, Walt would forget what it had felt like to scurry over to Jamaica Plain every morning. He would forget just how carefree and entertaining those times in the restaurant had been. Instead, his recollections would center on the restaurant itself: its physical space, which felt cramped in hindsight, and the single door in front that led out to the street, which made it so easy to trap people in the back. In every image that his brain conjured, in his daydreams and nightmares, a horrible sense of foreboding always lingered. And Walt realized quite soon after the shootings that he hadn't just lost the café, but his memories of the café as well. When a memory was filtered through trauma, it was no longer just a memory. And that hardly seemed fair. That seemed to constitute a larger act of evil for which no one person, no single gunman, could be held responsible.

But that morning, six days before the shootings, Walt felt no sense of foreboding whatsoever; he just registered the sound of the string of bells clanging against the inside of the door as he stepped inside.

"Walter!"

"Hey, Natalie."

The heavyset black woman who had been seated behind the cash register, reading the *Boston Herald*, rose slowly to her feet, walked around the counter, and embraced him. Natalie Bittles embraced everyone who came into the restaurant, unless they made it clear they didn't want to be touched. But curiously, in a city with a reputation for coldness, very few people stepped back from Natalie when she opened her arms.

"How are you this morning?"

"I'm good. You?"

"Wonderful." She pointed at his newspaper. "You going to find a job today?"

"I'm going to look over my options." Walt grinned and Natalie rested her right hand on her bad hip, which locked up on her all the time. Whenever she laughed, which was at the end of nearly every sentence she spoke, Natalie's head would roll back on her neck, onto the soft bed of her gray dreadlocks, and her mouth would open, but no sound would come out.

"How long have you been going through those employment listings now?"

"About two years." Natalie laughed some more while Walt waved his hand at her. "No, it's not what you think it is. It isn't that I don't want to work more than I do now. It's that every job in Boston appeals to me on some level."

Walt loved imagining himself in different occupations in the city: in scuba gear, feeding the fish in the main tank at the aquarium on Central Wharf (well, who wouldn't love that job?), in a suit behind a desk up in the John Hancock Tower, looking out over the city, doing some kind of complicated, highly lucrative task (he was a little fuzzy on the details for this one), being some kind of consultant for the Red Sox (again, a little fuzzy, but the job would have required him to sit in a box at Fenway Park for every home game). Whenever he daydreamed, the setting was always Boston, but Walt was always cast alone.

If he had felt a pressing need to change his life, Walt would have begun applying for real jobs by now, but he actually thought he had a pretty good setup. He worked as a superintendent, which gave him a free apartment right in the heart of Boston. In the afternoons, he sat behind the counter at Floyd's Cleaners, four blocks down Beacon Street from the building he managed. And every other week, he masturbated into a cup at the Brighton Cryobank for Oncologic and Reproductive Donors. Working at Floyd's was an easy job that paid very little but permitted Walt plenty of opportunity to read poems and chat with people, both of which he loved to do. Providing sperm at the cryobank was hardly a glamorous gig, but considering it was masturbation, Walt felt pretty well compensated for his labor. Working as a superintendent meant, more than anything, hanging around the building, which came naturally to Walt since—after all—he lived there. It also meant occasionally hiding from a tenant or two, which Walt could—and often did—do in his sleep. Because his expenses were so low—he didn't own a car or a cell phone, didn't have to pay for his utilities, and had defaulted on his student loans ages ago—Walt had figured out a way to live somewhat comfortably in a city that so many people complained was too expensive.

"Menu?" Natalie asked him.

"That's all right. How you doing over there?" Walt waved at Natalie's daughter, Mercedes, who was sitting at the table behind the register, drawing in a sketchbook. She was a big girl, with broad shoulders and a full, round face, around which her hair hung in thick, neat braids.

Mercedes looked up at him, her eyes big, brown, and unblinking. "I'm fine."

"You're fine, *thank you*," Natalie added.

"I'm fine, *thank you*," Mercedes repeated, rolling her eyes before she returned to her drawing.

Natalie and Walt watched her draw. "What grade are you in now?" he asked. He knew she was eleven but he had forgotten if that meant fourth or fifth grade.

Mercedes held up her hand with all the fingers spread apart.

"Fifth grade," her mother said. "And it's going to be fifth grade again next year, unless she starts getting her work done." She directed that sentence toward her daughter, who mouthed the last few words herself, her head rocking in imitation of her mother's.

"What subjects do you like?" Walt bent over so that if Mercedes raised her head she wouldn't have to look up to make eye contact with him. But she didn't raise her head. Walt was tall, about six-two, with dark, full black hair, jagged cheeks, and eyes set far back in his head. He had broad shoulders and a narrow waist. His body was lean from all the walking he did. He had a sense, just by virtue of the way girls in the Back Bay sometimes glanced at him and then glanced back, that he was still fairly attractive. In college he had known he was good-looking because girls had told him so. College was great. Now, though, it was harder to know for sure. Even with such uncertainty, Walt didn't attend to his appearance. He never had. He didn't own a comb. He didn't have *outfits*. He didn't have many nice clothes—one decent white Oxford shirt, one pair of presentable khakis. Today he wore what was more or less his customary uniform: a pair of jeans, and one of the sweaters his grandmother had knitted him for Christmas, this one a black cardigan with brown buttons, beneath which he had on a white tee shirt. Walt's grandmother had been knitting him sweaters for Christmas his entire life; he had, or so it seemed to him, an endless supply. Shoes, on the other hand, were a different matter. He owned two pairs: tennis shoes, which he never wore, and a battered pair of brown Doc Martens that he assumed would one day disintegrate on his feet.

Mercedes lifted her pencil, looked at what she had done, then added some shading. "I like art and math."

"Do you like English?" Walt stepped toward her and peeked over the top of her sketchbook. Mercedes pulled her drawing back and looked up at him, her lips forming a straight line between her large cheeks.

"He means reading and writing," Natalie said, and her daughter shook her head. "She doesn't like to read," her mother explained.

"That's probably because they've got you reading the wrong stuff. You should be reading poems. I still do, every day. When it's slow at work, I read poems. And I read poems at night, otherwise I can't fall asleep. That's the mistake they make in elementary school. Too much prose, not enough poetry." Walt didn't know anything about elementary school curricula, he was just quoting his grandmother's opinions on the subject. Mrs. Steadman had taught high school English for more than thirty-five years. She knew a thing or two about what students should know.

He waited for Mercedes to respond but she didn't. She just worked on her drawing. Natalie shook her head at Walt as she began to move slowly through the restaurant. He followed her.

The Early Bird Café was just one long, rectangular room with narrow tables on both sides and a hallway in back that led to the bathrooms and kitchen. On the walls, which were painted light yellow, were framed black-and-white photographs, all shot around Jamaica Pond over the years. They showed people, young and old, walking and playing and sitting around the pond. Natalie had taken all of them.

"You don't pay that girl any mind," Natalie said to him. "She's got to learn some manners."

Walt liked to think that, when he tried, he could connect with just about anyone in Boston, so Mercedes's aloofness had always irritated him a little. But he would have never implied as much to her mother. "She's just figuring things out," he said instead.

"She thinks she's already figured everything out. She's got a real stubborn streak. And she's fiery too. She could squash the boys in her class like bugs, my girl: a full head taller than every one of them. But what she doesn't want to do she just doesn't do."

They had arrived at Walt's favorite table, nestled all the way in the back in the left corner. Natalie pulled the table back so Walt could slip in. He draped his faded Patagonia jacket over the chair against the wall and motioned across the table.

"Sit down."

"No, Walter, I got a restaurant to run."

"Come on . . ."

She looked back over her shoulder at the empty café, leaned hard against the table—to take the weight off her hip—and then let herself fall back into one of the Early Bird's wooden chairs. She landed with a thud.

"Speaking of jobs, I think I should work here." He wasn't entirely kidding.

"What would you do?"

He gave this some thought. "I could do what you do. I'd host. I'm personable. I put people at ease."

"You think all I do is put people at ease? I order all the food, all the supplies. I do our taxes. I'm going to have to deal with Ramon. He didn't show up for work today. The second time in a week. That boy is driving us crazy."

Ramon was their short-order cook: a thin, wiry Hispanic kid with a wispy moustache and cheeks divoted by acne. He had only been working at the Early Bird for a little over a month and Walt had never had a conversation with him. He had tried, but Ramon had never responded to any of his questions. He had just looked through him: his face blank, his eyes staring ahead.

"All the more reason why you shouldn't be the hostess." Walt pictured himself standing at the door, chatting with customers the way he did with the tenants in his building. One of the reasons Walt liked being a superintendent was because it was so amusing, acting as if he cared about maintaining the building when in all honesty he didn't care a bit. But if he worked at the Early Bird, since he really *did* care about the restaurant, it stood to reason he'd do a pretty good job.

"How about this? If I end up needing a hip replacement, I'll interview you to replace me."

"I like that, but if you don't hire me, I'll still come here every morning, just to make you uncomfortable."

"It would take more than that to make me uncomfortable." She pitched her weight toward the front of the chair, preparing to rise, but Walt stopped her from leaving by placing his hands on hers. He loved getting her to talk about growing up in Port-au-Prince, about her grandmother, a Voodoo priestess, about how she saw America. He loved trying to see the world from her perspective.

"Tell me more about Voodoo."

"What do you want to know?"

Walt shrugged. "I don't know. What's the Voodoo conception of God like?"

She laughed. "We've been over this before, Walter. We don't *conceive* of God in Voodoo. We don't count him, like a . . . like a saltshaker." She pointed at the table. Natalie's French Caribbean accent swelled up behind every sentence her mouth formed, but when she used a word like *saltshaker* she was no longer quite speaking English anymore; then her voice sounded unmoored and would rush ahead for a second. "You are hungry for the spiritual, Walter. I believe that is why you are always trying to get me to talk about the Voodoo."

There was some truth to that. Walt's favorite poets summoned

God all the time; they spoke of divinity and resurrections and angels. His knowledge of religion was largely limited to their metaphors and descriptions. Regular church attendance was one thing his grandparents hadn't insisted upon after his mother became seriously ill; it was their one concession to the peculiar predicament he faced as a young boy. So Walt had grown up with the shadowy presence of religious belief all around him, but hardly any direct conversation about God.

The bells on the door sounded. Natalie looked over her shoulder again. Two women had walked in, also regulars like Walt. She waved them over to their favorite table, halfway back on the right, and they went about seating themselves.

"Where's Flora?" Walt asked.

"She's helping John in the kitchen." Natalie rose to her feet and began to head toward the front of the restaurant, but then thought of something and turned back around, her dreadlocks swinging limply behind her. She placed her hands on the back of chair on which she had just been sitting and leaned toward him. "Walter, you need to look after her for me. I worry about her."

"Why do you worry about Flora?"

"Because I think Ramon likes her."

"Really?"

She shut her eyes in order to simulate a nod.

Ramon pursuing Flora, that wouldn't do. He was a surly kid, and Flora was so sweet. Walt looked down at the table. He noticed a small brown spot on his left hand: much too big to be a freckle. Was it a liver spot? Was he actually beginning to get liver spots?

"What should I do about it?" he asked her.

The bells on the front door rang again. A woman had walked in with two children following behind her. "I don't know, Walter! You're a man, for goodness sakes! You figure it out." Natalie backed away from him, instinctively stepping around tables and chairs. "Remember, Agwe Tawoyo is watching, waiting. You can't let the days go by; we have very little time in this world."

Of course she was right; Walt knew that. The whole *carpe diem* thing. But why was she telling him not to waste time? Did Natalie think it was frivolous of him to spend every morning in her café? That hardly seemed fair. He was a paying customer, although Flora gave him a little break on his bill once or twice a week. Still, it wasn't like he didn't have a job; he had several. Granted they weren't high intensity forms of employment, but they counted. He was self-sufficient.

"Go get Flora for me, Walter. Tell her I need her out here."

And with that she turned around and returned to the counter at the front of the café. Walt quickly slid out from behind his table. As he walked across the width of the restaurant, he glanced at the black-and-white photographs that hung at eye level. One showed a boy standing next to a tricycle, another just the outlines of a couple with their backs to the camera, sitting on a bench, looking out over the Jamaica Pond as the sun set. Agwe Tawoyo was the spirit of the sea. He loomed large in Natalie Bittles's version of Voodoo because, as Walt had heard many times, he had swallowed her younger sister and both her brothers just south of Islamorada, Florida, when—many years before—the overcrowded boat on which they were all trying to journey to America capsized. To the casual eye, the photographs around the Early Bird Café seemed to focus on figures, but in every one of them the water of the Jamaica Pond could be glimpsed. This was out of deference on Natalie's part to Agwe's powers. In her mind, the Jamaica Pond was a gathering place for the dead. It was one of Agwe's special habitations.

Walt headed down the small hallway in back that led to the bathrooms and poked his head through the swinging door on his left. John Bittles was standing in front of a large griddle, using a spatula to fold over the sides of an omelet. Flora stood next to him, peeling a potato. She had a small mole above her lip and shoulder-length black hair that she wore curled, with the ringlets resting just below her ears. As always, she had a yellow ribbon in her hair.

"You're needed out front, Flora," Walt said. "Some people would actually like to see a waitress."

"Oh, listen to you!" Flora shouted over the hiss of grease. "I bet some people in your building would like to see a superintendent!"

John looked over his shoulder and grinned at Walt. He was a slender, tall black man with the top of his head shaved smooth and a beard peppered with gray. Beneath his white apron, which was splattered with egg yolks, he wore jeans and a black tee shirt. "Why does anyone need to see him?" he asked Flora. "He can't fix their problems himself."

Flora knocked John with her elbow. "That's true. When their toilets break, Mr. Walt has to call a man, someone with a real job, to take care of it. Then he doesn't pay any rent because he can call a plumber. How do you like that?"

John pointed at Flora's hands. "You're peeling away the whole potato." He stepped back from the enormous griddle, turning to Walt. "You ever met a Puerto Rican girl who cooks this bad?"

"I'm a good cook!" Flora knocked John with her hip. She was just a little over five feet and John was well over six, so—standing next to one another—they made a funny pair.

"Well, you're a bad peeler, that's for sure." John stepped forward to flip the omelet bubbling in front of him, his wrist tensing but the rest of his arm staying still. "Wait a second. I bet Flora's the only Puerto Rican girl you know, Walt. You don't get the Latinas up in Vermont, isn't that right?" John chuckled, his voice raspy and soft. Just saying the word *Vermont* always seemed to crack him up.

"I haven't lived in Vermont in a long time," Walt replied.

"Oh, but you carry the neighborhood you grew up in with you forever. You don't ever leave where you're from."

Walt's entire life was predicated on the opposite assumption: that by force of will, you could leave your hometown far, far behind, but he wasn't about to try to convince John of this. "Who's the omelet for?" he asked instead.

"It's my breakfast." John pulled out a plate from the shelf above the oven and flipped the eggs onto it. Then he walked over to the industrial-sized refrigerator in the corner and began to root around for some salsa.

"Look at him." Flora pointed at Walt as she followed behind her boss, the gored remains of a potato held in her hand. "He's already trying to get free food."

"Keep it up, Flora. You're just saving me money. I was actually going to give you a big tip today."

"Oh, I've heard that before, Mr. Walt. Now get out of here."

Walt rolled his eyes at John, who was laughing at him along with Flora, and let the door swing shut.

He returned to his table and sat back down. His eyes were drawn to the front door of the restaurant: the sunlight pouring through its glass, illuminating the dust in the air. Then the clouds shifted and it was overcast again. The wind suddenly gusted. Outside, a bike chained loosely to a stop sign fell over, onto the sidewalk. The weather was beginning to change. By the end of the day, it would be either raining or snowing, maybe both. He opened his *Globe* and began to peruse the job listings.

Flora walked out from the kitchen a moment later, a pot of coffee held in her hand. She passed Walt and walked all the way to the front of the restaurant. A couple had sat down in front and she wiped down their table and filled their blue coffee mugs. All the mugs in the café were blue; they matched the color of the front door. Walt watched Flora scribble down orders in the small spiral notebook she carried in her apron, one table after the other. Then she headed back toward the kitchen. As she approached him, Walt turned over his mug so that she could fill it.

"No coffee for you," Flora said. "Not until you find a real job."

Walt pushed the paper away. "You know, what I really want is to be the mayor of Boston."

She lifted the spout of the pot up just before the coffee spilled onto the table. "Why don't you run? Campaigning would be a normal day for you—going around the city, annoying people."

"Yeah, I'd like that stuff, but I imagine you have to file to be a candidate and paperwork has never been my strong suit."

She squinted at him; he had lost her there at the end. "The thing is, no one loves Boston more than I do. That'd be my platform. I love the T. I love the Back Bay. I love Jamaica Plain."

"You love the nice parts, like everyone. You should come to Mattapan some day, where I live. No one loves Mattapan."

"I'd make the whole city nice. That'd be my pledge as a candidate."

"How would you do that?"

"Well, I'd have to work the details out . . ."

"Well, those are a lot of details, Mr. Walt. Sorry, I think I might have to vote for someone else." Flora disappeared into the kitchen.

Walt knew how juvenile he sounded when he talked about his love of Boston. He knew that the more he extolled the city's virtues, the more he marked himself as an interloper. He knew, even, that the boyish nature of his enthusiasm was to a degree compensatory for the fact that he was feeling older and older in a city that was populated by, sometimes it seemed exclusively, college-age kids. But he couldn't help himself. He *was* an interloper, after all, and he loved—after having grown up in the less fashionable part of New England—living where he did.

When Flora returned, she refilled the mugs in the restaurant and took another order, this from a man Natalie had seated while the two of them had been chatting. After Flora dropped off his order, she stopped once more at Walt's table. He had begun to read the sports page.

"Why do you all read about the Red Sox in the middle of the winter? They play in the summer!"

Walt took a sip of his coffee. "But this is the hot stove season. This is when they make trades and sign free agents."

She shook her head, her curls bouncing on her shoulders. "Why would you want to read about a player on the team before he's played? I don't understand."

"If there's an article about the Red Sox in the paper, I'm required as a male New Englander to read it."

"That's the dumbest thing I've ever heard." She withdrew her notebook and took out her pen. "Now stop babbling and order something for breakfast."

Walt opted for an omelet with green peppers and mushrooms and a bowl of granola and yogurt. Flora jotted down his order before disappearing once more into the kitchen. For the next few minutes, while John made his breakfast, he read the sports and local sections of the paper. Walt never read the national wire stories. Instead, he read about the potential Red Sox lineup for that upcoming season, about a certain pothole in Roxbury that was deep enough to snap the axle on someone's car, about a grocer in Everett who was closing his doors

after twenty-eight years because he couldn't compete with the Bread
& Circus around the corner. Just as Flora reappeared with his food, he
learned that someone's sheepdog in Marblehead had turned eighteen.

He ate quickly. John was a great cook, and his omelets were
particularly good: always cooked through but never dry. While Walt
chewed his omelet and sipped his coffee, he looked out across the café.
Customers were seated at nearly every table, so Natalie had begun
to help Flora take orders and fill coffee mugs. Flora Martinez hadn't
always been the only waitress employed at the Early Bird. When they
hired her in June of 1999, John and Natalie already had another girl
working for them, but she quit a short time after Flora started and
Natalie decided not to replace her. The Early Bird was only open
through lunch anyway, Natalie had explained to Walt at the time,
and she wanted to keep their overhead low since the economy was
slowing down. Yes, she was a mystic, but Natalie Bittles knew how to
run a business.

As busy as the café had become, Walt knew that no one would
have the time to chat with him now, so when Flora swung by to pick
up his dishes, he asked for his check and she dropped it onto his table.
Flora hadn't charged him for the omelet; he only owed three-fifty. He
left a ten, grabbed his jacket and newspaper, and walked around the
table as she approached him. She stuck his money, along with the bill,
in her apron.

"Change?"

"No, keep it."

"Thanks." She smiled at him.

"Thank you. Hey, what's going on with Ramon?"

She rolled her eyes. "The boys in my neighborhood are *loco*."

Before moving out to Mattapan, Flora and Ramon had both grown
up in Jamaica Plain back when it was a Hispanic neighborhood, but
those days were gone. Like so many families, they had been priced
out and forced to move farther out of town.

She adjusted the yellow ribbon in her hair. "When my *abuela* asked
me to see if Natalie and John would hire him, Ramon didn't even
know how to cook. Not even toast! But my *abuela* wanted to help him,
because she's friends with his *abuela* and his *abuela* was worried that

her grandson was hanging out with the wrong kind of boys. Natalie didn't want to give him a job but John said yes. He was just trying to do me a favor." Walt tilted his head in confusion and Flora added, "Ramon's *grandmother* is friends with my *grandmother*."

"Got it. Sounds like too many *abuelas*."

"You're not kidding."

The two of them walked slowly toward the front of the restaurant. "I have an idea, Flora. Why don't you ask Natalie for the rest of the morning off? I'll take you over to the Museum of Fine Arts. Do you know John Singer Sargent? They've got that painting of his, 'The Daughters of . . .' something. Anyway, it's cool. We could look at it together."

He smiled at her and she rolled her eyes again. "Please tell me you don't walk around town grinning like you do here, Mr. Walt. Because if you do, some day someone is going to hit you in the head."

"I'm cagier than you think, Flora."

"You're what?"

"Tougher."

She laughed. "Oh, Mr. Walt. You are *not* tough. Good-looking, *maybe* on your best days, but not tough. And you're lucky too."

Walt knew that he was lucky, at least in one sense, but he wasn't sure what sense Flora had in mind. "What do you mean? I'm lucky because I live in Boston?"

She shook her head. "You're lucky because you don't have to be tough, not in your little world."

And now he was the one rolling his eyes. "My little world? We live in the same city, Flora." By which he didn't mean that the Back Bay and Mattapan were one and the same. He just meant they shared something together, some common experience.

"No we don't, Mr. Walt. You go to the museum yourself, I need to work; I need my tips."

They came to a stop at the cash register. Natalie was momentarily back behind the counter, ringing up a bill.

"Goodbye, Walt." Flora touched his elbow gently with her hand.

He looked down at her fondly. "Goodbye, Flora."

She turned and went back to work while Walt looked at Natalie and shrugged. "I asked her to take the morning off. She said no—she needs the money."

"I told you to look after her, not give her the day off!"

"I was freelancing."

"Well, you tried once, but try some more."

Walt handed her his *Boston Globe* so that she could give it to another customer. Natalie glanced down at its creased pages, her eyebrows wrinkling, her head shaking. "I've never understood, Walter. You went to Harvard, but you work at a dry cleaners. Why don't you use your degree?"

"Ah, see, that's your mistake. I don't have a degree from Harvard. Well, I have a master's, but they just give that to you if you pass your generals exam. I don't have a PhD. That's what I was supposed to get."

"Then why didn't you get it?"

Walt zipped up his jacket. He wasn't cold yet; it was a gesture of self-insulation.

"I was studying American poetry; you can't get a job on the basis of having studied American poetry. Well, you can become a professor if you have a doctorate, but in order to get a doctorate you have to write a dissertation, and I couldn't manage that." He noticed Mercedes sitting behind her mother, staring at him. "Still, I know a lot about poems." As if to prove his point, he nodded at the young girl. "Hey, maybe the next time you come to work with your mom, we can read a poem together. Wouldn't that be cool?"

Her big eyes just looked at him, unblinking.

Natalie stepped around the counter. "You don't pay her any mind, Walter." Once more she embraced him. "Have a great day," she said.

"You too."

"Try again with Flora tomorrow. You could really help her, I think."

"Do you?"

"Of course. She thinks the world of you. I don't know why, but she does."

They both laughed over that one, Walt audibly, Natalie without making a noise. Then he opened the door and stepped outside, into the cold. The Early Bird Café made Walt feel connected to Boston. That was the real reason he began every day by coming here. Otherwise, Flora was right; his world was a little one. But, in his defense, that was at least partly by design. Walt Steadman wanted to keep his world small because, by so doing, he thought it improved his chances of being able to stay in Boston. That was really all he wanted. He wanted to live in Boston, make enough money to get by, read his favorite poems on a regular basis, and have breakfast each morning at the Early Bird Café.

CHAPTER 2

When Walt was six, his mother began to act a little strangely. First he noticed his grandparents noticing. Then little things began to catch his attention, although he dismissed them with the nonchalance of a child. So his mother's right eye had begun to flicker regularly, like a candle. But that was fine because it didn't seem to bother her. And then he saw her left hand on the arm of the couch one night, shaking like a branch in the wind. Well, that was weird, but so what?

One morning, while he was eating breakfast with his grandparents and his mother was in the bathroom, brushing her teeth, she collapsed. Even now, twenty-three years later, he could hear the sound of her body crashing against the sink, then falling back onto the floor. He could see the look in his grandmother's face: shock and fear. His grandfather swooped up his daughter and the three of them drove her to Fletcher Allen Hospital, where she underwent a battery of tests that went on for days. Walt assumed that the tests were going to make his mom feel better. He went to school that week as he always did. But that Friday afternoon, when he stepped out of the playground and saw his grandfather standing across the street, waiting to walk home with him, he knew that his mother hadn't gotten better: that something was wrong, and his grandfather had come to tell him what it was.

The walk from Walt's elementary school to their home in South Burlington took about fifteen minutes. They passed several groves of trees, since swallowed up by housing developments, and a bunch of modest homes just like theirs: single-story, aluminum-sided residences with big American sedans parked in their driveways. As they walked, Mr. Steadman held his grandson's hand. He asked Walt if he had ever heard of something called multiple sclerosis. Walt hadn't.

His grandfather explained that it was a disease that made the cells in someone's brain and spinal cord have a hard time talking to each other. "When they can't talk," Andrew Steadman added, "then your body has a hard time working right. And it seems . . ." And here he choked up, which was so unlike him that Walt looked up into his face with outright fear. His grandfather kept everything on an even keel at home. He had served in World War Two and sometimes at night he would tell Walt stories about the battles he had been in. In every account, when Walt asked if he had ever been afraid, his grandfather always answered yes, which confused him. "Then how did you make it through, if you were scared?" Walt would ask. And his grandfather would lean toward him, as if he were sharing a secret. "You'd be amazed, Walter, at what you can accomplish when you're scared. The thing is, you can't be afraid of being afraid, because everyone is afraid at one time or another. You have to remind yourself that it's okay to be scared of stuff, so that when you are frightened, you don't freeze up. There's no shame in being afraid, remember that."

That day, Andrew Steadman looked scared. He started over again. "And it seems that there are two kinds of multiple sclerosis. One is called relapsing-remitting multiple sclerosis. The other is called progressive multiple sclerosis. The doctors think your mom might have the second kind. That means, over time, she might have a hard time, using her body and even her brain. But we'll help her, won't we?" And Walt remembered nodding his head vigorously and his grandfather patting him on the back. "Of course we will. We'll help her, and we'll help each other as well."

Months went by. Marion Steadman was on medication. She was seeing a specialist. Her eye still fluttered, but her hand didn't seem to shake as much. Everything went more or less back to normal, except Walt's mom had to reduce her hours at the Fletcher Free Library, where she worked as a librarian. Then, one Saturday, they were getting ready to go have a picnic on Grand Isle and Marion Steadman called for her mother from her bedroom. She had lain down to rest and couldn't get up. They called an ambulance. The following week, the doctors changed their diagnosis; Marion had relapsing-remitting MS, marked by pronounced attacks that left permanent neurological damage. Less than a year later, after another attack, she no longer had the use of her legs.

Walt didn't remember having a direct response to his mother's illness. Instead, he remembered his reaction when his grandfather built a ramp up to the front door of their house in order to accommodate his mom's wheelchair. Walt sat in the window and watched him work, refusing to help him set the posts or nail down the boards. "The ramp is so ugly," he remembered complaining to his grandmother. "No one else has one. It isn't fair." About this time, late one afternoon, Jason Rutovski called him over from across the street. Jason was a delinquent and a bully. His clothes were two sizes too small and he always had bruises up and down his arms from his dad, who beat him sometimes with a belt in their driveway. Jason was just a year older than Walt but he towered over him. Once Walt had made his way over to his weedy yard, Jason glared down at him, his nose wrinkled in disgust, as if the whole Steadman home had begun to give off some kind of odor. "Is your mom, is she—like—retarded now?" he asked Walt. Walt didn't know if having MS and being retarded was the same thing, he feared it might be, so in response he tried to punch Jason in the face, which was a big mistake. He got the crap beaten out of him.

From then on, just as his grandfather had said would happen, the three of them cared for his mother together. They helped get her dressed in the morning. They stretched her limbs in the afternoon. They bathed her at night. And slowly, as the years went by and the light seemed to go out in Marion's eyes, they discussed her condition less and less. There was no getting better with MS. The doctors had all told them that, but it took a few years for the harsh truth of the statement to sink in. And as Marion got worse, the Steadman financial situation also declined. Eleanor retired from teaching to care for her daughter, so they were living on one high school teacher's salary instead of two. Their medical bills, what Medicaid didn't cover, were extraordinary. They had to buy a van to accommodate Marion's wheelchair. Before they had watched their spending like everyone else did in their neighborhood. Now, Walt began to sense, they were distinctly frugal. As a young boy, not having a father had struck Walt as unfair and cruel at moments, but at those moments he had always reminded himself that he had his grandfather. Now that their lack of money was palpable, Walt thought more and more about his unknown dad, but in a different way from before. What they needed more than anything was to have another breadwinner around. They needed more help than they had.

To save money, Walt lived at home the first two years that he was a student at the University of Vermont. He majored in English. His selection of a major seemed less like a choice than just a natural outgrowth of his home life, where—every evening—Walt's grandmother read poems to his mother in the living room while Walt and his grandfather played checkers or Yahtzee at the kitchen table. As a boy, he never saw himself as someone who loved verse. Instead, he saw himself as a kid with a horrible TV situation: an old set with temperamental rabbit ears that only picked up the local ABC affiliate and PBS. He read because he had no other entertainment options, and he read a lot of poems because books of poetry were everywhere in the house, especially the poetry of Robert Frost. Frost was his grandmother's favorite writer.

All through high school, Walt had been reminded again and again of just how different his family situation was from those of his friends: not just that he had a sick mom and a missing dad and that he lived with his grandparents, but that his grandfather taught at South Burlington High, where he himself was a student. It wasn't until he went to college that Walt began to realize that his fondness—what he was more likely to call at that time his *comfort*—with poetry wasn't the only thing that he had acquired from his unusual upbringing. As a kid, he had grown up listening to his grandfather's jazz records. At parties, he knew when a Nirvana song was playing but he didn't listen to Nirvana himself; he listened to Miles Davis. So he knew a lot about jazz. And he knew how to care for someone with MS, how to maneuver a body whose muscles had atrophied. At the same time, he didn't know how to ski or play tennis. When his junior-year roommates complained about the road trips they had been forced to take with their parents, driving to Yellowstone, to Orlando, to the Grand Canyon, Walt remained silent in his bunk bed. The farthest the Steadmans had ventured from Burlington was Willsboro Bay, on the other side of Lake Champlain.

Through his childhood and early adulthood, through all the efforts he and his grandparents made to help Marion Steadman make it through her life, Walt came away believing that there wasn't much one person could do for another person to change that person's life. Granted, you could try, you could make gestures, but they were just that in the end—gestures. Of course Walt couldn't be sure, but he always suspected that his mother's condition had made him more self-involved than he might otherwise have been and a lot more fatalistic, even if his fatalism was hidden beneath a veneer of cheerfulness.

Halfway through his senior year in college, Walt decided to apply to PhD programs in English. He told the professors he approached for letters of recommendation that he wanted to continue his studies of twentieth-century American poetry, which was true, but just as much, he wanted to stay in school. College was, for him, like the Early Bird Café before he had discovered the Early Bird Café.

He applied to more than a dozen programs, including, for the hell of it, Harvard. When his application there was actually accepted, Walt immediately jumped at the opportunity to move down to Cambridge, even though the aid package presented to him seemed a little paltry. After matriculating, he learned that his acceptance had really been intended as a gentle rejection; no one in the English Department had expected him to accept such a small stipend to study and live in such an expensive place. No one imagined just how little money a kid like him would be willing to take in order to have an excuse to leave Burlington.

So at twenty-three, he left his hometown with no intention of ever returning, except for the occasional holiday and summer vacation. And his days suddenly became all about what *he* wanted to do, or didn't want to do, which was wonderful. He lived on campus his first year, then up in Porter Square his second. Once his coursework and exams were completed, however, and he came face to face with the terrifying task of trying to write a dissertation, Walt took his job as a superintendent and moved across the Charles River to Boston, the city where most of his favorite poets had either lived or passed through at one time or another.

Walt loved living in Boston, although with this love came more than a little guilt. By then his mother needed more help than ever. His grandfather had passed away back in 1997. There was even less money than before. And there were even more tests that his mother required: more physical therapy, more medication. His grandmother handled everything, never complaining, never asking Walt to move back home. And Walt, in return, tried not to think about Burlington. He told himself to take nothing for granted because he knew he was lucky to have what he did and that life was both very predictable and very unpredictable. On the one hand, he could collapse one morning in his bathroom and never be the same. On the other hand, at some point his grandmother would pass away—she would be eighty in a little more than a year—and then he would have to take care of his mother. So until that happened, he told himself to try to savor every day he spent as a resident of Boston.

After leaving the Early Bird that morning, Walt decided to go to the Museum of Fine Arts himself. Walt loved museums but only during the week, when they were quiet and still. He stared for a while at the Sargent painting he had mentioned to Flora in the café, "The Daughters of Edward Darley Boit." He looked at paintings by Matisse and Hockney and Warhol and imagined that they were being displayed not in a museum, but rather in a private home to which he had access but did not own. He imagined himself, that is, in proximity to wealth, but not in direct possession of it: that would have strained believability too much. When he picked up his dilapidated jacket at the coat check, he apologized to the girl behind the counter for taking up one of her hangers. She laughed. Then Walt headed to the Back Bay on the T, stopped by his apartment to grab his *Norton Anthology of Poetry,* and took a nice, roundabout walk to Floyd's Cleaners, where he sat through his five-hour shift. He chatted with the same customers he saw every few days, read poems by John Crowe Ransom and Richard Wright and John Berryman, cracked some jokes with complete strangers—some of which went over, some of which didn't—and then headed home at five.

Since he always had a good breakfast, and was on a tight budget, Walt never ate lunch, and because he never ate lunch, he was always starving in the early evening. There was a small deli across from his building and Walt usually swung by and bought a burrito and a Coke before going inside to his basement studio, but that night his routine was disrupted by the sight of a girl in the half-light, hunched over the doorknob of his building. He knew the silhouettes of all of his tenants and this girl wasn't a tenant. If she had been, he would have waited in the shadows until she had entered the building. Instead, he crossed the street and made his way toward her.

She was wearing a black wool skirt and black leggings, with big, clunky black boots on her feet. Walt noticed the boots when the girl stepped back and gave the doorknob a swift kick. The next thing he noticed was her parka, which was silver colored, puffy, and stylish. She was a good-looking girl, wearing an expensive outfit and acting miffed. In the Back Bay, she fit right in.

"Can I help you?" he called up to her.

She stepped back onto the top step of the building's entrance and turned toward him. "This lock is a piece of shit."

"Yeah, you can't put the key all the way in; if you do it won't catch." Walt skipped up the steps, slipped around her, and withdrew the key ever so slightly from the lock. Then he turned it with ease. "See?"

"Cool, thanks. One of my movers figured it out this morning but he didn't tell me the trick. The super was supposed to meet us here but he didn't show."

Walt straightened his posture. Well, this was unfortunate. He had assumed she was staying with someone, not that she was a new tenant. New tenants he avoided as much as possible, since they always had tons of questions and entirely too many logistical needs. Also, he preferred for new arrivals to discover over time that he wasn't the most responsible superintendent, by which point he hoped that his reputation as a nice, affable guy would make his flakiness more forgivable.

"That's my bad. I'm the super."

She held herself awkwardly, her head out over her neck, her torso pivoted on her hips, while she frowned at him. "Walt . . . Sneadman?"

"Steadman, yeah. I'm so sorry."

She unwrapped a Tootsie Pop from her parka and put it in her mouth. "Didn't you get the message I left on your machine?"

"The thing about my answering machine is," he ruffled his hair as he leaned back against the side of the building in an attempt to appear a little more boyish and a little less like a superintendent, "the *erase* button is really close to the *play* button and sometimes, you know . . . you can hit the one instead of the other."

She smirked at him. "Maybe you should think about making the jump to voicemail." She held out her hand. "Ginger Newton."

Walt tucked his book under his arm while they shook hands. The name meant nothing to him, at least not the first name. The last name made him think a little, because of the township. "Newton?"

She nodded.

Walt cleared his throat. "Whose place did you buy?"

By *you* he meant her parents, of course. By *you* he named her as rich and young, probably younger than all the other occupants in the building, but not that much younger than some of them.

"No one's. I'm staying in Blair Montgomery's apartment for the semester. That's what my message explained."

"Oh, okay." He liked how she said *semester,* as if the academic calendar applied to everyone. She had the whole thing down: the combination of presumptuousness and lurking displeasure, the great outfit, the tortured posture. And she was really attractive, he could see now, with the streetlight right above them, if in a more than slightly clichéd way. Her complexion was very light, her nose straight, with perfectly symmetrical, thin nostrils, and her eyes were a deep blue. She also had a mass of tangled blonde hair piled on her head and set in place by an intricate system of barrettes and pins, and a pointed chin toward which her entire face was drawn.

"You know Blair Montgomery, right?"

"Yeah, I know Blair. Good guy. He's in Brussels for a few months. He's working for Microsoft on the antitrust suit the EU has brought against them."

"Is he?"

Walt nodded.

"He sent me his key and said I could just show up. I didn't think I'd have a problem with the lock, or getting ahold of you." Ginger sucked her Tootsie Pop.

"How'd you swing the place? Are you and Blair related?"

She laughed. Her laugh was louder than he expected; it startled him. "Am I related to Blair Montgomery? That's hilarious. No, he's sort of a family friend. Actually I barely know him; he's, like, twice my age." Walt winced. "I decided I needed to get out of my dorm, do something a little different. I have this idea, for a project . . ." She stopped herself and pointed out at the street, toward a black Lexus parked in front of a fire hydrant. "Is there anywhere I can park my car?"

"Yeah, you have a spot in back."

"Cool." She bit down on the remaining candy, removed the cardboard stick from her mouth, and threw it in the bank of snow next to the stone staircase on which she stood. In the spring, Walt thought, once the snow has thawed, I'll have to pick that up.

They both walked inside. In the foyer, Walt tried as inconspicuously as possible to slip his *Norton Anthology* into his open mailbox. Ginger didn't seem to notice. "Do you go to Harvard?" he asked, as they made their way into the hallway. "I mean, that's where Blair went. Not that you would necessarily—"

"No," she jumped in, "that's where I go. But I didn't go to Saint Paul's, or wherever Blair attended boarding school. My family isn't into all that. I went to Trinity in New York. I'm a New Yorker."

Walt hit the button for the elevator. Apparently he was showing her up to her new place, half a day late but still. "So what are you, a sophomore, junior?"

"Junior. I'm in Eliot House—*was* in Eliot House—but my quad kind of fell apart." The doors opened and they stepped inside. Ginger hit the button for the third floor. "One girl's taking a leave of absence because she's having a nervous breakdown. Then the other two, you know, they're my *friends*, but only in the college sense. They told our RA about Sid. He knew, but they complained. Sid was a pretense; they were really complaining about me, see? I'm hard to live with; I get that. So rather than send Sid home to my parents, who are too afraid of him to feed him, I decided to look for my own place. Then I heard about Blair going out of town and everything came together, blah blah blah. And like I said, more importantly, I have this idea I want to develop—"

Walt interrupted her. "Who's Sid?"

"My pet boa constrictor."

The doors opened. The building had a "no pets" rule, but Walt had a strong feeling he wouldn't have the temerity to bring it up to Ginger Newton. They walked down the hallway of the third floor to the farthest door on the left, which Ginger opened without any problem. "Come on in," she said. Walt hesitated. She probably already had a list of complaints about the unit that she'd expect him to attend to right away. But she had walked in, so he followed her.

Blair's apartment was a one-bedroom that overlooked Beacon Street. Even by the high standards of the building, this apartment was a nice one, with hardwood floors, granite countertops in the kitchen, and a brick fireplace in the living room, in front of which a bare mattress had been placed, bordered on one side by two enormous duffel bags, their unzipped tops disgorging clothes like miniature volcanoes.

"Blair has a waterbed," Ginger explained, nodding at the mattress. "I hate waterbeds. I don't want to sleep in his room anyway; that'd be kind of weird."

But sleeping on a mattress on the floor, a few yards from a boa constrictor, was perfectly normal. Walt wandered over to the far corner of the room, where Ginger had set up Sid's large tank, along with heat lamps above and what looked to be an electric blanket below. He placed his nose against the glass. Sid uncoiled quickly, his tongue flickering out. Walt stepped back; he put his length right at three feet.

"Are you afraid of snakes?" she asked.

"I think I might be, yes."

Ginger laughed again. What kind of laugh was it, a nervous or a brash one? He wasn't sure. "Don't be. Sid's awesome, unless you're a rat."

He thought of this thing getting out of its tank and ending up in another tenant's place. Who the hell would he call then? He surveyed the room some more from his new vantage point in the corner. In addition to the duffel bags, a leather trunk had been dumped just in front of the counter that divided the kitchen area from the living room. Its lid left open, Walt glimpsed dozens of books piled within it. He wandered over to examine their titles: *The Scholastic Theology Reader, Aristotle in Outline, The Letters of Abelard and Heloise, The Sentences of Peter Lombard.* Everything else he saw was either written by Thomas Aquinas or had his name in the title. He picked up one of the thicker tomes, entitled *The Shorter Summa.* "Couldn't they make it any shorter than this?" he joked.

Ginger plucked the book out of his hand. "Don't get them out of order! There's a system in play here."

Walt stepped back, both from the trunk and from Ginger. What the hell was going on here? Was she flirting with him a little? Girls in the Back Bay flirted with Walt a fair amount, but usually before discovering that he was a superintendent, not so much after.

"I should let you unpack," he said.

"Why would I unpack? It's so boring." She crossed her arms. Her left foot was stuck out in front of her and pointed to the side, probably a vestige of childhood ballet lessons or something. She was an awkward thing. Then again, most girls her age, with her particular look and grooming, were awkward things. They cultivated awkwardness. And they all had such sophisticated footwear; it was remarkable any of them could stand.

She gestured toward her pile of books. "I'm a philosophy major. I'm all about the Scholastics." She caught herself. "They were philosophers—"

"I know who the Scholastics were," Walt shot back, although he was a little fuzzy on several details, such as when exactly they lived and what exactly they thought. "So you're getting a head start on your reading for next semester?"

"In part. Well, I'm reading this one," she picked up a thick book with a white spine, "for this course on the problem of evil in the medieval period I'm about to take, but I was going to read it anyway this break. The course is just an excuse." Walt glanced at the cover: Thomas Aquinas's *De Malo.* "Have you read it?" He shook his head. "Oh, it's awesome. It's a theodicy. You know, a defense of God as omnipotent, omnipresent, and perfectly good in spite of the existence of evil. The *De Malo* is behind this little project I have in mind. In English the title means *On Evil*, but isn't the Latin so much better?"

"Oh, so much."

She set the book down. "Don't make fun of Aquinas. He's my favorite philosopher. I'm getting ready to start my project first thing tomorrow morning, so I'm going to be inhabiting his worldview here for a little bit. That's how I like to work. You know, I don't just want to *study* an idea; I want to live it."

"What's your . . ." Walt hesitated to ask. Harvard undergraduates all had their little projects, he remembered that from the two semesters he had spent as a teaching assistant. Whenever he had handed out their paper assignments, immediately after class everyone would e-mail him and ask for an extension due to extenuating circumstances. *I'm presenting a paper at the World Bank that week,* one of them would explain. *I've begun my own foundation and we're having our first fundraiser.* That one was fairly common. *I'm traveling to Central Africa to build latrines . . . I have to help a gubernatorial candidate in California I interned for last summer with a speech . . . I'm beginning research on my senior honors thesis with a trip to Northern Mongolia . . .*

"Oh, it's silly," Ginger said, shaking her head. "Okay, I'm embarrassed to admit this." He gave her a few seconds. She twisted several times at her waist. "This is going to sound weird." She paused, composing herself. Walt didn't think her self-consciousness was fully felt. He was willing to buy that she was a little uncomfortable, but he suspected that—just a few hours into living off campus—she was already terrified of being deprived of a captive audience.

"All right, so my generation, you know, we are a really *clever* generation. We like *irony.* We like to look *through* things, get to the *heart* of stuff. We are *witty.* We are good at *banter.* And we are super self-involved. Even if you factor in that each generation of Americans since the end of World War Two has been more self-involved than the preceding generation, we are *really* self-involved. Every girl with an eating disorder from my high school is writing a novel about a girl with an eating disorder from my high school. So I decided, with my set of interests, and by virtue of the fact that I don't really like anyone my age, or at least anyone I've met who's my age, that I would try to write about something bigger than myself. Although *write about* isn't quite right." She bit at her lower lip. Actually, now Ginger did look genuinely ill at ease. "So, I have this idea. I'll interview women from all walks of life to see what they do to get by—what motivates them, what they care about. I want to hear how they face the evils of the world. It'll be a theodicy in the form of personal narratives. Something Aquinas might have written if he had been a Women's Studies major. The working title is *Girls I Know*."

Walt looked at her blankly. Actually he hadn't followed her. She wanted to imitate Thomas Aquinas by conducting personal interviews? And she didn't like people her age? But she seemed, in a sense, the perfect embodiment of someone her age, at least someone at Harvard. She had money. She was pretty. She was smart. He didn't know what to say and she was waiting for him to respond. "So it's going to be a book about Boston?"

"I hadn't thought of it in those terms—"

"Well, this is your lucky day. I'm an expert on Boston."

"Are you?" And she smiled at him, dimples hollowing out both cheeks.

"Yes, I am—all things Boston." And he thought, what the hell. She had appeared out of nowhere, after all. What did he have to lose? "Want a tour?"

"Right now?"

"Not by car. We'll go up to the roof; I'll point out some buildings, we'll freeze our asses off."

Now he was flirting with *her*, and that changed things; that required Ginger to reassess the situation. Walt stood there, waiting while she mulled over his offer. The worst-case scenario really wasn't so bad. She'd pass and he'd go across the street, grab a burrito, read some poems in bed, and fall asleep. The best-case scenario . . . well, he wasn't sure what the best-case scenario was. The two of them overlooking Boston, huddled together for warmth? That might be nice, or a looming disaster; he couldn't decide which.

"You know something?" Ginger shrugged. "This is my first night in Boston proper. Why not?"

CHAPTER 3

Ginger extracted a white knit cap and a matching pair of mittens from one of her duffel bags, unfastened several barrettes, and pulled the cap down tight on her head so that the ends of her blonde hair poked out from under. After they took the elevator to the sixth floor, Walt led her down the hallway and around the corner to a thick green door. Then he withdrew his bulky ring of keys and inserted one of them into the lock. He had to push against the door several times before it gave way. Inside the narrow stairwell was a light switch that he flipped. The two of them climbed up the seven steep steps, the cold air from outside swirling around their legs and feet. At the top, Walt leaned into the door that led onto the roof itself and propped it open with a cinder block he had lugged up years before.

They walked over to the front of the building. The night was cold and clear. Together they looked out over the low wall that ran along the edge of the roof. Below was Beacon Street, filled with honking cars and BU students shouting back and forth at one another as they set out for the bars. The enormous CITGO sign was just a few blocks away in Kenmore Square, in front of Fenway Park, and to their left was the Prudential building, massive and ugly, or so Walt thought. Back behind them was a wide patch of darkness, where the Charles River swelled to its widest width.

Walt waited for Ginger to comment on the view but she didn't and he reminded himself that she was a New Yorker, after all; she probably wasn't too impressed.

"So what's your deal?" she asked him. "How long have you been superintending?"

"Three years." He knew he had to come clean about his own academic background. "I dropped out of grad school at Harvard.

Well, *dropped out* is a little dramatic. I haven't written my dissertation."

"You were at Harvard?"

"Yeah, I was in the English Department. Meredith O'Shea was my advisor. She's an expert on American poetry. I guess she still is my advisor, technically."

"That explains why you were reading that anthology. How long has it been since you've met with her?"

"Three years."

"What happened?"

A stray snowflake suddenly appeared in the air, then another one: just the smallest webs of crystalline ice, floating in slow motion.

"I was going to write on Robert Lowell, the Boston Brahmin poet. The title of my dissertation was going to be *The Poetics of Yankee Peerage*. The idea was basically that Lowell's poetry was shaped by where he was born and the shadow cast by his family name. Not that original, I'm afraid. But when it came time for me actually to start writing, I couldn't come up with anything that didn't sound either really obvious or completely uninteresting. I tried for a while and then—eventually—I stopped trying."

Walt walked over to the side of the building that looked down on Mass Ave. Ginger followed him. He wanted to add, in case she didn't know, that graduate students abandoned their dissertations all the time. He was willing to bet, he might even have gone on to say, that a significant percentage of the Boston population was composed of people whose academic careers had flamed out: that if everyone who started doctorates in Boston completed them and moved onto academic postings all around America, the local economy would probably crater. But he kept these thoughts to himself.

"I'm not sure I'm sold on finishing my degree either," she said. "It seems like an excessive amount of time. Henry Adams said everything he learned in four years at Harvard could have been learned in four months."

"But he stayed four years, right?"

"That's true."

"And you're halfway through your junior year—"

"Yeah, but I'd rather work on my book, you know? Anyone can go to college."

The snowflakes had begun to thicken. She was thinking over his situation now, he could feel it. "What does it mean when you stop working on a dissertation? Do you still have health insurance?"

"I'm not sure. I think so." Actually his coverage had lapsed along with his fellowship, but Walt didn't want to disclose his uninsured status to someone like Ginger. She probably had some bionic coverage plan that let her see any doctor she wanted to without a referral or anything. "I'm still registered as a student," he added. "Last time I checked out library books, my ID still worked."

She stared blankly at him. His intention had been to link a working Harvard ID card with health coverage, but clearly he hadn't succeeded. He decided to start over. "No, I've been trying to find something to do with myself but it's hard. I feel like I could do just about anything and be happy, and then I realize that I'm happy now and I wonder why I would get a full-time job at this moment, since I'm content. But I'm about to turn thirty—"

"Thirty is the new twenty."

"That's easy to say when you're . . . how old are you?"

"Twenty."

"There you go." He tucked his chin behind the frayed collar of his jacket. "No, I have to do something here in a little bit, get started on the next part of my life."

She was peering at him intensely; it was a little unnerving. "So what are your days like? Take today, what did you do today?"

He tucked his hands beneath his armpits and leaned toward her. Walt loved talking about his routine, since he derived so much pleasure from it. "Well, I have breakfast each day at this place in JP, so I went over there. Afterwards I dropped by the Museum of Fine Arts. Then I went to work. I have a shift at a dry cleaners down the street."

Finishing with the dry cleaners wasn't quite the exclamation point he wanted but it was too late now.

"You go over to Jamaica Plain every morning for breakfast! That's so cute." She smiled at him, her eyes misty from the cold. Her white teeth flashed in the half-light.

Again, perhaps unintentionally, she had made him feel old. Walt decided to try to shift the attention away from himself before he revealed too much. "How much progress have you made so far on *Girls I Know*?"

"Not a lick. I start tomorrow." She fumbled with her pair of mittens. "I don't know how it's going to turn out, but I definitely needed to get out of Cambridge. I didn't want to be that cliché: the Harvard student who studies so much she loses her mind. But at the same time, I'm a Harvard student who was losing her mind because she was studying too much. But enough. I'm ready for my rooftop tour of Boston."

"All right, then." Walt pointed off the southeast corner of the building. "That's the John Hancock Tower. Sixty-two stories. I. M. Pei designed it. He's a . . . famous architect." Realizing that he had far fewer facts to relate than he had assumed, Walt paused. "The tower is in the shape of a rhomboid. It's cool, especially up close."

Ginger pulled a Tootsie Pop out of her parka. "What's your family like, Walt?"

"My family?" The question threw him off. Who met someone and then just asked him about his family? Especially someone older, since the general rule of thumb had to be that the older you got, the more complicated your family became.

"Family, that would be people you are related to by blood. Or I guess remarriage. Or adoption. Do you have any siblings? My mom is basically a socialite who claims to be a philanthropist. My dad's a classic New York liberal. I have one little sister, Beatrice. We call her Bee Bee. She's nine years old and claims to be afraid of snakes, but I don't believe her."

Walt pointed back across the building, toward Copley Square. "Trinity Church is down that way. It's Episcopal, I think."

"I wish we had Gothic cathedrals here in the States. Not neo-Gothic but the real thing. Wouldn't that be awesome?"

"I guess so . . ."

"It was a rhetorical question. You can let it go."

"Okay." But she had made him lose his train of thought regardless. Was she always so on? It made Walt's head spin a little, trying to keep up with her.

Ginger's teeth crunched through the heart of her Tootsie Pop. She threw the stick off the side of the building. It hung in the cool air, then dropped out of sight. "This tour sucks." She crossed her arms. "I can't see any of the things you're talking about."

"You have to squint a little—"

"And I want to hear about you! I like it, when I meet people, finding out where they're from, what they grew up doing, that sort of thing."

"You like finding all of that stuff out immediately?"

"Yeah, I'm impatient."

Walt put his hands in his jean pockets and looked down at his shoes. She was just so direct. You had to be either really rich or really drunk to be this straightforward and Ginger certainly wasn't drunk. In the three years that he had lived in the Back Bay and chatted with girls who at the very least looked and dressed somewhat like Ginger, Walt had never been asked to discuss his family. But she stood there, waiting, and she was relentless, that much was obvious.

"Okay, so I grew up in my grandparents' house in Burlington. My mom has multiple sclerosis. She's in a wheelchair. My grandmother takes care of her."

"That sounds awful."

He couldn't argue with that. Walt shifted on his feet. "She and my grandfather raised me. He died four years ago."

"What was he like?"

"Amazing. He fought in World War Two. Then he came back to Vermont and taught high school American history for the rest of his life. He loved nature; he was involved in all of these preservation projects around Burlington. And jazz, he really loved jazz. He gave me all of his music before he died."

"What about your dad?"

"I never knew him. My grandfather was my dad."

They looked out in the direction of the Common, hidden behind blocks and blocks of brownstones and parkways. She was right, there was nothing to see: just headlights and brake lights, the tops of cars and buses, and the bundled bodies of pedestrians, all dusted now with snow.

"My granddad's awesome." Ginger tossed a piece of gum into her mouth and began to chew it loudly. "My mom's dad. He's totally

politically incorrect—uses words like *Oriental*—but he's also got
that gallant thing working, so he'll always hold the door for you, or
help you with your jacket. Well, he wouldn't help *you*—he just helps
women—but I like that about him. He's chivalrous."

"Do you see him a lot?"

"I do. They just live a block up from us, on Seventy-fifth and
Fifth. But they travel through the winter. They have this yacht they
take around. Bibby, that's what we call our grandmother, she and
my grandfather are sailing in the Aegean now, so we're a little out of
touch."

"Hard to talk to people when they're on a boat, huh?" Walt smiled
with fake assurance.

"No, they have a satellite phone," Ginger explained, "but it always
cuts out."

The wind kicked up. Snow began to swirl. Ginger sat down and
nestled her back against the low wall in front of them. Walt sat down
next to her. What could he be expected to contribute on the subject of
satellite phones? He didn't even own a cell phone. He had never been
on an airplane. He had never been out of New England. He looked
west, in his mind's eye traveling past Allston and Brighton. She hadn't
been coy asking about his family, so he took that as an excuse not to
be coy asking about hers.

"So, I'm guessing your family has some connection to Newton,
Massachusetts?"

"They founded it, at least that's what everyone says."

"Did they come over on the *Mayflower*?"

"My mom's side, yes. My dad's side isn't so blue blood. They didn't
make it over here until the 1650s or so."

He couldn't help it; he thought that was all kind of impressive.
According to his grandfather, Walt's own family roots—restricted
to his mom's side, of course—all seemed to taper out in various
nineteenth-century French-Canadian brothels.

"Did any of your ancestors sign the Declaration of Independence?"

"Yeah, and the Constitution too."

"And they had cabinet positions?"

"A few, but boring stuff: Treasury and Interior, crap like that.

Nothing sexy like State."

"And no inventors, like Franklin?"

"No, they went from merchants to bankers pretty quickly." Ginger looked him over. "You don't have any candy on you by chance, do you?"

"No, sorry."

Once more, she peered at him.

"What?"

"I'm just trying to get a read on you. I can't quite tell if you're on the cusp of despair or actually a fairly happy person."

And he was ready, or at least not shocked this time, by her brusqueness. "Oh, I'm pretty happy, all things considered." Walt cupped his hands over his ears to warm them up. "I'll tell you my secret." He paused. His real secret was not a profound one. Provided he wasn't living at home with his grandmother and mother, he had plenty to be thankful for. But he didn't want to put it quite so bluntly so he tried the following. "I ask for so little of the world that surrounds me, I ask only to be allowed to appreciate it. That's all I need. I'm probably the happiest person you've ever met."

Ginger squinched up her nose. "That's not saying much, Walt. Everyone I know is miserable. Besides, I've always assumed happiness was overrated. Happy people, no offense, they tend to be a little dopey. Besides, what do you learn when you're content? That's what I don't get."

"Clearly, you've never been happy. When you're happy, you don't care if you're learning or not."

"I guess that's true." But she sounded unconvinced. "Aquinas thought a person's happiness depended upon the degree of his or her knowledge of God," Ginger added, "so ultimate happiness could only be achieved in death."

"But Aquinas spent his life in monasteries, right? So it was pretty easy for him to imagine a higher realm where people actually enjoyed themselves."

She seemed to take his comment seriously, which he hadn't intended. "Well, if you're right and you've figured out how to achieve true happiness on earth, that means you're a genius, so congratulations."

"I'm like Albert Einstein," he whispered, "only without all the math." He grinned at her, pleased with his little joke, but when she looked up at him her eyes seemed to empty and he caught himself. What if he had badly misread her, assuming that she couldn't have a care in the world? No, she really had to be in search of something to move off campus, even if she had the means to move into an apartment building in the Back Bay. You could be rich and unhappy of course, but it took a force of will on Walt's part to acknowledge this.

She hopped to her feet. "I could use some more gum. And a rat, too. My poor little snake needs to be fed."

"There's a deli across the street where we could get your gum." He stood up slowly. Now he was thinking too much, which always made Walt a little nervous. When his brain began to mull over something, the possibility increased that it might turn on itself. But what if Ginger's impulsiveness, what if all the chatter about Aquinas, all the chomping on Tootsie Pops, what if hanging out with him in the first place was all part of a more or less frenzied attempt to keep something at bay, something awful enough to get her to cook up this book project of hers just to keep herself busy for a bit? Well, if that was the case, then this girl really was a mess. But Walt wasn't sure he'd go that far. Now he felt himself coming full circle, felt the voice of the boy who had grown up on the wrong side of Burlington—the boy with the funny looking family—pipe up: *How much of a mess could you really be if your last name was Newton?*

"And there's an alley behind the deli where there are plenty of rats," he added, "but you're on your own there."

They began to walk across the roof, but then Ginger stopped abruptly and Walt followed suit, his feet slipping in the snow beneath them.

"One glitch in your master plan, it occurs to me." She looked up into the dark sky thoughtfully. "In your scenario, when you achieve true happiness by virtue of not asking anything of the world that surrounds you, that means you aren't giving anything either. So, in the end, you're all alone, and no one has been touched by your experience of pure bliss. Just a thought."

Walt didn't say anything. Ginger had put her finger on what had always haunted him about his little life in Boston. The flip side of inhabiting a world so small you could hold it in your hand was that such a world didn't matter to anyone else. That was the real reason he doubted the sincerity of his own jocularity: the way he had joked with Flora about wanting to be the mayor of Boston, the way he had just claimed affinities with Albert Einstein. Who was he kidding? What did he really have to be that happy about after all?

CHAPTER 4

Walt heard someone knocking on his door the next morning but he didn't get out of bed. Occasionally, one of his tenants drifted down to the basement to ask him about something, but he never let any of them know he was around. Neither did he ever lock his door, so when he heard it creak open and then shut quickly, he assumed that someone couldn't resist trying the knob before fleeing back upstairs. But then, a minute or so later, he heard a rustling and suddenly a girl's voice.

"Oh my God!" Ginger cried out. "You have records! You actually listen to records!"

He shot up in his futon. Ginger Newton was perched on her knees in the corner of his room, thumbing through his jazz records, which Walt kept in two milk crates.

"What the hell are you doing in here?" He checked his alarm clock. It was half-past seven in the morning. "I could be an ax murderer for all you know."

"I doubt a lot of ax murderers listen to Thelonious Monk." She flipped through more of his albums. "When I get excited about an idea, I can't sleep. I told you this last night in the foyer upstairs, after we bought our candy, and you said I could drop by whenever."

"After *you* bought *your* candy I might have said that, but I didn't think you *would* drop by whenever." Was she a little unstable? Walt had more or less dismissed the possibility the night before; now he wasn't so sure. At the very least she had a reckless streak, barging into his room like she had.

"Well, then you shouldn't have said I could. That's being insincere. I hate insincerity." She examined another one of his albums. "You really made a blunder, Superintendent Steadman, establishing an open door policy. I don't sleep much even when I'm *not* excited about an idea. I might start waking you up at four."

"So you're an insomniac?"

"Oh, come on, you aren't one of those people who has to label behavior, are you?" She pointed at the record in her hand. "Who is Jon Faddis?"

"A jazz trumpeter."

"Like Wynton Marsalis?"

"He's better than Marsalis." Walt glanced around his messy apartment. He was embarrassed not to have a TV. Did she think he was one of those people who made a point of *not* owning a television? Because he hated those kind of people. He was, rather, the kind of person for whom it was better not to have a TV at all than to have a shitty one, because there was nothing more depressing—he knew from his childhood—than having a shitty TV. Better to walk over to Daisy Buchanan's, the bar on Newbury Street, to watch Red Sox games than to have a six-inch screen and five channels.

"I don't know anything about jazz. Can we listen to some of these records?"

"Now?"

"Why not?"

"Because it's seven in the morning!"

"You're crabby when you wake up." She pointed above him, at the ceiling, where an enormous brown stain reached from above his bathroom door to the far side of his futon. "That's nasty."

"Yeah, it gets a little darker each day too."

"Maybe you should do something about it."

"I'm thinking of calling the super."

She rolled her eyes at him, then took in his room once more. "You're a real slob, Walt."

"I prefer the term *intellectual.*"

"I bet you do." She put the record back in the crate and relocated to the plaid La-Z-Boy recliner on the other side of his small oak desk.

"Did you let yourself into anyone else's apartment in the building this morning or just mine?"

"Like I said, I took the unlocked door as an invitation. It's not easy, you know, not being able to sleep. There are lots of hours to fill."

Walt reached over and scooped up the white tee shirt he had worn the day before. He put it on. "How long have you been . . . let me rephrase that: how long have you had trouble sleeping?"

"Since the middle of eighth grade. I woke up one night at three in the morning and couldn't sleep. I wasn't tossing and turning. I was *up*. So I went out into our living room and read on the couch until the morning came. And it was bliss. The phone didn't ring; Bee Bee wasn't being a nuisance. From that point on, I just started to get up at three or four and read until seven. Then, one night, when my mom couldn't sleep, she came out to do a crossword puzzle and found me there. She asked what I was doing and I told her I was reading, like I did every night. So she freaked out, of course, and took me to see a psychiatrist: a great guy, very Upper-West-Side-Jewish-Intellectual type back when there still was an Upper-West-Side-Jewish-Intellectual type. We met once a week for a couple of months, at the end of which he told my mom not to worry about me: that some people just don't need as much sleep as others. So that was that. My grandmother still worries about it. She's a labeler like you. She thinks *insomnia*," Ginger affixed quotation marks in the air with her fingers, "might be an early sign of epilepsy. She's epileptic-phobic, if that's a term. She has self-control issues, see?"

Ginger plucked his *Norton Anthology* off the edge of his futon. Walt had retrieved the book from his mailbox at the end of the previous night, and then fallen asleep in bed while reading it. She set the collection down on her lap. The pages plopped open, which made Walt squirm. He didn't like the idea of Ginger reading what he had — over the years — scribbled in the margins. She glanced down, then shut the book. "Want to know why I fell in love with Sid?"

"Sure."

"Honestly, I bought him just to annoy Bee Bee, since she's always had this irrational fear of reptiles. But then I discovered, the third day he had been home with us, that — like all snakes — he didn't have any eyelids. So he had me with no eyelids, I guess you could say. And we've been the perfect couple ever since."

"What a sweet story," he said. She flipped him off just as the phone started to ring. Walt didn't budge.

"Aren't you going to get that?"

"It's just a tenant, complaining about something. So since you were up all night, what did you do?"

"I read more of the *De Malo*. It's really cool. Aquinas doesn't just say, 'Look, don't question evil. God has a plan.' He doesn't claim that all evil can be explained. He even says that evil has to come from good, since God creates everything and what he creates is good. So he's not just following Augustine, like everyone else. Aquinas is rigorous. That's what I love about him. He's tough on his beliefs."

His machine finally picked up. "Walter? Walter?" It was his grandmother's voice, halting and confused. Mortified, Walt dove for the receiver on the far side of his futon. As soon as he picked up, a horrible, high-pitched screeching sound filled the air.

"Walter! What's going on?"

"Grandma, it's the answering—"

"I can't hear you!"

"My answering machine does this—"

Ginger started to laugh.

"Are you there, Walter?"

He waited for the racket to die down. "Yeah, I'm here."

"How are you?"

"I'm good. How are you?"

"Fine. We wanted to hear your voice. Your mother and I were at a chili supper at South Burlington High last night. Mary Higgins asked about you. We told her how happy you are in Boston. Do you remember her?"

"Of course. She taught algebra."

"That's right. She said you were a pleasure to have in class. Not great at math, but you tried your hardest. She and I retired at the same time, you know. Her husband's passed on too."

Ginger re-opened Walt's *Norton Anthology* while he cupped his hand over the phone. "Grandma, I'm sorry, I'm walking out the door—"

"Oh, we don't mean to keep you. We just wanted to check in. Would you like to say hi to your mother?"

"Sure."

"She's right here. Hold on a moment."

Walt heard them fumbling with the phone, the receiver falling onto the floor, then his grandmother scooping it up. There was a pause, followed first by his mom's labored breathing, and next her guttural groan as she began to speak. In the back of her throat, her vocal chords enunciated a *hello*, then her tongue stumbled over the *W* that began her son's name. Walt could picture her neck muscles tensing. He pressed the receiver against his ear. "Hi, Mom," he said. What followed was a more sustained grunt that he actually understood as a question. "I'm doing well. You sound good. How are you? How was the chili supper?" He let her go on for a little bit, no longer able to divine what she was trying to say. Then, once more he understood her. "I love you too," he said. And he remembered, when he was little, before she got sick, how they'd play checkers together after school. He thought of the picture of her as a little girl that still sat on the hutch in the living room: her arms extended out over her head as she jumped off a dock into Lake Champlain.

With his back now fully turned to Ginger, Walt glanced over his shoulder. She had curled her knees up under her chin and was reading, her face hidden behind his book, just her blonde hair visible, with its tangle of barrettes and pins. Through the receiver, he heard more fumbling, then his grandmother's voice once more. "Call us, Walter, whenever you get a chance."

"Okay. Bye, Grandma." And he hung up the phone.

Ginger peeked over at him. "Should I know who Theodore Roethke is?"

"Probably. He wrote some great poems."

"I've never heard of him. Or Jon Faddis. Maybe you need to tutor me, Walt."

"No, you'd ask too many questions." He looked over at the phone, now resting inertly on his bed.

"Is that hard, when your family calls?"

"Yeah, it is a little. I'd like to be there for them, but not if it means *being there* for them."

"I know what you mean. I'd have to kill my mom if I lived with her. Even though I love her, I'd poison her." She tossed his *Norton Anthology* onto the futon. Then she stood up. Walt noticed now just how nicely she was dressed: black stockings, a black skirt and turtleneck, and a green cashmere sweater. When she stretched her hands up toward the ceiling with a yawn, he caught a flash of skin as her sweater and turtleneck inched up her flat stomach. "So I've got my first interview for *Girls I Know* scheduled for nine this morning and I was wondering if you'd like to tag along."

Walt regarded her for a moment as a curiosity, which of course she was. She had moved over to his desk and was examining the papers he had strewn about.

"Where are you going?"

"The Dana-Farber / Brigham and Women's Cancer Center. I'm meeting with a doctor who does breast cancer research. I want to learn about a natural evil, not to mention *the* anti-female disease."

"How'd you find a doctor who would see you?"

"My dad knows someone who knows someone. Blah blah blah. What do you say? Are you in?"

"Sure." Could he really just skip breakfast at the Early Bird, all to watch Ginger Newton ask some doctor questions about breast cancer? Apparently he could. He grabbed the same pair of jeans he had worn the day before, conveniently discarded next to his bed, and stepped into them.

"I need to get my car keys, and a coat. I'll meet you outside in five minutes."

"We're going to *drive* to Dana-Farber?"

"Yeah, I need the practice. I just got my license in the fall, when my grandparents gave me my car. So, you know, I'm not much of a driver. I'm still learning."

That didn't sound too promising. After she was gone, Walt took a leak, brushed his teeth, put on his shoes, and grabbed another one of his sweaters, all of which he stored in a box in the closet. This one was dark blue with a turtleneck collar; it fit snugly under his jacket. He went outside to wait for her in front of the building. A couple of inches of snow had accumulated on the sidewalk. He was supposed to shovel and sprinkle salt after every storm. Well, that wasn't going to happen right now. He kicked at the icy steps with his shoe. The next morning, when Flora asked why he had missed breakfast today, Walt knew he wouldn't tell her the truth. He would never mention Ginger to her; he'd sooner die. But why?

He didn't have time to formulate an answer to his own question; Ginger darted out the door in her silver-colored parka, an enormous, black leather bag slung over her shoulder, a small, black leather journal clutched to her side.

"What's with the journal?"

"It's to take notes in, for *Girls I Know.*"

She hit her remote and the Lexus beeped from behind the fire hydrant. Walt had seen cars towed from this spot in under an hour, but Ginger's automobile had sat there for nearly a day; it too led a charmed life. They walked down the steps and across the sidewalk. From beneath a thin film of ice, he peeled a parking ticket from her windshield and opened the passenger door. "Didn't I mention, there's tenant parking in back?"

"Yeah, I just didn't have it in me last night to move my car."

"How could you, with all that Aquinas to read?"

"Exactly."

He stepped into the car, shut the door, and felt himself cocooned in leather. When she turned the key, the engine purred. "Do you know where Binney Street is, Walt? No, wait, we have some time before we have to be there. Let's go a roundabout way, open this engine up a little bit."

"Okay." He pointed straight ahead and Ginger whipped her car onto Beacon Street. It was clear, after less than a block, that she was a really terrible driver. She cut off other cars while whispering *Shit* under her breath and seemed capable of hitting her brakes only with the full force of her foot, so that each time they stopped the car fishtailed and the tires screeched. It didn't help that, while steering, she was also fumbling with the wrappers of several pieces of Bazooka bubble gum she had taken from a bag of candy she kept in the armrest of her Lexus. Walt noticed the pedestrians waiting to cross on the corner of Charlesgate East back away from the curb as they approached. When they came to a stop, he ran his hand against the polished hull of the glove compartment. "What a great car," he said.

She shrugged as they merged onto Storrow Drive, then flipped on the car stereo and skipped through her music by tapping a button on her steering wheel until she settled on something Walt didn't recognize. She rolled down their windows and held down another button so that the thrashing guitars got louder and louder until finally there was a wall of sound—pulsating and rhythmic—set between them. They careened alongside the Charles. The cold air made Walt's throat burn and his eyes water. He could see, to his right, streaks of blue beneath the ice on the river. He could see, to his left, Ginger's leg, encased in black stockings, extend ever so slightly as she accelerated.

"What is this?" he asked, pointing at the dashboard's equalizer, which was lit up like some kind of strategic defense warning system. As they raced along, it felt like the sound waves were pulling his heart out of its cavity, like there was no distinction between the inside and the outside of his body: just the music and the wind and nothing else holding him together."I can't hear you!" Ginger screamed. "I can't even hear you a little!"

CHAPTER 5

They met Dr. Sandra Keller in the doorway of her office on the third floor of the Dana-Farber / Brigham and Women's Cancer Center. She wore a lab coat over a pair of slacks and had black hair cut in a short bob and large, round glasses. "What a pleasure to meet you, Ginger!" she exclaimed, clasping her hand. Only then did she turn to Walt.

"Are you advising her thesis?" she asked him.

"Uh . . ." Walt looked at Ginger.

"Walt's a graduate student in English," she explained, as if that shed some light on his presence.

"Oh, welcome. Apologies for the cramped quarters. This is just my consulting room. I do most of my work in the lab across the hallway."

Her office was a tiny one with very little in it: just a metal desk that faced two chairs, a large screen affixed to the wall on the right, and a window on the left that looked out over a parking garage.

"I understand that your parents have done a lot for the hospital, Ginger." Dr. Keller pointed at the two chairs behind her while she circled around her desk. Ginger and Walt sat down.

"They do a lot of fundraising in general, yes. It's their thing." Ginger rolled her eyes at Walt.

"It's an important thing," Dr. Keller added.

They both nodded. Walt peered some more at Dr. Keller. He couldn't imagine that she was much over thirty-five. The two of them were probably closer in age than he and Ginger.

"So I assume you're pre-med?" Now seated herself, she rolled her chair up to her desk and leaned across it, toward Ginger.

"No, philosophy, actually. I should explain that this isn't a thesis project. It's just a book I'm working on: about women, about girls, all from different walks of life. I want to assess female experiences in American society in the supposedly post-feminist early twenty-first century."

At some point in the preceding twelve hours, she had reworked her terms, probably in anticipation of the audience she'd be facing this morning.

"I see. How interesting." Dr. Keller sighed reflectively. "And how is the college these days?"

"I don't think it's changed much. At least my dad never gets lost when he's back on campus. Neither does my grandfather."

"I'm Class of 1987." Dr. Keller pointed on the wall to the left behind her, where two diplomas hung next to one another: one for Dr. Keller's BA, the other for her MD. Both prominently displayed the Harvard crest.

Ginger pulled a digital voice recorder out of her bag. "Would you mind, Dr. Keller, if I taped our conversation?"

"Not at all. We should get started. I don't have too much time."

Ginger hit a few buttons, then placed the recorder on the desk. "Okay. We're here at Forty-Four Binney Street in Boston, talking with Dr. Sandra Keller. Dr. Keller researches breast cancer. Do you have patients as well?"

"I do. We all do here at Dana-Farber."

"So she researches cancer and treats cancer patients. What are you working on at the moment, Dr. Keller?"

Dr. Keller cleared her throat. "Well, until recently, I was on a clinical trial. We were looking at different two-drug combinations for oncologic treatment options. We finished that up last year and now I'm heading my own research team. We're trying to figure out how cancer cells detach from one another and move into the membrane lining of the ductal wall. This kind of breast cancer is known as *infiltrating ductal carcinoma,* but we're focusing on a certain kind of ductal carcinoma specifically that's called *medullary carcinoma.* Do you want to see what I'm talking about?"

Ginger nodded. Walt tried to focus, but he was acutely aware of the lack of caffeine in his bloodstream. He wondered if the Early Bird was busy that morning, if Natalie had seated someone at his table by now, if Flora missed seeing him.

Dr. Keller walked around her desk, over to the screen on the side wall of the room. She thumbed through a number of photos and images sorted in a bin in front of her, picked one out, and placed it on the screen. Then she flipped a switch that illumined the photo.

"This is what an infiltrating ductal carcinoma of the breast looks like when we detect it on a mammogram."

Walt saw a flecked black-and-white image of what looked like the profile of a planet. On the periphery, an inserted arrow pointed down toward a tiny little bright spot. That was it? That was cancer, that little blip?

"Here is a histopathologic image. That just means a microscopic close-up of a biopsy." She flung the photo onto the screen next to the one already displayed. It snapped against the metal bar at the top. "This one is dyed with hematoxylin and eosin stain. That explains the color." It looked like a satellite photo of a river, Walt thought, with purple hues and bends and swells. "And this is a picture of a mastectomy specimen. An actual tumor, a little more than three centimeters in dimension . . ."

It resembled an oyster. And suddenly, Walt found himself wondering what his mother's MS looked like. Not its effects, but what the disease itself actually resembled. And then, he thought of both his mother and grandmother not as his mother and grandmother, and not even as Marion and Eleanor Steadman. He thought of them as women, as susceptible to something like this cancer: some unique, gendered form of suffering and loss. In spite of all his mother's limitations, Walt didn't want her to die. He didn't want his grandmother to die either. All the family members left to him were women. Of course he had known this, but he had never thought about it this way before.

"*Ductal* carcinoma." Ginger sat with her back perfectly straight, in rapt attention. "That develops in the milk ducts of the breast?"

"That's right." Dr. Keller nodded and Ginger winked at him. "Nine years of Latin finally pays dividends in the real world." Walt smiled thinly at her. She was like a kid at an amusement park, having the time of her life.

"The prognosis for invasive ductal carcinomas is poor, although improving. Some of the means by which we treat early-stage ductal carcinomas include—"

"Excuse me, Dr. Keller, but I know you're pressed for time." Ginger blew a strand of hair out from in front of her eyes. "I guess I'm more interested in *why* you do what you do than what exactly you do. What led you to work on breast cancer?"

Dr. Keller turned off the screen and returned to the chair behind her desk. "I was always interested in medicine. My father was a pediatrician. He retired just a few years ago."

Ginger withdrew her journal from her bag, uncapped a pen, and began to write. "Do you have any close relatives who are cancer survivors? Cancer victims?"

Dr. Keller pushed herself back from her desk and crossed her legs. "Actually, my mother died of breast cancer when I was eight. It was probably a medullary carcinoma, but they would have had no way of determining that back then. Treatment was limited as well."

"Did she suffer a great deal, before she died?"

"She did, yes."

"And did you witness any of this suffering?"

"Of course."

"Did you see her die?"

Dr. Keller sat up in her chair. She looked down at her hands as she pressed them against the front of her desk. Her eyebrows wrinkled. "Excuse me?"

Walt was conscious now of his own body language, the way he had begun to lean away from Ginger, trying—as best he could—to disassociate himself from her.

Ginger set down her pen. "I'm sorry to be blunt, but I'm wondering if you witnessed her death. I'm curious, how that might have impacted you if you did."

She stared intently at Dr. Keller. Walt thought of her pet snake, Sid, its head probably hovering above its body at that very moment, looking inscrutably at something in Blair Montgomery's apartment. Really, what kind of twenty-year-old had this degree of self-possession? This cold inquisitiveness? He was fascinated and embarrassed at the same time.

"I did see her die, yes." Dr. Keller inhaled sharply, then blinked several times. She looked as if she had been struck in the head. "We were all in the room when she passed away: my father, both my brothers, my grandparents, and I."

"You must see people die all the time now?"

"I do a fair amount, yes."

"At those moments, do you ever think of your mother's death?"

Dr. Keller puckered her lips. She turned in her chair. She glared at the fancy little recording device Ginger had set up right in front of her nose. "I suppose, on some level, I do, yes."

"What was it like, growing up without a mother?"

"I, uh . . . I was under the impression that we were going to discuss my research . . ."

Ginger smoothed the folds of her skirt with her hand. "My book is about loss, to a large degree, Dr. Keller." She sounded distracted as she spoke: her voice softer than before, her manner less intense. "One of my organizing ideas is that girls become women by virtue of what they lose: childhood friends, a certain kind of innocent self-confidence, positive images of their own bodies, and on and on. So I'd be grateful about anything you could say about your girlhood."

Dr. Keller removed her glasses. "Well, it was hard. Like I said, I have two brothers; I'm the youngest. They were very kind to me growing up, at least most of the time—quite protective. And my father is still incredibly supportive. But, yes, it was hard. I remember little moments: getting ready for the senior prom and not having a mother to help me with my hair. That sort of thing, the little things. Of course there were larger things as well but those were harder to fathom for me when I was young."

They all sat there. Walt looked at Ginger, wondering what her next move was going to be. She looked over her shoulder, at the dark screen on which those gruesome and beautiful images had loomed. "How do you understand what you do?" she asked Dr. Keller, not even looking at her. "Do you tell yourself you're *fighting* cancer? Do you feel like you're waging a battle?"

"I don't think of it like that." Dr. Keller shook her head. "They're so adaptable, the cells. They're so relentless. We can slow cancer down . . . we *are* slowing it down, but we can't beat it." She put her glasses back on and touched her lips with the tips of her index fingers. "But for me it's more of a problem that you try to . . . I don't know if *solve* is the right word. Maybe *contain*. I don't see cancer itself as evil; it's an organic process: mutative, but still a process." She lapsed into thought. "Now, the suffering that it produces, that *is* evil, I think. The way my own mother suffered. That we do fight. I believe . . . every doctor I work with, we all believe that mitigating suffering on the part of our patients is incredibly important. It's central to our mission as care providers."

Once more, Ginger began to scribble furiously. "That's interesting that you used that word *evil*. Do you think a just God would permit cancer?"

"Oh, I don't know. I'm not a theologian."

Ginger looked surprised. "But of course you are! You work on questions of life and death and suffering—"

"Yes, but I don't frame my work in those terms. I'm a scientist." Dr. Keller's beeper went off. She lifted it out of her lab coat, looked at the number, and then switched it off. "I'm sorry, I have to run." She didn't look sorry at all. She looked eager to get back to cancer, to get back to anything other than Ginger's questions. Or Walt was misreading her. She was a woman, after all, and he didn't trust his readings of women. Or girls. Or, to be honest, men.

Ginger retrieved her digital recorder and Dr. Keller showed them into the hallway. She shook their hands. She wished Ginger good luck with her book. And then she was gone. They walked back to the elevator bank, then through the maze of hallways on the ground floor, until they found the doors through which they had first entered, and the garage where Ginger had parked her car.

"What's on your mind, kiddo?" She pointed her key at her Lexus and it chirped obediently.

Walt wondered where exactly to start, or if he should even start at all. "That was . . . that was a little tense in there, don't you think?"

"Not for me. Remember, I'm a New Yorker."

They got in the car and shut their doors. Ginger put her key in the ignition but she didn't turn it. She just strummed the steering wheel with her hands. The Lexus was an icebox; Walt could see his breath.

"I got carried away a little, didn't I?" she asked him.

"I don't know. Maybe a little."

She sighed. "The empirical types you really have to throw off, otherwise they'll just recite their boring talking points to you." She shook her head. "No, I got in the way. I pressed too hard. I was doing an imitation of one of those old duffers on 60 Minutes, in spite of myself."

She turned the key and the dashboard lit up. "What a dodge!" she exclaimed. "Saying you're a scientist and therefore don't think in theological terms. Give me a break!" A brief blast of cold air poured out of the vents but then the heater and seat warmers kicked in and they were comfortable, even cozy. She reversed out of their parking spot, nearly clipping her rear-view mirror against a column. Then, at the pay station at the bottom of the ramp, she unintentionally nudged the barrier gate with her bumper before slamming on her brakes. When they pulled onto Binney Street, traffic was at a standstill. It would have been so much faster if they had just walked.

Walt looked over at her. She seemed so small all of the sudden, so tiny and impulsive and young.

"I'll need to listen to this recording several times to figure out where I went off track." She puckered her lips, then abruptly leaned over, opened the glove compartment, and withdrew a handful of bubble gum. "The thing is, as a woman, you can ask another woman a direct question, but intonation is key. You have to balance empathy with straightforwardness." Ginger was driving west now on Beacon Street, toward Chestnut Hill. After running a red light and getting flipped off by a guy in a ComElectric truck going the other way, she gave Walt a sidelong glance. "What you thinking over there, loser?" She dropped the second 'r' out of the last word to imitate a Southie accent, which she did pretty well.

"I don't want to die," Walt said.

"Oh, there are so many airbags in this thing; we'd be fine." She veered around a pothole but not soon enough; they both bounced in their seats. She turned on the stereo, then immediately turned it off. "I need some new music. I'm so sick of Radiohead and Yo La Tengo.

Can I borrow some of your jazz?"

"Sure."

"Wait a second, I don't have a record player. I guess I could buy one . . ."

He had tuned her out. He was thinking of Flora: picturing her filling coffee mugs, taking orders, wiping down the tables, waiting for him to show up.

Ginger dumped her gum in his lap and Walt dutifully began to unwrap the pieces for her.

"Women like it when other women write down what they say," she observed.

"Is that right?" In spite of the scene he had just witnessed, Walt believed her. He believed anything a girl or woman told him about other girls and women.

"At least, they're inclined to like it, if you do it the right way. But I screwed up back there. Still, the key is just to keep at it. Start piling up the interviews. Maybe then, before I know it, I'll have a book."

As someone who had tried, and failed, to write a book, Ginger's observation struck a nerve with Walt. He looked out his window. He noticed the girls in the car next to theirs, the girl on the Gap billboard across the street, the girls waiting at the intersection for the light to change. The whole premise of her book was just ridiculous and he might as well tell her. It's not like he owed her circumspect silence. She was a kid, he reminded himself.

"Honestly, I don't think there are many editors out there who want to publish a theodicy in the form of personal narratives."

"I won't tell them it's a theodicy. I won't mention Aquinas once, either in the proposal or the introduction."

"You still need a central character, a single voice. All books need that."

"The Bible doesn't have a single voice."

"It has God's."

"But he changes all the time! One minute he loves the Jews, the next minute he's mad at them. Then he loves them again, then he floods the whole world." He handed her a couple of pieces of gum and she popped them into her mouth and began to chomp.

"The thing is . . ." he paused. "No offense, but you've led a pretty sheltered life, right? And now you want to write an account of women and evil—"

"*Girls* and evil. I think I'm going to use the word *girls* exclusively, since it signifies the potential for growth, rather than *women*, which just names the female as an appendage to the male."

"When did you decide this?"

"Just now."

They had inched up on the bumper of the car in front of them: a woman in a Volvo with two kids in back. The Volvo abruptly switched lanes and dropped behind them while the woman laid on her horn. Ginger flipped her off in her rear-view mirror. "Isn't that why we have bumpers?" she asked him. "Isn't a little bumping allowed?" She clipped one orange cone and then another one and then another one, all of them once lined up to indicate a lane closure ahead. "Are we even going the right way? Not that I care. I just like driving."

Walt squirmed in his seat. A snowflake hit the windshield, and then another. "I'm just saying, the book sounds like a stretch to me."

"Well, I appreciate your opinion. I really do. If you had gender reassignment surgery, I might even put you in it. Hey, that's an idea! I could interview men who decide to *become* women . . . I mean girls. Men who decide to become girls. Or boys who decide. Anyway, that could be *really* interesting, to get that perspective . . ."

Walt leaned his head back and shut his eyes. He felt the car swerve again and again. He listened to a more or less steady symphony of honking. Yes, the premise of *Girls I Know* was ridiculous. But, as he opened his eyes just enough to watch as Ginger withdrew her journal from her bag and balanced it on the steering wheel while she jotted down a note, Walt had a horrible realization. Oh shit, he thought. She's going to do it. She's going to write the stupid book.

CHAPTER 6

Walt first encountered the poetry of Robert Lowell in an undergraduate survey course his freshman year at the University of Vermont. They read two of his poems in that course: "For the Union Dead" and "Grandparents." Walt loved the first because it was all about Boston: the "Hub of the Universe," as his grandmother had always termed the city, quoting Oliver Wendell Holmes. He loved the second poem because it was the first one he had ever read in which a poet talked about his grandparents with unbridled fondness and sentimentality. "Grandpa! Have me, hold me, cherish me!" one line read. In the whole poem, Lowell never once referred to his own parents.

Three years later, when he decided to apply to graduate school and sat down to write a statement of purpose, Walt spoke of his interest in Lowell. For his writing sample, he submitted a paper he had written on "For the Union Dead." He didn't discover until he arrived at Harvard that studying Lowell was no longer fashionable in academic circles. The poet was thought to be too navel-gazing, and also too patrician. Nonetheless, Walt stuck with him, and when it came time to turn in his prospectus, he explained that he was going to write his dissertation on the influence of Yankee peerage on Lowell's verse. *I will submerge Lowell's work in its cultural context,* he wrote, *and argue that his confessional tone is both empowered and hampered by his privileged background.* The language wasn't that outlandish; everyone Walt knew in graduate school in the late nineties was *submerging* books and poems in their cultural contexts. But when he sat down in front of his laptop to begin his critical dunking, Walt froze up. And he remained frozen for years. All a far cry from Ginger's performance that morning, and Walt couldn't help but think that her confidence with Dr. Keller was to a large extent linked to her impeccable social background, whereas his writer's block had been caused, at least in part, by all the limitations he had felt growing up. A Harvard degree would have meant so much to his family that Walt had to fail in his efforts to achieve one, whereas no one in Ginger's world would care whether or not she finished her book and therefore she would be able to. He knew exactly what he was doing: oversimplifying his interpretation of how people performed by focusing exclusively on one factor, class. But he couldn't help it; when in doubt, it was the only way he *could* think.

After driving him around Boston for more than an hour in the snow, Ginger pulled up in front of their apartment building and dropped off Walt. She wasn't done for the day; she wanted to see if she could scrounge up an interview or two over at the Copley Place Mall, but Walt begged out, citing work he needed to do. Once she was gone, he shoveled the sidewalk around the building. He chipped away at the ice. He sprinkled salt generously on the steps. Then he walked over to Floyd's Cleaners for his shift. That night, he waited to see if Ginger would drop by. He listened to two Sonny Clark albums and Stanley Turrentine's *That's Where It's At*. Then he read poem after poem in his *Norton Anthology*: Wyatt's "They Flee From Me" and Andrew Marvell's "The Garden" and Louise Glück's "The Garden" and Theodore Roethke's "I Knew a Woman" and a slew of poems by Elizabeth Bishop, whom he really loved. He didn't linger on any of the verse; he just let the lines run by him again and again. He tended nowadays to skip over Lowell's poems when he stumbled upon them. They no longer made him think about Boston and what it would be like to come from a distinguished American family. Instead, they signified what he hadn't been able to accomplish. They were tiny, graphic embodiments of his own failure to become a scholar.

The whole time he read, Walt listened for a knock on the door, but there never was one. When he turned out his light, he felt a combination of disappointment and relief.

In the morning, he swore he heard her once more, rummaging around in his room, but when he shot up in bed he was alone. It was just a little after seven. He dressed and headed off to the Early Bird

Café.

He beat the rush hour. He had a seat on every train. When he arrived at the Green Street Stop, he stepped through the blast of cold air and made his way onto the platform and up the escalator. He walked as quickly as he could down Green Street, past the condominiums that were being built and the clapboard houses that leaned toward the uneven sidewalk. He passed the dog grooming store, then the bakery, then the post office. Finally he crossed Centre Street and walked up to the blue door that opened into the Early Bird Café.

Natalie met him just inside the door. "Walter! Where were you yesterday?"

"Something came up . . . with a tenant." Not a lie, but not the truth either. He saw Flora, pouring coffee for a couple a few yards away, and waved. She smiled at him. Then he noticed Mercedes sitting behind the register in a blue corduroy dress, the shade of which matched the front door. She was in the midst of filling saltshakers. "You're turning into a regular," Walt said to her. She said nothing in response.

"She's not a regular for long. School starts up next week." Natalie turned and looked at her daughter with her hands on her hips. "My love, the salt is supposed to go *into* the shakers, not onto the table." Mercedes stared at her mother blankly. "No, no, my love. Don't eye me like that. What have we talked about? Respect through what you say *and* how you act."

Mercedes took the large carton of salt, balanced in both her hands, and tipped it ever so slightly, its spout dipping over the edge of the table.

"Don't you dare!" Her mother stood there, staring, until Mercedes started to laugh, silently, just the way her mother did. "Oh, she will be the end of me," Natalie put her hand on Walt's shoulder. "What is the expression? Pushing my . . ."

"Buttons."

"Yes, pushing my *buttons*." And she chuckled to herself as she led Walt through the half-filled café, a few steps behind Flora, who was hurrying back into the kitchen to drop off an order for John.

"You missed some fireworks yesterday," Natalie said as they reached the back of the restaurant. "We had to fire Ramon."

"What happened?"

Natalie looked over her shoulder to make sure none of the other customers were within earshot. Then she waited for Walt to take off his jacket and settle into his chair before she plopped down onto the one facing him.

"Oh, it was something else, my friend." She let out a low whistle as she looked down at her nails on her left hand, which were long and unpainted. "So John comes to work at five thirty yesterday, as always, and Ramon is supposed to be here at six. As you know, we open at seven, which is when I come, only yesterday I was running late because Mercedes was tagging along, since she didn't have school."

"What does she do normally, in the morning?"

"Normally Nene takes her to school with her daughter, Kiki. She's Mercedes's best friend. They live just one floor below us. Then I pick them up after school while Nene works. Anyway, it's a little after seven when Mercedes and I get here and there is no Ramon. That means John has to do all the prep himself. He has to cut all the vegetables and fruit. He has to make the coffee and the oatmeal; it's not easy, making good oatmeal. He has to do everything. So he's rushing around and he's not so good early in the morning anyway, John. You would think a cook who wanted to open a breakfast place his whole life would be a morning person, but he isn't. But I wander."

Flora sped by them again, a tray filled with food balanced on her palm and shoulder, and Natalie, sensing that she would soon be needed up front, slowly rose to her feet. "To make the story short, he comes in—Ramon—a little after eight, and I'm being generous with the time. He comes in and he doesn't look right. His eyes are all glassy and he smells like he slept outside. When you make food for people to eat, you have to be clean! You cannot smell like someone's garbage can. So I go back to the kitchen with him to tell John that I need to speak to him but when John sees him he doesn't need to talk to me about it. He says to him, 'You can't cook today. What are you thinking?' And he tells him to clean out the kitchen instead, starting underneath the oven. And Ramon says to him . . ."

But Natalie couldn't bring herself to repeat the offending phrase. Instead, she waved it away with her hand, and then placed the same hand over her mouth. She looked as if she might cry. She shook her head. "What he said was very disrespectful of John as a black man, and as a restaurant owner, and as his elder. My daughter is sitting in the front of our café, the place we opened after everyone told us we would never be able to pay the lease, after seven banks turned us down for a loan. She is sitting there coloring while an employee of ours is disrespecting her father! Did you see her shoes this morning? They are real leather. When I was a little girl, I didn't know any children who owned a pair of shoes, and now I have a daughter and she has so many shoes, she has a holder for them that hangs from the doorknob of her closet." Natalie tucked in the chair on which she had been sitting. "I don't know why I am talking about the shoes. No, I do. It is because there should be respect for your elders when they have worked hard and can employ you. But Ramon showed John no respect, speaking to him the way he did, and he showed no respect to our family, showing up with dirt on his hands, smelling like a sewer rat. So we told him to leave and never come back—that we'd send him his last paycheck."

With that, Natalie flung her hands in the air, turned, and began to walk back toward the front just as Flora passed her going the other way.

"Did she tell you about Ramon?" she asked Walt.

"Yeah."

"I feel bad."

"Why?"

She walked into the kitchen to drop off her tray and returned with a pot of coffee. Walt turned over the blue mug on his table and she filled it up. "I should have never told John to hire him, not with what's going on in Mattapan."

Walt didn't get the connection. "What's going on in Mattapan?"

And she looked down at him: not like a teenage girl, but like someone older—someone who had seen so much more than he had.

"You're such a *niño*, Mr. Walt. Where's your newspaper?"

"I forgot to buy one this morning."

She tilted her head at him. "You must have met a girl."

"What are you talking about?"

"You're forgetting things, so you must have met a girl."

"Just because I didn't buy a *Globe!*"

"Mr. Walt, let me be honest with you." She sat down on the chair that Natalie had just vacated. Flora never sat down. Even though she always complained about her feet hurting, she never took a break. "You aren't going to be handsome forever. Pretty soon, the jokes you make and stuff, the way you mess up your hair, it won't work anymore. You'll have to do more than that. You should get a girlfriend before that happens. Besides, men who stay single too long get weird, like if you leave a dog locked up every day."

"Is that right?"

She nodded for emphasis.

"I've had girlfriends, you know."

She shook her head and then stood up. "I'm being serious. This is real advice."

She walked off to check on the other tables, her black ringlets bouncing against her neck. She had a round bottom that stuck out inside her jean skirt, underneath which she wore thick black stockings. Walt looked down at her feet. No fancy boots, just a pair of cheap pumps, the soles worn smooth. And he realized why he had no intention of ever telling her about Ginger. It wasn't just because Ginger was rich, although that was part of it. Obviously, it was because he liked Flora; he always had. That must have been why he had never been able to see her as a sister; he liked her too much. But he had never quite admitted this to himself, which was curious. It had taken Ginger's appearance in his life to make him recognize that he wanted to be with Flora.

He watched her now as she chatted with the other customers—writing down their orders, topping off their coffee—and tried to imagine the two of them together. Would they look a little funny, walking down the street? She was so small. Why did he ask himself such stupid questions? He wondered what they'd talk about outside of the café. That was a more credible concern. They couldn't discuss literature. Not that he and his old friends from grad school ever talked about literature, but they could, if they wanted to, and that was enough. Flora had probably never sat down and read a poem before. But that was just because the opportunity had never presented itself. He could help her with that; he could present the opportunity. Ginger had joked the day before about him tutoring her, which would be insane, but he could teach Flora stuff and she'd really appreciate it. And he'd learn from her too. He'd learn to see Boston from her perspective. Eventually he'd meet her family: all of those cousins that she was always complaining about, and her two sisters. He had always dreamt of having an extended family that didn't actually extend from his own. Maybe she could teach him Spanish too. That would be cool, if he learned Spanish, since he overheard it all the time on the T.

She walked back over to his table, flipping open the cover of her tiny notebook. "What will it be?"

"I think an omelet today."

"What kind?"

"You choose."

She rolled her eyes. "I don't have the time, Mr. Walt."

"Well, how about some sausage and Swiss cheese and . . . I don't know."

"Mushrooms are good with Swiss cheese. Why are you smiling at me like that?"

"What are you talking about?"

"Stop it."

"Okay. Mushrooms then. And some granola and yogurt on the side."

She dropped her tiny notebook into her apron. "You're acting funny this morning," she said, before disappearing into the kitchen.

For the next few minutes, while he waited for John to make his breakfast, Walt stared out at the restaurant. He watched Natalie seat a group of four businessmen. He listened to the faint sound of grease snapping on the griddle back in the kitchen. And he thought more about Flora. She was young; he wasn't sure exactly how young—he had never asked her how old she was—but she was young. What if it got weird between them? Where would he have breakfast then? But it could get weird between them without them ever going out, that was the thing. It was already getting weird, just by virtue of how he was thinking.

A few minutes later, she reappeared with his food and he thanked her while she sped off. The omelet was delicious. Walt ate the whole thing in a rush, the cheese dribbling out of his mouth, the hot pieces of sausage singeing his tongue. Then he had the granola and yogurt, a perfect complement. Before he had finished eating, Flora dropped his check on the table. There were people standing at the front counter now, waiting to be seated. Maybe Flora *did* like him, maybe she thought the world of him—as Natalie had said—but she still wanted to turn over his table; she needed the tips. She had charged him five dollars; Walt left eight. He grabbed his jacket and began to wiggle out from behind the table. Flora had darted into the kitchen to get some ketchup for someone and now she reappeared, the plastic bottle held in her hand.

She scooped up his money. "Thanks, Mr. Walt," she said. She bit her lip. "You know, you never talk about what you studied at Harvard. What's the use of knowing things if you don't tell anyone what you know? Why go to a fancy school in the first place?"

"Well, remember, I haven't really been *at* Harvard in a while."

"That's not what—"

"No, I see your point." He tossed his napkin onto his plate. "What would you think about the two of us reading some poems together? That way we could talk about them."

She peered at him skeptically. "Are you joking?"

"No, I'm serious. Would you like that?"

"Of course." She nodded, the yellow ribbon in her hair lifting up and then down. "Yes, I would like that very much."

"I'll teach you everything I know about poetry. We'll start with Robert Frost."

"Who's that?"

"My grandmother's favorite poet. A New England poet."

"Is he an important one?"

The fact that she took for granted that some poets were important made him smile. They were off to a good start. "Oh, yeah, he's important. We'll read a few of his poems together, once a week or so, and analyze them. I'll show you how to figure out their rhyme schemes. I'll tell you what a metaphor is. I'll explain stresses to you."

"What is a *stress*?"

"You'll see soon enough. When do you usually get off?"

"It depends how busy we are for lunch. We close at two, but I have to be home by three to take care of my nephew, Antonio, while my sisters work."

"What do your sisters do again?"

"They clean rooms at the Copley Marriott."

"Okay, well, I need to be at the dry cleaners by two. Any chance Natalie would let you off a little early every once in a while?"

"I think so."

"All right, so let's start next week, say Friday."

"Okay. I'll ask Natalie if that will work."

He started to walk to the front of the restaurant. He'd have to check out a copy of Frost's *Complete Poems* now and make some photocopies for her. That would mean going onto campus, which he always dreaded. He was afraid of running into his old advisor, Meredith O'Shea, and having her look through him. He was afraid of not seeing anyone on campus that he recognized.

Flora followed just behind him while Natalie walked the other way, leading a couple back to Walt's table. "Thank you so much, Mr. Walt."

"Oh, it's nothing."

"You know, I don't want to work as a waitress my whole life."

She stopped in front of the register. A party of three waited for a table but they were engrossed in their own conversation. He and Flora were, more or less, alone for a moment.

"You're not going to be a waitress your whole life, Flora."

"I know that." She looked down at her feet and he reached out, put his index finger just beneath her chin, and lifted up her head. In the flat light she looked tired and worn, with deep, purple circles under her eyes. On the one hand, hardly anyone looked halfway decent in Boston in the winter. But on the other hand, she looked *so* tired. And she was smiling at him—beaming, really. She was so excited to learn about poetry, of all things. She thought it would change her life. And he wondered if it had been fair of him to make the offer in the first place.

"I don't want to live in Mattapan forever," she said. "I want to live someplace pretty."

"You will. If you want that then you'll get it."

"Oh, it's that simple?"

"Yeah, it is. Look at me. I live in Boston and—growing up—that's all I ever wanted."

"You should have wanted more."

"You've never been in Burlington in January."

She didn't laugh at his attempt at humor. Instead she sighed, her bangs lifting off her forehead.

"How old are you, Flora?"

"Nineteen."

"That's it?"

"Yeah. Why, do I look older?"

He didn't answer her right away. He was doing the math. So she had taken this job right out of high school. This was what her diploma had made possible for her.

"No, you look nineteen, that just means I've got ten years on you. That's a lot, don't you think?"

She patted him on the cheek. "I can always just tell people who ask that you're my uncle. Goodbye, Walt."

"Goodbye, Flora." He watched her walk back toward the kitchen, then stepped toward the front door. He stopped in his tracks. They hadn't been alone after all. Mercedes Bittles had been watching them. She was finished filling the saltshakers. They were all lined up in front of her. She had her hands folded and was staring at him: studying him, or so he thought. Kids are too self-possessed these days, he decided. He was extrapolating from her alone; he didn't know any other kids, he couldn't recall *seeing* any other kids, although surely he passed them all the time in the streets of Boston.

"Have a nice day," Walt said to her as he pulled on the knob. The string of bells that hung from the top of the blue door rang out. Mercedes didn't say anything in response but Walt didn't notice. He had drifted off into another daydream: he and Flora walking down the street, holding hands, speaking Spanish to one another. For some reason, he had grown a goatee. She was wearing a thin, cotton dress.

It was spring; neither one of them had anywhere to go. She leaned into him as they meandered along: the whole city of Boston laid out before them, from Mattapan to Cambridge, every neighborhood and alleyway ripe for the taking.

CHAPTER 7

He came home to find Ginger lying on his futon, reading *The Sentences of Peter Lombard.*

"Where ya been?" she asked.

"I was having breakfast." The entire way home, he had been thinking about Flora, but now he felt her receding in his mind: disappearing over the horizon that separated the Back Bay from Jamaica Plain.

Ginger smirked at him from over the top of her book. "Are you sick of me yet? I wear people out, you know."

"You don't say." He tossed his jacket onto the floor.

"So you are sick of me! Be honest. Maybe a little?"

"Maybe a little."

She lowered her book as her eyebrows arched. "You don't have to be *that* honest."

"I'm just kidding."

She fluffed the pillow behind her, which was thin and flat and more or less unfluffable.

"Who is Peter Lombard anyway?" Walt plopped down on his recliner.

"Oh, he's an awesome Scholastic philosopher—twelfth century. Aquinas stole from him quite a bit, it turns out. I've been reading what the two of them have to say about charity."

"Do you even believe in God?"

"No, but I like people who do, especially when they really work at it. I think that's cool."

"But now you're interested in charity? I don't get it. The other night, you said you were studying evil—"

"Yeah, I realized—after our trip to Dana-Farber—that, you know, if I'm truly following Aquinas, the only way to understand evil is by juxtaposing it with charity. That's how I think Aquinas would understand Dr. Keller's desire not just to alleviate the suffering of her victims, but to try to save them in the first place. Technically speaking, her impulse in both cases is a *charitable* one. She's not trying to save *herself* from dying, after all; she's not self-interested. The thing you have to realize, for the Scholastics, is that *charity* doesn't mean what we take it to mean. It isn't about dropping off crap at the Salvation Army. Charity is about loving like God loves, loving people you have no need to love, loving the world so much it hurts. That's why I'm reading Lombard. He thought, when you acted charitably, you actually became a part of God. Isn't that cool?" Her blue eyes shimmered with intensity. "Aquinas's take is different. He basically says that God loves his created beings so much that he is willing to let them destroy each other. And when natural evils like cancer arise, if they prompt a charitable response like Dr. Keller's, then that's a good thing. God could get rid of cancer, see, he can do whatever he wants, but he chooses not to because cancer teaches us how to love more like God loves. Cancer is an evil, but, like all evils, it can produce a good."

Walt shook his head. "That's lunatic."

"I don't think it is."

A silence fell between them. Ginger flipped onto her stomach and propped her chin in her hands. Did he want her to disappear from his apartment, maybe even disappear from his life? Yes and no. He loved the fact that she was squirreled away in his studio while the rest of the city barreled along, but at the same time he wanted her to go away. He felt, as he looked at her, his brain becoming cluttered and confused. He wanted to undress her, but he wanted himself to remain clothed. He wanted to live near her, but he didn't want to run into her anymore. He wanted to understand the way she saw the world, but he didn't want to listen to her enumerate the details of her privileged existence.

She yawned, then pulled her sharp chin back toward her shoulder until her neck cracked. "I can't read in Blair's apartment all day and night. The radiator is too loud. Plus, I get distracted watching Sid. I can watch him for hours. So I was thinking of turning your place into my basement study."

"Help yourself," he heard himself say. "All that's mine is yours."

"See, Peter Lombard would love you. You're so giving."

He popped up the footrest of his La-Z-Boy, which squeaked loudly. Why, when he really wanted to ask her for space, did he feel compelled to invite her to take over his apartment? She threw him off balance. Almost the exact age as Flora, but she seemed so much older.

"What?" He shook his head but she insisted. "No, what?"

"I sure as hell hope you aren't the embodiment of some early midlife crisis I'm starting to have."

"I hope so too. Who wants to embody that?" She smiled narrowly, one of her guarded grins. No dimples appeared.

"Aren't your friends wondering where you are?"

"You *are* getting sick of me. I thought we went over this. I don't have friends, Walt."

"But how can that be?"

"I have odd tastes, clearly. What's your excuse? Where are your friends?"

"All over Boston. My two best friends, Max and Scott, both live in Arlington. They didn't finish their dissertations either. Mostly we hang out in the spring and summer, when the Red Sox are playing."

"Boys are so weird." She rolled onto her back and stretched out her arms. "That is nasty, by the way." She pointed at the stain on the ceiling above her, then glanced over at his alarm clock. Quickly she hopped off his futon. She was wearing jeans and a gray, zippered sweatshirt, a far cry from her outfit the other day. "Oh, shit, I'm running late. Want to keep me company on another field trip for *Girls I Know*?"

"I can't, I . . . uh," he suddenly remembered what he had planned for that morning, "I have to go to work early today—"

"You're lying."

"Not very well," he said under his breath. "Where are you going?"

"I'm talking to the director of a women's shelter over on Harrison Avenue."

"That's in Roxbury."

"So?"

"Well, you know, not a great neighborhood."

"I think I can handle it." She crossed her arms and stuck her foot out. "So aren't you going to tell me what you really have to do this morning? What do you have to hide? I thought you had discovered the secret to happiness."

Walt stood up from his La-Z-Boy and retreated, self-consciously, back toward his records. There was no polite way to put it, not that he felt any obligation to be polite to Ginger, who was not herself Miss Manners. "I make a deposit every other week at a sperm bank out in Brighton and I can't forget to go; they close out your lot number if you don't show."

"Deposit? Don't you mean a withdrawal?" Ginger looked at him, poker face intact. She was very good. In the game of language, she knew every move. "I've never been to a sperm bank. Want a ride?"

He actually could use a ride; taking the T out to Brighton was a huge pain. "What about your meeting in Roxbury?"

"She said I could just drop by anytime today. Come on! Let's get you over to Brighton to jerk off!" Ginger tossed his jacket to him, then opened the door and stepped out onto the concrete landing at the foot of the basement stairs. "Oh, I need to grab my journal, though."

Like a puppy, he followed her: up the stairs, into the elevator, then back down again after she had fetched her journal, zipped up her parka, and slipped on her boots. They took the hallway on the ground floor out to the lot in back, where—remarkably—she had parked her Lexus in the appropriate spot. Once more, Walt directed her onto Storrow Drive. Once more, his brain fogging over, he watched her right leg as it extended ever so slightly whenever she pressed down on the accelerator. *What am I doing with this girl?* he asked himself as they raced along the Charles, in a hurry for no reason. *What in the world am I doing?*

The Brighton Cryobank for Oncologic and Reproductive Donors rested on the ground floor of a nondescript, three-story concrete building off Market on Surrey Street. The sperm bank was itself ingeniously laid out, with entirely separate entrances and waiting rooms—one for ejaculators, the other for prospective buyers. On the floor above were two different clinics: one run by a clinical psychologist, the other by an ear, nose, and throat specialist. An accounting firm occupied the entire third floor.

Walt and Ginger walked through the unmarked door behind the building that led into the ejaculators' check-in and waiting room. This room was eggshell white, with tidy rows of chairs set around a pair of coffee tables. All of the chairs were empty.

He stepped up to the counter, behind which a large, ruddy-complexioned woman in loose-fitting white scrubs typed at a keyboard.

"Hey there, Kathryn."

The woman turned slowly in her chair. "Hey, Walt."

Kathryn wheeled her chair back to one of the large filing cabinets behind her desk and flipped through a few files before withdrawing Walt's, which she opened while wheeling back to the counter. She set the folder down in front of him. He signed and dated his name while Kathryn rolled over to another cabinet, this at the far end of the counter, where they kept the plastic cups, lids, and white paper bags. She wheeled once more back to where Walt stood and only then did she stand up. That was when she noticed Ginger, who had been lurking well behind the high counter, beyond her field of vision. She looked her up and down.

"She can't go back there with you," she said to Walt as she wrote her initials next to his signature.

"She's my ride." Walt smiled. Kathryn didn't look impressed and he added, because it seemed as if something needed to be added, "I'm going to give her a free tour of Boston afterwards." He turned to Ginger. "A real tour this time. Deal?"

"Deal."

"Well, don't he treat you right," Kathryn deadpanned. She peeled a sticker with his lot number on it from the sheet inside his folder and placed it on the side of the cup. "Room four is all yours," she said.

Walt took the cup and paper bag and looked over his shoulder, expecting Ginger to be right there, but she had already sat down in the waiting area. "Think of me, darling," she called out as she thumbed through a *McCall's*. While the donor rooms were filled with porn, the waiting room didn't push the envelope at all. Just the typical piles of outdated magazines, a few condensed books, and some pamphlets on STDs and high cholesterol.

He walked down the hallway to the right of the counter and entered the second door on his left. The masturbation rooms were all identical. They each had a sink with a small mirror above it, a chair in the corner, and next to the chair, a small TV with pornographic magazines and a few videos piled next to it. Against the wall, facing the sink, was an examination table: a vestige of when the cryobank had been an allergy clinic.

He turned off the dim light and stood there with one hand on the padded table. Walt never used any of the donor aids. The magazines were fairly tepid stuff, mostly *Playboy* and *Penthouse*, although occasionally someone would leave something raunchier behind. Still, they all smelled of unwashed men's hands. The videos had titles like *Bad to the Boner* and *I Know Who You Banged Last Summer*. They sounded more parodic than they did erotic; besides, the VCRs never worked anyway. He loosened his pants and made sure to remove the lid from the cup, so he wouldn't have to fumble with it while he ejaculated.

He began to touch himself. As was usually the case, he pictured Kathryn for a moment. Then he thought of the girl who worked at the deli across the street from his building, her pierced eyebrow, the apron she wore smeared with nacho cheese drippings. Where had she been lately? He remembered the Israeli student in the last class he had taught at Harvard: the one with jet black hair and leather everything. He always thought of her. Then he returned to the girl at the deli, now pressed up against the soft drinks dispenser with her pants off, her stomach and breasts splattered with melted cheese, her tongue heavy on her lower lip. And now she was lying with her back on the counter of the deli, her legs spread, and Walt was standing over her, until she pulled him on top of her, arching her back, and he was inside of her: his hands on her breasts, her mouth open, her head turned to the side.

When he was about to come, he made sure to dip his penis in the cup. Then, when he was finished, he replaced the lid and fastened his pants. He placed the cup in the bag. The whole time, he never thought of Ginger.

They headed back down Storrow Drive, the music blaring, the windows down. Walt imagined being stricken with a case of pneumonia and dragging himself to a doctor, who would ask him if he was dressing warmly enough for this time of year. Walt would answer yes, then confess that he had also been driving around town in a Lexus with the windows down. But of course this conversation would never take place because he would never drag himself to a doctor, since he didn't have health insurance.

The music suddenly cut out. Ginger was eyeing him from the heated seat of her starship. "What's going on in that brain of yours, Walt? You're biting your lip."

"Can we roll up the windows?"

"Oh, you are so no fun." As if responding to his request on their own, the windows suddenly rose. "Do you need a nap and a cigarette too, after expending yourself?"

Walt shook his head. "You are something else."

"Where are we going for my tour of Boston? Or were you just saying that at the sperm bank for show?"

"No, no—"

"You're a little sneaky, aren't you, Walt Steadman? You act like you're an open book, but some pages you don't want anyone to read." She grinned, pleased by her choice of metaphor, her perfect teeth peeking out over her bottom lip. "So I did another interview for *Girls I Know*."

"When?"

"Just now." Ginger opened her armrest and withdrew an empty bag of candy. She leaned over and opened the glove compartment. No gum, just wrappers. She growled. "While you were masturbating this morning, at least the last time you masturbated this morning, in the sperm bank, I chatted with the woman behind the counter."

"Kathryn?"

"Yeah. I was wondering just what a weird job that would be. So I asked her about it. She said she likes her job. They have really great benefits. She said some of the men can get pretty emotional about selling their sperm, that lots of guys can't produce their first time in. Did you have any problems?"

"No. She told you all of this?"

"I told you! Women unburden themselves to other women. It's just a fact." Traffic was bumper to bumper ahead: morning rush hour. Ginger slammed on her brakes. The tires screeched. Someone behind them honked. "Sorry, still getting that down. So I have a proposal. I'll let you off the hook with regards to my tour if you ride shotgun with me now on another interview."

"Ginger—"

"Please! I don't want to do this one by myself. It could be awkward." She tapped the steering wheel while he remained silent, trying to imagine what in the world would give her pause. "Come on, Walt! Say yes, otherwise I'll roll the windows down again and turn on the AC."

"Okay, okay. Who is the subject this time?"

"Well, as clichéd as it sounds, I feel like I should talk to at least one girl who works in the sex industry. Girls do exploit themselves; it's a topic I have to cover. So, do you have a favorite strip club in the area?"

"No!"

"You don't like any of them?"

"I don't know them! What do you think, I troll around strip clubs?"

"As opposed to being holed up in your dungeon all the time? God, I hope you do. But seriously, don't guys, every few months, gather together as a group and go watch women take their clothes off, kind of to boil off steam, like girls go and buy shoes?"

"No, we don't do that." He began to think. "I did go to one, years ago, for a bachelor party." This had been a party thrown for a friend of Walt's who had ended up, after his marriage, moving to Connecticut, never to be heard from again. Kind of a friend of a friend. Walt couldn't remember his full name: Mike Something.

"See!"

"It was an awful place. I've heard the nicest one in the area is in Providence. At least that's where Mo Vaughn always went."

"Who's Mo Vaughn?"

"Red Sox first baseman. Plays for the Angels now."

"Well, I'd rather see one that's on the sleazier side of the spectrum anyway."

Walt checked his watch. "It's definitely sleazy, I'm just not sure if it's open this early."

"Let's go see."

He directed her toward Chinatown in downtown Boston. First they cut through Beacon Hill and around the Common. Then they wound through the narrow streets that encircled the Opera House. Walt couldn't recall the exact location of the establishment, just that it was somewhere nearby. They passed an empty parking lot, then a couple of pawnshops, before turning onto Lagrange Street. On their left hung a flickering neon sign displaying a pair of legs above the phrase *Glass Slipper*. Ginger parked on the street and they went in.

The bouncer, an enormous black man, met them at the door. He asked Walt for ID and twenty dollars for the cover, which he didn't have. Ginger pulled several twenties out of the pocket of her jeans and handed him one. Then the bouncer waved them into the lounge.

The place was dark and empty: just a couple of cocktail waitresses in strapless tank tops, black skirts, and fishnet stockings, talking to one another, and a DJ with headphones on, hunkered over a control board on their left. Ginger chose a booth just to the right of a small stage and she and Walt sat down next to each other.

She looked around. "Why do you think the bouncer didn't ask for my ID? Maybe he thinks I'm a hooker."

"Not with the journal. I bet he thinks you're a Harvard kid working on a book."

"That's the meanest thing you could ever say to me."

They could just glimpse the top of their heads in the mirrors behind the stage. On their left was a steep staircase. A stripper walked down the stairs just as the DJ began to spin some techno music. The speakers, bolted on the ceiling above the front corners of the stage, were blown and the sound came out muffled.

The stripper had on a business suit that was about two sizes too small and was holding a briefcase that she set down in the middle of the stage while looking menacingly at Ginger.

"Her tits are busting out," Ginger said. "I wish my tits busted out." She opened her journal and jotted down some observations. One of the waitresses sauntered over. She was thin, bony really, and had dirty black hair tied off in a ponytail, dark eye shadow, and gold lipstick.

"What can I get you?" Like the dancer on stage, she looked at Ginger, not Walt.

"I'm writing a book about girls," Ginger said, sliding toward Walt and nodding at the space created next to her. "If you want to talk some about your life, I'd love to hear what you have to say."

Ginger had apparently adopted a different strategy for this locale than the one she had used at Dana-Farber: no digital recorder, no formal request for an interview.

The woman looked over her shoulder, then over at Walt. "You want something to drink?"

"I'm fine." The front door opened and a stab of light flooded the lounge before disappearing.

"It's a one-drink minimum per person," she explained.

"Then I'll have a Bud."

She nodded and looked at Ginger, who ordered a gin gimlet.

The waitress walked away. "Maybe not every girl will want to be in *Girls I Know*," Walt said with a grin.

On stage, the stripper had opened her briefcase and taken out an enormous dildo that she waved around like a fire hose. Ginger pointed up at the ceiling, where there were mirrors Walt hadn't noticed. The dancer walked up the stairs, then came back down minus the suit and dildo, in a black teddy. She put her arms around the pole in the middle of the stage and began to buck and twist, the lingerie slipping to the ground. Looking at the woman's back as it was reflected off the mirrors behind the stage, Walt noticed a purple stain on her skin.

"Birthmark?" he asked Ginger.

"I'm thinking more burn than birth." She nodded her head authoritatively. They both looked at it for a few seconds. "It's shaped like Rhode Island," she added.

The waitress came back with their drinks. She asked for twenty-two dollars. Walt pointed at Ginger, who gave her forty.

"So you're writing a book?" The waitress began to peel ones from a wad of bills.

Ginger nodded. "*Girls I Know*. You can keep the change."

"Thanks." She looked down at her. "Sheila," the woman nodded at another waitress, "can you check on the guy at eight?"

Walt couldn't see Sheila's reaction, the back of their booth was too high. Their waitress set her tray down on their table and squeezed in next to Ginger. After the stripper in front of them had crawled over to pick a twenty out of Ginger's hand with her mouth, she started to talk about her life.

"I ran away from home at thirteen," she began. "We were living with my mom's boyfriend in Rumford, Maine, a piece of shit town. I don't remember the guy's name. He had two kids. One of them was mental—really big and strong but would spit up his food and crap on himself. The other went to juvenile hall cuz he kept on trying to rape the girls in his homeroom. He was a year older than me.

"Mom was diabetic and didn't work. She got disability money because her left eye was no good. The guy she was with then was real fat. He didn't work neither. The two of them would sit around, drink, and watch TV. Whenever I was alone with him, he would smile at me in a fucked up way. He never touched me, though. I heard them talking about it one night and my mom was like, 'If you want it so bad go give it a try, just don't hurt her,' so I left.

"It wasn't like I meant to run away for good. I was just planning on walking around. I went into a grocery store and decided I was going to buy some cigarettes only I didn't have any money, so I swiped a pack and then out in the parking lot this guy came up to me and said he had seen what I had done with the Marlboro Lights and he was going to turn me in. I begged him not to; I actually thought he could get me into trouble, and he said he wouldn't but that I should get home and he'd give me a ride. So I got in his car with him.

"He took me to his house all the way up near Oquossoc, me screaming the whole way, pounding on the window. No one in any of the cars we passed looked over at us. When we got to his place he locked me in his basement. A couple times a day he'd give me food. There was a sink and shower down there. I'd go to the bathroom in the sink. A few weeks later he came downstairs with a mattress and another man. The man gave him money to rape me. I don't know how much. I found out later that the guy had taken out ads in porn magazines. 'Young Girl Who Likes Pain.' It took me a month of getting the shit raped out of me to figure out a way out of there. I ended up knocking the door down with a section of pipe when he was gone one day.

"I didn't feel like I could go home after that so I moved to Waterville, then Berlin, New Hampshire, then Manchester. I did tricks, worked in a convenience store for a while. I didn't look like I was thirteen no more. I got arrested for stuff, nothing serious, mostly just cuz I had nowhere to go. Then I started doing speed and LSD and other shit guys would give me to fuck them or suck them off. I'm eighteen now. I take Concord Trailways down from Manchester every Sunday afternoon and waitress and dance here through Wednesday. I can't dance on the weekends because they say my tits aren't big enough and I can't afford no enlargements. So I work and buy my shit down here for the week. One of my girlfriends looks after my boy while I'm gone in exchange for speed. I had him two years ago: Jayce. I work down here so it won't ever get back to him, how I make money."

A guy sat down at the booth behind them and their waitress stood up, picked up her tray, and went to get his drink order. As she walked off, Ginger wrote madly. Walt didn't say anything; he just watched her hand fly back and forth across the page.

A short time later, they climbed back into Ginger's car. She turned the key in the ignition, but rather than immediately hit the gas, she sat there for a moment, slumped over her steering wheel, the collar of her sweatshirt drooping so that Walt could glimpse the base of her neck, the ridge of her collarbones.

"Are you okay?" he asked her.

She rubbed her eyes, yawning. "I haven't slept in days. I mean *days*. And all the sudden, I feel a little down. Why is it always so overcast here? Honestly, I can't believe the Puritans stayed. I can't believe they didn't all just go back to England and become Anglicans."

Walt felt down too. Maybe it was because they had been running around all morning. He wondered what Flora was up to now. Then he watched Ginger bite at one of her nails. If the Puritans had gone back to England, that meant her ancestors would have returned as well.

She wouldn't have come into existence, at least not on this side of the Atlantic. He would have never met her.

"I can drop you off in the Back Bay," she said, shifting the car into drive. Once more they were on the move. "You just have to give me directions."

"Where are you headed?"

"I want to get over to that women's shelter. Sorry, I'd ask you to come but this is one trip I think I'd be better off doing on my own."

He wouldn't have gone along on this next excursion even if she had asked him. There was something deeply wrong about *Girls I Know*, something objectionable about driving around in a black Lexus and seeking out these stories, these experiences. The whole idea was indefensible on some level. Ginger must have known that.

Walt directed her back around the Common, onto Charles Street. Neither one of them spoke. When they neared Beacon he told her to take a left. "I know *that*," she snapped. "I'm not an idiot." For what seemed like a long time, they sat at the light on Arlington Street, then Berkeley, then Gloucester.

"Do you think it's a good idea," he asked out of the blue, "driving this car everywhere?" He wanted to dissuade her from going to the women's shelter but he didn't know how.

"Why?"

"I don't know; it kind of draws attention, don't you think?"

"Well, it *is* my car, and I'd like to learn how to drive it." As if on cue, she gunned the Lexus across Mass Ave and pulled in front of the fire hydrant that faced their building.

"Is it hard to get from here to Harrison Avenue?" she asked him.

"No, just take Mass Ave. It's the first street after Washington."

"Okay."

He unfastened his seatbelt but he didn't open his door. He was thinking more about the curious paradoxes that constituted Ginger Newton: the insightfulness paired with the naïveté, the fascination with others and the utter self-absorption. He wanted her to explain herself but he didn't know how to get her to do it. Instead, with a hint of exasperation, he asked her simply: "How did your roommates deal with all of your energy?"

She threw the car into park. "Well, one of them lost her mind. I think I told you about her. She claimed to hear me talking even when I wasn't around, but that's psychosis, you know? You can't blame someone else for that. Another one slept at her boyfriend's a lot. And the other one just slept around. Well, that's not entirely fair. She also ran her own student activities group, blah blah blah." She slapped her cheeks a couple of times. "Hey, you won't see me for a few days. I'm flying back to New York this evening. My parents are hosting a fundraiser for Habitat for Humanity tomorrow night and I promised them I'd be there."

"That would be the more modern notion of charity."

"Right you are."

He opened the door and stepped out onto the curb. "How long will you be gone?"

"Just until Sunday. Oh, listen to that. Maybe you aren't that sick of me."

He smiled. The funny thing was, as he stood there thinking about all her different attributes, Walt also imagined making a pass at her. He liked and disliked her all at once, as opposed to Flora, whom he just liked. And now, still standing there, still looking at Ginger, still thinking about hitting on her, he was also thinking about Flora.

"Good luck," he said, "with the interview, and the drive over."

She rolled all the windows down in the car and lurched back into the street. "See ya," she called out, hitting the accelerator. And in a flash she was off. Walt wondered how long it'd take her to realize she was going in the wrong direction.

THE EARLY BIRD CAFÉ

CHAPTER **8**

While Walt sat at Floyd's Cleaners and Ginger interviewed not just the director, but several women staying at Rosie's Place, a shelter for impoverished, homeless, and abused women, Flora finished mopping the floor of the Early Bird Café. She had already wiped down the tables, cleaned the coffee station, and swept the sidewalk in front of the restaurant. Now she lifted a chair off one of the tables, sat down, slipped her left foot out of her shoe, and massaged it in her hands.

Natalie stood behind the counter, counting the money out of the register, her lips moving each time a bill rustled in her hands. Flora could hear John back in the kitchen straightening up, the big metal garbage can knocking against the oven door. She looked out the window—so gray outside, and cold. Winter just went on and on, while summer was over before you knew it: a few spring days, then hot as can be, then the leaves falling and winter all over again.

"You need a good pair of shoes, a pair that will cushion those little toes of yours," Natalie said to her, not even looking up. She noticed all sorts of things without using her eyes; like if a customer tried to walk out without paying, she'd meet him at the door and ask if he was sure that he didn't want a little more coffee. Flora had seen her do that several times. And if she gave Walt a break on his bill more than twice in one week, Natalie would remind her that he wasn't just a friend of theirs but a customer too. But her talents were even more otherworldly than that. If you handed Natalie Bittles the whole stack of menus, she could tell you if one or two were missing. And if you found an article of clothing under a chair, say a scarf or a pair of mittens, she always knew who had left it behind. "That belongs to the woman who was wearing the brown trench coat," she would say, "the one who asked if we had cinnamon rolls." Or, "That hood attaches to the parka that the little boy threw on the floor. He was sitting right in the window, with a sitter. Couldn't have been his mom; no way that girl ever had a baby." Sometimes Flora felt as if the Early Bird Café was a part of Natalie's body—not something she had to think about keeping an eye on, but rather something connected to her, no less so than her arms and legs.

"My friend, you are deep in thought today. What's on your mind?"

Flora shook her head. "I'm tired, is all." Natalie seemed always to catch her when she was occupied with something she couldn't quite share. She slipped her left foot back into her shoe and began to massage her right one. Could she make it over to the Northeastern University Bookstore after they closed up the café? She wanted to buy a copy of Robert Frost's poems. She checked her watch. No, it was almost two-thirty; as it stood now, she'd have to rush to make it home before Pilar and Fatima went to work. Maybe she could go over after her shift on Sunday, when her sisters didn't work?

"Goodness, look at you! Chattering away to yourself. What are you thinking about, Flora?"

Flora shook her head again. She didn't want to mention Walt, or the prospect of reading poems with him. Over the last year and a half, ever since she had started working at the Early Bird, she and Natalie had talked so much about him. Flora had never met anyone who had gone to Harvard before. At first she had kept her mouth shut when she served him; she didn't want to say something stupid. But then, after a little bit, Flora started to tease him. Walt was so easy to tease. He wore these awful-looking sweaters and had that funny job as a superintendent. Still, he was a good-looking man, and he was educated, even if he acted like he wasn't. He had gone to Harvard, and now he wanted to teach her what he had learned there. It was all very exciting.

Natalie finished counting out the drawer. She put rubber bands around the ones, fives, tens, and twenties. Then she put the bills into the leather pouch that had *Wainwright Bank* printed on the side. She zipped up the pouch and walked around the counter, just as John stepped out into the hallway in back.

"You get that all cleaned out already?" Natalie asked him.

"You can look. It's clean. Shoot." John hated cleaning the kitchen. That was why they had hired Ramon. Now they were looking for his replacement, but neither John nor Natalie had asked Flora if she knew anyone who needed a job. And they weren't going to ask, either. Not after the way Ramon's time at the Early Bird had ended.

"I'll be back in a few," Natalie said to him, holding up the deposit bag. That was Flora's cue that she was free to go. She ducked around the register to get her purse while John waved the two of them away. He liked to smoke a cigarette in front of the café after they had closed, but the only way he could do that was if Natalie took the money down to the bank; otherwise she'd grab the cigarette out of his hand and snap it into two before he could get out his lighter.

Flora stood up and put the chair back up on the table: upside down, so its back pointed toward the floor. Then she stepped outside with Natalie. Some afternoons she'd walk down to the bank with her, but Flora didn't have the time today, so when they reached the light on Green Street, she stopped walking.

"You get some rest now, Ms. Martinez," Natalie said to her. "I don't like seeing you dragging your little butt around." And she reached over to shake her hand, catching Flora by surprise. Flora wasn't sure if they had ever pressed their hands together before. Even when Natalie had interviewed her for the job, after they were done talking, she had wrapped her arms around Flora's shoulder blades and given her a squeeze. When their palms met now, she felt the edge of a bill pinch against her skin. Twenty dollars. She shook her head at Natalie, who squeezed her fingers around the money. "Now listen to me. You go buy yourself some new shoes. I know you can't get much with twenty dollars, but you got some nice tips today, right? So use a little of that money on yourself. There's nothing wrong with doing that every once in a while. Go get yourself some new shoes. And when you and Mr. Walt sit down and start reading poems together, you can slip them off and run one of those bony toes against his shin."

Flora pushed her away playfully while Natalie rolled her head back on her neck, smiling. "Oh my friend, do not think I don't know what's going on in my restaurant. Never think that!"

The light changed. Flora stepped into the crosswalk. "Thank you,

Mrs. Bittles."

Natalie shooed her away. "Get moving now. Don't stand in the middle of the street!"

Flora waved over her shoulder and began to walk up Green Street, toward the T stop. There was a Payless right on Blue Hill Avenue, just up from where she lived. She could stop by on the way home and no one would know the difference. She was going to get herself a pair of flats this time; she always bought shoes that gave her some height, but what she really needed was a pair that was comfortable. After she paid for them, she'd have to hide them under her coat; she couldn't go home with a box of new shoes. And when she bought the book of poems by Robert Frost that weekend, she'd have to tell Fatima that Walt had loaned it to her. Otherwise she'd get mad at her for wasting their money. Fatima had been like that ever since Antonio was born. Each month, she worried they weren't going to be able to pay the heating bill. "What would we do if they turned off the heat?" she'd ask them during dinner. She didn't want to wrap Antonio in extra blankets because, when he was born, all the nurses at the hospital told her that was dangerous. But she'd have to use extra blankets if the heat was turned off. And Pilar would say that there was nothing to worry about, that NSTAR couldn't turn the heat off in the winter, even if you didn't pay. "That's against the law," she'd say. But Fatima would shake her head. "That can't be right, because if NSTAR couldn't turn off the heat, then no one would ever pay their bill, and the heating company would run out of money." They'd go back and forth like this, but Flora would never say anything; she'd just sit there, exchanging glances with her grandmother, thinking what a shame it was that none of them knew what they were talking about.

She pulled a token out of her purse and stepped through the turnstile. Flora loved taking the T, especially early in the afternoon, when it was never very crowded and she could always find a seat. The T wasn't like the bus. On the bus she always recognized too many of the people who got on, but on the T there were always people she knew she had never seen before. The T was nice and loud too, so no men ever tried to talk to her. A man might look you up and down, but he wouldn't say anything, and even if he did you could always act like you didn't hear him.

She waited for what seemed like ages for the train. When it finally pulled up, she took a seat right by the door. As they started to move, she thought some more about buying shoes. Even if Fatima didn't see a box, she'd notice the new pair soon enough and when she did, she'd start a fight right away. Flora argued with Fatima all the time. Everyone argued with Fatima. Their grandmother always said that death made some people sad and other people angry. Their mother's death three years before had made Fatima angry.

The train stopped at the end of the Orange Line: just one station past Green Street. Stepping onto the platform, she pulled the yellow hood of her parka up over her head. She pressed the Velcro down on the wide collar to cover her mouth. She wanted to disappear as best she could into her coat, not so much to stay warm but to keep from being noticed.

She walked off the platform, over to the bus lanes, and waited there under the rusted overhang for the #31, shifting her weight back and forth on her feet while she glanced around, hoping to see her cousin Carolina. If the pizzeria where she worked, just up from Forest Hills, was slow, they sometimes sent her home. But Carolina was nowhere to be seen. There were no girls waiting for the bus that day—just the three old ladies she always saw, the middle-aged man who wore his Taco Bell uniform, apron and all, underneath his parka, and the old man with the three backpacks who smelled like alcohol. Some of the other people waiting, about fifteen altogether, she recalled seeing before, but none of them had ever made an impression on her.

When the bus pulled up, she stepped quickly into the line that formed at its door. The key was to get a seat right in front. That way, if the boys from MS-13 showed up, they wouldn't hassle you as much. She sat down in the first row, just past the seats you were supposed to leave empty for the handicapped and elderly. The bus would idle now right up until the scheduled departure time. Then the troublemakers would rush on at the last minute. Where did they come from? They would suddenly appear, and you could feel everyone already on the bus sigh, everyone sit up a little in their seats. Especially the girls. They were bothering girls now, the boys from MS-13. It had something to do with initiations. Everyone knew this.

The door hissed as it shut. The bus lifted up on its tires. Flora wiggled her mouth out from behind her collar. Then there was a rap against the window. *You don't have to open the door,* she wanted to say to the driver. *They're late. They can wait for the next bus.* But the driver did open the door. He drove this bus every day; he saw these guys all the time. He wasn't going to leave them in the cold and piss them off.

Three of them stepped on. The first two were dressed almost identically: real baggy jeans, red bandanas on their heads, one of them wearing a Dallas Cowboys jacket with a *13* embroidered on the sleeve, the other one in a New England Patriots jersey with a giant *13* on the front. The last one of them wore a bandana and jeans but no jersey, no football jacket, just a black sweatshirt. He had terrible acne and a thin, crooked moustache. Flora recognized him right away. Ramon Gutierrez.

They gave their transfers to the driver. The boys in MS-13 always had transfers; they never paid in cash. Then they looked down the aisle. Flora stared out the window. She could feel their eyes on her. What was Ramon doing with these guys? Who was he kidding? If his grandmother found out how he was spending his time after losing his job she'd kill him.

They began to walk toward her as the bus pulled away. One of them was wearing motorcycle boots without the buckles fastened so they clicked as he walked. The man in the Taco Bell uniform had sat across the aisle from her, but when they reached his seat, he stood up and slid toward the back of the bus. The boy in the Patriots jersey took his place. The other boy, along with Ramon, sat in front of her. Both of them hung back over the seat, their arms dangling right in front of her face. Flora looked down at her hands.

The bus plowed along, their bodies all shifting whenever it turned or came to a stop. Flora could see, out of the corner of her eye, that the boy who had sat in front of her next to Ramon wasn't a boy. He was older and he had tattoos all up and down his neck: green and ugly, the kind men gave themselves in prison.

He opened his mouth and set his tongue, heavy, on his lower lip. All of his front teeth had gold caps. He leaned toward her. *"Chiquita,"* he whispered.

Ramon started tapping the back of his seat with his hands like it was a drum. The whole side of his face, around his eye and at the corner of his mouth, was twitching. He pulled the collar of his sweatshirt down past the collarbone and showed her the 13 tattooed on his neck, the skin around the numbers all red and swollen. "How you like that?" he said to her.

"¿Qué?" Why was he speaking in English to her? Maybe so the others wouldn't understand?

"I say, what you think of that?"

He leaned toward her so that his neck was right in her face. She turned away. He didn't smell right: sweat but also dirt and greasy food. He was grinding his teeth too; she could hear them scraping against each other. He had the crystal meth in his body; she was sure of it. She reminded herself that she had known Ramon for a long time — that in first grade, he used to cry every morning when his big sister dropped him off at school. And the boys would tease him. They would call him Ramon the crybaby. So there was no reason to be scared of him now. She knew where he came from. But if he was hanging out with boys in MS-13, then Ramon wasn't the same boy she had grown up with. They knew how to change people in that gang. They would give them drugs. They would beat them up. It made it easier for them to go out and hurt other people if they hurt each other first. You would think it'd make it harder but it made it easier.

"He's not in yet," the man said. His English was hard to understand. He had a heavy lisp and she couldn't place his accent — definitely not Puerto Rican. "Ask him what he has to do to get in."

She made sure not to look at either one of them. She stared down at her own shoulder. She felt her right arm shaking, like it was stuck in an electrical socket. Ramon took his hand and slapped himself on the cheek over and over again, laughing loudly, like a bird in a cage.

"You!" The man grinned at her. Where there were no caps, his teeth were yellow. "He has to do you, then he's in."

Her stop was coming up, but she was too frightened to reach for the cord. It didn't matter; someone else signaled the driver and the bus rolled to a halt. Flora put her foot in the aisle. None of them made a move. She rose to her feet, then walked to the front. The man with the gold caps got up and followed her while Ramon and the other boy stayed on the bus. Where were they going? And why was this man getting off here? He didn't live near her; she would have known him if he did.

Flora stepped onto the sidewalk. The man from MS-13 followed behind her. The other person who was getting off the bus, the man who had yanked on the cord, he always walked the other direction than she did on Blue Hill Avenue. She thought of trying to walk with him, but she knew he wouldn't let her. He would see this man and get away from her. So she headed home.

She wanted Blue Hill Avenue to be filled with people, but it was deserted. She thought of running, but she couldn't, not in her shoes. So she kept on walking. The man had fallen back. She told herself not to look like she was hurrying but not to stop walking either.

She could feel her heart pounding. Now he was getting closer again. The buckles on his boots clicked. They clicked faster and faster. He began to call out to her softly. "*Chiquita,*" he said. "*Chiquita.*" He was going to hurt her first, to make it easier for Ramon to hurt her later on. *Look at what I did to her,* he'd say to Ramon. *See? No big deal.* That was why he had followed her off the bus by himself. She began to swing her arms, like the white women she saw sometimes walking around the Jamaica Pond on the weekends. They would swing their arms and kick their heels up but never run. She tried to do this, to make herself go faster, but he was right behind her now. She could hear him breathing. She had to start running; she didn't have a choice. She clutched her purse to her side and tried to rush off, but it was too late. She felt his hand grab her shoulder hard as he spun her around.

CHAPTER 9

Three days later, Ginger took the shuttle back from New York. Looking out her window during the plane's final approach into Boston, the same thought as always struck her. It didn't feel like a *city* to her. If you didn't focus on the compacted, downtown skyline, the place nearly looked medieval: all the crooked streets, all the low-lying buildings. There were those people like Walt Steadman who took Boston so seriously. People who knew its history and the names of its neighborhoods and streets. They could tell you all about the Kennedys and Oliver Wendell Holmes Senior and Junior and how to get on I-95, which was otherwise more or less a mystery. But none of these factoids impressed her. At the end of the day, wasn't Boston really just a college town? A place where kids like her spent a few years before going elsewhere? It had been a city once, but it wasn't one anymore.

She picked up her car in long-term parking at Logan Airport and within a half-hour she was pulling into the small parking lot behind her new accommodations on Beacon Street. It felt funny to her, returning to Boston: to her sterile lodging in the Back Bay, to the university where she would soon be back in classes but on the campus of which she no longer lived. It felt lonely. The weekend had been a terrible one. Thursday night she met up with a couple of friends from Trinity. One was at Columbia now, the other took the train in from Princeton. Both of them just wanted to compare notes about their boyfriends, each of whom sounded identical to the other. At the fundraiser Friday night, her mother had introduced her to a boy who had dropped out of college but was still referred to as a "good catch," presumably because his family owned Northern New Jersey. Then, Saturday night, she ran into some friends of old friends when she was out having dinner with her parents and Bee Bee, so she had to hear more about who was seeing whom and the like. Among her age group now, there seemed to be an outbreak of attachment frenzy: everyone pairing up, everyone trying very self-consciously to make their relationships sound serious, not so much because they really *were* serious but because everyone was nearing the end of college and the one thing you were supposed to have at the end of college was a serious relationship. She didn't relate to this sensibility at all. Still, it was a little funny; over and over again while she had been in New York, Ginger had wondered what Walt Steadman was up to.

Ever since the end of her first year in college, no boys had interested Ginger very much, and the idea of a *boyfriend* hadn't interested her at all. She had had two. The first had been during her senior year in high school, but the minute they told themselves they were *dating* their conversations suddenly became awkward. They should have just lost their virginity together and not worried so much about how they were supposed to be acting as girlfriend and boyfriend, but they had been sucked in by convention. Never again, she had sworn afterwards, but then she started to see a boy right after first-year orientation at Harvard, mostly because she really believed he was different from everyone else: an aspiring geneticist from Cleveland who played the cello. But two months later, he had picked up squash and had decided to join a final club and that was that. By the end of her first year at Harvard, Ginger had so inveighed against dating that her roommate at the time had joked that if she kept at it she'd end up being a lesbian. *There are*, she wanted to say but didn't, *worse fates*. Beneath the veneer of liberalism, Harvard had consistently revealed itself over the years to be a stubbornly conservative place.

She deposited her suitcase just inside the door to Blair's apartment, poured herself a glass of water, and sat down at the kitchen counter. She thought once more of Walt, now not so much as a person than as a category. First of all, he was good-looking, by which Ginger meant— more than anything—that he was tall. In spite of knowing better, she had never been able to disconnect fully her ideal notion of masculinity from height, maybe because both her grandfathers and her father were tall. But Ginger knew plenty of tall, attractive guys who were her age and none of them appealed to her. Walt did, though, in a strange way. He wasn't brainy. She liked that. The brainy boys at Harvard had initially intrigued her, with their physics textbooks, bad skin, and scientific calculators. But invariably they ended up being more or less addicted to pornography and saddled—not coincidentally—with profoundly resentful views of women. They had been turned down just one too many times by the cute girls in their high school classes and now they were at Harvard, and still not getting laid, so they were bitter and awkward and not to be trusted.

In Walt's presence, Ginger didn't feel as if she were having a self-consciously *intelligent* conversation. She hated that feeling. Ever since she had started college, she had aligned herself against *wit* specifically and all of her generation's intellectual pretensions more broadly. She was well aware that she possessed most of these pretensions herself, but she blamed her cultural surround for that. She was trying her best to unlearn the worldview that was more or less ceaselessly being foisted upon her through bad TV (which took its toll even if you didn't watch television) and the mere mention of an upcoming Hasty Pudding show. Hence her turn to the Scholastics, with their genuine desire to make sense of the world around them and their absolute lack of cool. Just what she was looking for.

She drank her glass of water. Surprisingly, even after summoning Aquinas and company, Walt still held the stage in her brain. Why was that? He was a guy who read poems. That was unusual but not unprecedented. And there was his employment situation; that was kind of interesting. More or less all the guys she knew her age were going to emerge, twenty years down the road, as exact replicas of their fathers. But Walt Steadman didn't even know his father. That family story of his was genuinely depressing. But still, pitiful stories didn't usually work very well on Ginger. Why did his?

She was standing over Sid's tank when she heard a knock on the door. "It's open," she called out.

Walt stepped into the apartment, wearing jeans and a brown sweater with a stretched neck and loops of yarn hanging from the elbows.

"Hey," she said.

"Hey." He stood there, lurking. She did love the way those sweaters of his hung on his frame. Where did he get those things anyway? They had to be homemade.

"Look! Sid shed while I was gone." She pointed at the translucent tube of discarded skin that lay crumpled in the corner of his tank. "And I forgot to humidify the tank last week."

Walt had no reaction. Clearly he was anti-snake; one strike against him. He wandered over to one of the three bay windows that looked down on Beacon Street. "How was the fundraiser?"

"Boring. Someone started a rumor that Jimmy Carter was going to show up but of course he didn't. Then my Aunt Bee Bee got drunk and embarrassed my mom by flirting with this hedge fund guy. Do you know what a hedge fund is? No one seems to be able to explain it to me."

"Sorry, I can't help you with that."

She frowned and followed him over to the far side of the living room. "Maybe I should have majored in economics like everyone else. I'd like to understand that stuff and it's too boring to study on your own."

"As opposed to Lombard and Aquinas?"

"They're not boring. They just aren't flashy."

Walt didn't seem convinced. He squinted at her. "How many Bee Bees are in your family anyway?"

"Just two: my sister and my aunt. We have two Mitzys too. My mom and my Uncle Skip's second wife. WASPs are terrible at coming up with new names."

She walked over to her mattress, plopped down on it, and kicked off her clunky boots.

"So school starts up again the day after tomorrow?" he asked her.

"Yeah."

"I probably won't see you as much."

"Why do you say that?" Viewed from the mattress on the floor, Walt loomed over her. But he wasn't looking down at her. He was staring off to the side. And she got it now: why she had been thinking about him in New York. It was because, deep down, he disapproved of her. He thought she was spoiled. He thought the whole premise of *Girls I Know* was naïve; he had basically said as much. After first meeting him, after standing on the roof of the stupid building, she had just assumed that he was interested in her, but now she suspected that his feelings were more complicated than that. And Ginger liked complications. Complications, in her mind, were what made life worth living.

"Come here." She motioned him over. He stepped toward her slowly, slipped off his shoes, and sat down next to her. His sweater smelled sharply of mothballs and his eyes were glassy. She liked his languid quality. Nothing worse than overcaffeinated Harvard boys, babbling about their upcoming internships and what a drag it was studying for the LSAT. She put her hand up to his cheek. He made no move toward her. How odd. She rose up onto her knees and looked down at him. Viewed up close, from above, his hair revealed small, gray flecks. She pushed his bangs out from his eyes, bent toward him, and kissed him softly. He kissed her back, pressing his mouth up against hers. She pulled back. That was too much. She tried again. She kissed him as lightly as she could, so that even as their lips touched, a film of space flickered between them. This time he kept his distance. She placed her hands on Walt's collarbones and held him back while she kissed him. A minute passed, then another. She felt his breath on her face. She watched as his eyes closed, watched his mouth move against hers, watched as his nostrils flared and thinned. He fell back onto the mattress. She lifted herself onto his waist.

Outside, the light had shifted as the sun set. She unpinned her hair and unclasped her bra beneath her shirt. Then she leaned over and pressed her mouth against his. Why was she doing this? Was she trying to *make* him like her? How immature. Or had all the talk of dating down in New York actually made her feel a little insecure? Or was it simply because he was tall and smelled of mothballs? Maybe it was out of pity for him—a superintendent with an unfinished degree, a sick mom, a missing dad. Maybe it had nothing to do with him; maybe she was just out of sorts, having been mulling over *Girls I Know* more or less constantly since the book idea had first occurred to her. Maybe fooling around with Walt was just a way to distract herself. Or maybe she didn't want to be alone right then. Stepping out of the airport, Boston had felt so cold to her; it wasn't a city in which she'd ever feel at home.

He placed one hand beneath her shirt, against her breast. She began to loosen his belt. Why was she doing this? Could it be for all the reasons she imagined, all these reasons and more? She didn't see why it couldn't be.

CHAPTER 10

Walt woke up groggily the next morning. For a moment he was disoriented enough to place himself in Vermont, in his little boy's room. He knew he wasn't in his own apartment; the sheets didn't smell bad enough. But then he glanced around. He saw Ginger, sitting at the kitchen counter in a long tee shirt, immersed in *The Otloh of Saint Emmeram Reader*.

"Was that a real person?" He pointed at the cover.

"As real as any of us." She turned a page.

He wiggled out from under the white comforter. Something was digging painfully into his back. He reached down and pulled out a copy of the *Essential Writings of Bernard of Clairvaux*. On the pillow next to him was a photocopy of an essay on Norbert of Xanten. What the hell was with this reading material? He found his jeans and sweater at the foot of the mattress and wiggled into them.

Ginger set down her book. "It's not going to get all weird now between us, is it?"

He propped himself up on an elbow. "What do you mean?"

"Sex makes guys weird. Please don't get weird on me."

"I won't get weird on you. Don't get weird on me."

"Deal." She returned to her book. He ran his fingers through his hair, which was drenched with perspiration. "God, it's hot in here," he said.

"I keep the temperature up, just in case Sid wiggles out of the top of his tank." She took a long sip from the glass of water that sat next to her book. I should drink more water, Walt thought. He checked his watch—just a little after seven—and scurried into the bathroom to take a leak. When he returned to the living room, Ginger had already put on a black cardigan and a pair of jeans.

"I got to get moving," he mumbled. Flora hadn't been at the Early
Bird either Friday or Saturday and Natalie said she'd be out Sunday
as well, so Walt hadn't even bothered going over there the day before.
Natalie said Flora had called in sick, which was weird. Flora was never
sick. Actually, she was sick a fair amount, like everyone in Boston in
the winter, but she had always showed up for work.

Walt sat on the floor and laced up his Doc Martens. There he was,
thinking of Flora again. But now, the situation clarified in his mind. He
didn't want to be around Ginger. For ages, really ever since moving to
the Back Bay and managing to have a few dalliances, Walt had known
that rich girls weren't for him. He had generally discovered this
right around the same time that the girls in question realized that a
superintendent who worked at a dry cleaners wasn't their dream date
either. Still, he had pursued them. Why? Simply because they were
attractive, or conformed to what—growing up—he had learned to see
as attractive? What did he have in common with these girls other than
skin color? Ginger had mixed him up there for a little bit. She was
genuinely more eccentric than other girls he had met in the Back Bay,
but was she fundamentally different? He didn't think she was. Yes,
her props were different; rather than a yoga mat and an enormous
bottle of water, she had her works of Scholastic philosophy. But she
remained, nonetheless, pent in glass, just like those other girls who
looked and dressed like her—girls whose privileges formed a prism
around the world they encountered: bending its contours in ways
they could scarcely fathom. He didn't share a reality with Ginger any
more than he shared a reality with any of the other entitled girls who
lived around him. Girls whose parents bought them apartments and
cars and paid their college tuition with a single check at the beginning
of the year. He shared the same complexion but nothing more.

He rose to his feet. While he had been thinking, Ginger had
returned to her book. Now, as she read, her foot tapped the leg of
her stool and her index finger ran across the page, picking up a line
of text and following it through to its end, then picking up the next
line, one after the other. She didn't know what it was like to worry
about money. It wasn't her fault; she just didn't know. But Flora did.
So when he arrived at the Early Bird later that morning, provided

she had recovered from her mysterious illness, Walt was just going to ask Flora out on a date. They could still get together and read poems but he didn't want to use poetry as some pretext for flirtation. He just wanted to ask her out directly. And then, the next time he saw Ginger, he'd tell her about Flora. And Ginger, he assumed, would say that was fine. She'd probably think it was weird that he had even bothered to bring it up. She'd say she didn't care, but then they would both make sure not to run into one another for a few days, and those days would turn into weeks, and finally that'd be it. Once he mentioned Flora, they'd go their separate ways.

He told himself he should just leave the apartment—just offer a quick goodbye as he headed for the door. But he couldn't simply walk out. He felt an utter compulsion to engage her in a conversation, however briefly, about the decision he had made. Even if he couldn't tell her directly what that decision was, he needed to hear her process it.

"Do you think racial identification trumps class identification in America?"

She put her book down. "Yes, I do," she replied. She didn't need to be brought up to speed regarding his line of thought. She was forever up to speed.

"Always?"

"Always."

"Okay, but in interpersonal terms, wouldn't a middle-class . . . or let's say a lower-class white person, have more in common with a lower-class—I don't know—let's say Latina, than he would with someone of a higher class who might share his racial profile?"

"That's assuming the white experience of impoverishment mirrors the Hispanic experience. I don't know if you can assume that."

Walt gritted his teeth because he wanted to assume just that.

"You can't make race go away in America," Ginger observed. "Like in Britain, class issues are everywhere. In the US, race gets in the way of everything."

"And class too." Walt walked over to the door. Ginger hopped off her stool and followed him. "I disagree. Class divisions are surmountable in the US. That's what the American Dream is predicated on."

"The American Dream is predicated on racial divisions being surmountable too."

"But that's our Achilles' heel! That's the exception that proves the rule."

He opened the door and stepped into the hallway. "What's the rule?"

"In the end, Americans only believe in the power of money to change things. And since money can change social standing, class is always negotiable in the US. But racial difference isn't."

Walt sighed. Was she right? She exuded such interpretive confidence.

"Where are you headed?"

He shrugged apologetically. "I need to get some breakfast."

"Thanks for the invite."

"You can come . . ."

"No, no, go off by yourself. I was going to read some Peter Lombard this morning anyway, once I've had it with Otloh of Saint Emmeram. I think I left Lombard in your room, by the way. Can I go grab him once you've gone?"

"Sure."

He began to drift toward the elevators. She stood in the doorway to Blair's apartment, her arms crossed, watching him. "By the way," she called out, "what's the restaurant called where you eat?"

Of course he didn't want to tell her. What if she showed up? What if she decided to become a regular? But he was being paranoid. It's not like she'd ever spend an hour having breakfast.

"The Early Bird Café."

"The Early Bird Café . . . I like that. It's so hopeful."

"Isn't it? They're hopeful people, the owners. Natalie especially."

Walt walked off. "Have a nice breakfast at the Early Bird Café!" she hollered. Was Ginger making fun of him? Waiting for the elevator, he reconsidered how she might take the news that he was smitten with a waitress from his favorite restaurant. Maybe she actually would care. Maybe, coming on the heels of their sexual encounter, she would feel betrayed. He really couldn't be sure what her reaction would be. They had only known each other for a few days, after all.

Walt went down to his apartment to grab his jacket. His room smelled funny, like hardboiled eggs; he wondered if the odor was new or if he just noticed it now, having spent the night in Ginger's little Elysium.

Halfway to Jamaica Plain, he realized that—once again—he had forgotten to buy a *Globe* to read at breakfast. Flora would assume it was because he was still thinking about someone else, which was true, but not entirely true. More accurately, he was thinking about Ginger in order to no longer have to think about her.

And he felt, for the first time in years, for the first time since giving up on his dissertation and moving to the Back Bay, that he had made some progress in his life. Just in the last few minutes, Walt felt that he had accomplished something important and lasting.

CHAPTER 11

Natalie was filing her nails and talking on the phone when Walt arrived at the Early Bird. She cupped the receiver and nodded toward the back. "Seat yourself, Walter," she said. "I'll be by in a minute."

All of the tables were empty. It seemed unusually quiet. Since he didn't have a paper, he lifted a menu off the stack and made his way to his favorite table. When she hung up the phone, Natalie walked over.

"Where is everybody?" Walt asked her.

"It's Martin Luther King Day. People are sleeping in. Mercedes doesn't have school, but she had a dentist appointment. John's mom took her."

Flora walked out of the kitchen just then. When she saw Walt, she turned around quickly, but not quickly enough. He saw that her left eye was swollen, her cheek beneath it bruised and slightly green.

"No you don't! Get over here." Natalie beckoned Flora toward her and—when she was close enough—gave her a squeeze so that the girl's body disappeared for a moment into her ecosystem.

"What happened?" Walt looked at Natalie for an explanation.

"She wasn't sick after all. She lied to us—"

"I didn't want you to worry—" Flora pushed away from her but Natalie wrapped her hand over her mouth. "She says she was mugged, only the guy didn't take her purse. Does that make any sense to you?"

Walt shook his head while Flora slipped out from under Natalie's arms and went into the kitchen. She returned with a pot of coffee.

"It's nothing." She shrugged, looking down at the floor. "It's no big deal."

"It's no big deal!" Natalie put both her hands on Flora's shoulders and gently turned her away from Walt so that the two of them faced one another. "You don't say, when someone hits you in the face, that it isn't a big deal! You never say that. Your body is a holy thing." And she let her go, her head shaking as she walked back toward the front of the restaurant.

Walt sat awkwardly at his table. He didn't know where to set his eyes; he didn't want to study Flora's injuries, but he felt a need to take them into account, so he fidgeted.

"Do you want some coffee, Mr. Walt?"

"Sure."

She began to pour, then forgot to lift the spout. The cup overflowed.

"I'm sorry." She pulled a towel out of her apron and pressed it down on the spill.

"Here, I got it." Walt took the towel from her hand and cleaned up the mess while Flora continued to look away from him. A stab of sunlight from the front windows momentarily illumined her face; her left eye socket, purple and swollen, glistened. "I'm so out of it," she said quietly.

"Who hurt you?"

She shook her head. "Let it go, Mr. Walt."

"But how could anyone . . ."

The corner of her mouth pinched in. "Oh, there are men in Boston, there are boys, who can do this real easy." And she pointed at her face as if it didn't belong to her, as if it were sitting on a shelf in a store somewhere. "They can do this without any problem."

Walt found that so hard to believe. He was more naïve than he cared to admit.

"I don't want to be here." Flora touched her cheek softly with her hand.

"Why don't you ask Natalie and John if you can leave early today? I'll take you home. I mean, I'll ride home with you, if you want."

"I've just missed three days! I need to make some money." She examined her hands, biting her lip as she did so. "I can't stay here much longer." Walt said nothing and she added, almost to herself: "I need to get another job. I can't take the bus anymore. I need to work closer to home."

"Don't take another job! People here care about you."

"You're sweet." And she touched him on the forearm with her index finger. "Oh, I bought the Frost book this weekend. I bought some others too. They were on the same shelf, and all of them were on sale. You would meet me in Mattapan, for the tutoring, if I got a job there, right?"

"No, only in Jamaica Plain." He grinned at her. "Let's get together before Friday."

"What do you mean?"

"Let's have dinner. Would you like that?"

She took him in. Then she offered him a thin smile. "I can't. Not during the week. I take care of my nephew at night."

"Every night?"

"Every night. But you don't want to take out a girl with a black eye anyway."

"Sure I do. How about this weekend?"

Again she looked away. "I don't know if my *abuela* would approve. You're a little old."

"You don't have to tell her."

"Oh yes I do. Now especially." Flora walked back into the kitchen.

Walt flipped through the menu. He thought that had gone okay. At least she hadn't looked aghast at the idea of the two of them going out. She hadn't even seemed that surprised when he asked. He tried to imagine what they might do together. Maybe he'd take her to Bartley's in Harvard Square for a hamburger. Then they could see a movie at the Brattle Theatre. That would be a good first date. Actually maybe just dinner, and then ice cream afterwards at Toscanini's; that way they'd have more time to talk. He was thinking all of this through—his eyes breezing over the words on the menu, absorbing none of them—when he heard the bells on the front door clang.

Normally the restaurant was too loud for Walt to be able to hear the front bells, but he was the only customer, the only person—other than Natalie—sitting there at the moment. He looked up and saw a lanky guy step into the café, wearing baggy jeans with big pockets on both legs and a loose fitting, black sweatshirt, the hood of which was tightened around his head. Walt peeked back down at his menu. He considered ordering corned beef hash, one of John's specialties, but that was a serious commitment; maybe he should stick with an omelet.

His eyes lifted up again. The guy at the front of the restaurant wasn't wearing a parka or a jacket, and it was pretty cold outside too. That was odd. He was still standing just inside the door, his back to the nearly empty café, his jeans bunched up above his enormous sneakers. Only young men wore pants that big and not a lot of young men had breakfast at the Early Bird. It's cold and he's waiting for a ride, Walt figured. He returned to his menu. He could get an omelet with a side of grits. John made really good grits. Actually, Walt didn't know if they were uniquely good, since he had never had grits anywhere but the Early Bird Café. He wondered what exactly a *grit* was? Looking up once more, he saw the guy reach his right hand out and flip over the OPEN sign that hung on the inside of the door, jostling the string from which the bells hung. And then he watched as he pulled a gun out of his pocket and leveled it at Natalie Bittles's face.

Walt had never seen anyone draw a handgun before. He wasn't even sure if it was a real gun. It looked too small and stubby. And the guy holding it, in his baggy clothes, with his stooped posture, seemed to wield it more as a prop than a weapon. First he held it loosely in his fingers, dangling it almost like it was a set of car keys. Then he lifted it up way over his head, the short barrel pointed down at Natalie, and gestured with it toward the back of the restaurant. Natalie sidestepped around the counter. Then, abruptly, she raised her hands in the air. He must have told her to, although Walt hadn't heard him speak.

Natalie began to walk toward the back of the café. She moved slowly on her bad hip. Walt tried to act as if he was reading the menu, but he couldn't even make out any of the words. His hands were shaking. It was so quiet in the restaurant. He wanted to hear a truck lumber by; he wanted to hear the door open and see a large group of businessmen, burly businessmen, walk in. What am I doing, he wondered, sitting still like this? Am I too afraid to move? Or was he hoping somehow that he wouldn't be noticed, that the two of them would march right by him, into the kitchen, at which point he would run outside and flag down a squad car? He could hear Natalie's shoes scraping against the floor. He could hear the blood in his own body, rushing through his veins, his heart pounding up in his throat. The gunman hadn't taken any money out of the register. Was he going to rob them first, then on the way out empty the register? Should he take out his wallet right then, his emaciated wallet with the worn Velcro strip? What was he supposed to do?

They were nearly on top of him now. Walt stared right through the menu, through the table, through the flooring. He wanted to dig down into the ground and hide away. He thought of the gunman hogtying them. *We are going to be hogtied*, he whispered to himself, and in spite of the fact that his breathing was shallow and his arms and hands were fluttering, he thought of that word *hogtie*, which he was pretty sure he had never used before. He wasn't even quite sure what it meant.

Natalie stood in front of his table. She didn't appear to be the least bit frightened. She looked more angry than anything: her lips pursed, her eyes squinted, her heavy, round jaw set in stone.

"Get up," the gunman mumbled, sticking the gun out at him from behind her. "Get up!" he said again. Walt had been hypnotized by the gun: the squat barrel silver and gleaming. He had to lift his head to pull his eyes off the gun. He placed his hands on the table and rose to his feet tentatively, worried that his legs wouldn't support him. While Natalie stood there waiting, he squeezed out from behind the table and put his hands up in the air.

"Just what are you doing, Ramon? What in the world are you doing?" Natalie spoke loudly; she stuck her face out toward his. "You think you can come in here with a hood over your head and wave a gun at us? Shame on you, my son. Shame!"

Walt glanced furtively at the gunman. It *was* Ramon. And suddenly his mouth felt parched. He began to sweat.

She and Walt made their way toward the back wall on the far side of the café, the wall that ran into the hallway that led toward the kitchen and restrooms. When they reached it, they turned around, their heads knocking into the frames of the black-and-white photographs of Jamaica Plain that hung behind them. Walt peered at Ramon's face now, beneath the hood. His chin and cheeks were pocketed with acne and he still had his thin, uneven moustache.

Ramon stepped back from them, waving his gun at their midsections. Walt and Natalie had lowered their arms by now, simply because there wasn't enough room, standing as they were, with their shoulders touching, to keep their hands in the air. Walt felt bile in his throat. He thought he might throw up.

Ramon pulled down his hood. He wasn't wearing one of those stretchy nylon things on his head as he once had, and Walt saw that his black hair—short and spiked—was drenched in sweat. His teeth jutted out over his bottom lip, and his right eye—Walt also noticed—was twitching. He was swallowing over and over again, which made his Adam's apple bob. He didn't look altogether human; he looked electrically charged.

Walt told himself to run for the door. If he was shot in the back, the bullet might not make it to the front of his body, where the important organs were. That was what he said to himself. But he couldn't move. He was so scared, he was having a hard enough time just standing still. His knees were knocking together. His hamstrings ached.

They stood there, the two of them, against the wall. Ramon said nothing. He waved the gun at them some more, then jerked his head around, first to the left, then to the right, as if he were searching for something. He stared for several seconds at their shoes. Once more he checked over his shoulder, this time toward the front of the café. Walt wondered how it could be that no one had come into the restaurant this whole time. Was that just because Ramon had flipped the OPEN sign over? Was that really enough to keep the entire city at bay?

The door that led into the kitchen, just down the hallway on Walt's right, swung open and Flora stepped out, her head angled down as she counted a small wad of bills. Walt wanted to scream to her to run back into the kitchen, but he couldn't open his mouth. He couldn't speak; he was too scared.

She looked up at the two of them, standing there against the light yellow wall, wrinkled her brow, and then—when she made it out of the hallway and into the room itself—she saw Ramon and her hands opened, the money fluttering toward the floor.

When he saw her, Ramon inhaled sharply, his head jerking back.

He spoke to her in a rush of Spanish, the words running together. *I should have taken Spanish in high school,* Walt said to himself, *instead of French. If I knew Spanish, maybe I could ask him to let us go and he would listen, because I would be asking him in Spanish.*

"Ramon! Por favor, no! Ramon! Por favor!" Flora waved her hands in front of her face while Ramon's voice grew louder and louder.

"What the fuck—" John Bittles rushed out of the kitchen. His apron was splotched with dried yolk. He held a spatula in his hand. Ramon pointed the gun at him, then toward the wall.

"Get the fuck out of my restaurant!" John hollered. "Get the fuck out of here!"

"Get against the wall!" Ramon said to him. His speech was slurred and hard to understand.

"No! Ramon! No!" Flora began to cry, her head buried in her hands, and Walt wondered what she knew that the rest of them didn't.

"Get the fuck out of my restaurant!"

"John, get against the wall," Natalie said to her husband, her voice unwavering. Their eyes locked, then he walked over to her side.

Flora stood still, sobbing, and Walt reached out and steadied her by her shoulder, which was bony and fit into his palm. He wanted to tell her that everything was going to be okay. He wanted to say this, but he couldn't speak. His jaw was shaking. As gently as he could, he pulled her over to where he was standing.

Ramon was pointing his gun at John but looking around at all of them, his tongue darting out from between his lips over and over again, his right eye still twitching. He grunted something that Walt couldn't understand. He said it again and Flora moaned, her head still buried in her hands. Then, still pointing the gun at John Bittles, Ramon pulled the trigger.

The sound of the bullet discharging was so loud and sudden, Walt's hands instinctively covered his ears. He fell to the floor, coming down hard on his left knee, his body twisting awkwardly at the waist. He heard another shot. His eardrums stung. Glass from one of the framed photographs sprinkled onto him. He smelled plaster and dust and something else, something burnt. Another shot rang out. Walt's hands rushed to shield his eyes but they weren't fast enough and he felt—between his fingers—mush like applesauce while he heard, of all things, his grandfather's voice saying to him, *Walter, your face is gone. I see it there on the floor. You no longer have a face.*

He opened his left eye. He didn't try to open his right one because that part of his face had been turned to mush. He was lying on his back. He saw, on his hand, blood and bone and cartilage. He saw, on the ceiling above him, on the wall he was facing, flecks of blood spread out in patterns. He wondered why he wasn't dead. He had been shot, but it didn't hurt. Or maybe he *was* dead and that was why he heard his grandfather's voice.

He turned on his side and rose to his knees. Flora's body was folded back against the wall, her head turned toward Walt, blood still pooling where her left eye should have been. Her face had been melted in the corner, the skin rolled back from her cheekbone, the flesh turned inside out, but the rest of her was the same: the yellow ribbon in her hair, the narrow shoulders, her tiny feet. I look like that, Walt thought; my face is also ruined, only I'm a different kind of dead than she is. I'm still moving around.

He saw John Bittles's enormous shoes, pointed up toward the ceiling. Slumped sideways on his chest was Natalie. There was blood all about their bodies, rivulets of blood running along the floorboards, pooling and dripping: blood on the shattered photographs of Jamaica Pond, in Walt's own hair, in his mouth.

He could feel Ramon standing right behind him. He could hear him breathing. Walt pivoted at the waist. It hurt to turn his body this way.

Ramon glared at him. There was blood on his face and hands. His right eye was no longer twitching. He was breathing out of his mouth. He raised the barrel of the gun so that it was a foot or so from Walt's forehead. Walt could see the tiny, black hairs on Ramon's hand, flecked with blood. He could see blood on the barrel of the gun, and on his pant leg. He looked away.

On the cusp of death, Walt Steadman didn't think of Flora Martinez. He didn't think of Ginger Newton. Instead, he thought— remarkably—of his unwritten dissertation. He thought of *The Poetics of Yankee Peerage*. When you completed your PhD at Harvard, you had to submit a leather-bound copy of your thesis to the registrar. They would put it in the library. It had the title of your thesis and your last name on the spine, almost like a real book, and Walt thought now of his dissertation having been finished after all: of it sitting on a shelf in the sub-basement of Widener Library. One weekend, after he had been dead for a while, his grandmother would have arranged for someone from Burlington Health and Rehabilitation to drive her and her daughter down to Cambridge for the day. One of the librarians would have taken them deep into the stacks and there they would have looked at his leather-bound dissertation. The librarian would have stood next to them as they examined it, and Walt's grandmother would have explained to her that her grandson had written this book, not that it was a book, exactly, but it was right there in front of them—a part of the permanent collection of the Harvard University archive—and her grandson, Walter Steadman, had finished it before he was shot to death in a restaurant in Jamaica Plain.

He heard the click of the trigger, the sound of something catching, and then he assumed that he was dead like everyone else. And death, it turned out, wasn't such a big deal; it was just like living, only there was no movement or sound.

But then he heard breathing. He opened his left eye just as Ramon turned the barrel of the gun away from him. He peered at the handle, then at the trigger itself. I should run now, Walt thought, but he couldn't move; he was frozen in place. Suddenly the gun went off. Ramon's body fell backward as if it had been pushed off a diving board. Walt watched the gun clatter against the floor, spin, and then come to a rest. He smelled the burnt smell again; once more his eardrums rang.

Walt saw, on the floor in front of him, a wedge of skull and hair that had been ripped from the rest of Ramon's head. He vomited. Then he tried to shut his eye, his left eye, the one that still worked, but it wouldn't close. His whole body began to shake: his arms and legs, even his stomach. His stomach was convulsing. There was vomit all over his chin and neck. He crumpled to the floor, shaking, and realized that he had to get out of the Early Bird Café but that the only way to do that would be to crawl. It never occurred to him that he could walk. So he began to crawl toward the front door, because everyone around him was dead and if he could get out of the café he might not die. He crawled in a wide arc around the gun and Ramon's body. He could see light coming through the window in the front of the restaurant. He could hear the city on the other side of the blue door.

He heard a siren and assumed it was a fire truck—that one of the old clapboard houses had burned down and the fire department had been called. He thought this because he imagined the café as utterly disconnected from the rest of the city, with its carnage unknowable beyond its walls. But the siren howled right up to the door of the Early Bird. And then the door banged open.

A frigid blast of air whirled around him and Walt fell once more to the floor. He was terribly, terribly cold. He felt the cold settling inside of him; he felt his body freezing from within.

He wrapped his arms around his chest and squeezed himself tightly. The others had been shot to death; he had died from the cold. I'll miss the spring, he thought, when the girls start to wear miniskirts again. I'll miss having breakfast at the Early Bird Café.

He felt a hand grab him and press down sharply on his wrist. His muscles were tensing involuntarily now, his teeth grinding together. Without warning, his bladder released in a rush. And suddenly he was no longer held within his own body. He had floated above it and was looking down at his former, physical husk—watching it flop below him on the floor like a fish. He studied his old body as it twisted and jerked. And then he could no longer see or feel anything. He was in darkness, fast asleep.

CHAPTER 12

He thought he was home in Vermont, sleeping in his little boy's bed. He thought he could smell cheap ground coffee brewing in the kitchen. He thought he could hear his mother, trying to form words in the room next to his.

Then he felt cold air around him and—on his face—the sun shining dimly, and he knew he wasn't home. He felt himself lifted up and then down. He thought he might be dead: that death meant you were outside and could feel light but couldn't see it. Only that didn't sound right. Weren't you supposed to *see* light when you died?

Then he was inside again. He heard voices. He could feel people rushing by him. He smelled cleaning products. He felt himself lifted once more, up and then over. He felt his legs stretch out on a surface that was softer than the one he had just been on. He heard the sound of a curtain being drawn loudly and felt a hand pat around his waist and pull out his wallet from beneath his butt. Next it withdrew the ring of keys from his front pocket. He was being robbed. He wondered if maybe he was still there, in the Early Bird, only now he really was dead. Death meant you couldn't move while your body was being looted.

"Walter Steadman? Walter Steadman?"

He opened his left eye. He didn't dare open his right one, which he knew no longer existed, although he could still feel it. He told himself he was experiencing phantom eye syndrome, when victims of restaurant shootings think that their faces are whole when on the contrary they have been hollowed out and shattered.

A man in green scrubs was leaning over him. A woman dressed in white stood on the other side of the bed, looking at the man in the green scrubs. The man spoke.

"Walter, my name is Dr. Morris. You're in the Emergency Room at Mass General."

"Is my face gone?"

"No, it's not."

"I can't open my right eye. He shot me in the face."

"No, you weren't shot. You passed out. Do you remember being in an ambulance?"

Walt tried to shake his head but it hurt his neck.

"The ambulance brought you here. We're just going to check to make sure you're okay."

"I want to sleep. Can I go back to sleep?"

"Actually, someone is on his way down to evaluate you. Can you stay awake until he gets here?"

Walt didn't say anything. Dr. Morris had him sit up. He listened to his heartbeat, then pressed against the bottom of Walt's jaw, which made him wince. "You have a contusion there," he noted matter-of-factly.

He took Walt's blood pressure. When he was done, the nurse leaned over the railing and smiled at him. "Honey, I'm going to clean you up a little bit." She turned toward a cart behind her, on which were an assortment of cotton swabs and towels. She asked Walt to put his head back on the pillow. Then she dragged a garbage can over to the side of the bed and began—very gently—to dab at his face with the cotton swabs, throwing them into the garbage, one after the other, once they became saturated. She was wearing gloves, Walt noticed. He blinked and suddenly his right eye opened, good as new.

"How did you fix my eye?" he asked her.

"There was nothing wrong with it," the nurse said. "It was . . . you had blood and some bone there, but it wasn't your blood or your bone. It came off another body."

It was Flora's blood and bone and now it was in the garbage can on the side of the bed.

"Do you have any family in the area?" Dr. Morris asked him. "A girlfriend? A partner? Anyone you want us to call?"

Walt breathed through his mouth. The only person they could contact would be Ginger. If they called her, she'd rush right over in her black Lexus. She'd come in wearing some sort of outfit. Then, the minute she laid her eyes on him, she'd tell him his face was ruined. "You look like crap," she'd say. She wouldn't bullshit him any.

"Is there anyone you'd like us to phone for you, Walter?" Dr. Morris asked again.

"No, there isn't anyone."

The doctor scribbled some notes. While he was writing, the curtain drawn around the bed opened abruptly and another man stepped in, this one dressed in gray slacks and a blue dress shirt. His Mass General ID badge hung from the front of the breast pocket of his shirt. Dr. Morris leaned toward him and the two of them spoke in hushed tones.

When the nurse finished cleaning his face, she asked him to lift his arms up. "You've got—" she interrupted herself, "your clothes are very dirty."

Walt put his hands in the air and she pulled his sweater over his head. He smelled vomit and blood on its yarn and thought he might throw up again. "He shot everyone," Walt said to her, in part to excuse what a mess he was. His legs were shaking from the cold, from his urine, which had frozen in his pants. "He shot everyone he could."

The nurse shook her head sympathetically. She had him wiggle out of his jeans and handed him a thin, white gown, the back of which was open. He put it on without getting up from the bed.

"If you need anything, honey, you hit this button." She placed a small white keypad on the side of his bed, pointed at the call button at the top of the panel, and followed Dr. Morris into the hallway, drawing the curtain closed behind them. Once they were gone, the new doctor stepped over to the side of the bed.

"Walter, my name is Irving Schneider. I'm a psychiatrist here at Mass General. I understand you witnessed a shooting this morning?"

Walt said nothing.

"Would you like to talk about it?"

He grimaced. "I thought I was shot but I wasn't."

Dr. Schneider regarded him for a few seconds. "Did you know any of the victims?"

"I knew all of the victims. I saw them every morning." Walt stared at a fold in the white sheet that covered his lower body. Dr. Schneider stared at the same spot.

"They're all dead, aren't they? Flora and John and Natalie?"

"Yes, they're all dead."

Walt looked down at his hands. His knuckles were swollen and dusty. "The restaurant felt so small, when he was shooting the gun. That's why none of us tried to run; there wasn't enough room to move." He felt a need to explain why he had stood there, waiting to be shot. It seemed like the most important question he had to answer.

"Would you like to tell me more about it?"

"No, I'd like to go back to sleep."

"Why do you want to sleep?"

"I don't know. Because I'm tired? Honestly, I just want to go back to sleep. Can I go back to sleep?"

Dr. Schneider put the tips of his fingers together. "Yes, if you want to, Walter, you can go back to sleep."

He heard voices. Feet shuffling, doors opening and closing, the sound of squeaky wheels on tile floors. He opened his eyes. He didn't know where he was. The room was painted white. There were railings on either side of the bed. A TV was mounted in the corner of the room. Then he remembered that he was in Mass General. He rubbed his hands against the bed sheets, which were crisp and clean.

The drapes in the room were drawn but in between them he saw a faint band of light so he knew it was still daytime. On the other side of his bed stood two police officers. Standing behind the officers was a heavyset woman in a white smock.

"Walter Steadman?" One of the officers asked, stepping forward and placing his hands on the railing of the bed. His Boston accent flattened the second syllable of his first name.

Walt nodded by blinking his eyes once, slowly.

"I'm Officer Sullivan. This is my partner, Officer MacCaffrey. We responded to the shots fired this morning, at the Early Bird Café."

Officer Sullivan was bald and heavyset, with pronounced cheeks and a thick, black moustache. Officer MacCaffrey had a narrow face and a long, flat nose. He was slightly taller than Officer Sullivan and didn't react at all when his partner gestured toward him.

"Not a scratch, huh, bud?" Officer MacCaffrey stared down at him.

It felt like an accusation. "I hurt my neck, and twisted my side," Walt explained. "And my jaw is bruised."

"Yeah, but I thought you were hit for sure."

"Me too."

The two officers exchanged glances. Officer MacCaffrey let out a low whistle while he shook his head.

"Can you tell us what you saw this morning?" Officer Sullivan asked.

"I think so."

Officer MacCaffrey abruptly ducked into the hallway and out of view. When he came back, a guy wearing a wrinkled blazer and a faded red tie followed behind him.

"Walter Steadman?"

"It's Walt."

"Walt, I'm Detective Flager. I've been assigned to this case. How you doing?"

Detective Flager was noticeably older than the two officers. He was shorter too, with black hair matted down thinly against his forehead. His black eyes were set far back behind his cheeks, which were rounded and red. Still, below the neck at least, he wasn't as bulky as the two officers, and Walt wondered if they had on bulletproof vests. He wondered why he hadn't worn a bulletproof vest to breakfast this morning. But it turned out he wasn't shot, so the vest wouldn't have helped.

"I'm not thinking right," Walt said.

Detective Flager turned to Officer MacCaffrey. "Frank, go see if you can find that doctor."

Officer MacCaffrey left the room again while Walt pushed himself up in bed. He was still in his white gown.

Detective Flager stepped around the bed. He lifted Walt's battered wallet from the table in the corner and then set it back down, next to his bulky ring of keys.

"So you're a Harvard student?"

"Was. I dropped out."

"And you're from Vermont?"

"That's right." The detective must have taken a look at his student ID card and expired Vermont driver's license.

"But you live in Boston?"

"Yeah."

"Whereabouts?"

"In the Back Bay. Beacon and Mass Ave."

Officer MacCaffrey stepped back into the room. "They're paging him," he said to Detective Flager.

"Do you have any family in the area, Walter?" Detective Flager turned back toward him. "Anyone you'd like us to contact? Girlfriend? Roommate?"

"No." Walt stared at the white wall that faced his bed. Again he thought of Ginger. It wouldn't be right, phoning her, not after he had dismissed her for being too spoiled. But still, he longed to see her burst through the doorway, her cheeks rosy from the cold.

"We're going to need a statement from you, at some point . . ."

His eyelids felt very heavy. They shut on their own. A moment later, he had drifted back to sleep.

Walt was awoken by the door to his room opening. It was dark outside. Officer Sullivan, the one with the moustache, was sitting in a chair by the window. The detective leaned against the wall facing the bed, his arms folded in front of his chest.

A clean-shaven man in scrubs, probably in his mid-thirties, stepped in from the hallway. He picked up a clipboard attached to the end of Walt's bed and looked down at it thoughtfully. The door opened again and a nurse walked in. Walt could see, through the doorway, the other officer from earlier in the day standing there.

The doctor handed the clipboard to the nurse and stepped over to the side of the bed.

"I'm Dr. Walker," the man said. "How are you feeling, Walter?"

"It's Walt, actually."

"Sorry. So how you feeling, Walt?"

"I don't know. I'm a little confused." He pushed himself up in the bed.

Dr. Walker nodded. He listened to his heartbeat, checked his blood pressure, and asked him to stare at a small bead of red light at the end of a pencil-shaped metal implement he had taken out of his shirt pocket. When he was done, Walt asked what time it was.

"A little after five." Dr. Walker put his index finger under Walt's chin and gently touched his bruised jaw. Then he stepped back from the bed. "Well, he's looking good physically," he said to Detective Flager. "Psych still needs to sign off, then we can release him. Or, if he wants, we can keep him for the night." He turned to Walt. "It's up to you."

Walt thought of his lack of health insurance. He imagined spending the night and then getting some insane bill. But maybe Boston had a rule about surviving a shooting; if you did, you were entitled to a free night of hospital care. Maybe that was why no one had asked him about his insurance situation.

"I don't think I need to stay," he said. "I'm okay."

Dr. Walker studied him. "Give yourself a little bit of time, before deciding one way or another." He underscored the advice by smacking his lips together.

"Thanks, doc," Officer Sullivan called out as Dr. Walker and the nurse walked out of the room, sounding every bit like a cop. Walt didn't say anything.

Detective Flager unfolded his arms and stepped toward the foot of the bed. "Walt, we need you to tell us what you saw this morning, but we don't want you to try to talk if you don't feel up to it. If you think you need to rest some more, you go ahead and do that, but it's better for us if we can take a statement from you sooner rather than later. Do you understand what I'm saying?"

"Yeah." Walt was afraid now of shutting his eyes and being inundated by images of the dead. It was how ugly they all looked; it was the unexpected anger he felt toward their lifeless bodies that he wanted to avoid feeling.

"I don't want to sleep anymore," he said. "I want to talk."

"All right then. I have a tape recorder here." Detective Flager held out a small device that had been in the palm of his hand the entire time. "I'm going to ask you to speak into it, if that's okay." He held it out toward Walt, then quickly pulled it back. "Wait, let me make sure this thing is rewound . . ."

While he fumbled with the recorder, Officer Sullivan rose slowly to his feet and stepped toward Walt, who made eye contact with him.

"He tried to shoot me too," Walt said. "Ramon did, but nothing happened." He felt a need, in front of someone who had come upon all the bodies, to try to justify his existence. He felt as if he owed him an apology.

"So you knew the shooter?"

Walt nodded. "He had been a short-order cook there. John and Natalie had just fired him. Flora wasn't surprised when she saw him. She started crying right away, like she knew what he was going to do. And she had bruises on her face. Someone beat her up just a few days ago."

When he said Flora's name, he felt as if he were falling, as if the sound of the letters themselves released a trapdoor that opened out into space.

Detective Flager whispered "Testing, testing," into the tape recorder, then played the words back.

"You're a lucky man," Officer Sullivan said to Walt. He ran his thick fingers along the bed railing. "The gunman had a Walther P22. It's a terrible gun. If the barrel nut is just a little too tight it jams. That's probably what happened when he took a shot at you. The nut jammed up."

Walt didn't know what a *barrel nut* was. He didn't think to ask. He'd just sat there. "I should have tried to run," he mumbled. "I wanted to, but I couldn't."

"No one runs in restaurant shootings." Officer Sullivan rubbed his moustache with his index finger and thumb. "No one ever runs. Besides, the kid had KTW ammo: Teflon-coated brass bullets. You get hit by one of those and it will kill you. They can go through concrete, those bullets."

"All right, we're ready to roll here," Detective Flager said. He announced the date, time, and Walt's full name into the recorder. Then he handed it to Walt. He could hear the wheels laboring to turn. The red light on the top of the tiny machine flickered with uncertainty. It wasn't a fancy device, like the one Ginger had.

"He was in *Mara Salvatrucha,* the gunman," Officer Sullivan added. "Fresh tattoo on his neck. He just joined, the piece of shit."

"It's not your statement, Tommy," Detective Flager interjected.

"I know, I'm just saying."

"What's *Mara Salvatrucha*?" Walt asked.

Detective Flager snickered at Officer Sullivan, who patted Walt on his shoulder. "It's nothing, bud. It's nothing at all."

CHAPTER 13

Walt told them everything he could remember. But it turned out he didn't have much to tell. He could describe Ramon entering the Early Bird, and the way Natalie had spoken to him, her voice steady and scolding. He could picture the dollar bills fluttering from Flora's hands, and John standing there, a spatula in his hand, yelling at Ramon to get the fuck out of his restaurant. He recalled how Ramon had held the gun, how his head had jerked around, how his eyelid had twitched. But after he spoke of the gun going off, Walt really had no more testimony to give. He could visualize the blood splattered on the wall behind Flora and Natalie and John. He could recall the burnt smell made by the bullets as they exited Ramon's gun. And he could hear the sound made by Ramon's body as it dropped, lifeless, to the floor. But Walt didn't know how to put these images and smells and sounds into words, so he found his voice dipping and cutting out until he had nothing left to say and fell silent.

He handed the tape recorder back to Detective Flager and asked if he could take a shower. The detective said of course—that in the meantime he'd hunt down some clothes for him. "The ones you were wearing are pretty far gone, I'm afraid," he added, as he and Officer Sullivan stepped out of the room. After they were gone, Walt walked into the bathroom and locked the door.

He undressed and stepped into the shower. For several minutes he let the water run down his face. Then he scrubbed his chest and arms. He rubbed soap on his stomach. His body seemed spindly and flaccid to him. I should be working out, he thought. He washed his soft butt and his thin legs and finally his hair.

When he was done, he still didn't want to get out of the shower, so he sat on the tiled floor with his knees up beneath his chin and his arms folded over his eyes. The water streamed against the top of his head. He listened to it pour down on him, then dried off and let himself out of the bathroom.

On the hospital bed he found a pair of gray sweatpants and a red sweatshirt that said *Boston* on the front in blue, raised letters. He put the clothes on. He placed his old wallet and keys in the pocket of his new pair of sweatpants. Then he sat down on the side of the bed. The door was open a crack and he could see Officers MacCaffrey and Sullivan standing there, talking in low voices, and he realized for the first time that they were guarding his room.

Dr. Schneider, the psychiatrist who had visited him in the emergency room, dropped by. He reintroduced himself. He asked Walt how he was feeling. Walt shrugged. He asked him if he was sure that he wanted to be released, and when Walt said he was, Dr. Schneider inquired if he knew anything about post-traumatic stress disorder. Walt said he had heard of it. Dr. Schneider asked him if he knew any of the symptoms associated with PTSD. Walt didn't so he listed some: flashbacks, disturbing dreams, feelings of anger, of detachment, of fear, exaggerated responses to loud noises, and so on. He asked Walt if he wanted a prescription for some sleeping pills. Walt declined. Dr. Schneider encouraged him to make an appointment with a therapist. "I can recommend a few, if you'd like," he added. Walt said that was okay. "I have people I can ask," he explained, which was of course untrue. "Then I'll get the process moving on your release," Dr. Schneider said finally. And he shook his hand before heading for the door.

A few minutes later there was another knock and Detective Flager stepped in, carrying Walt's brown Doc Martens. Someone had cleaned them; for the first time in years, Walt could see the distinct, yellow stitching on the side of his shoes. He put them on.

"You need a lift home?"

He imagined standing on a T platform, strangers pressing up behind him, their faces buried in hoods and under hats. "Yeah, a ride would be great."

"I'll let the guys know," Detective Flager said, but he stood still.

"What is *Mara Salvatrucha*?" Walt asked him.

"They're a gang, originally Salvadoran but now Latino and Latina. The name is slang and doesn't really translate. It means *Salvador Forever*, or *Street-Wise Salvadoran*. They call themselves MS-13 as well. We don't know what the 13 stands for but they tend to advertise that number, on football jerseys and stuff. They go for tattoos too. Officer Sullivan mentioned that Ramon Gutierrez had a new one on his neck: *13* written in gothic numbers. He must have just gone through initiation."

Mara Salvatrucha. Walt mouthed the words. "And that's what they do, kill people in restaurants?"

"No. What they do, mostly, is traffic narcotics. They've been real active lately. We don't know that much about them. They're getting bigger, we know that. And they're very violent. They beat you up before you're allowed to join; each member beats you for thirteen seconds. If you try to quit they go after you with machetes. They like machetes. They're sick fuckers, by any standard. The worst we've seen on the Juvenile Crime Task Force, at least since I've been on it."

Walt rubbed his eyes. "Why would they have Ramon kill a bunch of people in a restaurant? Because he had been fired?"

Detective Flager shook his head. "I don't think so. It seems odd, to send a new member into a restaurant to shoot it up all by himself. I'm guessing he was there on his own business, but maybe he was looking to impress his new brothers as well. I don't know. You'll drive yourself crazy, trying to understand these fuckheads, because you can't. They've got screws loose. They'll go places you can't even dream of." He glanced at his watch. "Our investigation will move quickly. We'll do a ballistics analysis, toxicology report on the gunman's body, conduct some interviews, trace the gun, see what we can find. Basically, any information we get that helps us understand these guys is valuable. If something comes to mind, I want you to give me a call." He withdrew a card from his blazer and handed it to Walt, who put it in his wallet.

"Are the guys in *Mara Salvatrucha* going to come after me?"

"I don't think there's anything for you to worry about. Our protocol with cases like this one is to keep the names of witnesses out of the paper. But if you see someone and he gives you the creeps, you call me about that too."

"Okay. Thanks." Walt stretched out his arms and legs. His whole body was sore. He felt tired but at the same time anxious and still a little sick to his stomach. And he was so confused. "How could he shoot Flora? They grew up together. They had already beaten her up, those guys, it must have been them, and then he shoots her in the face . . ."

Detective Flager just shook his head.

There was a brief knock on the door before it opened. A nurse had some paperwork for Walt to fill out.

"Thanks again for your testimony." Detective Flager shook his hand. "I meant what I said about phoning. Don't hesitate."

Walt nodded as Detective Flager let himself out. With the nurse's help, he indicated his uninsured status on one sheet and signed the other, acknowledging his release. He couldn't bring himself to ask if he was going to get billed for anything; he preferred not to know. The nurse took the papers from him and the two of them stepped out of the room, where Officers Sullivan and MacCaffrey were waiting for him. Without saying anything, the three of them began to walk down the hallway.

They stopped at a bank of elevators; Officer MacCaffrey pressed the DOWN button and just as it illuminated, Walt—staring ahead at the shiny, gray doors—felt his stomach tighten. Walt tapped MacCaffrey on the shoulder.

"I don't want to take the elevator," he said, looking down at the floor, which seemed to be moving beneath him, rippling up and down. "I can't take the elevator." He thought of how cramped it would be inside, of how the doors could open on any floor and some angry teenager could step through them, pull out a gun, and start firing. Walt would be standing there, in between the officers in their bulletproof vests, with nowhere to go. The bullets would rip into and through him, splattering his skin and blood and bones on the wall behind him.

"That's fine, bud," Officer MacCaffrey said. "We'll take the stairs. You could use the exercise, Tommy."

"Oh, and you're a triathlete," Officer Sullivan replied. They followed the EXIT signs to the end of the hallway, then took four flights of stairs down to the ground floor. Outside it had begun to rain. There was a squad car pulled up right in front of the main entrance to the hospital and Walt followed the two officers over to it.

Officer MacCaffrey opened one of the passenger doors while his partner circled around to the driver's side. Walt had never been inside a squad car before. It smelled of cream cheese and cigarettes. Officer Sullivan slid open a small window in the plastic partition that separated the back seats from the front, flipped on the windshield wipers, and whipped the car around. "Where are we taking you, Beacon and Mass Ave?"

"That's right."

"You can forget about Storrow Drive," Officer MacCaffrey said. "They got that lane closed. Take Charles Street."

Officer Sullivan took his partner's suggestion and headed toward Beacon Hill. Outside their windows, Boston set up around them beneath a hazy film of rain, impersonal and innocuous. They passed underneath the elevated T stop on Cambridge Street, then through the roundabout. A dispatcher's voice came in loudly over the police radio and Officer Sullivan turned down the volume.

"So what'd you study at Harvard?"

"American poetry."

"You don't say."

No one said anything for several blocks. The storefronts of antique shops and florists, one after the other, were lined up on Walt's side of the street. On the opposite side were mostly nice restaurants and bars, plus a few clothing boutiques. All the buildings in this part of town were redbrick Colonial, nestled against one another neatly: the way he thought all of Boston looked before he moved here.

"Isn't it a little out of the way, having breakfast over in JP, if you live in the Back Bay?" Officer MacCaffrey asked.

"Yeah, but it's my favorite place. Or at least it was . . ." His voice trailed off. They turned onto Beacon Street. It was quiet, just a few people out walking their dogs in the rain, holding umbrellas at awkward angles. Walt read the names of the cross streets as they passed them: Berkeley, Clarendon, Dartmouth, Exeter.

Officer Sullivan caught him talking to himself in his rear-view mirror. "Hey, it's still a safe city, bud. Remember that. It's much safer than it used to be. You were just in the wrong place at the wrong time."

"Right."

"But even so, you made it out okay," Officer MacCaffrey added.

"Someone likes you up there." Officer Sullivan winked at him. "Still, I wouldn't dive right back into things. If I were you, I'd think about taking a few days off. Go talk to someone, a therapist or, you know . . . someone. A priest or chaplain. You a religious guy?" Walt shook his head. "Well, then maybe a therapist. Your buddies might think it's weird, but let me tell you, I've seen a shrink before and I'm glad I did."

"I don't have the money to see a therapist," Walt said. They came to a halt at a streetlight. When they started to move again, he added: "I don't own a place in my building. I'm the superintendent."

Officer MacCaffrey twisted in his seat, but not enough to be able to see Walt. Instead he stared at his partner. "What does that mean, you oversee the place and you don't have to pay rent?"

"Yeah."

"Sounds like a pretty good deal."

"You should look into it," Officer Sullivan said to him. "Your wife would love to get you out of the house."

"You have no idea."

They sped along. Officer Sullivan raised his voice for emphasis. "This kind of stuff can work on you, that's all I'm saying. You might feel all right now, but then in a week or a month you could be all fucked up. That's what it was like for me. Four years on the job and my first partner gets shot in the neck in Roxbury, his wife pregnant with their second kid. He made it through, barely. I think I'm fine and then, a few weeks later, my own boy mouths off to me and I smack him clean across the face. Split his lip. I'd never laid a hand on him before. You see what I'm saying?"

"Yeah," Walt mumbled.

They crossed Mass Ave and rolled to a stop against the curb. There was the usual bustle on the sidewalk: students streaming by, cars honking. Nothing had changed. Officer MacCaffrey whistled. "I do like the Back Bay. Check that out!"

Walt cupped his hand against the window. *That* was Ginger, sitting on the steps of their building, her hair combed down on one side, smoking a cigarette. It wasn't raining in the Back Bay, or at least it wasn't raining on her, and Walt was reminded of what it was like to look at Ginger for the first time. She really was beautiful.

He tried to open his door but he couldn't; there weren't any levers on the inside. Officer MacCaffrey stepped out onto the sidewalk and let him out on the curb.

"You take care of yourself, bud," Officer Sullivan said to him.

"Thanks for the ride."

Officer MacCaffrey shook his hand. "Take it easy."

Walt squeezed the policeman's hand, which was calloused and thick. "And thanks for getting me out of there."

"Don't thank me; thank the Walther guys for making a gun that jams." He slapped the roof of the car, then climbed back in and shut his door. A moment later, their squad car had merged into traffic and was gone.

Ginger had stood up. She waited for him on the steps. He walked over to her.

"Oh Jesus Christ," she said to him. She opened her arms but he stepped back. How could she already know? She had probably started to monitor police frequencies for her book, something like that.

"When did you start smoking?"

"Tonight. It was so boring sitting here, I bought a pack of Newports. I thought you were dead, Walt. I was driving over to Cambridge, to the library, and I had the radio on. I *never* have the radio on. I thought you were killed, I swear to God. I almost drove right into the Charles River."

He wrapped his arms around his chest.

"Were you there when it happened?"

He nodded.

"You lost your jacket?"

He nodded again. And then, the oddest thing. He began to shake, and it wasn't even that cold outside. He shook so hard, he thought he was going to fall over. She put her arms around him. "I can't go downstairs," he said.

"No, no, you shouldn't. You come up with me." She squeezed him tight.

They walked up the steps, through the foyer, and took the elevator to the third floor. In her apartment, Walt noticed a printer now sitting next to her trunk, with pages and pages piled on top of it. Ginger scurried around the room, scooping up sheet after sheet with both hands.

"I've been transcribing interviews, inputting notes," she muttered apologetically. The printer was brand new; there was a discarded box in front of the fireplace. For the first time since he had known her, Ginger seemed nervous. Walt took off his shoes and sat down on her mattress, right where they had had sex the night before. He watched her dart into the kitchen. He wondered where the bodies of Natalie and John and Flora were right then. In a morgue somewhere in Jamaica Plain? What were their families doing? Where were the members of *Mara Salvatrucha*?

"You need to get some sleep," Ginger called out to him. She brought him a glass of water that he gulped down. He was thirsty and tired. His body—still intact, still functioning—had its needs.

She set two fluffy pillows behind his head. She pulled her plush comforter up over him. All this great bedding owned by someone who never slept. He shut his eyes and confronted Flora, dead on the floor, the corner of her face gone, her cheekbone exposed, her mouth stretched unnaturally.

His eyelids popped open. "I'm not going to be able to sleep," he said.

She crouched down next to him. "Don't even try to sleep. Just lie still for a little bit."

But he wanted to sleep: like he had slept in the ambulance and the emergency room and in his own room in the hospital. He just wanted to sleep and sleep. I should have taken the prescription for the sleeping pills that the doctor offered me, he thought. Ginger hadn't moved. Up close, he could see the pinprick pores of her skin and the cracks in her lips. She didn't seem real to him. Her face was made out of papier-mâché. *I will never have breakfast at the Early Bird Café again*, he said to himself. *I will never again fall into the depths of unblemished sleep.*

CHAPTER 14

But Walt did fall into the depths of unblemished sleep. Hours passed without a single disturbing image barging into his unconscious, without a single discordant sound or hallucination. Walt slept the sweet, black sleep of the living dead.

He awoke to the sound of a key turning a lock and suddenly he was back in the Early Bird Café. He rolled off the mattress, onto the floor, and curled up into a ball, waiting to be shot. He didn't try to run; no one runs in restaurant shootings. He heard footsteps approach him. He held his breath and then, unable to wait any longer, opened his eyes.

Ginger tossed a shopping bag at him. Inside was a brand new parka: blue and puffy like hers, with zippers on the side.

"I'm not sure if I got the size right, but baggy parkas are in. It's what the cool kids are wearing."

She shed her own coat, tossed her white knit cap onto the floor, and shook out her hair. "It's cold as shit out there," she said. "Colder than it gets in New York. I'm sick of it."

He was still processing the parka. Of course he couldn't accept it. She wasn't giving him a CD she liked, or a book. It was a coat. But he needed a coat, and he didn't have the money to buy one himself. So what was he going to do, wear several sweaters whenever he went outside? Just the day before he had decided that he wasn't going to have anything more to do with Ginger, in part because he disapproved of her background, but now this background was offering him a parka. He could feel his moral indignation crumbling. It was such a nice coat, that was the thing. And it could get so cold in Boston in the winter.

He stood up and tried it on. The parka wasn't baggy at all; it held his body snuggly, as if in a cocoon.

"Thanks so much, Ginger." She hugged him, lifting up on her toes. Through all of the Gore-Tex and insulation he could feel none of her body. He took the parka off and sat down on the floor. It was Tuesday, the first day of the new semester. He knew that. "Shouldn't you be in class?"

"I don't like going the first week, during shopping period. I hate to watch the professors sell their courses. I hate the way students walk in and out. So I'm going to start next week, when things get more serious."

Walt shrugged. "I always liked the bustle at the beginning of the semester. At least I liked it more than the midterms." Ginger, it was clear, preferred exams to chatter. She was looking him over, studying him; Walt felt compacted, as if he were some pebble that she was stooped over.

"He pointed the gun right at me," he said. "It jammed. The barrel nut jammed. Otherwise I'd be dead." He held his hands out in front of him as he spoke, the palms up. It was a gesture he had never used before.

"Unbelievable. The paper said he was in a gang?"

"*Mara Salvatrucha*. MS-13."

"That's it."

They fell quiet again. It didn't feel awkward, just very still.

"Just to witness something like that . . ." Ginger shook her head slowly. She sounded equally appalled and intrigued, but Walt wasn't focused on her tone. "Every morning, at the Early Bird, I'd read the *Globe*," he said. "But I'd skip all the scary articles, about murders and rapes. Not consciously but subconsciously. I'd linger over the local interest pieces and the sports page and the job listings. I was meticulously preserving this pristine image I had of Boston, more or less from my childhood. 'The Hub of the Universe.' That crap."

He stood up and picked his new parka off the floor. She scooped up her winter garments. They drifted out of the apartment, into the hallway.

"I set up an interview yesterday morning with a woman who runs an outreach program for teenage runaways. Want to tag along? We could head over there now."

"I don't know . . ." He couldn't imagine spending a day in Ginger's car, circling around Boston, but he didn't want to be alone either. He paused when the elevator doors opened. Again he imagined being stuck inside when a gunman started shooting, but he weighed this fear against the prospects of taking the stairs and his laziness won out. He stepped inside and hit the button for the ground floor.

They stepped out into the hallway. Apparently they were going on another excursion after all. Halfway to the back door, an awful smell—thick and soupy—poured over them.

"What the hell is that?" Ginger held her arm up to her nose. It was coming from the basement. They descended the concrete steps. Ginger hung back while Walt flung open the door to his room.

Half the ceiling had collapsed. On his futon, clumps of sewage gurgled. More dripped out from the hole where the stain had once been.

Walt doubled over from the stench. He cupped his hands over his face.

"Oh God," Ginger called out from the stairwell. "Oh shit! Literally. Walt, I got to go upstairs; I'm going to puke."

His eyes teared from the smell. He began to scurry around his studio. The deluge had missed his desk, so Walt was able to carry his laptop out the door, but everything on or near his futon was ruined. He couldn't help but notice that all of his Lowell books, which had been neatly stacked on the far side of the room ages ago and were now covered with dust, had been spared. Walt threw all of his unsullied clothes, including an armful of sweaters, into the hockey bag that had sat on the floor of his closet since the day he moved in. His grandfather's recliner was also destroyed, but his records and his record player were okay. He dragged those out into the stairwell next. All the times he had imagined evacuating from his studio, he'd estimated needing only two minutes, but it had taken closer to ten; he was more tethered to the place than he had been willing to admit.

"We can bring it all up to Blair's place," Ginger shouted down to him from the hallway on the ground floor.

He lugged his hockey bag up the stairs, then went back down and fetched more of his belongings. "No, I can't," he said.

"Why not?"

He couldn't explain why. Moving in with Ginger simply because the ceiling in his apartment had collapsed didn't feel right. Besides, she was an insomniac who owned a snake. One at a time, he carried up his two milk crates filled with records, then his record player.

"Come on, just stay with me."

"I can't." He was visualizing the whole arrangement once more. The problem wasn't so much Ginger's insomnia or her snake, or even his complicated feelings about her; the problem was the Early Bird Café. He felt too close to Jamaica Plain where he was, too close to the shootings. "I think I have to move away," he said.

"Back to Vermont!"

"No, I don't mean . . ." But he didn't know what he meant. He was at a loss.

She crossed her arms and peered at him again, her upper lip curled, as if she disapproved of his indecision. "Walt, after a near death experience, aren't you supposed to do whatever it was you always wanted to do? Aren't the scales supposed to fall from your eyes?"

He nodded and tried to think about what he wanted to do with his life but it was hard, in the midst of all the chaos going on downstairs. What if he died from contracting some awful sewage disease, this after surviving a restaurant shooting the day before? But that wasn't going to happen. Ginger was right; he had been given a second lease on life. "I think," he said slowly, "I think I want to write my dissertation." That was what he had thought of, after all, on the cusp of death. He had thought of *The Poetics of Yankee Peerage* sitting bound and finished in the sub-basement of Widener Library.

"You should do that! Without thinking too much about it. You should just do it! Move back on campus and focus on finishing your degree." Ginger's head was a blur of nods. The mere idea of his unfinished doctorate must have been driving her crazy all this time. She grabbed the straps of his hockey bag and began to drag it down the hallway. "Come on, I'll give you a ride to Cambridge."

He watched as she lunged down the hallway. "Hold on a second, Ginger."

She stopped walking and leaned against the wall to catch her breath.

"I don't think just driving over to Harvard makes much sense. I should call first, see about housing availability, find out if someone who disappeared like I did can even apply for accommodations—"

"No, Walt. Don't overthink it. If you call, it will take them forever to figure out what to do with you, but if you just show up you never know. I've got to believe that no dorm is ever completely full. There's a ton of attrition on campus; it's like the Children's Crusade." She headed off again, her wiry body straining beneath the weight of his bag.

He caught up to her and placed his hand on her shoulder. She staggered to a halt. "You know, Ginger, this is my life. Give me a minute. Please."

She nodded. "Sorry, I can get carried away."

He inhaled several times through his mouth, both to calm his breathing and also to avoid the smell of sewage that had attached itself to his clothes. "Okay, so first off, there's my job here: the building stuff I have to deal with."

"Do you actually deal with that stuff? I'm not trying to be a bitch, I'm just curious."

"No, I don't really. But there has to be someone around here who does, at least hypothetically."

She grinned at him, dimples and all. "I can be that person, at least for a little bit. We can put a note up in the foyer with my contact info. No one will think twice."

He was really thinking about doing this, which was shocking. He had this great setup—well, it wasn't *that* great but it sustained him— and he was about to give it up. Not in order to take a new lease on life. Even if that did appeal to him, he would never have given up a free apartment in Boston to pursue something as amorphous as a new life. No, he was scared. He was scared of living where he did. He was afraid that members of *Mara Salvatrucha* might come looking for him in the Back Bay. That was why he was willing to rush off to Cambridge.

He grabbed one of the straps of his hockey bag. Together they dragged it toward the door in back that led out to the parking lot. Outside, the wind was whipping. They made their way over to Ginger's car.

"Someone has to phone the property management company down in New York so they can deal with the sewage, and hire a new me. Their number is on the fuse box in the basement, of all places."

"No problem."

The trunk of her Lexus popped open and the two of them lifted his bag up and in. Walt had the nagging sense that he was forgetting something crucial but he had made up his mind now. He was ready to get moving.

"I can shovel the walks in the meantime too," she added. "It's no big deal, none of it is." She put the heel of her boot against the back bumper of her car and looked up at him. "You need to get out of here. After something like that, you have to start over."

That seemed indisputable. What if, for example, in a week or so, he awoke, got dressed, and ended up on the T, on the way to the Early Bird? What if he made it all the way to the blue door? He could see himself doing that. But he couldn't picture himself back on campus. He thought of having her drop him off at his friend Scott's apartment in Arlington instead. But then he'd have to explain what he was doing there and he wouldn't be able to do that without mentioning the shootings and he didn't want to mention the shootings. So as ridiculous as it sounded, moving back on campus made sense too, particularly if he started to work on his dissertation again.

They grabbed the rest of his stuff and pushed and pulled it all outside. With the car loaded up, they peeled out of the parking lot, onto Mass Ave. The Harvard Housing Office was located in Holyoke Center, right across from the Yard. Ginger parked in the absolute middle of Harvard Square, in front of a fire hydrant, in the taxi queue, with cars and pedestrians streaming by. Inside, even though there were just a couple of people waiting for help, Walt was instructed to take a number. When his number was called, he explained his situation to the woman behind the counter. She didn't bat an eye while he spoke, she just covered her nose with her hand. Then she spent several minutes typing at a computer. He'd be lucky to get housing for that coming fall, she let him know, not to mention anything sooner, but you never knew. She typed and typed. She moved around her mouse, her eyes narrowing. Then she phoned over to Perkins Hall and confirmed the recent opening of a room. "Well, it's the fourth floor," she said into the receiver. "That explains it." She spent several minutes consulting a waiting list, just to make sure the room didn't meet the requirements of anyone already looking for accommodation. Then she walked back over to Walt.

"You're in luck. A room has opened up in Perkins Hall. It's a fourth-floor walkup."

Walt turned to Ginger. "I lived across from Perkins Hall my first year in graduate school. If someone had told me that, four years later, I'd be living on the other side of the street—"

"It could be worse," she said.

The woman tapped the counter with her plump fingers. "We'll need a check up front for the semester: $2,600. That includes the meal plan."

"Up front?" He hadn't anticipated this development. He had assumed that they would bill him and that, when the bill arrived, he would call his grandmother and tell her something. Not about the Early Bird Café. He would never tell her about that. She would be so terrified, she'd want him to move home immediately. So instead, he'd explain that he was trying once more to write his dissertation and that—in order to get down to business—he had moved back on campus. And she'd tell him she was thrilled that he was giving the doctorate another shot, but that sadly they didn't have any money to help pay for his room. So Walt would throw the bill away and wait to be kicked out of the dorm. That was how he had imagined it would play out.

Ginger put her hand on his shoulder. "I can pay it, Walt—"

"No, it's fine."

"Honestly, it's no big deal."

"That's crazy, Ginger." He turned back to the lady behind the counter. "What if I don't want the meal plan?"

"You're required to get it."

"You have to eat, Walt. Come on." Ginger pulled her checkbook out of her bag and began to write.

"I'll pay you back," he said hollowly. And he thought of the parka she had bought him, and now the housing and meal plan. His debts were increasing, along with his hypocrisy. He felt a twinge in his stomach and caught his breath, aware that he was close to crying. He missed his father; the man he had never known. When everything fell apart, you were supposed to lean on your dad, not a girl you just met.

Ginger tore the check out of its booklet and handed it to the woman, who placed it in a drawer beneath the counter. She turned back to her computer and typed furiously for a little bit. She asked for Walt's student ID card and typed some more. Then she printed out a housing and meal contract and indicated where he needed to initial and sign. After placing the completed form in a tray to the right of her computer, the woman walked over to the far wall behind her, on which dozens and dozens of keys hung from rows of hooks. She plucked a single key from one of these hooks, then ran a plastic card and Walt's ID through a reader before handing everything to him.

"You're going to be in room 427. This opens your dorm room. This keycard gets you into the building. They have to run your ID card before you can eat, no exceptions, so don't forget it."

Walt put the keys in the pocket of his new parka.

The woman folded her hands together. "The floor you're going to be living on is hot. People complain, but you can't get your money back on account of the heat."

Walt shrugged. "It's not my money anyway," he said.

It was meant as some kind of joke, but the woman didn't laugh. She just stared at him.

They drove through Harvard Square, around the Science Center on Kirkland Street, before taking a left onto Oxford. Perkins Hall was just a little ways up on the left. Ginger did a U-turn and stopped in front of the main entrance.

"I can take my stuff in. You just idle here."

"No, I'll help you."

"Seriously, I can do it."

She didn't argue with him. He ran in his hockey bag, then his laptop and books. He saved the records for last. After everything he owned was piled in the foyer of the redbrick building, he came back out to the car. Ginger rolled down the passenger window.

"Let me give you my cell phone number." She passed him a pen from the glove compartment and he wrote the numbers down on his hand. Then she had him read his new phone number off his housing contract and she punched it into her phone. "Check in with me first thing in the morning," she said. "I want to know how you're doing."

He didn't want her to leave him. He couldn't believe he had actually done this. He had uprooted himself. He had given up a free apartment in the Back Bay: granted, one filled with sewage, but still. He had never acted like this before.

"I have to find out when Professor O'Shea has office hours," he mumbled to himself. And suddenly he remembered his bulky ring of keys. He tossed them onto the passenger seat, then looked at Ginger. "I'm not your charity case now, am I?"

She shrugged. "That depends on your definition of charity."

He leaned in the window and reached out to her. Their hands fumbled together.

"Thank you, Ginger."

"You smell like cabbage, Walt. Raw sewage smells like cabbage. Who knew?"

"You're going to have to air your car out."

"I'm not sure if airing it out will be enough." She gave him a wink, then checked her side mirror. "Good luck." He thought she meant in general, but she added, "With *The Poetics of Yankee Peerage*. Don't let the aristocracy off the hook!"

Before he had withdrawn his arms completely from the interior of her car, she hit the gas and took off.

CAMBRIDGE

CHAPTER 15

By the time Walt had dragged his stuff up the stairs to the fourth floor of Perkins, he was drenched in sweat. He took off his shirt, sat on the stark, bare mattress, and glanced around at his accommodations. The room was tiny: maybe fourteen feet long, ten feet wide. The bed was set on the left side, just inside the doorway. In the far corner was a single window that looked out on one of the law school dormitories, separated from Perkins Hall by a scattering of oak trees and a parking lot filled with cars. A small desk was positioned in front of the window: its surface uncluttered, its chair tucked neatly up against it.

Walt managed to wiggle open the window slightly. He set his crates of records at the end of the bed, and his record player and laptop on his desk, next to the phone. He needed to call his family and let them know where he was, but he couldn't handle that conversation now. A dresser stood against the wall, facing the bed. Walt unpacked his clothes. Just before heading off to take a shower, he checked the ceiling to be safe. No stains, but the paint was flaking off, probably because the building was so overheated.

He didn't see anyone in the hallway or the bathroom. Back in his own room, he put on a fresh pair of boxers and a tee shirt. It was unnervingly quiet in the dorm. Occasionally he heard the patter of feet but never any voices. No shouting or laughing, no dull roar of traffic from outside. He didn't know what to do with himself. He debated going for a walk but decided against it. He didn't want to try now to make a pale imitation of his old routine.

So he flipped through his records, settling on Art Pepper's *Living Legend*, and plugged in his headphones. He shut his eyelids but they flipped open. Being alone in this room, in this dormitory, scared him. He reminded himself that members of *Mara Salvatrucha* would need a keycard to get into Perkins Hall. He pictured them swarming the housing office, shooting the woman behind the counter, and taking all of the keys. But they'd still need to know how to program a keycard so, when they swiped it, it opened the door to this particular dorm. And even if they managed to get into Perkins Hall, would they really bother to climb up to the fourth floor? He remarked to himself that they probably wouldn't. He remarked to himself that he was surely safer here than he would be anywhere else in Boston. Still, he wasn't convinced. He decided that he didn't like the voice in his head that *remarked* things.

He got out of bed and rummaged through his hockey bag, looking for his *Norton Anthology of Poetry*, but it was back in his apartment, on his futon, beneath a pile of crap. That left him with just his Lowell books. He picked up his worn copy of *Lord Weary's Castle* and began to read, but just a few pages in, he drifted off to sleep.

Several hours later, he was awoken by a soft, persistent knock. He opened his door to find a short, chubby guy in jeans and a Harvard sweatshirt standing in the hallway. The guy looked to be in his mid-twenties. He had a scraggily beard, black hair that hung down to his shoulders, and wire-frame glasses.

"You just move in?"

Walt nodded.

"I'm Javier. I live right there." He pointed across the hallway, through an open door, into a room strewn with books and clothes.

"I'm Walt."

When Javier smiled, his glasses rode up on his nose. "I figured they'd fill your room pretty fast, even though this has got to be the worst graduate housing in the whole university."

"Yeah, it is a little hot up here."

"Everyone walks around in his underwear. That's why it's an all-male floor. Get ready to see a lot of back hair."

"I can't wait."

Javier turned and walked back into his room, returning a moment later with a coat in his hand. "Want to grab some dinner over at Dudley House?"

Dudley House was the graduate dining hall. Walt checked his watch. It was a little after six; he had slept away the whole afternoon. "Sure." He plucked his own parka off the floor. "Nice coat," Javier said, as the two of them began to descend the stairs. On the first floor, just in front of the doors that led outside, he pointed down the hallway. "There are three art history doctoral candidates on this floor. Pretty cute, you know, at least by grad school standards."

Walt sighed at the thought of no longer running into BU undergraduates on the sidewalks of the Back Bay, not to mention Ginger. They stepped out into the cold and began to walk down Oxford Street. Javier pulled a plaid hunter's hat with fur-lined earflaps out of his coat pocket and put it on. "Are you just starting a doctoral program?" he asked Walt.

"No, re-starting one, in English." He paused. "I took some time off," he added.

Javier nodded. "I study the economics of public education. How we fund our schools, and how our funding mechanisms contribute to educational inequality. The approach is mostly micro. This is my first year."

The sidewalk was slick with ice and every few steps one of Walt's shoes slipped out from under him. He envied Javier's *mostly micro* approach. Whatever the fuck that meant, at least it was an approach. By contrast, Walt's critical strategy seemed to involve endlessly reading the same poems over and over again without ever establishing an interpretation of any of them. To soak up some warmth, they cut through the cavernous Science Center, shaped like an enormous Polaroid camera, and then plunged back into the winter. They entered Harvard Yard through Thayer Gate. As undergraduates circled around them, their conversation petered out. They made it to the far side of the Yard, then up the steps of Dudley House, yet another redbrick building on campus. In the large foyer, they were surrounded by other graduate students, most of the men disheveled, many of the women dressed in clothes that Walt knew—just by summoning an image of Ginger—were unfashionable.

They hung their coats on the racks that stood against the wall on their left. Then they stepped through the double doors in front of them, which opened out to a large room filled with tables and chairs. To their right was the cafeteria itself. They joined the line of students that snaked off in that direction.

"What are you working on?" Javier asked. Walt realized that he had been patiently waiting for the past ten minutes for his intellectual autobiography.

"Oh, I'm interested in the poet Robert Lowell." They handed their ID cards to an attendant, who swiped them and handed them back. Walt picked up a tray.

"What were you doing during your time off?"

"I was a superintendent of an apartment building in the Back Bay." The two of them parted company as they pursued different dining options. Walt served himself a helping of chimichangas, then some mashed potatoes, and finally a piece of apple pie. He had forgotten all about the odd combinations of food that typified Harvard dining. He skipped the salad bar. With the cafeteria behind him, Walt looked out at the dining area. There were small, round tables on the periphery of the room with students scattered here and there, never more than two or three sitting together, and two long, rectangular tables in the center of the room where a lot of people were eating by themselves: books propped up behind their trays, napkin dispensers being used to weigh pages down. Javier gestured toward a table in the corner of the room and Walt followed him over, choosing to sit in a chair on the far side so that his back wouldn't be facing the double doors that led into the hall.

Javier began to eat immediately. "So you were working as a superintendent . . ."

"Yeah, my academic project kind of stalled out there for a while." Walt didn't want to go into all that. What he really wanted to discuss, he realized, was Ginger. Since meeting her, he had yet to mention her existence to anyone. "I just met this rich Harvard undergraduate. She moved into the building where I used to work. She's writing a book. She asks women to talk about what they do for a living, to describe their encounters with *evil*, and she records what they say and then transcribes it. She thinks that all the interviews, added up, will constitute some kind of theodicy. That's a defense of God's omnipotence and—"

"I know what a theodicy is," Javier interrupted. He continued to eat.

"Kind of crazy, huh?" Walt leaned into the table.

"Actually, I think it sounds interesting."

Walt took a bite of a chimichanga, then sampled the mashed potatoes. "Yeah, well, she's definitely committed to it. Works on it day and night." Javier seemed to be studying him, perhaps as a cautionary tale of what could happen if you ran out of steam as a doctoral candidate. "The ceiling of my apartment collapsed this morning," Walt added. "All of this sewage poured out onto my stuff. I took it as a sign that maybe it was time for me to move back on campus." He had already decided, at some point in the last few minutes, not to mention the shootings.

"That's disgusting," Javier mumbled. But he continued to eat. For the next few minutes, he offered a string of statistics having to do with the funding of public school education and Walt nodded and said over and over again, "Is that so?" He tried to offer his own observations, about Lowell and confessional lyric, about Boston in the 1960s, but they sounded vague and unlearned by comparison. Javier asked a few questions about Ginger, but Walt had already discovered—just in discussing her book idea—that speaking about her made him miss her, so he gave nondescript, bland answers. Then, to keep their conversation going, but at a safe distance from his own life, Walt turned to baseball. Javier had grown up in Pittsburgh so the Pirates were his team, but he said he could root for the Red Sox too because they were in the American League. They debated the merits of the designated hitter for a little bit, but by the time they began their walk back to Perkins Hall, an unfortunate silence had descended between the two of them. There was, Walt recalled now, a lot of silence shared among doctoral candidates at Harvard. In the three years that he had been away, the feel of the place hadn't changed much at all.

CHAPTER 16

Walt woke up early the next morning. He had slept on the bare mattress, in his clothes. He needed to pick up some stuff for his room: linens, a bath towel, some toiletries, maybe a desk lamp. He dressed and headed down Oxford Street toward Harvard Square. It was neither raining nor snowing but something in between. In the Yard, yellow ropes had been set up to keep the students off the snow-covered grass. There were little Bobcat bulldozers at work, clearing the walks.

It wasn't even eight o'clock; all the stores were closed. It occurred to him that he should grab something to eat, but he didn't want to go over to Dudley House. The idea of having breakfast there, rather than at the Early Bird Café, depressed him. Then he realized that he wasn't even that hungry. Maybe the whole breakfast routine had just become an excuse to see Flora. Maybe, now that she was dead, he would skip the meal altogether.

But no, he still wanted a cup of coffee and a small bite of food. He crossed Mass Ave, went into the Au Bon Pain there on the corner, and waited in line for several minutes. A homeless man dressed like Napoleon asked if he had any spare change. The woman behind him spoke loudly to herself, saying over and over again, "No, I didn't put it there. No, I didn't put it there." Walt ordered a small coffee and a Danish. He paid, got his change, then had to move to the end of the long counter to wait to pick up his order. As he stood there, he realized an obvious wrinkle to his new life that he had somehow overlooked. He had no income. Now that he was on the other side of the Charles River, working at Floyd's Cleaners made no sense; the commute would take forever. Besides, he wasn't about to ride the T through Boston; he was too frightened by the idea. So he'd have to call Floyd and tell him that he quit. And he couldn't just look for another job, not right away, not if he actually wanted to get started on his dissertation. He had to at least give himself a chance at being an academic. Not to mention, the very idea of sitting in another cramped dry cleaners somewhere in Cambridge, or sitting behind a cash register *anywhere* in Boston for that matter, scared the hell out of him. He couldn't believe he had done it all those years.

When the three-digit number printed on his receipt was called, he picked up his food and beverage and grabbed a seat in the corner, alongside the window. He put his back against the wall. A few feet from him, another homeless man slept with his arms in his lap and his head on the table. Although the bathroom was all the way in the back of the restaurant, he could hear a man behind the door clearing his throat loudly and spitting, again and again.

The pastry was dry. The coffee was piping hot and burnt tasting. Walt ate quickly. He was terrified the whole time. It would have been a really easy space in which to shoot a bunch of people.

When he had finished his Danish, he dumped the rest of his coffee into the garbage can and hurried outside. He saw Ginger reading a newspaper in front of Out of Town News, the newsstand in the center of Harvard Square. Walt considered darting down Dunster Street to avoid her altogether, but he couldn't make himself run away. Instead, he walked toward her.

"What are you doing?"

He had startled her. She had been engrossed in whatever article she was reading. "I go to school here, remember?"

"Right."

She folded the paper under her arm. "How was your first night?"

"Okay, I guess."

"You should see your old stomping ground this morning. They've had to tear out the whole sidewalk to fix that pipe that burst. They've turned off the water to the building." She began to walk toward Harvard Yard. Walt walked with her. They waited for the light to change, then crossed Mass Ave. Halfway through the intersection, a car going the other way honked and Walt jumped. Ginger grabbed him by the elbow and they made their way onto the sidewalk that ran alongside the brick wall that separated the Yard from the rest of Cambridge.

"God," she said, "you're a mess, aren't you?"

He shook his head, but when brakes screeched behind them he jumped once more. "I think I'm mad at Boston—at the city. I'm pissed at the buildings and the traffic. I'm mad at the pedestrians. Isn't that ridiculous?"

"No, it's not. It makes sense." She took out a cigarette, cupped her hand over the end, and lit it. She inhaled, then coughed profusely. "I'm having trouble picking up smoking. I thought it was addictive. Whatever."

He took in the sharp pleat of her pressed, black pants. He noted her thick, gold earrings. Flora had died in a pair of cheap pumps and Ginger was wearing those clunky boots of hers. He felt anger toward her too, for all of her nice things, including the nice things she had given him. It was unfair, but that was how he felt.

She blew a stream of smoke out over his head. "What are you thinking?"

He made fists in the pockets of his jeans. He was so crabby all of the sudden, which was unlike him. Or was it? He wondered if the shootings had somehow rewired him inside, making him more volatile, more antagonistic. "Do you ever feel guilty on account of all that you have?"

Ginger squinted as she formulated a response. "Not *guilty*, exactly. I think about inequality, yes, but it's not my fault that I have the background that I do. We don't choose our families."

But Walt wasn't ready to concede such a thing. Not now, not after what had happened in the Early Bird Café. Ginger could have renounced some of the privileges that had come with her upbringing. She could have insisted on going to a public school in New York City. She could have demanded that her parents pull no strings to help get her into Harvard. She could have insisted on paying her way through school. When her grandparents had offered her a Lexus to drive around Boston, she could have said no. But let's say she had done all of those things. What would that have meant? How would her sacrifices have improved the world? How would it have caused the dissolution of MS-13? It just would have meant that she wouldn't have had a Lexus to drive around Boston. It would have meant that she wouldn't have been able to pay for his dorm room.

He thought of all of the hurtful things he felt tempted to say, just to inflict some pain on a person who had only been trying to help him. "I think I need to be by myself for a little bit."

Her nose wrinkled skeptically. "I'm not a shrink, but I don't know if you should be alone right now."

"I think I need to be alone." He squeezed her shoulder and turned to walk off.

"Hey! Do you know what I just read in the paper, about MS-13? There are girls in the gang too. Isn't that interesting?"

Her cheeks had spots of red in them and the cold seemed to hang in her blue eyes, making them opaque and distant. She was thinking about her book. She couldn't help herself.

"That is," Walt said. "That's just fascinating."

She smiled at him—the smile that came without dimples—as he trudged off. He went back out the same gate they had entered. What had he been thinking, about buying bed sheets and bath towels? He had to hold onto what little money he had. He walked up Oxford Street, back to Perkins Hall. Up on the fourth floor, he wandered into the common room at the end of the hallway, looking for a phonebook. An Asian man in faded white briefs was eating a donut and underlining in a chemistry textbook. Another man, in what looked like a swimming suit, was grading a pile of papers. Neither one of them looked up when he entered. Walt took the phonebook from the table in the corner and went back to his room. He began to call Martinez families in Mattapan, saying—each time someone picked up—that his name was Walt Steadman and that he was a friend of Flora's. People hung up on him, one after the other. When he rang the seventh number, the girl on the other end recognized his name the moment he uttered it. "You were her friend from the restaurant," she said. "The one who went to Harvard!"

"Yes," Walt said, "that's me."

"You were going to teach her, so she would be able to get a better job?"

"That's right." He could hear her on the other end of the line, speaking in Spanish to someone. He heard chatter in the background. "Are you one of Flora's sisters?"

"Yes, I'm Pilar."

The voices in the background grew louder. Now he could hear a baby crying.

"I would like to come by, to express my condolences."

"You would like to what?"

"I would like to see you all, to tell you how sorry I am."

She was repeating what he said in Spanish, to a chorus of replies.

"Do you need the books back?"

"The books?"

"The ones you gave Flora to study."

She must have meant the books of poetry Flora had mentioned picking up. Flora must have told them that he had given her the books. Otherwise they would have been mad that she had spent her money on them.

"No, no," he said. "Keep them, please." He paused. "Can I come by?"

He heard more Spanish, then a rustling on the other end, and finally Pilar's voice, speaking slowly and clearly. "No, you shouldn't come over here; it's not safe. Thank you for calling."

"I can take a cab?"

"It's no good. It's not safe. And our house, it is so small. The funeral is Friday, at Saint Thomas, on South Street. I will call you and tell you what time."

"Okay, I'll be there."

But she didn't ask for his phone number. She wasn't going to call him. They didn't want to see him. He wasn't family. All the time he had spent in Boston, living by himself, and Walt had never felt as alone as he did right then. He hung up the phone and sat at his desk, wondering how he'd fill the hours in front of him.

CHAPTER 17

Days went by. Walt descended into a hole of his own devising. He inhabited a space of half-light. He slept in snatches. He had terrible nightmares, all utterly transparent. In one, he was stapled to the floor of the Early Bird Café, his arms and legs spread wide. Ramon stood above him, shooting around his body, but getting closer to him each time. In another dream, he was already dead, or at least as dead as was possible in one's own dream. Rather than place him in an ambulance, the paramedics threw him into a garbage can. Then someone took the can and began to empty it into a dumpster. Walt tried to stop himself from tumbling into the bin with the rest of the garbage but he couldn't. He was too dead to prevent himself from becoming deader.

In his dreams, as he walked down city streets, pedestrians crumbled into pieces as he approached, swirling up into thin air, diffused. In his dreams, bullets entered his body, opening holes out of which his organs fell, and he scrambled to shove his intestines and his liver back where they belonged, scrambled to grab his flailing heart and return it to its yawning cavity.

He waited for Ginger to call him but she didn't. She was just giving him the space he had requested, he knew that, but he couldn't bring himself to call her, or his family, or any of his friends. He knew that these people might very well ask him if he was finally making progress on his dissertation, now that he was back on campus. And he wasn't making any progress. He was still just reading poems, still feeling blocked as a writer. It wasn't enough for him to tell himself that he was reinvesting in *The Poetics of Yankee Peerage*. The days were too long, and besides, simply working on a doctorate didn't seem like an appropriate response to what he had witnessed in the Early Bird. But he had no idea what would.

Each night, he had dinner with Javier. He told him more about Ginger. About how she was trying to inhabit the philosophy of Thomas Aquinas ("That's just showing off," Javier interjected), and how she was learning to drive in a black Lexus. ("That is appalling on so many different levels.") He even tried, at one point, to explain to him what he had seen that morning at the Early Bird Café. He described Ramon lining them up against the wall, and the melee that ensued, but Javier wasn't able to follow his account. "I don't understand; what the fuck is a barrel nut?" he asked. "How could you think you were shot if you weren't? And how the hell did the gunman shoot himself in the head by mistake? Does that actually happen? How does that happen?" And Walt could only respond to each question by saying, "I don't know," over and over again, because he had no idea what a barrel nut was, and he didn't understand how he had convinced himself he was shot when he wasn't, or how Ramon Gutierrez had taken off the corner of his own skull with a gun that, a moment before, had been jammed. All of what had transpired remained a mystery to him.

The more time he spent in Perkins Hall, the more accustomed Walt became to encountering grown men in bikini briefs, typing away on their laptops. It was a different sort of reality.

More days passed. Each morning, Walt would wake up and bring a cup of coffee back to his room from Au Bon Pain: usually his only expenditure of the day. Then he would sit at his desk for a few minutes and consider the poetics of Yankee peerage. Next he would retreat to his bed, where he would read Lowell on the subject of his illustrious family, his manic depression, the breakdowns of his marriages, his complicated friendships, and so on. Eventually he would drift off to sleep, sometimes waking up after the light had shifted in the afternoon, after one of his nightmares, with no clue where he was, the sweat having pooled beneath his chin, his books having fallen onto the floor.

Three weeks into his new life in Cambridge, even though he couldn't afford to, Walt went out and bought a new edition of the *Norton Anthology of Poetry*. Now, a little earlier each day, he would quit work on his dissertation and instead thumb through its thin pages, returning to the old poems he knew so well, only now unadorned with his past scribbles. He didn't read any of the newer poems that had been added to the collection in this, its most recent printing. Instead, he stuck with John Donne and Robert Herrick and E. E. Cummings. He read poems about sitting on pregnant banks and women loosening their hair and men transfixed by hands as small as rain. He had read these poems so many times that his lips actually anticipated the lines before his eyes reached them, mouthing the words so that the poems hung in the air before and after he read them, echoed and reformed like acoustic clouds.

One morning, after finishing his coffee, Walt decided to go and work in Widener Library. It didn't feel right, just sitting around in his little room after having his life spared by a jammed barrel nut. And his body had begun to resist the many naps it was being invited to take. So he grabbed his copy of *Life Studies*, Lowell's collection of poems all about his family, and headed off. He made his way down Oxford Street and past the Science Center. He cut around Memorial Church. Widener Library loomed right in front of him. In the winter, the Harvard groundskeepers placed wooden planks over a small section of the front steps that led up to the library and shoveled this area alone. The snow that piled on either side of the planks remained untouched throughout the winter. It was piled high now on either side: craggy and dirty and frozen solid.

He climbed the steps, passed in between the massive Corinthian columns that extended from the top of the stairs to the roof, and presented his student ID to the guard seated at a desk just inside the door. The guard glanced at the picture of Walt on his Harvard ID, taken his first day as a graduate student, then up at Walt, then back down at the picture. Walt grimaced apologetically. He ascended the main staircase to the second floor and entered the Loker Reading Room, which spanned the entire width of the building. Outside, beneath the eaves, the pigeons were nestled against the high windows in bunches, waiting out the winter. Down below them, inside, the students had carefully scattered themselves among the tables, leaving at least two chairs empty between them. Walt sat in the far corner of the room, just in front of a bookcase filled with a complete set of the *Dictionary of National Biography*. Off to his right, a row of four Ionic columns separated the room from a smaller alcove, also filled with bookcases and reading tables, as well as plush chairs set off in pairs, with large standing lamps perched between them.

He told himself that he was claiming this as his new workspace, not because it made some sense for a graduate student to spend his days in a library, but because it was quiet and filled with people whose identities had been checked upon entering. Then he opened *Life Studies*, but he couldn't read any of the words. He was too distracted. Instead, he folded his hands across the pages and closed his eyes.

Growing up, Walt had been surrounded by decent people. His grandfather, a history teacher and a preservationist. His grandmother, an inexhaustible caregiver to his mother and also *such* an English teacher. She would diagram sentences from his papers to identify why they were clunky. With her pencil held lightly in her fingers, she would emend dangling modifiers in the *Burlington Free Press*, but she never called the paper to complain that none of them knew how to write well. That might have hurt someone's feelings. At Christmastime, the Steadmans would dutifully send out their small donations—to the Red Cross and the United Way and the Vermont Land Trust. In the winter, the thermostat in the Steadman home was never set above sixty-two degrees, even if that meant dressing Walt's mother in an extra pair of pajamas. True, heat was an expense they needed to keep down, but it wasn't just about money; it was about not wasting resources.

Flora and Natalie and John were unlike the Steadmans in so many ways, but they were all alike insofar as they were all decent people: not strident or judgmental, just decent. And now, when he thought about what he should do with himself in the wake of what had happened at the Early Bird—because he had to do something more than what he was doing now—Walt decided that he should try to do something decent: something to help someone other than himself, something charitable, if that was the right word. A gesture that would acknowledge that he knew just how lucky he was to be alive.

And that was when he thought of her, for the first time since the shootings. She was the perfect person for him to try to help. Even though she had never laughed at one of his jokes, even though she was his least favorite person from the Early Bird Café, she was also—along with him—one of its only two survivors. So Walt decided right then to reach out to Mercedes Bittles.

MERCEDES BITTLES

CHAPTER 18

She woke with a start, the door to her room slamming open, the knob hitting the frame of the bed. That was how small the room was; you couldn't open the door without hitting the bed. She didn't fit in the room; she didn't fit in the bed. What was going to happen to her old bed now, and the soft pillows she had slept on? Where were they going to put her brass headboard, and the green bookcase where she had kept her drawings? What was going to happen to their table in the kitchen, the one she had got the red paint on? They were going to have to empty their apartment in JP. When they did, where was everything going to go? It wouldn't fit in her grandmamma's little house. It wouldn't fit in her Aunt Chantal's apartment, or in Aunt Denise's place either.

"Time to get ready for school," her grandmamma said, looking down at her. "No dilly-dallying now, Sweetness." Her voice would climb a ladder so it was higher at the end than it was at the beginning. Every sentence of hers was like this, set on a ladder. Momma's voice had been a raft in the water, bobbing up and down after every word. If they had had a raft, she would have met her momma's sister and her two brothers. They didn't make it from Haiti because the water took them down. It filled their throats so they couldn't breathe no more. But Momma made it. Then, once she was on land, years later, the water came and got her and took her away. And the water took her daddy too.

"That bus won't wait for you, Sweetness, so do your grandmamma proud and get up and get dressed."

Her foot was stone cold, having drifted out from under the blanket during the night. The blanket smelled funny, like something left in a drawer for too long. That was how the whole place smelled, especially the sheets on her bed and the couch in the living room. And the TV had antennae on the top of it, what Grandmamma called "rabbit ears." The little house, just half a house, was too cold. There wasn't a draft. Like in their place, there had been that one window that didn't shut all the way and the cold seeped underneath it, until her daddy fixed it. Then it was as warm as could be. Her grandmamma's house was just cold: the faucets on the bathroom sink, the handle on the refrigerator door, the two chairs on either side of the kitchen table, the kitchen table itself. Cold, cold, cold, and all of it with that funny smell.

She missed her bedroom, with the white curtains and the radiator that ran along the wall, hot to the touch. She thought of the time her momma had brought home those little pieces of cardboard with the paint colors on them and said she could pick whichever color she wanted for her walls, so she picked the card that said *Perfectly Purple* and that next weekend, after the café closed, she and her momma painted the whole room. They put blue tape on the light switches so they would stay white; everything else they painted.

"You hear me now, child? You get up out of that bed." Her grandmamma's voice faded as she walked into the kitchen. Mercedes had to remind herself that her mouth didn't open anymore, at least not to make words. Otherwise she might say, *Yes, Grandmamma*. Otherwise she might say, *Where's my green bookcase going to go, Grandmamma? The one I used to keep my drawings on? I know where my drawings are, in the big suitcase in the little living room, but I want my bookcase back. Are they going to bring it over, when they clean out the apartment?* But she didn't say any of these things because her mouth didn't open anymore to talk. It opened for food and milk and to yawn and sometimes when a sneeze came out of her mouth instead of her nose, which she couldn't do nothing about. Otherwise her mouth was always shut tight.

She dressed first, then went into the bathroom. She brushed her teeth real carefully. She brushed the tops and back behind the teeth in little circles, just like she was supposed to, so she wouldn't ever have to go to the dentist again. Then she spat out the toothpaste, rinsed her mouth, and brushed them all over again. She tried not to look at herself in the mirror. Her hair didn't look right. It was all crinkled and wild, but Grandmamma's fingers were too swollen—on account of her blood being bad — to braid her hair.

At the kitchen table, waiting for her, were two pieces of toast and a bowl of cereal. Mercedes sat down and started eating.

"No one expects you to be a chatterbox, Sweetness, but when Taneka and Tashawn talk to you at lunch, you might want to talk back. Otherwise they might think you don't want them to sit with you." Her grandmamma stood at the counter, pouring herself a cup of coffee in one of her tiny little cups. She didn't have any mugs. What had happened to the mugs in the café, the blue ones that matched the blue door? And the photographs on the walls that her momma had taken over the years? Where had they all gone?

"Mrs. Garner says they told her you just sit there and don't say anything when they talk to you. You can't make friends if you don't talk! Don't you want to have friends at your new school? Wouldn't that be nice?"

But Mercedes did have a new friend. She told herself that quiet and her were friends. She told herself that was the only friend she needed in Watertown.

"I think that would be nice." Grandmamma took a loud sip of her coffee. "You could have Taneka over this weekend to play. You got all of them dolls and dresses. You two would have a good time. Yes you would."

Mercedes took a bite of her toast, burnt at the corners. She took a spoonful of her cereal: soggy Raisin Bran with barely any sugar. Her daddy would say, *Your grandmamma's going to heaven, but God won't let her in the kitchen.* When people would ask him why he became a cook he would say, *Shoot, it was a matter of survival.*

"Girl, I'm going to lose my mind, talking to you, if you never say anything back."

Mercedes finished eating and poured herself a glass of milk. Grandmamma moved into the living room. She didn't have her wig on yet. She wore her white stocking cap and her red bathrobe that had threads coming out of the bottom of it. She looked out the front door. "Mercedes, the bus is pulling up. Mercedes!"

She was looking at the picture of her daddy on the kitchen counter while she drank her milk. It was taken when he was in the army. He was in a uniform. He was a fine looking man, with his big hands folded in his lap. That was where she got her hands. She could have been a boxer with her hands, her daddy had joked with her. He would make her a full breakfast, every morning, before going to open the restaurant. He would leave it for her, wrapped in tin foil. Each day, it was like opening a present.

Grandmamma helped her into her blue coat and handed Mercedes her yellow backpack. Then she put her hands on her shoulders. "The world is just going to keep on going on," she said. Her left eye was all milky in the middle, her right eye just a little in the corner. "It ain't right, but that's how the world works. No point sitting at home with your grandmamma. I can't teach you a single thing that the world will want you to know. So you got to go to that school. Besides, it's a good school! If I lived one block over, you wouldn't be going there. So when your teacher calls on you, as hard as it might be, I want you to open your mouth and give her an answer to her question. You think your momma or papa would want you sitting in a classroom, not talking when you were called on? You think they would want that? So you act good today, and get yourself an education."

She gave her a hug. When Mercedes opened the door, the cold was right there, waiting. "You be strong, Sweetness," her grandmamma hollered after her. She didn't know how to be the quiet's only friend. "Remember, Jesus loves you. Jesus is looking down right at you saying, 'My, that girl is going to be a *strong* girl. She's getting her tests out of the way early in life, so no cross afterwards will be too heavy for her to carry.' You know that's what he's saying. You know it." Mercedes didn't turn around; she just kept on walking through the cold. "I love you, Sweetness. Grandmamma loves you."

The sidewalk felt cold through her shoes. It never seemed this cold in JP. Watertown was colder. They put her here, in a town named after water, to try to make her sink. *But I'm not going to sink*, she said to herself. She said to herself: *Remember, your momma is a raft in water. Your daddy is a big hand, holding a skillet. The water is not going to rush into your mouth. You just don't talk and you'll float on by.*

Up the four steep steps of the bus. There was Taneka on the left, and Tashawn on the right. They just alternated their outfits. One day

Taneka wore the red turtleneck, the next day she wore the green one. Then, the day after that, she'd wear a shirt over the red turtleneck but it was the same turtleneck. She didn't have nothing to wear. And Tashawn just had that one sweatshirt that said *Boston University* on it, and the black sweater that was too short in the arms.

"Taken," Tashawn said. "All these seats in front are taken."

Shoot, no seats were *taken*. Only a dozen of them had to take the bus to school! They were the only black kids *in* the school. She went all the way to the back, where the heat didn't reach. The seat was so cold on her bottom, she about wanted to cry out. Why did everything have to be so cold?

The bus lurched forward. Another day of school. She felt the water up in her throat, up underneath her eyes. She took her fingers and squeezed them together so they hurt. *No water is coming out of me,* she said to herself. *Not one drop.*

In the hallway she just kept on walking, right past the other kids. No point slouching; she might as well let the boys see that she was bigger than they were. She might as well let the girls worry about her bumping into them. She didn't look down at them either; she kept her eyes straight ahead, like she was her daddy, marching in the army.

They all moved to the side of the hallway when they saw her coming, like water when you ran your hand through it. She heard their fake-whispered comments, just like they wanted her to. "Her mom and dad were shot dead." "I heard they were drug dealers." "I heard, instead of shooting her, they cut off her tongue. That's why she can't talk." "I heard *she* killed her parents. She'd be in jail, but she's too young, so she's here instead."

It was a game. They were trying to get her to talk. The whole school. The redbrick school on the hill. Lowell Elementary School. Even the building wanted her to talk. It would say to her in the morning, *Don't you want to call your best friend, Kiki, back in JP and tell her how big this school is? How pretty it is: red bricks and white cement like frosting in between? Don't you want to tell her about the playground? How there isn't one scratch on the jungle gym? How everything here is so clean? Don't you want to tell her?*

Homeroom. Mrs. Greene was taking them through their social studies assignment. They were studying the American Revolution, which was caused by people wasting tea and then men dressed like lobsters getting mad and other men riding horses in the night as fast as they could, which was dangerous back then because there was no electricity and it was real dark.

They were going around the room. It was Mercedes's turn.

"Mercedes?" Mrs. Greene smiled at her. Mrs. Greene always smiled at her. "Please tell the class what you got for number five. Who said 'Give me liberty or give me death?'"

Be the quiet's only friend.

"Mercedes?"

"She ain't got a Mercedes!" Tashawn shouted. "She takes the bus."

Wild laughter skittered across the room.

"That's enough out of you, Tashawn Garner, unless you want to spend the afternoon in the principal's office. Is that what you'd like?" Mrs. Greene never smiled at Tashawn.

"No."

"All right, then. Mercedes, we're on number five."

Stand like a rock in a pond. In the Jamaica Pond. Let the water sit around you. Do the rocks ever look bothered by the water?

"Mercedes?"

They were still laughing, Tashawn and Shahid, all the way in the back. What was so funny? They took the bus too. When they made fun of her, they were just making fun of themselves. Tashawn was doing fifth grade for a second time, on account of how much he liked to laugh and tease and not pay attention. Taneka had told her this back when she was trying to be her friend. So now, he was in the same class as his younger sister. But he didn't seem to care.

"Mercedes?"

Make a fist under the desk so no one will see it. Remember that morning Daddy taught you how to punch? He had boxed in the army. He knew just how to hit someone, just how to make a fist. *You curl your fingers up into your palm*, he said to her. *Then you leave your thumb on the outside. No, like this.* His big, cracked hands, folding over hers. *Then you aim just a little higher than their nose, so when they lift up you land right where they're going.* And her momma interrupting, saying, *You teach her how to talk to someone making a fist. You don't teach her how to fight. What's the matter with you?*

"Mercedes? Number five? No? Okay then. Carol, what do you have for number five?"

That's right, let the big black girl do her thing.

The worst part of the day was the cold ride on the school bus in the morning. Lunch was the second worst part of the day.

Going through the line was easy. The ladies in the white aprons didn't talk or listen to the school kids. If what they did was called cooking, then they needed another word for what her daddy did . . . what her daddy had done. Where were his spatulas and his pans? Where were his aprons? She took her tray to the table that had Mrs. Greene's name written on a piece of cardboard in the middle of it, then walked down to the far end, where the black kids in her class all sat together. There were four of them in one class and only eight in the rest of the school. In her old school, you couldn't sit back when you were bored and count up the black kids; you wouldn't have had enough time.

"Taken," Tashawn said, pointing at the bench on the far side of the table, right in front of her. "Taken, taken, taken. You're going to have to sit all the way at the end."

"What if she tips us over, like a seesaw?" Shahid was pushing them all along. Tashawn got the idea to be mean to her from him. "Hey, you leave any of them mashed potatoes for anyone else, or did you go ahead and take them all?"

Taneka pointed at her. Mercedes knew what she was thinking. She was getting ready to make fun of her. Her first try at playing the lunchtime game. The first week, she had said she was going to take care of Mercedes. They were going to be best friends. But then Mercedes never opened her mouth and Taneka must have decided it wasn't any fun, trying to be friends with a girl who wouldn't talk. *I'm sorry,* Mercedes would have explained, if she still made words, *but I can't be your friend. I am the quiet's only friend.*

"Who's going to buy you fancy clothes next winter, huh?" Taneka's finger wagged. "Not your grandmamma. She ain't going to buy you nothing new. She's too poor."

She snickered at Mercedes's light blue, cable-knit sweater. Her momma's favorite color. The color of the door of the restaurant. *We'll paint it blue,* Momma had said, *so that God will come for breakfast.* Because God is in all things but he is especially in water and blue is the color of water. After you have drowned, the next day, when the sky is no longer black, when the storm is gone, then the water is blue.

"She won't be a Mercedes then. She's going to be a Buick." Shahid looked around. Just for a moment he was out there all alone, waiting. Then the laughter came and he nodded his head knowingly.

"She's going to be a Toyota with no hubcaps," Tashawn said.

"She's going to be the school bus with no seats," Taneka said.

The other kids took their turns, but Mercedes wasn't listening. She was looking hard at the lunchroom table. It was white, but if you looked long enough you could see little specks of color: gray and red and brown. She looked for the specks of color.

CHAPTER 19

"I know," Mrs. Bittles was saying that same afternoon to Mr. Walt Steadman, the not-so-young man who was paying her a visit. He had knocked on her door for a good five minutes, and explained who he was for another ten, before she let him in. Now they were sitting at the kitchen table, waiting for the coffee to finish dripping, and she didn't know what she had gotten herself into. The way he kept on smiling, his whole face squinching up, made her distrust him. He said he had found them through Denise. What was that girl thinking, giving out her mother's address to some man on the phone? He could have been a member of the gang that did the shooting! Didn't she watch the news? When he said he had eaten breakfast at the Early Bird every morning for pretty near three years she thought he was exaggerating, but he did seem to know all about John and Natalie—had probably seen her son more than she had over that time. And now he was sitting at her kitchen table and she was talking about her granddaughter . . . the strangeness of it all.

"I know, she probably shouldn't even be in school at all, but she was already behind in her studies before. If she falls further behind now, how is she going to catch up? Besides, I don't want her cooped up with me every day in this tiny little place. She'd have nothing to do!"

He was just sitting there, hands folded on the table, thinking Lord knows what. She felt judged. Not that she owed him an explanation, but still.

"She had to come live here," Mrs. Bittles continued. "I couldn't move in with her; John's place was too expensive. First I thought I'd keep her in school in Jamaica Plain—just take her over there each morning—but that would have meant one bus and two T lines just to get there. More than an hour each way, four hours for me all told, going and coming. Four hours! Her best friend's mom, Nene Beauchard, said Mercedes could live with them during the week, but I'm not going to put my granddaughter in someone else's home right now! Not to mention, that's a Haitian family and they're different, I must say, just the way they do things. So I got her into a school here in Watertown that is supposed to be real good. The James . . . Russell . . . Lowell . . . Elementary School."

Mr. Steadman's eyes widened. "James Russell Lowell, he was the poet Robert Lowell's granduncle."

What the heck was he talking about? Mrs. Bittles waited to see if he'd explain himself but he didn't so she went on. "We're in the district, on account of them closing the Coolidge Elementary School around the corner." She paused to see if *Coolidge* set off any bells in Mr. Steadman's head. It didn't appear to. Her eyes drifted over to the picture of John on the counter. Outliving a child . . . there was no burden worse. Friends had told her as much but now she knew herself. Her heart couldn't break any more after this. "I tell her to be thankful for her opportunities, like a girl is going to be happy switching schools in the middle of the year, with her parents dead . . ." She shielded her eyes from his. Crying in front of a stranger just wasn't right but she couldn't help it. She was so weak now; she was a different person than before.

Mr. Steadman said nothing. He just sat there. You'd think, if you were paying a visit to someone you had never met before, that maybe you'd show up clean-shaven. Mrs. Bittles sniffled loudly. "John and Natalie should have never rented an apartment like theirs." Thinking about the decisions they had made just drove her crazy, but she couldn't stop herself. "They should have bought something small, built up some equity. That's what I told them. I wanted one of my children to own a home someday, since I never have. But they were in a hurry for the good life. They were too good for anything else. And I'm so old now . . . I got the Type Two Diabetes. I got a knee that hurts me pretty much always. My left eye is no good at all. My right eye ain't much better." She sighed. The coffee was ready. Mrs. Bittles shuffled over and poured them both a cup, then sat back down.

Mr. Steadman thanked her for the coffee. He took a sip, then coughed into his hand. "Couldn't Mercedes have moved in with one of her aunts or uncles?"

"Randy's in jail. Dontrelle Junior should be. Chantal can't take care of that big dog of hers, much less a girl. My youngest, Denise, she's got a good head on her shoulders, but she's got three kids herself and nothing I'd call a husband. Where's she going to put a fourth? Besides, I don't want Mercedes over in Roxbury, not now. This is where she belongs. In the summer, before school starts up again, we might have to rethink things." He nodded and Mrs. Bittles added, just so there wasn't any misunderstanding: "We didn't always live in Watertown. We moved from Roxbury when Dontrelle Senior took a job as a custodian at Boston Scientific. They had a factory here up until last year. Then they closed it. He died on the job, had a heart attack. That factory was where they made the little tiny things that clean out your arteries. But God bless him for being gone now. I wish I was with him, to be honest."

She removed her glasses and rubbed her eyes. She couldn't stop mulling over John and that wife of his. What were they thinking? "You know, they could have saved more, instead of always putting it back into the restaurant, and buying Mercedes all of those clothes. Shoot, she's got more to wear than I do, and she gets bigger every day!" She didn't think Mr. Steadman was following her but she didn't care. "They got insurance for the stuff they bought for the restaurant with the money the bank loaned them, the ovens and the silverware and the tables and the chairs, but John didn't have any life insurance! Now the bank says they can't sell anything from the café for more than cost. Is that right? A crazy Puerto Rican makes the ovens in the kitchen worth less? Explain that to me."

Mr. Steadman just shook his head. She went on. She couldn't help it. She had so much on her mind, and not a soul to share any of it with. She had to shout so loud when she called her best friend, Lynette, on the phone, her throat hurt afterwards. Denise had too much on her plate as it was; she couldn't take on all of her worries. And the rest of her children weren't what you'd call listening types. "I got my Social Security and Dontrelle Senior's pension, but I'm too old to raise a little girl. Look at me! I'm an old lady." She rapped the table with the arthritic knuckles of her left hand. "I take my granddaughter to the dentist, then I don't ever take her home again. The one son of mine with his head screwed on right, killed by a Puerto Rican he taught to cook. That about sums it up."

She put her glasses back on, too angry now even to think of crying. Carefully, she pressed her fingers down against the sides of her wig. It didn't feel like it was on right. She would have liked to have excused herself and done some rearranging but she wasn't going to leave this man alone, not with her granddaughter on her way home from school. What if he trapped her in the bathroom? What would happen then? Not that he seemed like the type, but the real dangerous ones never did.

"Mercedes won't do her homework," she added. Since she was complaining so much she might as well cover everything. "Where she sets her backpack down when she gets home is where she picks it up the next morning. I know I should be helping but I can't do schoolwork, not at my age, not with these eyes . . ."

Mr. Steadman took another sip of his coffee. He cleared his throat. "Well, that's kind of the reason I came by, Mrs. Bittles. I'd like to help Mercedes with her studies. I was thinking we could meet once a week or so."

She tilted her head, not following him. "Come again?"

"I'd like to help her study. And I'd like to teach her about poetry. One of the last things her mom told me was that she didn't like to read much, so I'd like to help her with that. Reading is kind of what I do."

"You work as a reader?"

"No, ma'am, I'm a graduate student at Harvard. I study literature."

"You go to Harvard?"

"Yes, ma'am."

"Do you have an ID or something?"

"Sure." He pulled out his wallet and handed over the card. She looked down at it, then up at him.

"It's a funny picture . . ." he muttered apologetically.

"Aren't you a little old to be a student?"

"Graduate students are older."

"Hmm." She peered at him. She had heard of these scams on the television. People would say they were going to help you do something and the next thing you knew they were using your name to get credit cards and buy all sorts of things. "And you want to help Mercedes with her schoolwork?"

"Yes, I would like to. I feel so bad about what happened. I want to do something to help and I think this is what I could do best, on account of what I've studied."

She held his ID just beneath the lenses of her glasses before handing it back to him. "You want to tutor my granddaughter?"

"That's right."

She squinted, trying to get a read on him, but who was she fooling? At the other end of the table, his face was just a blur.

"I can't pay nothing."

"Of course not."

She felt sure that she was overlooking something. "You'd come over to the house?"

"I could, yes."

"We spend our Sundays at church. I have to clear her mind of all that Voodoo talk her momma gave her."

"I was thinking more during the week." He paused. "What day is it today?"

What kind of man didn't know the day of the week? The kind of man whose job was studying literature, that's who. "Friday." More than three weeks had passed since the shootings. It felt more like three minutes.

"Right. How about Mondays?"

"Mondays are fine." Mrs. Bittles heard the tires of the bus wheeze to a stop outside. She rose to her feet to get the front door. Mr. Steadman followed her from the kitchen into the small living room, around a big black suitcase and a frayed green couch. He stood back while Mrs. Bittles pulled open the door.

Cold air swirled in, and then her granddaughter filled the doorframe. Lord, she wouldn't keep her mouth shut now, would she? When they had a visitor?

"How was school, Sweetness?" Mercedes stared over her shoulder.

"Do you remember Mr. Steadman? He used to eat breakfast at your parents' place." She couldn't bring herself to say *The Early Bird Café*— hadn't uttered the phrase once since the shootings. "He's offered to help you with your schoolwork once a week. He studies at Harvard. Why don't you say hello?"

Mercedes tilted her head at him.

Mr. Steadman stepped forward. "Hi, Mercedes. You can call me Walt."

"You can call him Mr. Steadman," Mrs. Bittles corrected him.

Mercedes didn't call him anything. She said nothing. She stepped back from both of them. She set her backpack down and struggled to get her coat off. Mrs. Bittles watched her squirm. Was it tight in the sleeves? My goodness, the girl just grew and grew. She walked into the kitchen to get something to eat. Mrs. Bittles followed behind her.

"I was thinking we could look at your homework together," Mr. Steadman said, poking his head in from the living room. With Mercedes home, there wasn't room for all three of them in the kitchen. She just filled up space, this girl, and not just on account of her size. She had always had a way of making people shy away from her.

He went on. "I could dig up some poems for us to read, just like we talked about that day. Remember? Over the Winter Break?"

Mercedes pulled a piece of bread out of the freezer and dropped it into the toaster. Then she withdrew a jar of strawberry jam and a stick of butter from the fridge. When the bread popped up, she took a knife and smeared butter and jam all over it. She set the plate of toast on the table and poured herself a glass of milk. The carton was just about empty, and Mrs. Bittles had gone to the store just three days ago. How was she going to keep this place stocked with food?

Mr. Steadman looked at his watch. "So I guess a quarter to four is when you get home? How about we say four o'clock on Mondays?"

"That would be fine." Mrs. Bittles walked around her granddaughter and placed her hands on her round shoulders. "Now you say *thank you*, Mercedes. Mr. Steadman is a busy man. He's making time to help you with your studies, so you say *thank you*."

Mercedes ate her toast. Her grandmother looked down at the top of her head. Mr. Steadman looked down at his feet.

"We'll have plenty of time to chat. I'll see you on Monday." He waved goodbye through the doorframe. Mrs. Bittles walked around the table and followed him into the living room. She handed him his parka, draped across the back of the couch. A nice, stiff coat, it must have kept the cold out real well.

"She hasn't opened her mouth since it all happened," she explained, her voice hushed. "Not one word. It's about enough to drive you crazy."

"Well, hardly any time has gone by."

They both stepped over to the front door. "I consider myself to be a fairly wise woman, Mr. Steadman. I raised five children in Roxbury. I buried my husband, and now a son. I saw things as a little girl, and then as a young woman . . . awful things. The looting right after Dr. King was killed, when they desegregated the schools, when everybody got messed up on the crack cocaine. I have seen a number of things. But Mercedes Bittles," she looked back through the doorway, then lowered her voice some more, "Mercedes Bittles is something else. She is just stubborn enough to make things real hard on herself. You should know that. The things Mercedes don't like she *don't like*. She's the stubbornest eleven-year-old I have ever seen, and I've seen a number."

He was rethinking things, she could tell. He was wondering what in God's name he had gotten himself into.

She opened the front door for him and he stepped out onto the cracked stoop. At some point, this tiny, one-story brick home had been split into two separate units. Mrs. Bittles's door was the one on the left: cracked open now just enough for her to stick her head out at him.

"I'm a good teacher, Mrs. Bittles," he said, suddenly looking away from her. That wasn't too convincing. He handed her a scrap of paper. "I wrote down my phone number for you. Please call, if something comes up. I'm just trying to help out. I feel terrible about what happened."

She took the paper from his hand and held it just in front of her nose. "What kind of chicken scrawl is this?"

"We won't work on penmanship." Standing on the bottom step,

Mr. Steadman could look her straight in the eye, without having to
bend over. He was tall like her boys, but he smiled too much. His
daddy should have taught him not to go around Boston smiling at
people he didn't know. "She'll be fine, Mrs. Bittles," he added, his
head a blur of nods.

And then she saw it clear as day. He was one of those types: a
dreamer, like her daughter Chantal—always assuming that at some
point a good job was just going to fall into her lap, that things would
take care of themselves. Mrs. Bittles let the door swing out into the
cold, crossed her arms, and lifted her chin at him. "How in the world
do you know that, Mr. Steadman? How in the world do you know?"

CHAPTER 20

Walt walked over to Mount Auburn Street and caught the #71 bus. Snow had begun to fall: big, wet flakes. He sat right behind the driver and stared out the window nervously, until he glanced around at the other passengers, none of whom seemed energetic enough to go on a shooting rampage. What a disaster that had been. Why had he called Mercedes's grandmother *ma'am*? That was a word he was pretty sure he had never used before. He had been so nervous—first talking to Mrs. Bittles, but even more so after Mercedes showed up. She didn't care for him much; that was obvious. And then, Mrs. Bittles had agreed to his little plan when it was clear to him that she didn't want to, and probably just as clear to her that he didn't want her to. Both of them trying to do right by Mercedes, while she sat there and glared at them. And what had he proposed, exactly? They were going to read poems together, just the way he and Flora had planned to do? The more he thought about it, the more embarrassing the whole thing was, on so many different levels.

He stepped off at the Harvard Square Stop and began to walk back to his dorm. Why had he felt so nervous out in Watertown? Because he had never been in the home of an African-American family before? The chipped coffee cups in Mrs. Bittles's kitchen, the cheap Formica table, the sagging couch, the way the furniture held the cold, the shitty TV in the corner of the living room, these were all the same props that had constituted the drabness of his own childhood. Still, it was different. Mrs. Bittles didn't *know* what his childhood home looked like. When he said *Harvard* her eyes had widened. He hated that. In graduate school, he and his friends had joked about the reaction they'd get when—home for vacation—they mentioned where they went to school. *Dropping the H-bomb*, they called it. But the word exploded for different reasons in Watertown than in Burlington. Harvard was more a real estate entity in Watertown than a school; it had been gobbling up land in that township in recent months, mostly for an envisioned expansion of the law school. The *Globe* had been all over the story. So when he said *Harvard*, it didn't necessarily make Mrs. Bittles think he was smart. It probably just made her think that he was privileged.

Back in his room, Walt grabbed his copy of Lowell's collection *The Dolphin* and headed for Widener. He didn't want to work; he wanted to go to sleep. The hour he had spent in the Bittleses' home had emptied him of all his energy, but the idea of being alone in Perkins Hall didn't appeal to him. It was too quiet.

He made his way back through campus. The snow continued to fall. The groundskeepers were already sprinkling salt on the walks. Walt loved this kind of snow, the kind that took its time falling. He cut through Harvard Yard, up the steps of Widener, and then into the library itself. He had to wait in line to show his ID to the guard; Friday night and the library was packed. He took the marble staircase up to the second floor.

He noticed Ginger right when he entered the reading room. It was impossible not to. She was sitting at the center table, her work spread out all around her: what looked like photocopies of newspaper articles. She had ignored the two-seat buffer to which everyone else adhered and had more or less taken over the entire middle part of the table. She was this little bead of perfection, surrounded by the nerdy and neurotic: kids chewing on pencils and grad students with their faces three inches from the screens of their laptops.

He stood on the other side of the table and watched her work. She appeared to be reading eight or nine articles at once, and highlighting lines from all of them. Whenever she pressed the yellow highlighter against the paper, it squeaked loudly, echoing off the green-coffered ceiling and the bookcase-lined walls. The students in her general vicinity squirmed with annoyance in their seats.

Finally she looked up. Her eyes narrowed as she scooped her papers into a messy pile. "You look like shit. Are you growing a beard?"

"Not by design. I just stopped shaving." He pulled back the chair facing her and plopped down. He had to peer around the enormous brass desk lamp bolted to the center of the table to see her face. "What are you working on?"

She shrugged noncommittally. As he looked at her, Walt realized Ginger wasn't a bead of perfection. The skin beneath her eyes was gray. Her white turtleneck was dirty, and her hair needed to be combed and washed. Every time he had seen her, he had always scanned her head to foot, noting her outfits and accessories, but he suspected he had never just looked into her face as he did now, without distraction. Her eyes seemed hollowed out and sad, let down by the all too subdued world that surrounded them.

"I had another good interview yesterday, this one with that woman who runs an outreach program for teenage runaways. We were scheduled to talk earlier, remember?"

"I do."

A student three chairs down from Ginger cleared her throat loudly and stared at the two of them with visible rage. They rose from their chairs and walked out into the hallway. Alongside the walls, circulation terminals were set on waist-high tables. Students tapped keyboards and peered at the screens.

Ginger stuck her foot out in its ballet pose and folded her arms across her stomach. "You haven't called me, Walt."

"I'm sorry, I've been hunkered down."

"Getting a lot of work done?"

"Not really." He noticed band-aids wrapped around the tips of each of her fingers. She caught him staring. "I've been at war with my cuticles," she said. "I can't stop chewing on them."

"Are you okay?"

She shrugged once more. "I'm trying to make sense of too much— for my book. I want to piece all of this human experience together. The goals I set for myself are so ridiculous. And then, in trying to reach them, I start to go a little crazy." She blew at her hair, which lifted off her forehead. "At night I can't stay in my apartment anymore. I just drive around. I hate being here so much; I really do. I asked my father, if I can get a contract for my book, if he'd let me drop out of school. He said he'd think about it. But enough. I don't want to talk about my crap. How are you?"

Walt didn't want to talk about his crap either, but he tried. "I'm okay, I guess. I'm having these stupid nightmares; they're embarrassing."

"All nightmares are stupid, when you think about them. That's what makes them so scary." She straightened her arms and then crossed them again. "Okay, can I be honest with you? Just now, I was reading about MS-13. Newspaper articles mostly. I feel a little funny about it too, almost like I should ask your permission."

"Why in the world do you want to research MS-13?"

"Because there are girls in the gang and I want to interview some of them for my book."

He looked at her incredulously. "Are you being serious?"

She nodded and he turned and slowly made his way to the top of the marble staircase. Then he stopped. As much as he wanted to, he couldn't just leave her there in the library. Perhaps the way it worked was that everyone had a certain number of points they could use leaving people behind and he had used up all of his when he had left his family in Burlington, so now he was no longer capable of letting people go. But that didn't quite work as a theory. He had let plenty of friends go since graduate school. He had forgotten about all the residents from his old apartment building in a matter of days. So he didn't know why he couldn't walk out on Ginger. He didn't know why he felt obliged to stand at the top of the stairs and wait for her to make her way over to him, but he did. He waited. And finally, after what seemed like an inordinately long time, she sauntered over. She was wearing jeans that had silver stitching around the pockets and down each leg. He could see the trace of her hipbones, pressing up against the denim, as she moved. Once she was within arm's reach, she placed her hand on his elbow.

"I know it's insensitive of me, Walt. I realize that, and I'm sorry. But I can't *not* look into MS-13. I have to."

Walt looked over her shoulder, at all the students jotting down call numbers and scrolling through lists and lists of books. He was supposed to be doing that. He was supposed to be tracking down articles and critical studies on the poetry of Robert Lowell. Instead he had been huddled in his little dorm room, reading around in the

Norton Anthology and concocting his plan to help Mercedes Bittles.

"What?" She puckered her lips. "No, what? You're thinking something."

He shook his head.

"Come on, Walt."

He sighed. "Okay, I'm just curious. What's it like to be so driven? To be so focused? To never stop? To just go and go?"

She sat down on the top step of the staircase. "Oh, it's awful. It's real bad."

He sat down next to her. Slightly below them, halfway down to the ground floor, was a mural signed in the upper left-hand corner by John Singer Sargent. It depicted a dead World War One soldier, his body crumpled and lifeless, his round green helmet perched atop his sunken head while a winged female angel lifted his soul up to Heaven, beneath a banner that read *Death and Victory*.

"Can I ask you something, Walt? Since that morning in the café, have you ever wanted to learn about MS-13, or Ramon Gutierrez? Have you ever felt any curiosity?"

He studied the Sargent mural. The angel had flowing golden hair and fantastic breasts, one of which Sargent had topped with the hint of a pink nipple, but the dead soldier looked like a pile of dirty clothes. He had no heft; nothing spilled out of him. Walt wondered if Sargent had actually ever seen a dead body.

"No, I've never thought of Ramon, except—in my nightmares—as some homicidal monster. And I haven't thought of *Mara Salvatrucha*," his face grimaced as he said the name, "except when I've been sitting in a coffee shop, or in my dorm room, and imagined being shot. I haven't tried to understand how it would be possible for anyone to do what Ramon did, or what those guys do. I haven't . . . I don't think I can think in those terms."

"See, that's why you study poetry, which is cool, don't get me wrong, but I don't study poetry. I'm a philosopher; I study truth claims. I try to answer questions; it's just the way I am."

A librarian passed behind them with a cart filled with books, one of its wheels squeaking loudly.

"What if I told you *not* to research MS-13? What if I said it had to be off limits? You wouldn't stop, would you? You wouldn't be able to. You'd keep on combing through newspaper articles, taking notes."

She swallowed. "Yeah, I probably would. I am very driven, I'd never deny that."

Several students coming up the stairs stepped around them, their overloaded book bags tugging them sideways. At some point, large backpacks with padded straps, what Walt had used as a student, had gone out of fashion.

"I didn't mean to insult you just then, when I said you study poetry, not truth claims."

"No, you're right." He was wondering now, on the heels of his trip out to Watertown, what it meant for him to care about poetry in the first place. Maybe his attachment to verse was really mostly sentimental. Maybe that explained why he couldn't bring himself to write his dissertation; he looked to poetry for some sort of comfort, which was why—when he had thought of helping Mercedes the other day—his impulse had been to offer her the same thing he had offered Flora: poems. As if they might make some sort of difference.

"I found the daughter of Natalie and John Bittles. You know, the owners of the Early Bird? Her name is Mercedes. She's living with her grandmother in Watertown."

He hadn't planned on telling anyone about the tutoring. That way, if the whole thing ended up being a train wreck, no one would have to know. But now he realized that he wanted Ginger's opinion; he wanted to see what her reaction to his undertaking would be.

"How'd you find her?" she asked.

"I went through the Bittleses in the phonebook. Denise, John's little sister, gave me her mother's address in Watertown. She told me not to bother calling, that her mother would hang up on me. So I went over there. Starting on Monday, I'm going to tutor Mercedes once a week: help her with her English assignments, maybe give her some poems to read."

Ginger squirmed in her designer jeans.

"You think it's a bad idea?"

She rubbed her fingers together so that her band-aids turned, like gears without grooves. "To be honest, it makes me a little uncomfortable."

"How so?"

"It's the whole 'white guy from Harvard, tutoring the black girl' thing—"

"That's a thing?"

"Kind of."

"How did you know she's black?"

"Well, her parents were black. Their pictures were in the *Globe*."

"They put their pictures in the paper!"

"It's a big deal, that shooting, Walt. There were several stories: biographical bits about the victims, about Ramon. Don't worry, you've never been mentioned."

He was grateful for that, not just because he was afraid of MS-13, but he wouldn't be able even to try to tutor Mercedes if she had any idea that he had seen her parents killed. And thinking of their lifeless bodies now, collapsed on the floor of the Early Bird, he winced at the thought of their deaths being confirmed in the paper, as if such an announcement alone made their passing irrevocable. "I'm trying not to fixate on the race stuff," he said. "I'm just trying to help her, person to person."

"I admire that. Like I said, I don't like the idea in general; it feels too well intentioned to me, and condescending, but that doesn't mean I think *you're* being condescending. I know what you're trying to do is a good thing . . ."

But she sounded so unconvinced. He cleared his throat. "You said something awhile ago that bothered me. That rule of yours, that money is the only thing that can make the world a better place—"

"That's not what I said! I said Americans only *believe* in the power of money to change things. And I was referring to social standing." Her mouth scrunched up. She was deep in thought. "But if you want to extend my claim, I'll accept your premise. We have, as a culture, monetized charity. People don't go out and invite a homeless person in for dinner, for example. They give money to an organization that is supposed to help the homeless. Or they give a homeless person a dollar. But that isn't, by Scholastic standards, a charitable gesture. It isn't loving like God loves. It's giving someone a dollar bill. Big deal."

Walt had wanted to point out that his whole venture in Watertown was partially intended to refute Ginger's assumptions about the singular power of money to change things, but he realized now that by refuting this he ended up somehow conforming to her Scholastic notion of charity, which he didn't want to do either.

"You know," she interrupted his train of thought, "you don't have to become a community volunteer just because you survived a restaurant shooting."

"I'm not trying to become a community volunteer. I just want to be a halfway decent person."

"Well, that's *really* ambitious. Maybe you should just stick to community activism instead."

"I think maybe you should finish your degree before you dole out advice."

"I think maybe you should finish *your* degree before *you* dole out advice."

She was something else. A brat, but adorable in her own, curious way. And suddenly, if for no other reason than because she was such a brat, he felt drawn to her. He wrapped his arm around her. She leaned her head against his shoulder.

"Mrs. Bittles says Mercedes hasn't spoken since the murders. By the way, the girl doesn't even like me—she never has."

Ginger put her hand on his knee. "Doesn't it suck? You just want to help someone but the possibility exists that merely by trying to, you'll piss the person off."

He immediately thought that she must have meant her paying for his dorm room. "And then you wonder what you were thinking in the first place," he replied. "You question your own motives. Maybe you weren't being selfless at all. Maybe you were just trying to make yourself feel better."

She lifted her hand from his knee and placed it on the far side of his neck. "Then you hear the ghosts of all those New England Puritans, all their skepticism about being charitable in the first place. 'People have to help themselves,' they say. 'You can't save someone else.' Aquinas was so lucky he died in the 1200s, before all of his beautiful ideas were ruined." Her hand moved up to his cheek. She turned his face toward hers.

"Oh, the stupid Puritans," Walt whispered.

"They made a mess of everything." She kissed him once, slowly, almost clinically. "The more they asked of themselves and others, the more they fucked things up."

He kissed her back. Behind them, at the circulation terminals, students combed through electronic databases and recalled items that had been checked out by other users. Walt heard the same cart with the squeaky wheel pass behind them. He told himself that she was just a stubborn New Yorker with a dumb idea for a book, and that he was just a sentimental Vermonter who thought the world would be a better place if everyone could simply appreciate the same set of poems. Poems, incidentally, all written by white New Englanders. He told himself that the two of them were ridiculous, making out in the middle of the library. He thought of Flora. But he didn't stop kissing Ginger. In spite of where they were and how different they were, he didn't want this moment to end.

CHAPTER 21

"I would use a comma here, instead of a period, since the word that follows isn't capitalized. I think you meant to use a comma."

Mr. Steadman was seated right next to her, at her grandmamma's kitchen table. He was reading an assignment of hers that had been due two days before, although he had no way of knowing that, since Mercedes hadn't told him. Mercedes hadn't told him anything; she had just produced the essay from a bent, blue folder in her backpack. At the top of the page she had written A Report on a Great American. What followed was a two-page essay on Paul Revere's Midnight Ride.

"And maybe you could vary the way you refer to him. You know, instead of saying *Paul Revere* each time. Sometimes you could say *he*, or just *Revere* is okay."

She blinked as slowly as she could. She tried to look at the inside of her eyelids. Revere was a beach too. Her daddy had taken her there once. That was a long time ago; when she had held his hand, it had been up around her shoulder.

"Did he carry two lanterns on his horse?" Mr. Steadman shifted in his chair. He was too tall to sit at the table; his legs kept getting stuck. When they had come over on Sundays, her daddy had never sat down in the kitchen; he had always stood over in the corner.

"How could you carry two lanterns on a horse? You'd need a good lantern holder—like a cup holder today. That was a joke."

Mercedes just stared at the page: her back straight, her hands folded in her lap. Mr. Steadman had a voice that was easy to tune out. She curled the fingers of her right hand up in her palm, leaving her thumb on the outside. *I am a boxer*, she said to herself. *I am in the army.*

"No, I'm pretty sure they put the lanterns in the . . . what do you call it? The church windows. The Old North Church. Weren't the lanterns there?"

She shrugged. Enough about the lanterns. She watched him scribble something in the margin. Now she'd have to rewrite the whole page. You could look at a person's hands and know how hard they worked. Her momma had always said that. Mr. Steadman's hands were real soft, like melted butter, but Grandmamma's hands were cracked and hard, like a loaf of bread left on the counter for several days. Her daddy's hands were creased in the palms from holding spatulas and pans, but his fingers were soft from having egg yolk run over them every day. His hands had always smelled good too, like pepper and strawberry jelly and hash browns. She wanted hands like her daddy's, hard and soft together.

"So the British came by sea. That's interesting. I had forgotten that." Mr. Steadman nodded. "So that means two lanterns. *Sea* refers to the Charles River, as in they crossed the Charles River? Is that what you're trying to say?"

That was what she was trying to say, but the words in her head didn't come out the same on the page. They got turned around. She didn't nod, but she blinked again, slowly. She liked the idea that her eyes were still seeing when her eyelids were shut. That meant, whenever she was sleeping, her eyes were looking at her momma. Because her momma lived in dark things now. When you were dead, that meant you went into water and dark things.

"Let's try to make that clearer." Mr. Steadman drew an arrow to the part of the sentence that he had already underlined and wrote something else in the margin. His hand moved real fast when he wrote, almost like it wasn't connected to the rest of his body. "You know, we aren't too far from the Charles River. It's just down that way." He pointed at the refrigerator, which was rattling like it always did. He was a strange man, Mr. Steadman. He seemed old and young at the same time. She didn't think it was right that he was alive. He should be dead, like her parents and Flora. Ramon was dead too. Her parents had given him a job, which meant, every other week, they had paid him money, but then they took his job away because he was disrespectful so he killed them. He killed Flora too. And she was so nice. She had always worn a yellow ribbon in her hair.

Mr. Steadman held the paper up to read it, then set it back down. "This is interesting, what you've got here. It's called faulty parallelism. Basically that means one half of the sentence doesn't match the other half."

What was he talking about? She couldn't follow him. If he was a teacher, why didn't he talk like her other teachers? Why did he use words she didn't understand? Grandmamma was in the living room, turning the pages of her *Herald* as loud as she could, just to make sure they remembered she was there.

"I would maybe think of rewriting this bit here," Mr. Steadman said. "Sometimes, if a sentence gets really long, you can clean it up by turning it into two sentences. It seems like this sentence wants to be two sentences."

Mercedes wasn't listening; she was thinking of Tashawn and Shahid in school that day, when they asked her what she was going to do for parent/teacher conferences in the spring. "They don't let no grandparents come to parent/teacher conferences," Shahid had said. "Yeah," Tashawn had added, "otherwise they would call them grandparent/teacher conferences." He puckered his cheeks when he looked at her. He didn't understand that she was big boned. He called her fat.

Mr. Steadman handed her the essay and she put it back in her folder. "If you want to show me the next draft you can. When is it due?"

Mercedes put the folder in her backpack and zipped it up. What did he mean by *draft*, the air coming into the house?

"Are there any other assignments you have, English assignments? I'm afraid I wouldn't be able to help you much with math."

What did he mean by *English*? Was that language arts? What about their library unit? Did that count?

"So is that it?"

She nodded as she pushed back her chair. She figured she didn't need to sit there if they didn't have any more work to do. But her grandmamma wouldn't let her go into the living room and watch TV, not that there was anything good to watch, since they didn't have cable. That meant she'd have to go back into her little room and sit there on the bed, staring at the walls. She hated that room; it was so small.

"Hold on a second." Mr. Steadman pulled out some sheets of paper, fifteen or so. He put them on the table. "I photocopied some poems that I thought we could read together. Does that sound like fun?"

No, it didn't sound like fun. She tilted her chair back and imagined herself falling over and knocking her head against the oven—everything going black, her momma coming to her in the darkness, her arms spread wide.

"These are all poems by Robert Frost," Mr. Steadman was saying. "He was a great poet. He was born in . . . the late 1800s, I guess. Actually, I'm not sure when he was born. He died in the sixties, the 1960s, I know that. He's my grandmother's favorite poet."

That was funny to think of Mr. Steadman having a grandmamma. Would she look a lot older than hers or about the same? Mercedes imagined that the two of them would look the same kind of old, on account of both of them being grandparents.

He began to thumb through the poems. His eyebrows kept wrinkling. "Let's see here . . ." He was nearing the end of his bundle. He was finding something in the poems he didn't want her to see. Maybe her momma was in the poems. When you read the words, you heard her voice. Momma was in the chalkboards at school too, like she was in her eyelids when she slept at night. She wasn't in the chalkboards once they had been written on; at the beginning of the day, when they were clean and looked like black water, then her momma was in them.

"Here's a nice little poem." He seemed relieved. "It's called 'A Time To Talk.' I'm going to read this one. Next time you can read. We'll take turns." He cleared his throat, paused, and started to read the poem.

When Mr. Steadman read out loud, his voice changed. It got deeper and steadier. It was harder to tune out. Her daddy's voice had always been real steady. Even when he was mad, it stayed steady. That was how Mr. Steadman sounded now. Mercedes thought one of his friends should tell him that he should always talk like he talked when he read his poems. She wondered what Mr. Steadman's friends were like. Maybe he didn't have any; otherwise, why would he have always come to the café by himself?

It didn't take him long at all to read the poem, even though he was pausing between the words and speaking real slow. "I'm going to read it once more," he said. Mercedes was glad because she hadn't been able to concentrate very well the first time through. He coughed into his hand and then started to read it all over again. She listened carefully.

In the poem, a man is working on his land when a friend on a horse calls out to him from the road. The man asks what he wants. *What is it?* But the friend doesn't say. So the man just goes up to the stone wall that runs along the road to chat with his friend.

There didn't seem to be much to the poem at all: just these two men, the land where the man was working, the stone wall, and the road. But Mercedes liked how you could list all of the things in the poem, kind of like a recipe. And she liked listening to Mr. Steadman read it.

When he finished the poem for a second time, the two of them sat still. "See, this poem is about how we all need to talk," Mr. Steadman said finally. "Even if we have other things to do, or stuff on our mind, visiting with other people is important. Being alone is important too, but you can't always be alone. Every once in a while you have to talk to your friends." He slid the sheet of paper toward her. "You keep that. You can read a poem of that length just about anywhere. Like at lunch, if you want. That's what I used to do—"

She stood up, her chair tipping back and just missing the door handle of the oven. He had tricked her with the poem. He had made her think that listening to it would be just like listening to music, or looking at something beautiful, like one of her momma's photographs. But he was trying to teach her a lesson through the poem. He *was* like a teacher, even if he didn't sound quite like one. Mr. Steadman wanted her to see herself as the man in the poem who was working on the land; and he wanted her to see him as her friend. But he wasn't her friend. He was a grown man! He had read the poem just to make her think she had to talk to everyone. Like her grandmamma, like Mrs. Greene, he was trying to get her to talk for no good reason, just because the quiet scared him.

She walked out of the kitchen, down the hallway twenty feet, and into the bedroom in which she didn't fit. She slammed the door behind her. She could hear the refrigerator humming. She could hear Mr. Steadman's chair squeak beneath his weight. She had never liked him. Whenever she had seen him in the café, he had always gotten under her skin. He was one of those guys who thought he was funnier than he was, who thought he could just make people like him because he laughed at his own jokes. He had always tried too hard with her and now he was trying extra hard because her momma and daddy were dead. He shouldn't have invited himself over like he had. That wasn't right. He shouldn't have been going all over town, always thinking he was welcome everywhere, because he wasn't. There were parts of Boston where he belonged and parts where he didn't and he should have known that, being a grown man and everything.

"Mercedes!" Mrs. Bittles slapped her paper against her knee and marched into the kitchen. "Mercedes Bittles! You get back here right now! You sit at this table until Mr. Steadman is done teaching you. Mercedes!"

"That's okay." Mr. Steadman rose to his feet. "I should be going anyway." He picked up his pile of papers, except for the poem he had just read to Mercedes; he left that one on the table.

"No, that's not okay. That's disrespectful." She cupped her hands around her mouth. "Mercedes Bittles! You come back to this kitchen right now!"

The two of them stood there, waiting for her to reappear, but she didn't.

"Mercedes!"

Mr. Steadman crossed his arms. So he was cold. Well, she wasn't turning the heat up for him; that she just could not do. "Oh Lord, this child." Mrs. Bittles put her hands on the kitchen table. "A sixty-eight-year-old woman, trying to talk sense into an eleven-year-old. How am I going to pull that off?" He didn't say anything. "Was she paying attention, when you were correcting her paper?"

"Yeah." He nodded, but he didn't sound too convincing.

"Thank you for your time, Mr. Steadman." No sense standing around. She walked him into the living room, where he scooped up his coat, and over to the front door. He turned the knob and stepped out onto the stoop. "I'll have a talk with Mercedes about respecting the readings you give her. You can bet on that."

"Please don't, Mrs. Bittles. I don't want to force anything on her."

She didn't understand. How was he going to teach that girl anything if she didn't respect what he said? Why was everyone afraid of setting children straight these days? That was why, when she'd get on the bus, none of the kids would give up their seats for her. They'd let her stand in the aisle, on her bad knee, because no one was telling them how they were supposed to act. But she couldn't tell Mr. Steadman how to teach. That was his business. "All right then," she said.

He nodded at her and headed off. She watched him trudge down the street, his head bobbing in front of his body like a turkey's. She had a pretty good feeling how this would turn out. He'd come over a few more times and sit at the kitchen table with her granddaughter. He'd try with her, but just enough to be able to tell himself he had done a good deed. Then he'd stop coming altogether. After a couple more weeks, they'd never see him again.

Mercedes watched Mr. Steadman walk down Dewey Street from the small window behind her bed. She watched his breath swirl up around his head in the cold. He was headed toward the bus stop on Mount Auburn. He must not have a car. What kind of fool would take a bus in the cold to look at homework of hers that had been due two days before? She watched him tuck his chin up underneath the collar of his parka. He thought he knew her family because he had seen her parents in the café every morning, but Mr. Steadman didn't know her family. He didn't know anything about her. Whatever her momma would say to him at the café, she'd say to everyone. She was just being friendly. And he had tricked her with that poem. He was out of her view now. She let the curtain go from her hand and lay down on her tiny bed. She didn't like the room she was in, or her grandmamma's little house, or the way she cooked, or Mr. Steadman, or going to school, or being at school. She didn't like Tashawn or Taneka or Shahid or any of the other kids who just stared at her. She didn't like being cold all of the time. She didn't like Watertown. There was nothing in her new world that Mercedes Bittles liked.

CHAPTER 22

Walt walked to the end of Dewey Street. He waited ten minutes for the #71 bus, then another ten. He considered just walking home, but then of course the bus would clamor by while he puttered along, so he waited and waited. Finally it pulled up. He paid the fare and took a seat right behind the driver. Standing outside, he hadn't been nervous at all, but the minute Walt found himself in this confined, public space he began to sweat and fidget. There were teenagers grouped way in the back of the bus; that was the problem. If one of them opened fire, even if Walt wasn't himself shot, the resulting accident would probably kill them all.

In an effort to calm himself, he thought back to his session with Mercedes. Telling her it was important to talk . . . that was so stupid, so disingenuous. What he had really been saying was that he found her refusal to speak irritating. No wonder she got up from the table and left. But the session had gone off the rails well before that. Why had he mentioned faulty parallelism to an eleven-year-old? And he had told that stupid joke too: lantern holder. He cringed at the thought. Like a kid whose parents were just killed was going to laugh about a lantern holder.

Back in Perkins Hall, he took the stairs up to his room, stripped down to his underwear, and stretched the phone over to his bed. He couldn't put it off any longer; he had to call home. His grandmother picked up on the first ring.

"Hello?"

"Hi, Grandma."

"Walter! Where have you been? Oh goodness. Marion! It's Walter. We've been calling and calling you!"

"I'm sorry; I've been meaning to phone."

"That's not like you, to disappear for so long. A couple of weeks, yes, but a month!"

"I know. I'm sorry."

"We were thinking of calling the police. Your phone would just ring and ring. The machine wouldn't even pick up."

"Actually I moved out of my apartment. I'm living back on campus."

"You're living back on campus! At Harvard?"

And of course this was one of many reasons why he had put off phoning them. They would be so excited to hear where he was now. They would jump so quickly to conclusions.

"Yes, back in Cambridge."

"Are you giving your dissertation another try?"

He paused, on the cusp of delivering the first of what he suspected might be several half-truths. "Yeah, I am."

"That is so wonderful." And he had to listen now as she repeated the news to his mother in the background. "We're so proud of you, Walter. You're giving it another try!"

"It's more complicated than that, Grandma. So I had to give up my apartment, as well as my job at the dry cleaners."

"You quit your job at the dry cleaners too?"

"Yes." He could picture the questions lining up in her mind: old-fashioned propeller planes, waiting to lift off.

"But how are you going to support yourself?"

"Well, that's the problem. I've got a little bit of money left . . ." He had very little in fact. That was one of the reasons he was phoning now. Walt needed a handout.

"How did you pay for the room?"

He considered lying about this too, claiming to have built up a little nest egg over the years, but there was no way she'd ever buy that so he went with the truth, which was really much worse than any lie he might have dreamt up. "A girl gave me the money. She's a friend, a tenant in the building over in the Back Bay. She said it was no big deal."

"How can paying for someone's dormitory room not be a big deal?"

"Well, it depends—"

"You have to pay her back, Walter, right away."

"I will, as soon as I can."

"As soon as you have the money. You can't owe someone that kind of money! You need to pay her back."

"I know." He looked out the window, at the law school students scurrying off to their classes. In mere months after getting their degrees, they would all have respectable jobs as corporate lawyers and clerks and whatever else Harvard Law graduates did. They would have steady income for the rest of their lives.

"I wish we had more money, Walter. I wish you didn't have to worry about anything other than your doctorate."

"It's my own fault. I wasted a lot of time—"

"There are just these expenses we have. Medicaid doesn't cover everything."

"I know, I know."

There was a pause.

"I'm sorry," Walt said. "I've let you both down; I know that."

"Don't be ridiculous, you're back at Harvard! We're so proud of you . . ."

"No, I've let you down."

". . . I wouldn't know where to start on a project like yours." Mrs. Steadman let out a loud, melodic sigh. Talking about his academic work always put her in a good mood. "Robert Lowell! What a complicated poet. What a complicated man. I just wouldn't know what to say."

"It's been such a strange year so far . . ." Walt had wanted to change the subject but he let his voice trail off. He was tempted to tell her right then that they had taken him out of the Early Bird Café on a stretcher. The police thought he had been shot. He could be dead now. He wanted her to know that. Compared to a dead person, he was getting a lot accomplished. But she wouldn't understand. She would think he had lost his mind. "How's Mom?"

"Good. Resting right beside me at the moment. She's been eating very well lately. I know she'd love to see you."

"I'll visit soon. I need to put some things in order but then I'll come up, maybe in the early spring?"

"That would be grand."

He paused, unsure how to switch subjects again. "Hey, Grandma, I have a question for you. What kind of poems do you think an eleven-year-old would appreciate?"

"The same kind of poems a thirty-year-old would. Good poems."

"What did you give me to read when I was that age?"

"Frost, mostly. *Mountain Interval*."

"But he's so rural."

"But he's a great poet."

"Yeah, but there are a ton of references to death in his work. I had forgotten about them."

"Yes, I suppose that's true."

"Well, I can't read poems about death to an eleven-year-old!"

"Why not? Eleven-year-olds know about death."

"Yes, but some eleven-year-olds know too much about death."

"Walter, you're speaking in riddles. What are you talking about?"

Again, he had to fudge matters a little. "It's a tutoring program, Grandma. Harvard set it up, to give back to the community. I'm tutoring an eleven-year-old girl whose parents were killed in a shooting."

"Oh my goodness. That's awful."

"Yeah, it's pretty bad." His grandmother meant the shooting. Walt, at that moment, meant the tutoring.

"But what a wonderful thing for Harvard to do." And her voice sounded buoyant again. Educational outreach was just the sort of thing to cheer up Eleanor Steadman.

"Isn't it?"

"Yes, it is. A school like that, with all of its resources, should give back to its community. Plus, what a great extracurricular activity for you."

"That's what I thought. But we had our first session today and she didn't say a thing."

"You have to give her time. Children don't just open up to strangers. They're taught not to do that, you know."

"That's right."

They shared the crackles of the phone line for a few seconds.

"Do give Mom my love."

"I will." He could hear her tell his mother he loved her. "She's very proud of you, Walter. She's just smiling away."

He waited for the phone to be passed to her but his grandmother didn't follow the normal script. "I have an idea," she said. "How about I send you my old book of Frost's poems? You could loan it to the girl."

"But it's your favorite book!"

"Oh, I don't need it. I have all the poems stored in my head anyway. You can send it back to me when she's done with it."

"Okay then, sure."

"Give me your dormitory address."

He did, along with his new phone number. She repeated all the information while writing it down. It seemed to take forever. When she was finished, they shared a brief, awkward silence.

"We're going into town today." She spoke deliberately, which meant she was thinking about something else. "Your mother has a doctor's appointment. We'll stop at the post office on the way in and I'll send the book, along with some money."

"No—"

"It won't be much, just a little to help you get resettled in Cambridge. I wish I could send more."

"Please, Grandma, don't say that."

"Oh, but it's true." There was yet another pause. He could almost hear her mind working. She was thinking about his financial situation, about their financial situation. "Oh, Walter! What kind of girl has money like that? Money to pay for someone's dormitory room! Money just to give away!"

"She's not like us, Grandma," he said. "She's just so rich. She's not like us at all."

CHAPTER 23

Mercedes Bittles shut the door behind her and rushed toward the school bus, trying to get there before the cold stung her face. She could feel her hair, bulging up in clumps beneath her gray wool cap. It was her daddy's cap; he had given it to her. She could smell him in it: hand soap and eggs and the way his skin smelled that there weren't any words for. Now that her hair wasn't braided, it filled the cap up so that it was snug on her head.

She stepped onto the bus, her right hand making a fist in her coat pocket: the knuckles tight against her palm, the thumb on the outside. When you punched someone, you had to aim just a little higher than his nose, so when he lifted up his head you landed your fist right where he was going. Her long underwear beneath her jeans made her legs itch. It was a Wednesday, but the days didn't matter anymore. When the weekend came, there was nothing to do—no good television shows to watch, no nice place to go for a walk, like the Jamaica Pond. On the weekends, after the café had closed for the day, she and her daddy would walk around the pond. Even in the winter, when the ice made it so you couldn't see the water, you just had to believe it was still there . . . even in the winter, they would go for walks around the pond.

She moved down the aisle. Was it ever going to be too cold for this bus to run? It was a rickety thing; the cushions of the seats were all torn and Tashawn would pull the spongy insides out when the driver wasn't looking and toss them at her.

"Whatcha going to do when your grandmamma dies?" Tashawn called out to her as she took her seat in the back of the bus. "Everyone's grandparents die. They got to, they're so old. Where you going to live then?" He looked over at his sister but Taneka didn't say anything.

She seemed to be getting tired of teasing her.

"Ain't you got an uncle in prison?" Tashawn dropped his arms over the back of his seat. The sleeves of his parka didn't reach his wrists. "I guess you can't stay with him when your grandmamma dies. You wouldn't fit in his cell, with your fat head." He glanced back at Taneka, who was staring out the window. "Yeah, that's right, not enough room for your head."

The bus hit a pothole and Tashawn nearly fell over. He turned around in his seat. He was still talking, but no one was listening. Mercedes set her backpack down. From the right pocket of her blue coat she withdrew the piece of paper that she had folded into fourths. It was the photocopy of the poem that Mr. Steadman had read: "A Time To Talk." She unfolded it.

When she first read the poem by herself the day before, she thought it was real simple, but the more she read it, the more complicated it got. Now she wasn't sure if the way Mr. Steadman had explained its meaning was right. She thought the man who spoke in the poem was trying to convince himself that he liked talking to his friends when they came by but that he didn't, really. He made conversation just because he felt he had to; that was what Mercedes thought. The man who spoke in the poem wasn't being true to himself. Her momma had always said you had to be true to yourself and that meant doing what you knew was right even if other people tried to get you to do something else that was bad, like drugs or disrespecting someone old or crippled or using bad language. By not talking anymore, Mercedes was being true to herself because her words were in the water with her momma and daddy and if she spoke she would be speaking words that weren't hers and she wasn't going to do that because she loved her momma and her momma had always told her to be true to herself. She loved her daddy too, which was why she walked down the hallway at school with her back as straight as could be— even though she was taller than pretty near everyone *in* the school— because her daddy said how you carried yourself said a lot about how much pride you had. He said the more pride you had, the straighter you'd keep your back, so she tried to keep her back as straight as she could. She thought of her daddy standing in front of the griddle at the restaurant, his back perfectly straight, and her momma standing at the register; even though her hip hurt her when she stood she always got to her feet whenever the door opened.

She read the poem nice and slow. She almost didn't have to look at the paper to hear the words in her mind. She liked how short it was, and how all the letters were lined up evenly on the left side, like a sheet pulled up straight on a bed with its corners turned in. Her daddy knew how to make a bed so that when you pulled up the sheet to go to sleep it felt cold and clean, like no one had ever been in it before. And the sides of the bed would be real neat too, with the top sheet wrapped around and under the mattress so it was smooth and straight, like the sides of a candy bar.

She read the poem over and over, read into and between each word in every line, moving the images around in her mind's eye, trying to figure out what the man might have been thinking before he was called away from his work. She decided he was a sad man. His wife had died. They had had a child together, a boy who had grown to be big and tall, but he had died too, in a war. That was why all these people were coming by. They were checking in on the man because they were worried about him. The thing was, they made everything worse for the man by visiting him all the time. They should have just left him alone to do his work. He had to take care of his crops so that, when the summer was over, he'd have something to sell to the farmers who lived all around him. The farmers would buy what he had grown to feed their cows, but if he didn't have everything ready for them then they'd buy from someone else and he wouldn't have any money when winter came and the table in his kitchen would be cold to the touch. The man had to work extra hard now because his son couldn't help him dig and plant and harvest; he had to do it all himself. And when he was done at the end of the day, his wife wasn't there to make him his dinner. He had to cook for himself and he wasn't a good cook. He was going to heaven when he died, but God wasn't going to let him in the kitchen. The only time the man felt okay was when he was working on his land because he could forget about everything and just concentrate on the dirt. So his friends made him feel worse when they dropped by, not better.

When the friend spoke to him in the poem, the man wanted to ignore him but he wasn't strong enough to do it. He didn't know how to be the quiet's only friend. So he went up to the stone wall to say words that weren't his. Mercedes thought, if the poem had gone on a little longer, that the man would have ended up saying he was sorry for breaking his silence. She thought he would have sat down in the dirt and scolded himself for talking like he had: saying stuff that didn't need to be said, that didn't come from his heart. She thought that was what the poem was about, not what Mr. Steadman had said it was about. She thought the poem was about how empty it felt to talk when you didn't want to in the first place.

Mercedes was so immersed in her own thoughts, she didn't look up any of the times the bus stopped to pick up the other kids. She didn't hear Shahid call her watermelon head from the front of the bus as he stepped into the aisle. She didn't hear the others laugh and repeat the phrase. She didn't hear Tashawn say that she smelled old and stinky like her grandmamma's house. She didn't hear Shahid say it wasn't much of a house, where Mercedes Bittles lived. She didn't hear Tashawn say the house wasn't big enough for her watermelon head. When they came to a halt in front of Lowell Elementary School, she didn't feel the bus lurch as it came to a complete stop. She didn't hear the brakes screech, or the door wheeze open. And she didn't see Tashawn until he was on the seat in front of her, his hand reaching out toward her.

"Whatcha got there, Toyota?" He snatched the paper away before she could stick it back in her coat pocket. He looked down at the piece of paper, his eyes narrowing. He snickered at her. One of his front teeth was gray, she noticed. Another one had a little hole in it.

She tried to look right at him, right into his brown eyes. *Don't let him think you care*, she said to herself. Tashawn's eyes were dumb looking and big. He had dark freckles all about his nose and cheeks. His neck was too big for the opening of his shirt.

He stood up on the seat and held the piece of paper up in the air. She told herself not to try to snatch it back. She told herself to sit real still and maybe he would just let it go. But he didn't let it go. He tore it to shreds. Bits of paper sprinkled into the aisle of the bus, onto the seats, onto Mercedes's daddy's wool cap. Like leaves from the trees around Jamaica Pond, she thought, sprinkling on the walking path in the fall. Like little Haitian children who couldn't swim, tumbling into the ocean without a raft.

CHAPTER 24

That same morning, Walt was awoken by the phone ringing just a little after eight. When he picked up, he heard Ginger's voice, and cars honking in the background.

"What are you up to?"

"Reading," he lied. He didn't want to admit that he had been sleeping, not to someone who never did. "What are you doing?"

"Driving around." Her speech sounded garbled, as if she had marbles in her mouth.

"You don't sound good." He rolled out of bed and started to get dressed, pinching the phone against his ear with his shoulder. He heard tires screech and loud honking.

"I'm tired but I can't sleep. I'm *really* tired. I could use some company."

"Why don't you park in Harvard Square? We can have a cup of coffee."

"How about I pick you up at Out of Town News in ten minutes instead? I want to keep moving."

"Okay." He stood there, with the receiver pressed to his ear.

"Walt?"

"Yeah?"

"That's interesting, just then, how you didn't hang up." Suddenly she sounded more like herself. "I wonder if you have separation anxiety stemming from the Early Bird. You couldn't hang up just then because subconsciously you feared that once you disconnected you wouldn't be able to reconnect. I'd be dead. That also explains why you don't call me. You're afraid I won't pick up; you're afraid you'll phone and someone else will answer and say I'm dead."

"That's a riveting theory." Walt tried to summon the sarcastic tone necessary to make it sound as if he were dismissing her observation without a moment's hesitation. "I thought you studied Aquinas, not Freud."

"Aquinas is more like Freud than Freud is like Freud."

"I don't understand what that means."

"I'll see you at Out of Town News." And Ginger hung up.

Her Lexus stunk of cigarettes and fast food. The back seat was filled with books, candy wrappers, and empty cups of Dunkin' Donuts coffee. Beneath the front passenger seat, at Walt's feet, was a pile of disemboweled *Boston Globes*, on top of which sat an eyelash curler and Ginger's copy of *De Malo*, its pages dog-eared, coffee stains on its cover.

"What the hell is going on in here?" he asked, wiggling into his seat.

The car lurched forward, grazing a student on a bike. He scowled at Ginger over his shoulder and in response she honked her horn. "What, do they have to ride those things even in the winter?" They began to inch through Harvard Square. "Sorry, I can't bring myself to clean out my car. I'm having some kind of early, twentysomething midlife crisis."

"That's funny, because I'm having some kind of late, twentysomething midlife crisis."

"Aren't we a match." Ginger chomped her gum as they sat at a red light. The tips of her fingers were still encased in band-aids. Walt noticed more coffee stains, these on the sleeves of her beige sweater. She flipped on the radio; Walt flipped it off.

"So what's with the driving around?"

"Oh, it's just . . . I'm accumulating a lot of do-gooders in my book, you know? Too many girls trying to make the world a better place." The light changed and she hit the gas. Pedestrians in the crosswalk ahead scurried toward the sidewalk. They drove through Brattle Square and turned onto JFK Street. "But girls aren't just victims of evil. They're also perpetrators. That's what I was trying to tell you in Widener. That's why I want to interview girls from MS-13. I hate that kind of pity feminism where women come across as only acted upon, you know? I don't want my book to be like that."

They took the Larz Anderson Bridge into Allston, and from there passed through the winding streets of North Brighton, by the motels and diners and sub shops, and toward—of all places—the Brighton Cryobank for Oncologic and Reproductive Donors. Since the shootings, Walt had forgotten all about the sperm bank. He tried to picture himself returning there now but he couldn't: not with the awful sightlines presented by the winding hallways, not with the scraggily men who were often milling about in the waiting area.

"So you're just riding around, trying to find girls to interview from MS-13?"

"*We* are just riding around."

"All for *Girls I Know*."

"All for *Girls I Know*."

Presumably, it was okay for Ginger to include him in her adventure around town; once he was invited into the cocoon of her Lexus, he was supposed to feel impervious to the threats posed by MS-13. Pathetically, though, in her car, he *did* feel impervious to the threats posed by MS-13. He knew that no trauma awaited him in this Lexus. A fender-bender perhaps, but nothing worse. The windshield might just as well have been bulletproof.

"Why don't you just take the Orange Line for a few days—look for the Latinas with 13s tattooed on their necks."

"I did ride the Orange Line for days, Walt, but nothing came of it so I changed my approach."

"Well, you're not exactly Woodward and Bernstein, in your fancy car."

"I'm not trying to be Woodward and Bernstein. I'm a philosopher, remember?"

"Yeah, I remember." He rolled his eyes at her while she rolled her eyes at him.

They ended up on Cambridge Street, which Ginger took back across the river, swinging onto Memorial Drive. Then they raced alongside the Charles, cutting back into Boston on the Longfellow Bridge. Ginger clearly knew her way around the city now.

"Where are we going?"

"I was thinking East Boston, around Maverick. I have to give Roxbury a break here. Mattapan's a possibility, but I haven't had much luck—"

"I don't want to go to Mattapan." He wasn't about to visit Flora's old neighborhood, in this car, with Ginger. He'd sooner walk back to Cambridge.

"Okay, East Boston it is, then." Traffic was stopped on Storrow Drive. Ginger turned a dial and Walt felt his seat warm up. "So have you tutored Mercedes yet?"

"Yeah, just the other day."

"How'd it go?"

"Honestly? It was the longest hour of my life. She can't write a coherent sentence. I made all of these corrections but I don't think she understood the logic behind any of them. Then I tried to be funny. I made a joke about a lantern holder. On a horse. Having a lantern holder instead of a cup holder."

"Ooh, that doesn't sound too good."

They lapsed into silence. After passing into East Boston through the Callahan Tunnel, Ginger turned onto one side street after another. As she drove, she peered down alleyways. Whenever she spied a group of teenagers standing on a corner, she'd slow down to look them over. They, in turn, would stare back at them. Rich kids in daddy's car. Or at least one rich kid in daddy's car, but none of the adolescents checking them out knew there was any difference between them. From the outside, they could only be paired together.

"So what do you think, members of MS-13 are just hanging out, waiting to be interviewed by aspiring writers at nine in the morning?"

"I'm not an aspiring writer. And I don't know. Maybe some of them are."

"You're being voyeuristic and naïve. Plus, who's to say, if you find a few of these girls, they'll be able to speak any English?"

"I know some Spanish."

"Not their kind of Spanish." Walt tried to get her to glance over at him but for once she didn't seem inclined to look him in the eye. "I don't get it. You disapproved when I told you that I wanted to help Mercedes with her schoolwork, but you're comfortable driving around town, trying to talk to female gangbangers."

"Yeah, I'm a hypocrite, and I'm immature." Her head tilted. "Immaturity is a funny thing," she observed. "Even if you work on it, it doesn't really go away. You can't will it out of yourself, like other things."

Their car drifted into the opposite lane, causing a van to swerve. Its driver honked at Ginger, who yanked on the steering wheel so sharply that they almost hit a delivery truck coming out of an alley on their right. That driver honked as well. Maybe assuming that a fender-bender was the worst sort of accident they might have was being a tad too optimistic. They came to a halt at a red light.

"You know, my head is sort of spinning," Walt said. "I kind of need to get back to Cambridge. If you see a T stop—"

"Wouldn't that scare you, taking the T?"

She had a point but right then he didn't care.

"Let me just give you a lift. I don't know what the fuck I'm doing anyway, except obsessing." She shook her head. "I'm definitely obsessing." She turned the car around, to a cascade of blaring horns.

"Maybe you should just focus on your coursework here for a little bit. You seem to be stressed out—"

"I'm doing my coursework! I'm studying the problem of evil, remember? That's one of my courses. Everything's related: my book, my classes. Everything. That's the point I want to make in *Girls I Know*. What I want to propose, the framework I'm stealing from Aquinas, is really simple. What happens if we don't think of *evil* as an entity, or as a set of simply malevolent choices or biases, but rather as a part of the fabric of existence? If we appropriate Aquinas's desire to see the world holistically, as a system in which all of the parts are mutually dependent and connected, then are we able to rethink *evil* in such a way that better helps us to understand why people act the way they do?"

Walt waited for her to answer her own set of questions, but Ginger remained silent, so—assuming she wanted a prompt—he blurted out, "Well, are we?"

"I don't know; I haven't finished the book yet." They raced through the Sumner Tunnel. Traffic was lighter in this direction. In a matter of minutes, they were back on Cambridge Street. This part of town had always struck Walt as bleak: the storefronts all in need of a fresh coat of paint, the sidewalks cracked and uneven. It didn't help that the sky was so gray, the clouds low and thick and indistinct from one another.

By the time they made their way onto Mass Ave, traffic was heavy. They snaked their way back by Out of Town News, then headed up toward the graduate dormitories. Right in front of Perkins Hall, Ginger whipped her car around, coming to a stop with her back wheel on the curb. Several graduate students, trudging off to class, stared.

"Walt, do you think you have post-traumatic stress disorder?"

"I think you need to get some sleep, Ginger—"

"I think you do. I was reading about it the other day: PTSD. I think you definitely have some of the symptoms."

There were a few disorders he felt tempted to associate with Ginger, starting with hyperactivity, but he wasn't going to bring them up now. He wanted nothing more than to get out of her car, in which he had been incubating for what seemed like several hours.

"Why were you reading about PTSD?"

"Because I care about you, dumbass."

There was a coldness to Ginger's personality, one that she tried to mask with playful humor, but a coldness nonetheless. She cared enough about him to read about PTSD, but not enough to leave MS-13 alone. She was worried that he was suffering trauma on the heels of the Early Bird Café shootings, but she thought nothing of dragging him through East Boston, looking for gang members affiliated with the person who had killed three of his friends. Walt was willing to accept that people were a bundle of contradictions, but all of Ginger's contradictions seemed inevitably to serve her own interests and fixations. And he felt, as a result, as if he had absolutely nothing to offer her. If she hadn't died, Walt could have taught Flora about books and ideas, but Ginger knew more about that stuff than he did. She was the kind of person who had to learn everything herself, which was a shame, because it would have been nice for him to have someone nearby who needed him. Instead, he lived in a city—perhaps a great one, he was no longer sure—to which it didn't matter that he had survived a bloodbath.

He stepped out of the car, into the cold winter, and shut the door behind him. And, as was her custom, almost instantaneously, Ginger slammed her foot on the accelerator and was gone.

CHAPTER 25

The following Monday, Mercedes slid her paper toward Mr. Steadman. It wasn't any good; she knew it. First of all, the assignment called for two pages and she had only written about five lines. She had written it during class, but she hadn't turned it in. She was going to see if Mr. Steadman could fix it up for her. Then she was going to give it to Mrs. Greene the next day.

She watched Mr. Steadman's face while he read her sentences. He looked like he was sitting on a hot griddle. His mouth kept bunching up in the corner. Whenever the refrigerator made its clanking sound, he would jump slightly in his seat and his knees would hit the edge of the kitchen table. He looked real uncomfortable. Even though it was all his fault that he was uncomfortable, since he had decided on his own to come out to Watertown to tutor her, she still felt a little bad for him.

He picked up her paper and, holding it above his head, read her essay again. She could see him mouthing the words. Then he set the paper down.

"Have you ever been on an airplane?"

She shrugged. He was asking her that because she had written about Orville and Wilbur Wright. They were going to take a vacation that summer, Mercedes and her momma and daddy. They were going to fly to Florida; her momma had been looking into it. That was going to be her first trip on an airplane.

"I've never been on one." That surprised her; at his age, he had never flown once? He glanced back over the sentences. "I never really got the Wright brothers. Was it a plane, or more of a glider? In the pictures, it always looked more like a glider to me."

Mercedes didn't know the difference between a plane and a glider.

She didn't care. She wondered if he was ever going to mention her momma and daddy. This was the third time she had seen him since her parents had been killed and Mr. Steadman hadn't said a word about them. Instead, all he did was talk about her writing, which she didn't care one bit about. She wanted him to mention her daddy's cooking. She wanted him to tell her what he and her momma had talked about that last time she had seen him in the café, when her momma had seated him and then stayed and chatted for a little bit. She wanted to know where he had been when he had found out they were all killed. She wanted to know how he had reacted.

"Each of your sentences looks the same. See how they each begin with the same words?" He started doing his circling thing again. "It's a good idea, for your reader's sake, to vary things. Do you know what I mean?" She didn't say anything. The refrigerator was really making a racket today. She stared at her grandmamma's kitchen table. It had smudges in it you couldn't get out, no matter how hard you tried: dirt way down in it.

He raised his voice. "You need to work more on this. Can you rewrite it and let me look at it again next week? Maybe you can get an extension. That's when you ask your teacher for more time. When I was in school, I was very good at getting extensions. That's a joke. Well, not really."

There he went again, with the forced grin. And he had been doing so good that afternoon. He rubbed his hair with his hand. It stood up on its ends, then fell back onto his head. He was always rubbing his hair, kind of like he was nervous. Grown men weren't supposed to be nervous, were they? Her daddy had never been nervous. What did Mr. Steadman have to be nervous about?

He pushed the paper toward her. Mercedes put it in her blue folder, the one she had bought with her momma in August right before school started. Then Mr. Steadman slid the large book he had brought with him right in front of her. She had noticed the book under his arm when he had stepped through the door but she had pretended she hadn't. Now she looked it over carefully.

"I've got something for you," he said. "It's my grandmother's old copy of *The Poetry of Robert Frost*. She just sent it to me. You can borrow it for a while, if you want. That way you can read around in it yourself. You know, you can take it to school, read it at lunch, if you feel like it. Or on the bus to school. No one will ever stop you from reading, unless you're supposed to be listening in class. Otherwise you can always read."

That wasn't true. Tashawn stopped her from reading the other morning. What Mr. Steadman should have said is that no one had ever stopped *him* from reading. He was just assuming that what happened to him happened to everyone else. That wasn't right. Her momma always said you had to try to see things like other people did, that the dark spirits grew stronger when everyone just assumed the way they saw the world was the way everyone else did.

"There's one poem I thought we could look at. It's called 'The Pasture.' It's really short. Actually, it's your turn to read. Do you want to read it?"

She stared at the dirt smudges in the table. What other things made the dark spirits grow stronger? She couldn't remember. What if she forgot the things her momma had taught her? What if she forgot someday what her momma's voice had sounded like?

Mr. Steadman opened up the book and began to read the poem very slowly. He read through it once, paused, then read it again. The words made her heart go up into her throat. There was a little calf in the poem. The calf was standing next to its mother. When the mother licked the calf it almost fell over. Mercedes told herself she was the calf. She saw herself standing next to her momma. She felt her momma in the poem, reaching out to her, touching her. She felt her heart in her throat and the water come up behind her eyes. The way you stopped the tears from coming was to breathe through your mouth and squint a little. She had figured that out on the school bus. She needed to keep from crying, to keep the tears inside of her so that she could be strong. She told herself she was a rock on the edge of Jamaica Pond. Did those rocks cry? No, they did not. Even though there was water all around them, those rocks didn't cry.

"Would you read that again, Mr. Steadman?" Her grandmamma was standing in the doorway; Mercedes hadn't heard her get up from the ugly yellow chair in the living room, the one that creaked every time you put your hands on its arms.

The refrigerator sputtered again, then grew quiet. Mr. Steadman read the poem once more. When he was done, Grandmamma walked back into the living room.

"It's okay, being quiet," he said to her. He shut the book. He slid it back in front of her. It was kind of like he was saying he was sorry for the other day, when he had told her that everyone needed to talk. She got up from the table slowly, so he wouldn't think she was mad, and headed for her room.

"Don't forget the book." Mr. Steadman held it out toward her.

Was he really going to let her borrow it? She hadn't believed him, since it was such a big book, and so old looking. It must have been worth something. He handed it to her. It was heavy in her hands. She walked out of the kitchen just as her grandmamma walked back in. A few strides later and she was in her little box of a room. She turned to shut the door, then paused. Did they talk about her after she left the room? They must, right? She decided to keep the door open a crack and listen. It almost made her feel bad, on account of how easy it was to hear them, but they should have known that and lowered their voices; it wasn't her fault.

"This thing," Mrs. Bittles pointed at the refrigerator, "it's been breaking down for three years now, but it hasn't broken yet."

Mr. Steadman didn't say anything for a moment. "Mrs. Bittles, what would you think about the three of us meeting somewhere else next week, just for a change of scenery? There's this Armenian bakery around the corner on Mount Auburn. The bus goes right by it. We could meet there." He paused. "Would that be okay?"

"You want to take my granddaughter into a restaurant after her parents just died in one?"

"It's not a restaurant; it's a . . . it's a bakery." He was tripping over his words a little. "I just think our sessions might go better if we were somewhere else. Mercedes would hear other people having conversations. Maybe she wouldn't feel quite so self-conscious."

"What in the world do they serve in an Armenian bakery?" He didn't seem to have an answer for that one. Her grandmamma spoke up again. "The girl might as well go into Harvard Square if she's going to go anywhere. She isn't going to feel any less self-conscious, sitting in an Armenian bakery."

"There is a café right in Harvard Square: the Greenhouse Coffee Shop."

"You really want to buy my granddaughter a meal once a week?"

"I didn't mean . . ."

"Mercedes!" When her grandmamma called out her name, she jumped. "We got a question for you, Sweetness. Come on in here."

She walked out of her room and down the tiny hallway, still holding the big book Mr. Steadman had loaned her.

"Sweetness, Mr. Steadman was wondering if you'd like to meet him in a coffee shop next week to do your lessons. Would you like that?"

She nodded.

"You can't miss it," Mr. Steadman said to Grandmamma. "It's right across the street—"

"I know where the Greenhouse Coffee Shop is! John knew the old cook. Not the one working there now, the one before. Neither one of them knows how to make an omelet." Once more she frowned. "I hadn't budgeted us taking the bus back and forth every Monday. No, I had not budgeted that."

She and Mr. Steadman exchanged looks. Mercedes had seen her parents look at each other like this when the subject of money came up. It seemed like adults only talked about money when there wasn't enough of it to go around.

Mr. Steadman reached into his jean pocket and pulled out five dollars. He handed it to her grandmamma. He wasn't even doing his little forced-grin thing right then. He didn't seem pleased at all.

"All right then," Grandmamma said. She showed him out. Mercedes followed them to the door. Mr. Steadman stepped off the stoop, onto the uneven walkway. With the door still open, only her grandmamma's back turned, he waved goodbye to Mercedes. And it was funny; for a second there, she almost waved back.

CHAPTER 26

A week went by, and then another, and then another. Several more times, Ginger swung by to pick up Walt for one of her jaunts around the city. She was still looking, to no avail, for girls from MS-13 to interview. Walt would complain and complain about these field trips, but most of the time he still opted to run around with her. They had takeout in her car one night in front of the Harp and Bard in Dorchester. They had coffee in a parking garage just up from Lewis Wharf. They had bagels in a traffic jam in Coolidge Corner. Ginger was more or less living out of her car now.

When she could no longer stand the music they had been listening to, when she was momentarily tired of discussing *Girls I Know*, Ginger would ask Walt what he was up to. He was not an easy person to get talking. True, she had barely known him before the shootings, but she was still convinced that he was different now from before: less carefree, his demeanor less silly. She found that if there was silence for a time he might fill it with words but otherwise, in the face of direct questioning—her preferred means of engagement—he would say hardly anything. So she practiced inhabiting silence with him, which was hard but also served a purpose, since—like Walt—many of the subjects for *Girls I Know* were inclined to speak only in the wake of stillness.

Over time, he filled in the details of his tutoring enterprise. He told Ginger about spending an afternoon in the library at the Harvard School of Education, flipping through elementary school curricular and teaching guides. He had read up on the importance of lesson plans and worksheets. He had relearned terms he had forgotten, like *topic sentence* and *transition sentence*. He explained at one point that he and Mercedes were now meeting at the Greenhouse Coffee Shop in

Harvard Square. Initially, the girl's grandmother sat at the table with them, flipping through her *Boston Herald*, but by the third week she began to drop her granddaughter off and run errands. While they sat there, Walt would go through Mercedes's homework assignments with her. When they were done with her schoolwork, he would read a few Robert Frost poems to her and then they would go their separate ways. Listening to the description of their routine always made Ginger wish she could interview Mercedes for her book, but she knew enough not to ask Walt if that would be okay. She was not, it turned out, completely without restraint.

The first week of March, Ginger interviewed a corrections officer from the women's medium-security prison out in Framingham. She spoke to the highest-ranking female in the Boston Sanitation Office. She had a pastry with a Poor Clare nun from Jamaica Plain. She still spent her evenings driving slowly through questionable neighborhoods, looking around for girls she might get to know. Sometimes she gripped the steering wheel of her Lexus so tightly, the tips of her fingers went numb. Sometimes her jaw ached from clenching her teeth. At three, at four in the morning, she would turn off the car stereo once more and imagine herself asking Thomas Aquinas for clarification of his views on the existence of evil. She loved this game of hers. She would picture him seated in the passenger seat of her car, his Dominican tunic spilling onto the center console. *What I still don't understand, Tom,* she would begin, *is this idea that good must come from evil. You make it pretty clear that God isn't responsible for the evil that humans produce. But then you end up saying that good comes from evil, which makes it sound like you're defending God from the charge that he's responsible for everything that's wrong in the world, which he kind of is, since he's omnipotent and created the universe in the first place.*

Aquinas would shake his head slowly. *No no no, Ginger,* he would say. *For someone who claims to appreciate my work, you could stand to read it more carefully.*

That's a little harsh.

I'm sorry, that's how we teach in the Middle Ages. So what I argue is that everything in the cosmos, including evil, is part of God's design, even if he didn't create evil.

But what about the person who is a victim of evil? What about the child who loses her parents? What about the waitress who is shot to death at work? Good comes from that?

And Aquinas, sighing, would fold his hands in his lap. *Of course it does, Ginger. If you were to submerge yourself in the space that evil occupies, you would see that good in fact does come from evil, and that evil exists only dependently on the choices that humans make.*

And Ginger, very likely on the Turnpike by now, because it got so tedious after a while, crawling around Boston's winding streets, would respond by hitting the accelerator, just to see if the speed might make Aquinas flinch. But he never did. *Are you being serious, Tom? What good can come of losing your parents in a shooting? I mean, come on! How are we all better off because of that?*

The more animated she grew, the more Aquinas would settle down in the passenger seat, his voice growing fainter and more subdued. *Better off? When in human history did people start to talk like this? Okay, imagine evil as a blank space, like the blank space at the center of a spider's web. God's design surrounds this blank space and makes use of it. It is not for us to decide how we are better off by virtue of his design. Leave that to God. But, I'll say it again, if you were to encounter this blank space yourself, you know, perhaps step outside this automobile of yours, then you would begin to understand. There is evil out there. I don't deny it. But good comes from evil; God makes sure of that. By the way, the American educational system is doing a number on you. You should get out while you still have half a brain.*

And so it would go, into and through the early morning, until the streets were bottled up once more with traffic and Ginger sat in rush hour, the smell of nicotine thick in her Lexus, her eyes drawn, her bladder probably permanently damaged from not having relieved itself for so long. While she was fairly certain that her talents as a driver had improved, the states of mind in which she operated her vehicle were much worse, so she swerved across lanes and irritated other motorists now just as frequently as before, although for different reasons. Still, she was, in her own way, happy. That is, she knew how she wanted to spend every day and night. She knew what to do with herself. And for Ginger, nothing was more important than that.

CHAPTER 27

Mercedes stepped aboard the bus to school on Monday, the fifth of March, her daddy's old wool cap pulled down tight on her head. She moved to the back. Tashawn called out to her but she didn't even hear what he was saying. She told herself Tashawn's voice was a radio station that she didn't have to listen to. If you told yourself not to listen to someone and you were strong enough, you could do it; you could just tune a person out.

Tashawn and Shahid had been trying harder and harder to get a reaction out of her. They teased her for being tall and having a fat face and living with her grandmother. They told her she smelled like wet blankets. They told her she had a stinky butt. Mercedes never said anything in response. She had started to bring the book of Frost poems Mr. Steadman had loaned her to school. She read it on the bus and at lunch. Sometimes she would take a peek at it during class. She found that if she kept the book open on her lap during recess, even if she wasn't actually reading, the other students usually left her alone.

The Friday before, she and her classmates had filed into the gymnasium after recess. It was picture day. They stood in line. One by one the photographer and his assistant called them forward. The photographer wore an ugly corduroy blazer. He had a bushy moustache. While the lady who worked with him told each child how to sit on the stool they had placed in front of a blue screen, the photographer would tease the children to try to get them to smile. Mercedes's grandmamma had ordered one photo. She was going to put it on the kitchen counter, next to the picture of Mercedes's daddy in his army uniform. Her daddy wasn't smiling in that photograph, so Mercedes told herself she didn't have to smile in hers. But when it was her turn, the photographer decided that he really wanted her to smile. "Come on, now!" he said to Mercedes. "Show us those pearly whites!" He had to pull back his tripod a few inches to fit her head into the frame. "Give us a smile, sweetheart!" But she wasn't going to smile; she had made up her mind. Finally the man glanced down at her order form. "One big smile, Ms. Mercedes Bittles," he said. She could tell he was frustrated. "You know, your parents aren't going to be happy with me if you aren't smiling in your picture."

She took her seat in the back of the bus and pulled *The Poetry of Robert Frost* out of her yellow backpack. Then she leaned her head forward so that it rested on her left forearm, on the back of the seat in front of her. That way, while she read, it looked like she was sleeping. Some of these poems she didn't get at all. She'd read one after the other and not understand what they were about, but then she'd find one that would speak to her. When a poem spoke to her, it reminded her of the way her momma had talked. Her momma was like a poet, she decided, although she hadn't written down what she had said. But the way she had talked, it was like she had been a poet.

She found the poem she had been looking for: "Birches." This was the one about a boy swinging from the branches of birch trees: how he'd bend the branches and how they'd never quite straighten up again. She liked the idea of trees remembering that you had played on them. She liked the whole poem, even though she didn't understand every bit of it. The boy was all alone in the poem, playing by himself, that she understood. And the way Mr. Frost described what it was like to swing—kicking your feet out, swooping toward the ground— it made her want to do it herself. But then there was the stuff at the end of the poem, about earth being the right place for love and how one could do worse than swing from birches, and that stuff she didn't follow.

She read the poem again as the bus creaked and swayed. Mercedes liked how, each time she read the poem, she noticed something different. Last time, in bed the night before, she had noticed how much water was in the poem. There were "ice-storms" and "rain" and "snow-crust": water frozen and unfrozen. She thought that was kind of neat. Now the poem made her think about all of the trees around Jamaica Pond. She thought of swinging out over the water, where the souls of her momma and her daddy were. Was she ever going to see that pond again, the place where she had spent so much time? It seemed so far away now, almost like it didn't even exist anymore.

When she heard the brakes of the bus screech, she shut her book right away. They were stopped in front of the school. She saw Tashawn, walking down the aisle toward her, instead of lining up like he was supposed to. She fumbled with her backpack. She had to get the book in there before he saw it. She couldn't let Tashawn ruin it because it didn't belong to her.

"Whatcha got there?" Tashawn stood in front of her now and Mercedes was so nervous, she knocked her backpack onto the floor by mistake. He had noticed how much she had been reading lately. Just the day before, at the end of recess, he had walked by her, staring down at the book the whole while.

"Hey, watermelon head! I said, whatcha got there?"

She stood up and held the book high up above her head with her left hand.

"Oh, you still reading that book, huh? Let me see that."

He grabbed at Mercedes's elbow. He had never touched her before, just torn up that piece of paper with "A Time to Talk" on it and called her names and made fun of her. She didn't like the feeling of his fingers on her coat. It made her real angry.

"Come on, Tashawn," Taneka called to her brother from the front as the doors hissed open.

"Give it to me! Give me the book!" He tugged harder. He was pulling her arm down. "Give it to me!" he screamed again. He had Cocoa Puffs breath. She made a fist with her right hand just the way you were supposed to, with her thumb on the outside. She told herself to wait and see if he'd stop yanking at her. He didn't stop. When she swung, she aimed higher than it felt right to, so she was swinging down at his forehead, but when Tashawn saw her fist coming at him his head jerked up just like her daddy had said it would and she hit him right in the nose. There was a loud snap. Her daddy hadn't told her there'd be a snap.

Tashawn let go of her arm. He fell straight back. When his head hit in the aisle, it bounced up. Blood ran out from his nostrils, which were all crooked now, down both cheeks. The other kids stood at the front of the bus, staring at her. She could see the driver's eyes widen in the rear-view mirror. He hopped up from his seat, shooing Shahid and Taneka and the others down the steps. Then he rushed over to where Tashawn was lying: his eyes closed, his lips quivering. The bus driver bent over his face, then looked up at Mercedes, his head shaking slowly.

"You broke his nose." The man had never spoken to any of them before; he had hollered at Tashawn to stay in his seat, but Mercedes had never heard him just talk. Her heart was racing. She was sweating and scared. "Girl," he said, "you are in some serious trouble."

CHAPTER 28

The phone rang in Walt's room that morning. It rang and rang. When he was finally roused from his sleep, Walt assumed Ginger was calling him. He thought of Ginger whenever he heard the phone ring, and when cars nearly hit him at intersections, and when he noticed people chewing gum. He slid off his bed and picked up the receiver.

"Hello?"

"Mr. Steadman?"

"Yes?"

"This is Mrs. Bittles, Mercedes's grandmother."

"Oh, hi." Walt stumbled over to his desk chair and sat down.

"I'm afraid we can't meet with you today. Mercedes is grounded. She got herself into a fight at school this morning, broke a boy's nose. An eleven-year-old girl, breaking someone's nose; can you imagine that? She's been suspended today and tomorrow."

"I don't understand." Walt slapped himself softly on the cheek, trying to wake himself up. "She just hit someone? That doesn't sound right."

"I told her if she explained herself, maybe I'd let you work with her, but she wouldn't say nothing. She's in her room now. I took away that book you loaned her. She's not going to get any ice cream after dinner either. That's it for punishment; there's not much else I can take away."

Give her back the book, Walt wanted to say, but he knew it wasn't his place to offer parenting opinions. "Did you speak to the principal directly?"

"I did. They have a no-fighting something or other. *A no-fighting policy,* that's what she said."

"Did you meet with her?"

"I spoke to her on the phone."

"Did you meet with her in person?"

"No, I didn't. I . . . Well, what am I supposed to do with Mercedes while I'm at her school? I can't take her with me! She's been suspended."

"Right, of course." And a curious thought occurred to him— another one of his bad ideas—but he went with it anyway. He was in this deep, that was the thing. And nothing he had tried with Mercedes thus far had worked. "Can I meet with the principal?"

"You want to meet with Mercedes's principal?"

"Someone needs to."

"She's already missed school today. One of the secretaries dropped her off. I had to give them permission to bring her home, since I didn't have any way of picking her up. When the lady got here with Mercedes, I had to sign a form."

"It's not that she missed her classes today, Mrs. Bittles; it's that we need to know what's going on there."

She seemed to give that some thought. "So you want to go talk to the principal, just to find out how Mercedes is doing there?"

"Would you mind?"

She breathed heavily into the phone. "I suppose not . . ." But she sounded unconvinced.

"Then you need to do me a favor. You need to call the principal's office and tell them I'm coming by. No, tell them I'll be calling to make an appointment to see the principal. Tell them I'm her tutor."

"You want me to call them to tell them that you'll be calling?"

"Yeah. Otherwise I show up and, you know, there's no parental or guardian consent."

"Hmm." Mrs. Bittles gave that some thought as well; Walt could hear her tongue clicking in her mouth. "I always went right over to their school, if Dontrelle Junior or Randy got in trouble—*when* Randy got in trouble. John never did. Well, once he punched this little thug, but no one got real upset about that. He just knocked the wind out of him; he didn't break his nose. But I always went in. I just . . . I'm so much older now. I'd have to take a taxi up there, unless Denise could drive me, but she works during the day." She coughed a few times. "It's not on the city bus route, you see, the school."

"I'll take care of it, Mrs. Bittles."

There was a pause. "Thank you, Mr. Steadman."

Mrs. Reynolds, the principal of the James Russell Lowell Elementary School, could not meet with Walt until Wednesday at eleven in the morning. Later that day was out of the question, her secretary explained when Walt called; so was Tuesday. So Walt spent that afternoon and the following day reading poems in his dorm room and at Widener. He looked for Ginger more than once in the periodical room but he never saw her. He waited outside Sever Hall when her course on the problem of evil ended but she didn't emerge. He knew it was silly of him not to just phone her but he couldn't do it. He *was* worried she wouldn't pick up. What if she had been in a car accident? Or had just moved back to New York? So he waited for her to call him in his dorm room and — when he trudged through campus — he kept an eye out for her, even though he felt that she was very far from Harvard these days. In all honesty, he felt as if he would never see her in Cambridge again.

Wednesday morning, he shaved off the beard that, through neglect, had begun to form on his face: a beard that seemed to have stalled at a level just past moderate scruff. *Am I somehow genetically programmed,* he asked his reflection in the mirror, *to be incapable of completing things?* After shaving, he cut off some of the tufts of hair that hung over his ears and attended to all of the scruff on his neck. Then he showered and put on his nicest clothes: the pair of khakis he never wore and his white Oxford shirt.

Mrs. Bittles was right; the city bus only took him to the center of Watertown. From there Walt had to walk several blocks over to Orchard Street, which led up to the school. The homes he passed along the way were beautiful: big and expansive, with bikes and Big Wheels scattered in front of them, next to the bare remnants of snowmen. The edge of winter seemed to be blunted ever so slightly. Walt wore his parka, but he didn't zip it up to his neck. He didn't feel pinpricks on his cheeks as he walked; when he inhaled, his nostrils didn't sting.

The James Russell Lowell Elementary School sat atop a hill. It was the quintessential New England schoolhouse — red brick, white mortar, with a small tower that rose up above the roof, perfectly centered above the front pediment—only the school wasn't quaint; it was a big, looming structure. Walt made his way up toward its entrance, passing the playground on his right, which was encircled by a black chain-link fence. Then he climbed the five steps to the front door and pulled it open.

He began to walk down the empty hallway. The walls on either side of him were decorated with student artwork and posters announcing upcoming fundraisers and school activities. Through closed doors, Walt could hear the carefully enunciated voices of teachers. A custodian rounded the corner and asked him who he was looking for. He led Walt to the principal's office. The door opened into a rectangular room. A long wooden bench extended off to his left. Directly in front of him, a counter ran the length of the room, maybe twenty feet. Two women worked behind a pair of desks that were lined up behind the counter, a small portion of which was hinged. Back in the corner was a door that appeared to lead to the nurse's office, marked as it was by a large cardboard thermometer. The woman at the nearest desk stood up and asked if she could help him and Walt explained that he had a meeting scheduled.

"Mrs. Reynolds is still in her ten o'clock." The woman pointed at the open door on his right. "You can wait for her in her office, if you'd like, or out here."

Walt opted for Mrs. Reynolds's office. He took a seat in one of the two wooden chairs that faced her desk, the surface of which was swamped with papers. Behind it, in front of a window that looked down the street he had just walked up, rested a dusty computer on a crooked stand. On either side of the window were filing cabinets: their drawers open, with papers bulging.

Mrs. Reynolds entered in a rush, clutching a manila folder in her left hand. "I'm sorry, I'm sorry," she said. "I hate being late."

Walt stood and turned to shake her hand. Mrs. Reynolds had her gray hair piled in a small cone atop her head. She was wearing a white turtleneck and a pink poodle skirt that pinched her sharply in the waist. "It's fifties day," she explained. "The kids don't all get it—well, the fourth graders do, they're doing a unit on the 1950s—but it gives the faculty a chance to have some fun." Mrs. Reynolds circled around her desk and tossed the folder on top of the papers that were already piled in front of her. "Apologies for the mess." She pointed at the wall on Walt's left, where boxes were stacked, some with papers spilling out. "We put in a requisition for an extra bookshelf three years ago but it hasn't turned up yet. I'm not holding my breath." Then she let out a sigh, plopped down in her seat, and folded her hands together. "So you're tutoring Mercedes Bittles?"

"Yes. Well, I'm helping her with her reading and writing. I can't help her with math or anything like that."

"Mrs. Bittles said you're a student at Harvard?"

The name of his school, if it was still his school, if it had ever been his school, hung in the air. "A graduate student, yes."

"Are you in the School of Education?"

"No, the English Department."

"Oh." Mrs. Reynolds looked surprised. She settled some into her chair. "Well, I had a chat with Mrs. Greene this morning—that's Mercedes's homeroom teacher—and she told me that Mercedes has had a tough start here, as I'm sure you know. She's had some problems with the other African-American students, and problems in her homeroom, where she hasn't been participating or turning in her work on time. Apparently she hasn't spoken in her art class either, although it seems she's a good drawer."

Walt decided not to mention that he himself hadn't heard her voice, at least not since her parents had died. "What kind of problems is she having with the other African-American students?"

"They're picking on her."

"I don't understand. Do they know why she's here? Do they know what happened to her parents?"

"Yes, they do, but these kids aren't thinking about that. They just see a girl who won't talk. They see a girl who has nicer clothes than they do. It resonates, even with eleven-year-olds. And the other kids . . . well, Mercedes towers over most of her classmates, and since she started here halfway through the year she's an unknown entity. So the other kids keep their distance. Our student body is not, I'm sorry to say, as diverse as we would like it to be. Now we can, and we do, treat bullying very seriously." She picked up a pamphlet from the corner of her desk and handed it to Walt, who read the cover: *The James Russell Lowell Elementary School Family Handbook*. "We define it on page sixteen, if you care to take a look . . ."

Walt opened the handbook and read the paragraph-long definition, as well as the bullet-pointed section entitled *Building a Bully Free School*.

"That said, we can't intervene every time a child says something obnoxious to a classmate. We can't control them to that extent, and sometimes when we try to, it makes things worse. What would help . . ." Mrs. Reynolds caught herself. She seemed a little nervous now. "Let me put it this way. My sense, from what I've heard, is that some of our kids are just trying to get a reaction out of Mercedes. If she could come out of her shell a little, that might help a lot. Now I know she's traumatized, but I did mention to Mrs. Bittles when we first met that we have a good school counselor. She's not full-time; we share her with the rest of the schools in the township. She's here on Tuesdays. If you could perhaps reiterate that option . . ."

Walt nodded.

"Our concern is that, once a child begins to act out in violent ways, it often escalates. We don't want that to happen with Mercedes. She's a part of the Lowell Elementary family now and we'd like to see her flourish."

"I would too. So would Mrs. Bittles." Walt sat with his hands clenching either arm of his chair, trying to think of a day in the life of John and Natalie Bittles's daughter. "So is she alone all of the time when she's here, or are there other quiet students that she can hang out with?"

"Again, what I'm hearing, and what I've seen myself—at least on the playground—is that she's quite isolated. The really quiet ones usually are." Mrs. Reynolds flipped open the manila folder she had brought in with her and held it up to read. Walt could see Mercedes's name typed on a label on the front flap. "Her test scores are a little low, at least for Lowell. Is she making progress in her work with you?"

"I think so. Her writing seems a little . . . choppy to me, but I don't have anything to compare it to. We've been reading some poems together. She doesn't seem to have studied much poetry."

"What are you reading?"

"At the moment, Robert Frost."

"Isn't that a little challenging for her?"

"They're good poems. That's what kids respond to, regardless of age, I think. Good poems." Walt wasn't entirely sure if he thought this but he knew his grandmother did so he spoke with the borrowed strength of her convictions.

"Well, you're very ambitious. Do you have any plans to introduce her to some African-American poets?"

"I hadn't really considered that."

"I just thought the self-identification might help." She shut the manila folder and slid it—along with the rest of her paperwork—over to the side of her desk. "We try to make sure that the kids are being assigned ethnically and racially diverse authors."

Walt nodded. "I was thinking of doing Emily Dickinson next. I guess I could . . ." But his mind went blank trying to think of an ethnically or racially diverse poet.

"If you've planned it out, that's great. I was just asking, that's all." She checked the clock hanging behind Walt. "Mercedes is back from her suspension today. She should be in the cafeteria now. Let's go see how she's doing."

She sped around her desk and out of the office. Walt had to practically jog to keep up with her. In the hallway, they passed a really convincing Buddy Holly and a not-so-convincing Johnny Cash, their students following behind them in crooked lines, like ducklings, several of the boys wearing jeans and white tee shirts with their hair slicked back, a few of the girls in brightly colored skirts.

"So what are you going to do when you finish your PhD?" Mrs. Reynolds asked him. As they motored along, she looked this way and that: at bulletin boards and in classrooms. At one point, she waved at the same custodian who had walked Walt to her office.

"I don't know, I guess look for an academic job."

"You aren't interested in elementary school education?" She tilted her head at him. Her beehive tilted even more.

"No. I mean, I've never really considered it before."

"But you're a tutor?"

"Yeah, that's true." Although it didn't *seem* true; it seemed like a counterfeit identity, as did his claim to be an academic.

"Tutoring isn't for the faint of heart. Here we are." She gestured toward a pair of double doors down a short hallway. They walked up to them and pressed their faces to the glass.

Adults meandered around several long rows of low tables at which children sat, laughing and eating and drinking milk. Walt counted, among the teachers, two James Deans and a woman in a red wig. Mrs. Reynolds noticed her at the same time. "Oh, so Sharon went with Lucille Ball. It was either that or Doris Day." She pointed off to the left. "It drives us crazy," she said, "how the kids self-segregate. We thought about assigning seats but the PTO didn't like the sound of that. 'Shouldn't the kids be able to have lunch with their friends?' the parents asked. 'Well, let's let them make new friends,' that was my response, although it didn't carry the day, I'm afraid."

In the far left corner, at the back of the room, he saw the table at which Mrs. Reynolds pointed. Three black kids had pulled away from the rest of their classmates and were seated together, eating their lunches. One, Walt noticed right away, had a splint taped to his nose and was hunkered over his tray. At the far end of the table, off by herself, was Mercedes. He didn't see her face, he just saw his grandmother's Frost book, propped up on the table, and assumed she was nestled behind it.

"I can't make out . . ." Mrs. Reynolds wiped her breath off the glass.

"She's the one at the end, reading."

"Oh, is that right? Oh yes, of course." They stared at her. "She's got my grandmother's collection of Robert Frost poems," Walt added. "I loaned it to her."

They waited to see if she'd put the book down but Mercedes didn't. The smell of pigs-in-the-blanket seeped through the door, along with more laughter and shouting. Walt tried to visualize the cafeteria of his own elementary school but he couldn't. *Maybe she'll just forget it all*, he said to himself with feigned optimism. *Maybe, over time, these days will just become a blur.*

He stepped back from the doors. Mrs. Reynolds led him down the main hallway, back toward the front entrance. A middle-aged Elvis Presley passed them. Behind him were two columns of youngsters, their noses running, their tiny fingers streaked with watercolors.

"If you weren't content in academia, I'd tell you to think about teaching in an elementary school," Mrs. Reynolds said. "Greater Boston needs people like you; every school in this area needs young teachers."

"I'm not that young; I'm twenty-nine."

"Oh, you're a spring chicken! Boston can make you feel old because it's such a college town. That's why they invented the suburbs." She extended her hand. They were just inside the front doors. "But I'm sure you love research and writing an awful lot," she added.

Walt squeezed her fingers tightly. "Actually, I hate the research," he said. Maybe all this time, he had just been waiting for someone to ask him if he enjoyed what he was trying to do, because he felt himself leap at the opportunity to explain himself. "I don't even know if you could call what I'm doing research. I love reading poems, but I can't bring myself to look at any articles about poems. And I can't seem to write a word of my dissertation. It doesn't feel important enough to me."

Mrs. Reynolds's head recoiled in surprise. "Why don't you keep my number handy, then. Give me a call and I'll put you in touch with some teacher accreditation programs."

"The thing is, Mrs. Reynolds, teaching Mercedes . . . that doesn't come easily to me. It's—"

"Oh, Walt!" She cut him off with a piercing laugh as she led him out the doors, her hand patting his back. "Are you kidding? Teaching these kids doesn't come easily to anyone."

CHAPTER 29

Walt phoned Mrs. Bittles the minute he got back to his room. He told her what Mrs. Reynolds had said about how some of the African-American kids were picking on Mercedes and how she kept to herself. He mentioned the counselor who was available on Tuesdays, at which point Mrs. Bittles interrupted. "She won't speak to anyone she knows, so they think she'll talk to a stranger?"

"Sometimes it's easier to talk to a stranger," Walt replied, but he didn't press the point. He asked if they could reschedule the tutoring session from Monday for the following afternoon and Mrs. Bittles said that would be fine. Then they both said goodbye and hung up.

Walt spent the rest of the day thinking about the Lowell Elementary School and listening to Miles Davis at his desk. He played *Porgy and Bess* and then *Sketches of Spain* right afterwards, in just the order his grandfather had always recommended. Then he put on *Kind of Blue*. He imagined himself standing in one of the classrooms he had passed earlier in the day, holding a thick piece of chalk in his hand, calling on these kids to explain the difference between a comma and a period, or asking them to read aloud something they had written. Whatever elementary school teachers did, he imagined himself doing it.

In the late afternoon, he walked across the hallway and knocked on Javier's door. He had to knock two more times before his hallmate answered.

"Hey, can I ask you something?"

Javier was in a discolored pair of Calvin Klein underwear. Clearly he had been sleeping. He rubbed his eyes. Without his glasses on, his face seemed narrower.

"You've got five minutes, Walt. I'm taking a two-hour nap and then I'm going to the library."

"Okay. So, as an expert in the economics of public education—"

"I like the way you're starting—"

"What would it be like to teach elementary school?"

"Brutal. You're on the front lines. That's real teaching—teaching that changes lives—but it'd be brutal."

"But it's important work, right? No one would deny that."

"No one would." He yawned. "Wait a sec, Walt. Are you thinking of becoming an elementary school teacher?"

"No, Mercedes's principal just brought it up."

"Who's Mercedes?"

"A girl I'm tutoring out in Watertown. Her parents owned the Early Bird Café."

"Wow." Javier stood there, scratching his bellybutton. "Why were you talking to her principal?"

"Mercedes beat up a kid, so I thought it made sense to go over there and get a feel for the situation."

"God, you're hands on."

"Yeah." Walt looked down at the floor. "Mrs. Reynolds, the principal, said Greater Boston needs young teachers like me."

"Greater Boston needs whatever it can get in terms of teachers."

"I figured as much."

Javier left the door open and returned to his bed. When he plopped down on his mattress, dust billowed into the air. "If you were spending all day in an elementary school classroom, you'd never write your dissertation."

"Oh, I'm probably not going to write my dissertation anyway."

"Seriously?"

Walt held up his empty hands. Javier peered at him. "Listen to me for a second, man. That's a rough life you're talking about. Your first day, you'd show up and you wouldn't have the supplies you'd need. You'd have to use a restroom where the urinals are six inches off the floor. Some kid would puke on himself and look to you for help." Javier breathed deeply. "You'd be broke too."

"But academics are broke."

"Yeah, academics are pretty broke. You'd be *really* broke, especially out of the gate."

Walt stepped through the doorway, into Javier's room. Briefly, he glimpsed his profile in a small hand mirror that stood propped against the wall on top of the dresser. He had no visible scars from the shootings at the Early Bird Café. He looked the same as before, maybe a little thinner but otherwise the same. "I don't care about money. I want to do something with my life—even if it's hard, even if it doesn't make me rich. I want to feel good about myself at the end of the day, you know? Does the world really need me to write a book about how Robert Lowell's poems are shaped by the fact that his family had money?"

Javier stared at him blankly. "You tell me."

But Walt said nothing for a moment. Earlier in the day, when he had been talking to Mrs. Reynolds, he had told himself that he was neither a tutor nor an academic, but in fact that wasn't entirely true. He *was* tutoring—maybe not very well, but that was work he was actually doing. "I've always been more or less broke. Who cares? It's not like the rich are any happier. They're not; trust me."

He was thinking of Robert Lowell and Ginger Newton: the only two rich people he had ever gotten to know, and one of them just on the page. Javier grimaced at him. "Tell me they're a little bit happier?" Walt shook his head. "Oh great," he groaned. "I'm as broke as you are, and you're telling me our level of happiness is pretty much standard? That's just great."

Walt told him to go back to sleep and drifted across the hallway into his own room. When he had first decided to try to help Mercedes Bittles, when he had imagined becoming a halfway decent person, Walt had summoned the image of his grandparents as teachers. He had told himself to do a version of what they had done their whole lives, not figuratively but literally. It turned out there was no distinction in his mind between being decent and being an educator. Maybe all along, without quite being aware of it, when he had used the one word he had really been thinking of the other.

CHAPTER 30

Walt was up early the next morning. He dressed and made his way down to Harvard Square, where he picked up a *Boston Globe* so he'd have something to look at during breakfast. Then he walked over to Au Bon Pain, ordered a coffee and a croissant, and grabbed a table right next to the side door that opened onto Dunster Street. That way, if a gunman walked in the main entrance, he could make his escape and run into the barbershop across the street. That was where all the cops got their hair cut.

He spread his paper out in front of him. *Look at me,* he said to himself. *I'm reading a newspaper and having breakfast, just like I used to do.* He took a bite of his croissant and told himself that he was going to read the *Globe* all the way through—take in the hard-hitting news stories as well as the articles about the Red Sox farm system. So he looked down, above the fold, at the front page.

There had been a sexual assault the day before. Two, in fact. A couple of girls had been raped in Foss Park over in Somerville, on the Cambridge side of the Charles River. Witnesses had reported a large group of assailants, male and female. Both of the victims were deaf. One was in a wheelchair. They tore off both the girls' clothing. After sexually assaulting them, they left them there, naked, on the ground, in the cold. Next to the girls, they placed a football jersey with the number 13 on it. They smeared blood from the girls on the jersey.

When Walt read about the blood on the jersey, he pushed the paper off the table, onto the floor. He stumbled outside, over to one of the payphones in Harvard Square, and dialed Ginger's cell phone number. She picked up immediately.

"Fancy that! A call from Walt Steadman." There was a lilt in her voice that he hadn't heard in a while. She was peppy again.

"How did you know it was me?"

"You're *out of area*. No one else I know is ever *out of area*."

"What are you talking about?"

"Oh my God, you don't know what caller ID is, do you? You've never used a cell phone! That's so cute. Oh, Walt, you still have your virtues, you little caveman."

He would have none of it. He cleared his throat. "Congratulations. Your big break. It looks like you know where to poke around today."

"What are you talking about?"

"Foss Park . . ."

"You read the newspaper this morning!"

"Yes. Let me guess; you're racing over there right now?"

"I'm making my way."

"Running red lights?"

"I'm not sure I like your tone—"

"How can you read a newspaper article about two girls being raped and then just rush over to the scene of the crime?"

"It's not what you think, Walt. I'm not going there in the hopes of finding some straggler from MS-13. I'm just going because I'm trying, to the best of my limited abilities, to submerge myself in the space that evil occupies."

"I don't understand what that means."

"I don't either. Not yet. It's experiential."

"All for your book?"

"Yes, all for my book."

A teenager carrying a sleeping bag and a guitar case emerged from the Harvard Square T Stop. He plopped down about ten feet from the bank of payphones and took out his guitar.

"I don't think you're behaving very charitably, Ginger."

"What do you mean by *charity*, Walt?"

He paused. For the last few weeks, he had been thinking about this word quite a bit, and whether or not he could redefine it in some way. Because, although he hated to admit it, he thought what Ginger had said weeks before was right: the more closely charity was associated with money, the less like charity it seemed. He had felt this over in Watertown when Mrs. Bittles had asked him for money to cover the bus fare to go into Harvard Square. When he had handed her five dollars, the transaction hadn't felt like a charitable one. Neither had he felt compassionate, or philanthropic, when he had subsequently purchased food and milkshakes for Mercedes at the Greenhouse Coffee Shop. These were just expenditures, all predicated on a misunderstanding of his financial situation. Spending money he couldn't afford to spend just made him resentful, and charity couldn't come from resentment; it had to come from something else.

"I think," he said slowly, "charity is when someone tries to see the world from someone else's perspective."

"That's not bad. I like that." She had blown a bubble into the phone; he heard it pop. "So why aren't I being charitable, going to Foss Park?"

"Because you should go to the hospital to check on the girls who were attacked."

"Well, that *would* be charitable, but so is going to Foss Park. Aquinas says you should try to understand the shape that evil takes in the world in which we live. Then the benevolence of God's design actually becomes easier to see, rather than harder. It's counterintuitive."

The teenager began to tune his guitar.

"I'm so sick of you mentioning Thomas Aquinas." Walt cupped his hand over his ear so he could hear her.

"I am too."

The teenager began to strum his guitar and sing. Walt crouched over the phone, trying to block out the city around him. He thought of all the poems he had studied in which music loomed so large: not just the rhythm of songs and ballads that influenced verse, but the evolution of poetry itself from singing. "Ginger, have you ever thought about how incredibly *unpoetic* our relationship is? All the noises and distractions that are always going on around us? All the bustle? All the traffic jams we've been stuck in? We never just sit by the Charles, on a picnic blanket—"

"I can't hear you, Walt!"

"There's a guy playing a guitar right next to me. I think it's a Bob Marley song."

"We need a worldwide, ten-year moratorium on Bob Marley

covers."

"I was saying," Walt tried again, "the intersection of our lives hasn't been very poetic."

"No offense, Walt, but when you say shit like that, it makes me so glad I don't read the kind of stuff you do. Literature makes you look for scenes in your life that don't exist. You know why they don't exist? Because life doesn't have an arc or a trajectory. Life just unspools. It's messy and repetitive and boring and then—I guess in your case—suddenly terrifying. But it doesn't have an arc."

"I disagree. I mean, even if you're right, I don't want to believe that my life is just unspooling. I want it to have a point." If faced with the choice of misreading reality through art or confronting the lack of meaning in reality itself, Walt Steadman wanted to misread the world, again and again. He wasn't like Ginger Newton, not remotely. He wasn't really interested in reality; he never had been. "Please be careful," he added.

"Okay, Grandpa. Now look, this time you hang up on me. Consider it part of your PTSD therapy. Go on now. I'm waiting."

Slowly, gently, he placed the receiver in its cradle so that it depressed the tongue of the payphone. Then he began his walk back to Perkins Hall.

CHAPTER 31

Ginger took the McGrath-O'Brien Highway into Somerville. Foss Park sat just past Broadway; it backed up against I-93. This part of town didn't feel much like a neighborhood. There were some homes, interspersed between shop fronts and apartment buildings, but the sidewalks were empty. Mostly there were just cars, funneling into and out of the city.

She took a left at Broadway, where the corner of Foss Park jutted out, and passed playground equipment, and then a pool house. In the far corner of the park sat two baseball fields that she circled around before getting back on McGrath-O'Brien. She could make out basketball and tennis courts now, and just beyond them, a squad car parked up on the grass. Yellow police tape marked off a wide area where several benches faced one another. That must have been where the girls were sexually assaulted, and where the other girls had watched them be sexually assaulted. Almost a dozen people stood around the police tape. Ginger had no intention of joining them. She wanted to submerge herself in the space that evil occupied, but she didn't want to gawk at a crime scene.

She decided to circle around the park once more. As she neared the playground for the second time, she glimpsed two girls sitting on a bench, and a third standing in front of them. They looked over at her, through the chain link fence, as she drove by slowly; they looked at her looking at them. Again Ginger turned onto Broadway, but this time she pulled over, grabbed her black leather bag, and hopped out of her car. She almost left her cell phone on the passenger seat where she had flung it after talking to Walt, but she remembered it at the last moment and slipped it into the front pocket of her jeans. Then she walked around the pool house and across the dirt soccer field before stepping onto the path that led from the soccer field through a small grove of bare trees to the playground. From a distance she could hear the girls talking, but as she approached they grew silent. The one standing was a white girl; the two sitting were both black. So they weren't in MS-13. How old were they? Sixteen, seventeen? She couldn't tell.

"How you all doing?"

The girls looked her over. Ginger stood still on the path so they could take her in.

"You the girl in that black Lexus?" The white girl standing in front of the bench nodded at her. She was lanky and wore a green Celtics jacket and dark, stiff jeans. Large hoop earrings hung halfway to her collarbones. Beneath her jacket she had on a white turtleneck, the collar of which was frayed.

"Yeah, that was me."

"Is that your car?"

"Yeah, that's my car."

"Shit, that's a nice car." The girl turned from her and looked at her friends seated on the bench, both of whom grinned at her. The girl on the right had her tongue pierced and a dark blue stocking cap pulled down low on her forehead. She was wearing baggy red sweatpants and an oversized gray sweatshirt.

Thinking it might accredit her in some way, Ginger withdrew her digital recorder from her bag. "I'm writing a book," she said. "Do you all want to be in it?"

"What kind of book?" the girl with the stocking cap asked.

"It's about what girls do to get by: what kinds of jobs they have, the sort of trouble they can find themselves in, the mistakes they make, how the world treats them, how they treat the world . . ."

None of them said anything.

Ginger checked her watch. "Aren't you all supposed to be in school?"

They looked at her some more. The girl who had yet to speak pulled out a pack of Camels from her unzipped, black jacket. Each of the girls took one. She extended her lighter toward them, one at a time, and then leaned back and took a long drag. As she did so,

Ginger noticed the way her round stomach peeked out from beneath her tee shirt, hanging firmly over the top of her jeans. She had to be at least six months pregnant.

"Someone give you that car so you could drive around and ask girls questions?" The girl who was standing crossed her arms. Her doughy, white cheeks had streaks of red in them and she had red hair and thick, red eyebrows as well.

"No, my grandparents gave me that car. I don't know why; I think to annoy my parents."

The girl turned her back to Ginger and looked at her friends. They were talking, the three of them, but just with their eyes. Ginger tried her hardest to understand the language that was being used right in front of her: the system of head nods and shakes and slow blinks. But it eluded her.

The girls smoked their cigarettes. When they were done, they all threw their butts onto the path and the tall girl walked off, followed by her friends. Halfway to the playground, the pregnant girl turned back toward Ginger. "Aren't you coming?" she asked.

"Let's just talk here." Ginger pointed at the deserted bench.

"It's too loud. There's a picnic table over by the supermarket. You can buy us something to drink."

Ginger kicked at the path with her boot. She didn't want to leave with them, but what was she going to do, just let them disappear? This might be the only chance she'd ever get to talk to girls like this. So she headed off after them.

The girls made their way slowly across the soccer field and around the pool house. They crossed onto Broadway. When they passed her car, the girl in the Celtics jacket ran her hand across the hood. At the corner, they took a right. By now, Ginger was just a few steps behind them. They cut through the parking lot of a Star Market and passed the entrance to the store. So much for buying them drinks. Ginger looked for a picnic table but didn't see one. The girls turned into an alley that ran along the side of the building. Ginger stopped walking.

"Where are you going?" she asked.

The tall white girl in the Celtics jacket turned around and shrugged at her. "They must have moved the bench cuz they didn't want us sitting in front of the store, but we can hang out here. It's cool."

"No, I'll talk to you guys over in the park, otherwise—"

"We can't stay in the park! Her boyfriend's looking for her." The girl nodded at her pregnant friend.

Ginger stared at the white girl, who stared back at her. She hadn't interviewed a trio of girls like this, a group of friends. All her other subjects up to now had been individuals. "All right." She took one step into the alley, and then another. Finally she walked halfway down and stopped; she wasn't going to go any farther. At the end of the alley, a high wall ran out from the supermarket, in front of which were two dumpsters lined up next to one another. Around them now, in the air, hung the smell of rotting food and refuse. The tall white girl, the ringleader—or so it seemed—walked out to where Ginger stood and leaned against the side of the building. Her friends hung back behind her.

The white girl nodded at her boots. "Those are nice."

Ginger said nothing. She took note of the pregnant girl, who had drifted up toward them. The other girl was standing back by the dumpsters.

"Don't you have questions to ask?"

Once more Ginger took in her surroundings. She noticed, at the far end of the dumpsters, a stack of empty liquor boxes piled on top of several old, rusted pipes. Out of one of the pipes she saw one rat, and then another, scurry out. She turned on the digital recorder she still held in her hand. "Okay, well, for starters, why don't you tell me your name and how old you are?"

"What's *your* name?" The girl circled around her so that Ginger had to turn to maintain eye contact. Now she was facing the opening of the alley.

"My name's Ginger."

Several of the boxes back by the dumpsters came crashing down behind her. Ginger jumped. The girl back there had picked up a pipe and was hitting the boxes with it.

"How old are *you*?" The white girl leaned back against the wall and placed her left sneaker behind her butt.

"I'm twenty," Ginger said.

And where are *you* from?"

"New York." The girl looked past her, over her left shoulder, but Ginger resisted the temptation to follow her gaze. She wanted so badly to connect with her. If she could get this girl to open up, the others would too. So she told herself just to be in the moment: to trust this girl enough to have a conversation with her, but to make sure the conversation had an edge to it. Otherwise they might simply talk about nothing.

"So did you hear what happened in Foss Park last night?"

"Yeah."

"Pretty awful, huh?"

The white girl looked at her, frowning.

"Do you know anyone in MS-13?" Ginger asked.

"No."

"Have you ever had any encounters with members of MS-13?"

"Are you fucking crazy?"

Ginger looked over her left shoulder, back to where the girl with the pipe had been standing, but she wasn't there anymore. She dropped her digital recorder into her bag and turned to run, but it was too late. She felt something thick and heavy strike the back of her head. Then she fell toward the ground.

CHAPTER 32

Mercedes and her grandmamma were late to the Greenhouse Coffee Shop, but it wasn't their fault. The bus usually pulled up at ten minutes after four. That gave them twenty minutes to make it into Harvard Square for Mercedes's four-thirty meeting with Mr. Steadman: more than enough time. But that day the bus was late. They waited and waited. Finally, what had been harmless sprinkles of snow turned into spitting rain. The umbrella was back at the house, in the tiny closet in the corner of the living room. Her grandmamma's wigs couldn't get wet—the rain ruined the fibers—and she only had a scarf on her head. Mercedes thought her grandmamma would call off the whole thing: that they'd go back to the house and she'd have to spend one more afternoon sitting in her tiny room. But Grandmamma didn't budge. She just put her hands over her scarf, while Mercedes slipped the Frost book underneath her sweater and made sure her coat was buttoned up all the way. They waited in the rain until the bus came so she wouldn't miss being tutored by Mr. Steadman.

By the time they pulled into Harvard Square, the rain had turned back into snow. She and her grandmamma crossed Mass Ave, rounded the corner, and stepped inside. The Greenhouse Coffee Shop was the ugliest restaurant Mercedes had ever seen: all green wood, with worn green carpet and a large mirror that ran the length of the back wall. Green lamps hung from the ceiling. Wooden chairs with faded, crimson-colored seat cushions were scattered around tables. The cushions weren't red; they were *crimson*. That was the Harvard color.

Mr. Steadman got up from the table where he had been sitting and met them just inside the door. "Rain got you, huh?"

"It most certainly did. That bus just wouldn't come." Her

grandmamma was definitely not pleased. She had grown tired of coming all the way into Cambridge once a week. *Shoot, he showed up at the house the first time without anyone even inviting him! Then, pretty soon, we're taking the bus all over town! That ain't right.* That was what she had said earlier that afternoon.

Mercedes unbuttoned her blue coat and withdrew *The Poetry of Robert Frost.* It was perfectly dry.

"I'm going to go across the street to the hardware store and buy an umbrella," Grandmamma said, "in case it starts raining again." She sighed for Mr. Steadman's benefit but if he noticed, he didn't act like he did.

After her grandmamma had left the coffee shop, the two of them walked over to the table where Mr. Steadman had been seated. It was on the far side of the restaurant, right against the wall. He always faced the front, Mercedes had noticed. She took the chair opposite his. The mirrored wall ran off to her right and she could see the swinging doors that led into the kitchen in back. She placed the Frost book on the table, kind of hoping that Mr. Steadman would just start reading some of the poems aloud. She liked listening to him read.

"Did you bring any homework with you today?"

She shook her head. Funny, she hadn't thought to check her backpack for any assignments. She had remembered to bring the Frost book but that was it.

"Do you not have any homework or did you just not bring any with you?"

She shrugged.

Mr. Steadman took a sip of his coffee. They didn't have mugs at the Greenhouse Coffee Shop, just these little cups and saucers, half of them chipped.

"Or, since you were out of school for a few days earlier this week, maybe you missed some assignments. Is that right?"

Mr. Steadman seemed to think they had more homework than they really did—at least more writing homework.

"This afternoon, I was thinking about how I might be able to help you more with your work, and I came up with this checklist." He pulled a sheet of paper out of his parka and unfolded it. "After you've written one of your essays, what you do is go through this list and check to make sure you're doing all the things we've talked about. That's why it's called a checklist. See?"

He passed her the sheet, a big smile on his face. Why did teachers get excited about stuff like this? She placed the paper inside the front cover of the Frost book.

"So you got him right in the nose, huh?" He grinned at her, like they had some kind of understanding. She glanced down at her hand. The day after, her fingers had swelled up from hitting Tashawn. They were still a little sore. Her daddy hadn't told her that would happen.

"I'm sure he deserved it, but you should try hard not to hurt anyone again. When you get in trouble, it makes your grandmother worry. And hitting people never solves anything."

It was funny, though. Just that morning, Taneka had asked if she could come over sometime and play with her dolls. She said she didn't have to talk any if she didn't feel like it; it was all the same to her. She said her brother was a stupid ass. She said her momma had told him he got what was coming to him. So even though everyone was telling her that hitting people didn't *solve* anything, Mercedes figured they just felt like they had to say that, because Taneka was being nice to her now, and no one was bothering her on the bus anymore. So if stuff wasn't *solved*, at least it was better than it had been, and all because she had punched Tashawn Garner in the face.

The waitress dragged herself over to their table. She was tall and had a long face. She wasn't anything like Flora. She didn't smile and she wasn't pretty and she never wore any ribbons in her hair.

"What'll it be?" She looked down at Mr. Steadman. She never looked at Mercedes, which bothered her. The waitress always acted like she wasn't there.

Mr. Steadman handed her his menu. "I'm fine for the moment. Mercedes, why don't you order for yourself."

But she couldn't order; she didn't have a menu to point at. He was trying to get her to talk again. She stared down at the table. It was a smelly restaurant. The pancakes she had ordered that one time were all overcooked, and sometimes powder would come up through the straw when she drank her milkshake.

"Mercedes?"

Be the quiet's only friend.

Mr. Steadman looked at her. The waitress looked at him. "Why don't you give us a second," he said. She shrugged and walked away.

Mr. Steadman picked up the salt and pepper shakers and then set them down again. His eyebrows were all bunched up together. He seemed to be thinking real hard. "I'm trying to help you, Mercedes," he said, "but I'm not sure what I'm doing. I've never tutored anyone before, and I guess I feel like it's hard to know if I'm doing a good job when you never say anything."

She didn't see how Mr. Steadman could complain about *her* not speaking. She didn't come into *his* grandmamma's house and ask to tutor *him*. You couldn't get mad at someone who had never asked for your help in the first place. That wasn't right.

"Maybe you think it's okay not to talk to me because you think I'm like everyone else in your world, but I'm not like everyone else. No one is like anyone else." He looked around the restaurant, like he was hoping to see someone he knew. Mr. Steadman didn't seem like the kind of person who knew a lot of people. Her daddy had known all kinds of folks. Every time they went into a restaurant, he had known someone.

"Or maybe you feel like you don't need to talk because of what you've been through, what you're going through. But you know, a lot of people experience awful things, even older people. Like with me. I never knew my dad. He's never been involved in my life. I don't know one thing about him. I don't know where he lives, or what he looks like, or what he does. I don't even know if he's still alive. And my mother, she's been sick for a long time. She's got multiple sclerosis. Do you know what that is? It's a disease of the central nervous system. She can't do much herself. My grandmother takes care of her." He shook his head. "I'm not saying I've faced things like what you're facing, I'm just saying people all have different things that make them sad and angry. That's all I'm saying."

The waitress came back to take their order. Mr. Steadman looked at Mercedes, waiting for her to say what she wanted. She just stared at the table. What was he trying to prove? Were they meeting so that he could help her with her schoolwork and read poems together, like he said, or was he just trying to get her to open her mouth?

"I'm guessing strawberry milkshake?" He waited to see if she blinked or nodded, some sign of agreement, but Mercedes didn't move a muscle. If he wanted her to talk, she'd just turn to stone and see how he'd like that.

Mr. Steadman turned back to the waitress. "A strawberry milkshake," he said. "And I'll have more coffee, please."

The waitress took the menu and walked away.

Mr. Steadman played with the salt and pepper shakers some more. He took a few packets of artificial sweetener and passed them through his fingers, one after the other. She really should have brought some schoolwork along, but she forgot to. Ever since breaking Tashawn's nose, Mercedes had had a hard time concentrating on anything. It was scary, hurting someone like that. Her momma would have been so disappointed in her. She could just see her, standing in front of her with her arms crossed. *If I didn't hit him, he would have ripped up Mr. Steadman's book!* she would have said, trying to explain herself. But her momma would have shook her head. *That doesn't make what you did right, my love. You did the easiest thing. Hitting is always the easiest thing to do. You know that.* And she would have nodded and buried her head in her momma's tummy and cried. But now she couldn't do that. Now she had to be strong. And her momma couldn't hug her because she was water now. She was a spirit in the water that made up the Jamaica Pond.

"I was listening to *Kind of Blue* the other day," Mr. Steadman said out of nowhere. "Do you know that album? Anyway, the musicians didn't rehearse. Miles Davis just brought in these sketches he made of different scales and melodies and they took it from there. Isn't that crazy?" He looked out the window, not out at the people but up at the sky, all filled with snowflakes. "I think that's pretty crazy."

She knew who Miles Davis was because her daddy loved jazz. He used to play it in the kitchen when he cooked. Not at the Early Bird, they didn't have a stereo there, but at home. But why was Mr. Steadman talking about Miles Davis to her? Because she and Miles Davis were both black? Why did he have to try so hard? He should have just stuck to what he could talk about without getting all fidgety, like Robert Frost. That was what he should have done.

She watched a waitress make her way out of the kitchen doors, a tray filled with food balanced on her shoulder. Even from where she was sitting she could tell the waffles were burnt around the edges. The woman was just a few feet away from them when a customer pushed his chair back and knocked right into her. The tray went flying, dishes crashed onto the floor, and just like that, Mr. Steadman dove right under the table. Mercedes had never seen anything like it. An adult diving under a table! And then he was standing there, brushing bits of food off his sleeves while two busboys rushed over to the mess, one of them holding a broom with half its bristles missing.

"Sorry about that." Mr. Steadman looked around as he picked up his chair. A lady one table over couldn't take her eyes off him either, so Mercedes wasn't the only one staring. He sat down and scooted himself back in. Now what would make a grown man act like that? He glanced back over his shoulder, like he was mad at the waitress. When he turned back around, he was all out of sorts: hair standing up, eyes all wide. He was real angry, she could tell, but why? Maybe he was embarrassed and for some reason it came out as anger.

"You know, you're pretty much the only person I've ever bought food for," he said. He looked down at his hands. He didn't know how to make a fist; he put the thumb inside the fingers. "I'm not a rich person, even though I go to Harvard. The rich kids at Harvard are the undergrads. The ones without any money are the grad students. I'm a grad student. My grandparents were schoolteachers. My mom can't work. The only reason I can live on campus is because a rich girl paid for my room. I don't know why I'm telling you this."

So she was right; when he had given her grandmamma the five dollars to cover bus fare that day, he had been upset about it. He had never planned on paying for her food either; that had just been Grandmamma's assumption.

Their waitress came over and poured some more coffee into the empty cup sitting in front of Mr. Steadman. He dumped a few packets of sweetener into the coffee and took a sip. His eyes pinched at the corners. "No, I guess I'm telling you all of this because I want you to know that I don't have much money myself. I never have."

He wasn't making much sense, though. If he didn't have much money, how had he paid for all of those breakfasts at the Early Bird? And why wasn't he working right then if he needed cash? Maybe he couldn't find a job. But her daddy said there were always jobs, if you looked hard enough. The first job he had in a restaurant, he had found himself. There wasn't a sign up or nothing, it was just a real busy restaurant right in Roxbury, off Smith Street, and he had gone into the kitchen to ask if they needed some help. He started working right then. They gave him an apron and in five minutes he was chopping vegetables.

"I hate this place." Mr. Steadman sniffled, then cleared his throat. "I mean, this is a terrible cup of coffee—truly terrible."

She wasn't really listening. She was still thinking through the stuff he had just said. Mr. Steadman had always kidded around with Flora. Now another girl was paying for his room at Harvard? That didn't seem right. She thought maybe her momma had figured him all wrong. Maybe Mr. Steadman wasn't such a good person after all. Maybe he wasn't truthful.

The two of them sat there until the waitress returned with her milkshake, but Mercedes didn't want it now. She sat very still. Mr. Steadman rubbed his eyes. He seemed like he was kind of falling apart right in front of her. There was something going on. He was keeping something from her—had been ever since he had shown up that first time at her grandmamma's house.

He sniffled and put his head in his hands. She wondered what she would do if he started to cry. She could picture him doing it; that was the thing. He might start crying any second. She wasn't sure if she had ever seen a man cry, except on TV. None of the men cried at her momma and daddy's funeral; they just bit their lips. If Mr. Steadman started crying, she'd get up and go find her grandmamma. She wasn't going to sit in a coffee shop with some man who was crying. She wasn't going to do that.

"I'm sorry," he said. "I'm just not myself today. I'm a little upset with a friend of mine. She's really stubborn. She's writing a book and she wants to put some people in it who aren't very nice. I don't know why someone would want to do that. That doesn't seem like the sort of book we need."

She wondered if the girl writing the book was the same girl who had paid for his room. She kind of figured she was the same girl because she didn't think Mr. Steadman knew too many girls, even though he was nice and tall. If he knew a lot of girls, she figured, he wouldn't have the time to meet with her every week. And since, it turned out, he didn't have much money, maybe there weren't many girls that wanted to get to know him.

They sat there until her grandmamma came back. Then Mercedes got up and left him there, her milkshake untouched, the book of Frost poems pinched under her arm. She figured she didn't have to give the book back right then. It belonged to his grandmamma, so it hadn't cost him any money to loan it to her.

Her grandmamma looked over at Mr. Steadman while Mercedes put her coat back on. Not that she could make him out at that distance, but she must have sensed that something wasn't quite right. Mr. Steadman was staring out the window again, up into the sky, at the snow, away from all the people in the square, almost like he was afraid of them.

Grandmamma bent over her. "How did it go today?" she asked, her eyes squinting, trying their best to get a read on her. She wasn't holding a new umbrella; they must have been too expensive.

Mercedes didn't say anything.

CHAPTER 33

Walt asked for some more coffee. He didn't want to walk by Mercedes and her grandmother at the bus stop so he sat in the restaurant for several minutes, then paid the check and made his way outside. He walked up Mass Ave in the snow. What the hell was the matter with him, venting to an eleven-year-old about his mom's MS? And had he really complained about buying Mercedes a milkshake? He needed to see a therapist. But how would that work? Even if he could afford to see one, what would he say? He didn't know how he was *feeling*. He just knew there were things that were upsetting him: obvious things, like the shooting, but less obvious things as well. He was still pissed that, when Mrs. Reynolds had mentioned racially and ethnically diverse writers, he hadn't been able to think of one. How would a therapist make him feel better about that, by giving him a reading list?

He walked alongside the wrought-iron fence that cordoned off Harvard Yard from the rest of Cambridge. He had been going over Mercedes's assignments for weeks now and she had never been prompted to speak. The way she sat there sullenly across the table from him . . . she made everything feel so weird. Like when he had mentioned Miles Davis and her lip had curled up. That wasn't fair; he had been listening to Miles Davis his whole life. She wasn't giving him a chance. When *he* was a kid, if an adult asked you a question, you answered it. Even if you felt so down you could barely imagine how you could make it through another day, you still answered the question. He wanted Mercedes to understand that. But of course that was unfair. If he had grown up in Boston, he would have been able to talk about his neighborhood or some childhood experience all the kids in the area shared: some familiar field trip they had all suffered through. But he didn't have anything like that, and once more he felt tied down to the very smallness of his own upbringing, and to the limited range of references that grew out of this smallness: the jazz music that, for him to mention to Mercedes, sounded like special pleading, and all those poems about rural New England life, a world away from Boston in 2001.

He cut through the Science Center, deep in thought. If he had grown up in Boston, he probably wouldn't have reached out to Mercedes at all, not if that meant going into Watertown for the first time. That was why Boston was made up of neighborhoods and townships, so everyone could stay where they understood how the city worked. If he had been from Boston, he would have never gone from the Back Bay to Jamaica Plain for breakfast every morning. If he had been from Boston, a white guy still named Walt Steadman, only from Charlestown or Everett, he would have never witnessed the shootings in the Early Bird Café.

Nearly to his dorm, he recognized the plaid hunter's hat bobbing ahead of him and called out to Javier, who turned around and waited for him to catch up.

"Are you coming back from Widener?"

Walt shook his head. "No, I was in Harvard Square, tutoring Mercedes."

The rain from earlier in the day had frozen, encasing cars and tree branches and streetlights in ice.

"How'd it go?"

Walt sighed as they stepped into the foyer of Perkins Hall. "Not so good. It started off okay. I tried to imitate something that Professor O'Shea had us do in her Keats course my first year here. She'd give us these checklists each week that we were supposed to fill out for every poem we read. We'd have to list speakers and addressees, the principal metaphors, the rhyme schemes, and so on and so on. So this afternoon I decided I'd write up a checklist for Mercedes to use for her writing assignments. That way, she can go through it when she's finished an essay and make sure that her nouns go with her verbs, that she isn't starting each sentence with the same word, that she isn't using a comma where she should be using a period—"

"My God, tell me you are not this boring when you talk to her. Please tell me you aren't."

Walt shed his parka quickly so he wouldn't start to perspire as they climbed the stairs to the fourth floor. "Isn't it okay if I'm a little boring? I'm her tutor after all."

"Now I really feel sorry for her. Before I thought I did but now I really do."

Three of the Chinese mathematicians who lived up on their floor passed them in the stairwell, smiling and nodding while looking down at their shoes.

"So the checklist didn't win her over? Imagine that."

"It gets worse. This waitress dropped a tray behind me and it freaked me out. After that I was all over the place. I told Mercedes about Ginger. I told her that my mom has MS. Actually, I might have told her about my mom before the waitress dropped the tray; I can't remember."

"I didn't know your mom has MS."

Walt was silent.

"Man, I think you need to get out more."

"I know."

They opened the doors to their rooms.

"What are you going to do until dinner?" Javier asked.

"I think I'm going to give Ginger a call." In spite of not approving, he did want to hear how her afternoon in Foss Park had gone.

"I'm going to take a nap. Wake me up at six?"

"All right."

Walt shut the door behind him, picked up the phone, and dialed her number.

"Hello?"

The voice on the other end was a woman's, but it wasn't Ginger's. "Who's this?"

"This is an attendant at the Mount Auburn Emergency Room. Who are you trying to get ahold of?"

"Ginger Newton." He heard a rustling sound on the other end. "Hello?"

"Could you describe her to us?"

"She's got blonde hair, blue eyes. She's really pretty. Twenty years old . . ." The woman was repeating what he said. "What's going on? Is she hurt?"

"An ambulance brought her in a short time ago. She was assaulted in East Somerville. She suffered serious head trauma."

"I'm sorry?"

"She was assaulted—"

Walt let the phone drop out of his hand. He put his parka back on and rushed out of his room. He skipped down the stairs, out onto Oxford Street. Then he began to run. He ran through campus, then down JFK to Mount Auburn Street, where he took a right. The snow turned to rain. He ran as fast as he could, but he kept on slipping on the sidewalk and he was out of shape so he didn't move that quickly. He told himself he had to keep running, but then he began to jog, and finally—panting—he slowed to a hurried walk. Serious head trauma meant she could die before he got there, like Flora and John and Natalie had died. What would he do then? The traffic streamed by him, the cars kicking up water, dousing his legs. If she were dead, he decided that he would leave the hospital and follow Mount Auburn Street until it took him out of town. But the road probably didn't go all the way out of town; it probably circled somehow back into Cambridge, back into Boston. He would have to get on another road to escape the city. At some point he would need a compass. But he didn't know to read a compass. His grandfather did, but he was dead. And Ginger was probably dead as well. People around him, people he cared for, they were all dying. Through some hideous trick of fate, he had become an angel of death. And for the first time that he could remember, for the first time since moving to Boston, Walt missed Vermont.

THE POETICS OF
YANKEE PEERAGE

CHAPTER 34

Walt sat outside the emergency room at the Mount Auburn Hospital. He wasn't allowed to see Ginger; since she was the victim of an assault, he needed permission from her immediate family. The Newtons had been notified. They were on their way.

An hour passed, and then another. People stumbled in: a guy with a messed-up leg, a woman whose hand was wrapped in blood-soaked paper towels, a little boy in his father's arms. They would go up to the counter to the right of the swinging doors that led into the emergency room itself. Then whoever was hurt would be rushed off, through the swinging doors, while their friends or family members or acquaintances found a chair in the waiting room and took a seat. Except for the boy's father; he went in with his son.

Almost four hours after he had arrived, Walt watched a man, a woman, and a little girl enter from outside, their footsteps echoing loudly on the floor. The man introduced himself to one of the women behind the counter as Edward Newton. He was wearing jeans and a black leather jacket. "I'm looking for my daughter," he said loudly. "She was attacked." His voice had all kinds of edges to it, like it could turn into a shout or a whimper, depending. He glanced around the room anxiously: his jaw clenched, his eyes bloodshot, his hair parted severely to the left. The woman next to him wore a silk scarf around her neck and a long black trench coat. The young girl standing between her mother's legs had on snow boots and a white parka.

Walt stood up and walked toward them. As he approached, the little girl turned toward him and he saw that she was wearing flannel pajamas beneath her parka. She looked wide-eyed and scared, her nose running, her hand clutching a dirty stuffed animal—maybe a pig, it was hard to tell. Mrs. Newton looked like her eldest daughter, with the same bone structure and the same blonde hair, only her face was fuller. The three of them didn't look like Yankee royalty. They were just a family, a disoriented one, standing together in a hospital.

Walt reached out his hand. "Mr. and Mrs. Newton," he said. "I'm Walt Steadman. I'm a friend of Ginger's."

Mrs. Newton fumbled with his hand, squeezing his fingers tightly. "Oh, yes, Walt. You're her friend from Vermont, right?"

Walt nodded.

"I'm Mitzy, this is Edward, and this is Bee Bee." Mitzy held her daughter by the shoulders while Bee Bee stared down at the floor.

Edward Newton began to say hello but cut himself off when the doors to their left swung open and a doctor in green scrubs walked out. The doctor had thin black hair and flushed, puffy cheeks. He introduced himself and shook all their hands. Bee Bee he patted on the head.

"Your daughter has a fractured skull," he said to Edward and Mitzy. "We've completed the preliminary neurologic assessment. She has a grade one concussion, a broken nose, and lacerations on her right cheek. There's a deep contusion on her chin. She lost three of her front teeth. It appears that she was hit in the back of the head with something heavy but—luckily—not pointed. She probably incurred the injuries to her face when she fell forward. She was lucky; the fracture is a small one. It'll heal on its own. If it had been bigger, she could have popped a blood vessel, in which case her condition might have been critical."

Mitzy blinked and blinked as she took in the information. "Is she going to be okay?"

"She should be fine. We're going to do a CAT scan shortly to check her brain functions."

"Could her brain be . . . damaged?" Edward Newton asked.

"I don't think so. She's responsive. She knows where she is and who she is. It's standard procedure when someone suffers head trauma to do a CAT scan." The doctor coughed into his hand while they all stared at him. "She's resting now. She's conscious, but she's in a lot of pain. We don't like to sedate someone with head trauma until we've established the full extent of their injuries. You're welcome to come back and see her, but I need to reiterate: she's missing teeth, her nose is badly broken, her chin is really swollen—"

Mitzy and Edward exchanged frightened glances. "We want to see her right away," Mitzy said. "Please, right away."

He motioned for them to follow and the Newtons began to walk off. Walt stood still, until Mitzy reached back and grabbed him by the wrist. "Come on, Walt," she said.

They walked through the swinging doors and down a winding hallway. All around them, through doorways and behind drawn curtains, machines beeped intermittently. IV stands and folded wheelchairs were strewn on either side of them. Walt thought of his mother. He thought of Ginger Newton becoming his mother. He thought of his own body: so unbroken, so unsullied.

They turned sharply through a doorway. A row of drawn green curtains greeted them. The doctor pulled back the one on the far right, revealing a large hospital bed. Walt and the others stepped toward the railing.

Ginger was lying with her head propped up on three pillows, motionless, staring at the ceiling. Her chin was purple and round and swollen out across her neck. The right side of her face was scraped and puckered and her nose was bright red, its bridge puffy like an uncooked sausage—twisted and raw.

"Oh my God." Mitzy Newton turned away. She put her hand across Bee Bee's eyes. "Oh dear God." She began to sob. Edward put his arm around her.

Walt said nothing. He studied Ginger's face. He searched for the features he had seized on when he first met her—for the pointy chin, the straight, thin nose, the perfect white teeth—but they were all unrecognizable now. He bent over her ear. "Ginger, it's me. It's Walt. I'm here with your family. You're going to be fine."

She cleared her throat. "Don't be mad at me, Walt," she said. When she spoke, blood pooled in her mouth.

"I'm not mad at you."

"You should be. You should be pissed at me."

But looking down at her, Walt felt no anger at all. He just thought that she was beautiful; or at least, he thought that there was nothing that could happen to her body that would make her any less beautiful to him. He really did care about her. She was too driven and self-absorbed and entitled for her own good, but he really cared about her.

He stepped back from the bed as Mitzy Newton squeezed in next to him.

"Oh, Mom," Ginger moaned.

"Sweetie." She grabbed her daughter's hands.

"Oh, Mom, it hurts so bad."

Edward scooped up Bee Bee, who had begun to cry.

"Everything hurts," Ginger whimpered. "Everything just hurts so bad . . ."

They stood around her bed until she was wheeled away for her CAT scan. Then Walt, Mitzy, Edward, and Bee Bee returned to the waiting room. They pulled some chairs into a circle. Bee Bee curled up with her head in her mother's lap. Mitzy ran her fingers through the girl's hair, over and over again, but Bee Bee didn't close her eyes. They sat in silence for what seemed like a long time, until another doctor came out to tell them that the CAT scan had been completed and the results had been sent along to the radiologist on call. Ginger was resting now. There was nothing to do but wait until the morning.

Walt wasn't the slightest bit tired. He didn't feel like going back to Perkins Hall. Outside, the night deepened. Bee Bee finally drifted off to sleep. He exchanged awkward smiles with Ginger's parents. He accepted their thanks for rushing over to the hospital. He told them how sorry he was that this had all happened and both Mitzy and Edward nodded. Then once more they lapsed into silence.

"Do you remember," Edward asked his wife suddenly, "do you remember that morning when Ginger announced that she wanted to read Charles Darwin's *On the Origin of Species*? She couldn't have been more than thirteen years old. So I dug up my old copy from college and she set up at the kitchen table." He turned to Walt. "Have you ever watched Ginger read?"

"I have, yes."

"So you've noticed the way she runs her index finger over the lines of text, again and again? The way her feet are always tapping and tapping?"

"Yeah." Walt grinned as he recalled that morning in Blair Montgomery's apartment, when he awoke to find her reading at the kitchen counter.

"It can drive you crazy," Mitzy added.

Edward brushed the hair from in front of his wife's face. "So she read and read. For days she read that book. I don't know how long it took her, but after about a week or so she announced that she had finished it and she thought Darwin was right and I remember I asked her why and do you recall what she said?" Mitzy smiled, her eyes glistening. Edward continued. "She said, 'I think he's right because, when you read his book, it doesn't feel like he's trying to convince you he's right. He's just telling you what he's learned.' I'll never forget that."

"This was right before she sent you off looking for Gibbon's *Decline and Fall of the Roman Empire*," Mitzy added.

"Yeah, the guy at the Strand got a kick out of that one—a thirteen-year-old dying to read Edward Gibbon. I'm not sure if she finished that project."

Mitzy leaned forward and gently squeezed Walt's knee. He couldn't help but notice that her wedding ring had a diamond that was the size of a postage stamp.

"We had a cleaning lady during Ginger's first year in middle school . . . Edward, what was her name? I'm forgetting everything."

"Mary, I think. No, Margaret."

"Yes, of course. Margaret. Well, Margaret was from Bensonhurst and Ginger was just obsessed with learning about her neighborhood. She would ask her question after question. 'Where do you buy your groceries?' 'What are the names of the restaurants on your street?' 'What does your apartment building smell like?' It was quite embarrassing. So then, one afternoon, she didn't return from school. We had finally given her permission to come home with the Clarkson twins and their nanny. They lived in our building. So I phoned their mother and, sure enough, her daughters were sitting with her, having an after-school snack, and mine was nowhere to be found. She had taken off by herself right after school ended, claiming that her father was meeting her on the corner of 91st and Amsterdam. Well, I absolutely freaked out. I phoned the cops, the fire department, everyone. And then, an hour later, Ginger waltzed in. She told me she had gone to Bensonhurst by herself; she had taken the subway out to Brooklyn to have a look around." Mitzy smiled while Edward rubbed the back of her neck, her eyes brimming with tears. "She was working on her book even then. She's always been working on her book."

She began to cry very softly while her husband massaged her shoulder. And Walt, too self-conscious to say anything, too self-conscious even to move, just stared at the floor. Of course it had never occurred to him that a family like Ginger's would have ever had anything to cry about, but here they were, worrying that their daughter might never be the same. In his own way, he had always been something of a snob.

CHAPTER 35

He spent the rest of the weekend with the Newton family at the Mount Auburn Hospital. That wasn't his intention. Mitzy and Edward were just incredibly inclusive: inviting him to come along the following morning when they were told it was okay to visit their daughter in her room, asking if he wanted to get a bite to eat with them in the afternoon, giving him a lift back to his dorm in their rental car in the evening. They must have known, Walt assumed when they dropped him off, that their daughter had paid for his room and board, but neither Mr. nor Mrs. Newton drew any attention to their own generosity, and so Walt remained silent on the topic.

The CAT scan report confirmed no damage to Ginger's brain, but the doctors didn't want to release her until Monday. It was best for her to stay in bed, one of them explained, not simply so that she could rest, but also because a person who experienced head trauma could seem fine, and then a day later, she might forget what her phone number was, or where she lived, or even her own name. So they needed to proceed cautiously.

They moved Ginger out of the ER Friday night, into a second-floor room that overlooked Memorial Drive and a slice of the Charles River. There was a little waiting area down the hallway, and each time they were herded out of her room, Mitzy, Edward, Walt, and Bee Bee would gather together there to pass the time. They'd play Old Maid and Go Fish. Sometimes other families would be waiting there as well and Mitzy would ask them how they were doing and a conversation would ensue. Other times the room would be filled but no one would say anything; Bee Bee and one or two other children would watch cartoons on the TV mounted in the corner while the adults thumbed through newspapers or stared at the walls.

Early Saturday morning, a plainclothes detective came by to interview Ginger about the attack. Walt wondered if the man knew Detective Flager, who had interviewed him after the shootings at the Early Bird Café. Maybe they were all trained together, or attended the same conferences? But he didn't ask him. Later that day, when a doctor came by to set her nose, Ginger told her family and Walt to get lost. He listened to her scream from the hallway. Most of Sunday she slept, although the nurses woke her every two hours in order to ask her where she was born (Roosevelt Hospital, Upper West Side, New York City) and what her middle name was (Penelope).

When Walt made it up to Ginger's room Monday morning, he met Mitzy just as she emerged from the doorway. "Oh good," she said. "You're here. I was hoping you'd keep Ginger company while I run some errands."

"Of course."

Mitzy adjusted the burnt orange scarf that was tied loosely around her neck. "I want to make sure there's food in her apartment, and I've been asked to check the heat lamps that keep that awful snake of hers alive. Ginger's just had a bath. I think she's getting a little stir crazy."

"That doesn't surprise me."

She rolled her eyes. "Nor me. Edward took Bee Bee back to New York early this morning so she wouldn't miss any more school, but I'm going to stay through the week, maybe more, depending on how Ginger's doing. Hey, look at this." She pulled a thin newspaper out of her black leather purse and showed him the front page of the *Harvard Crimson*. On Friday the *Globe* had run an article about the attack in its metro section, but Ginger hadn't been identified in the story. The *Crimson* piece from that morning carried a picture of Ginger above the fold.

"That's the photo they took for her student ID her first year," Mitzy explained.

In the picture, Ginger was looking right into the camera, her hair hanging down just above her eyebrows, and grazing her shoulders on the side. Her mouth was slightly open—caught somewhere between a smile and a frown—and her skin was ivory white, as if earlier in the day she had stepped off the *Arbella* in Salem. Mitzy sighed, then carefully tucked the paper back in her purse, making sure not to crease the photo of her daughter.

"Thanks, Walt, for everything," she said.

"It's the least I can do," Walt replied. He watched her make her way down the hallway and turn toward the elevator bank. Then he knocked softly on the open door and approached Ginger's bed.

Her injuries seemed to have settled more on her face. Her nose remained puckered and red, but her cheeks were also swollen now, the cuts on her right side glistening. The once purple bruise on her chin was now more fuchsia in color. When she looked at him, Ginger offered the briefest of smiles, one made with her lips pursed. Her hair was still wet from her bath. Walt pulled up a chair and sat down.

"How are you doing?"

She looked askance. "My head feels like a cantaloupe, or I guess how I think a cantaloupe would feel if it had cognition."

"I never liked cantaloupe very much. Those stringy seeds." He tried to grin affably. "Are they discharging you today?"

"Yeah, this afternoon." Gently, cautiously, she touched her own face with the tips of her fingers. "I guess the cops found my car last night—what was left of it. That's why those girls did this to me; they just wanted to take my Lexus for a spin."

She coughed into her palm. When she opened her mouth, he saw the raw gums where her front teeth were once moored. She told him to turn away while she spat into a plastic bowl that sat on the tray that extended out on an arm from the wall, on the far side of her bed. Then she wiped her mouth with the back of her hand. "They took my boots off my feet. Did I tell you that? Of course they stole my bag, that you'd expect, but to take someone's shoes . . ."

She said nothing for moment. She was still looking away from him. "I know what you're thinking, Walt. You're thinking I went to Foss Park because I'm spoiled and sheltered—"

"That's not—"

"No, it's okay. You're right. It's kind of true, some of it at least. I *am* privileged and pampered, my family *does* have money, and I've been surrounded mostly by people whose families also have a lot of money. When I came up with the idea for *Girls I Know,* I just assumed that I had to ignore my own background in order to write about people who had less than I do, or at least had lost more than I had. I was trying to write a book from the inside of my Lexus without ever telling my reader that I was writing the book from the inside of my Lexus. Well, you can't do that. It just doesn't work. I need to tell my reader where I'm coming from. I need to be confessional. There's a lot about *Girls I Know* that's compromised; I realize that. I thought this before but now I *get it*. I'm not going to bullshit anyone. People who write theodicies are people who have the luxury of thinking about evil; they aren't generally people who are suffering inordinately themselves. And I want to write about that. I want to write a theodicy that's also about writing a theodicy. And I don't care if the whole thing sounds crazy. I want to talk about Scholastic philosophy, because we all need to think more about the way people tried to understand the world before penicillin and roller coasters in order to get to the fundamentals of human existence. That's my position."

Walt was silent. On the heels of her apology to him the other night, he had hoped that they might have a discussion about the two of them: about whatever it was that constituted their strange relationship. But she wasn't interested in that; she was really just giving herself a pep talk. And he loved that about her—her doggedness, her determination. Even if it was incredibly exasperating, he still loved it. He wanted to tell her right then how much he cared for her without saying exactly how much he cared for her, but he didn't know how to compete with *Girls I Know*. He didn't see the point in even trying.

"It's going to be a great book, Ginger."

She pushed herself up in bed, squinting in pain. "I don't care anymore. I don't care if it's great. I don't care if no editor wants to touch it. I just want it to be *my* book."

The curtain was drawn across the window on the far side of the bed and Walt got up and opened it. It was an overcast day. As he sat back down, he noticed once more the lacerations on her right cheek, the skin pink and raw.

"You were right," he said. "Racial divisions probably aren't surmountable in the US."

"What makes you say that?"

"I'm just thinking about the tutoring I'm doing. Mercedes doesn't trust me and it doesn't really matter what I say. There's just this barrier. Not to extrapolate solely from my own experience—"

"You have more than one. What about at the Early Bird? From what I gather, that was something of a melting pot."

"Until everyone was shot to death."

"Except you." Ginger coughed again loudly. She took a sip from a glass of water set on the tray and then cradled her head in her hands. "Guess who's got a three-hour block with a dentist set up for the day after tomorrow?" She yawned, covering her mouth with both hands. "I need to shut my eyes, Walt. I'm so tired. I'm catching up on years and years of missed sleep."

"I'll just be down the hallway." He tapped her forearm and she fumbled for his hand before squeezing it. Halfway to the door, she called out to him and he turned around.

"Can you just indulge me for a second. Please. Remember, I've had a rough few days here, with the bludgeoning and everything."

"Of course." He sat back down.

"All right, so you know, I can't read because I get a headache, which means when I'm awake I've just been thinking. And, I can't help it, I've been mulling over the shootings you witnessed, and watching Spanish-language soap operas. I have to work on my Spanish; you can't live in America in the twenty-first century and not know Spanish. But mostly I've been thinking about the Early Bird, and what Ramon did. I can't speak to the murders of John and Natalie Bittles. He killed them out of anger, I guess. He was mad that they fired him; I don't know. I suppose he tried to shoot you because you were a witness. But with Flora, I kind of wonder if he knew what MS-13 was planning on doing to her and if maybe he killed her out of charity. A misguided notion of charity, but still—charity."

Walt recoiled in his chair, his mouth open slightly. She was really going to do this—subsume Flora's death to her grand design? And he was going to sit there and listen?

"I know it sounds obscene, Walt, but bear with me. For the moment, I can't help it, Aquinas is my signpost. That'll change when I finish this project. Really, it will, but for the moment I just have to keep on working through this frame, this way of seeing the world. I just want to understand the terms I'm using. I'm not trying to be annoying, or insensitive."

He pressed his fingers against his mouth and breathed slowly through his nose. Ginger had never met Flora. She had never heard her talk or laugh. She hadn't seen what her face looked like after being shot. He resisted the urge to judge her for being callous and overly intellectual. Having been through what she had with the bruises and missing teeth, with the fractured skull and the broken nose, Ginger was easier to forgive now than before. He was done with judging and criticizing her. He would just wait for her on the other side of *Girls I Know*. That was fine. He was good at waiting. He would wait until she was done with her book and then he would tell her he loved her without saying he loved her, exactly. He would tell her how much she meant to him, even with all her privilege and self-involvement, even in the wake of Flora's death. For now, though, he just wanted to understand what she was trying to get at with *Girls I Know*. "Okay, so tell me. What would Aquinas say about Ramon Gutierrez? What would he say about the girls who attacked you and took your boots off your feet? What would he say about these people doing awful things in the world his God supposedly made out of love?"

Ginger cradled her swollen chin in her hands; she sneezed, then moaned in agony. "He would say that even the most deplorable creature, the figure most saturated with evil, still attests to God's benevolence, because in choosing to do evil, that figure affirms the freedom that God has granted him. He would say that even the most fallen reflects something benevolent and beautiful in God's design."

CHAPTER 36

Mrs. Bittles rubbed her eyes. It was Sunday evening; she was dead tired but she couldn't sleep. There was just so much to think about. This past weekend had nearly put her under. What was she going to do with this child? She paced around the house like a caged animal, most of the time her nose in that big book Mr. Steadman had loaned her. That afternoon, she sat at the kitchen table for hours, fiddling with some essay of hers: thumbing through library books, checking off stuff from a sheet, some kind of to-do list. All that was fine, but the whole time, she never stopped eating! The girl needed to be getting out more. Maybe she should call Denise and not ask but tell her to invite them over the next weekend. So that would solve one day, maybe two if her daughter let them spend the night, but what would happen in a few months, when school let out for the summer? How in the world would she keep her occupied then? And what about that fall, when Mercedes was supposed to start middle school? How was that all going to work out?

She heard a soft knock on her bedroom door, which was halfway open, and set her *Reader's Digest* down on her lap. She loved the "Drama in Real Life" stories—people getting buried alive or crashing in airplanes, but always coming out okay, always making it through—although she hadn't been able to read more than a page or two at a sitting since John had died. He was the child that had made her most proud: owning his own business, working as hard as he did. She had seen them lower him into the ground, but he wasn't dead to her; she was still waiting for him to walk through the front door.

Mercedes stepped to the side of her bed. She had on her green pajamas, the ones with the outlines of little frogs scattered all over them. Her grandmother squinted at her.

"You're going to need to give me money for a milkshake if you want Mr. Steadman to tutor me. He don't have enough money to pay for me himself."

She tried not to act surprised, hearing her granddaughter's voice. "Then why did he ask us to start meeting him at places where you have to pay for food and drinks?"

Mercedes shrugged.

She set her glasses down on her bedside table. "Are you learning anything from him, anything useful?"

Mercedes nodded.

"All right then. You get back into bed."

Mercedes walked out of her room. A moment later, Mrs. Bittles heard the springs on the girl's bed squeak. She tossed the *Reader's Digest* onto the chair against the wall and turned off the light. How much did they charge for a milkshake at that place? Didn't matter. Her granddaughter had finally said something.

Mercedes hated Monday mornings. She hated every morning, but Mondays she really hated: waking up and having to start a whole new week. For breakfast, Grandmamma tried to make Eggos, but she burnt them pretty good in the toaster. Her daddy had always made her waffles with the iron they had. She wondered what had happened to it.

Some days Mrs. Greene could be kind of interesting, but not that day. The morning went by real slow. At lunch, she and Taneka sat together. Then, in the afternoon, they had their self-guided study time. Not even Shahid and Tashawn made any noise. School was about as boring as it could be.

The minute she stepped through the door of her grandmamma's house that afternoon, they turned around and rushed off. Her grandmamma didn't want them to keep Mr. Steadman waiting again, she explained, which meant they had to take the earlier bus. So they hurried over to Mount Auburn and sure enough, the bus was right on time; they ended up in Harvard Square with more than twenty minutes to spare. Her grandmamma didn't want to get a table because that would have meant ordering something. So they looked at the papers at the newsstand right next to the restaurant. Then they walked across the street to the hardware store because they needed to buy some mousetraps. Mice were coming into the kitchen from behind the refrigerator. Mercedes heard them in the morning, when her grandmamma flipped on the light, scampering back into the wall.

Dickson Brothers Hardware didn't sell a simple mousetrap; all theirs were complicated plastic things where the mouse would crawl in and a little door would shut behind him and he'd be stuck there, breathing in the dark. Grandmamma wasn't interested in that kind of contraption. "Made of cheap plastic," she said to Mercedes, having opened up the box and looked at one. "And four dollars apiece! Four dollars!" So they went back to the restaurant and stood there in front of the glass counter, staring at the pies lined up in rows, her grandmamma acting like she was thinking of buying one.

When Mr. Steadman arrived, he didn't look the same as before. His eyes were all tired and he had lines in his cheeks. How old was he anyway? It was hard to tell because he was old in some ways, like how he read poems out loud, but young in others, like the way his head bobbed when he walked. But he looked like he had gotten older, just in the last few days.

"Am I late?" he asked her grandmamma.

"No, we're early."

Mr. Steadman held a small book in his hand, with a pen clipped on the front. He glanced at the pies himself. "Doesn't that coconut cream one look good?"

Grandmamma nodded. Mercedes's daddy's favorite pie was peach cobbler. Her momma's favorite pie was lemon meringue. Mercedes didn't have a favorite pie; she liked them all.

She and Mr. Steadman followed the hostess to a table back in the far corner while her grandmamma excused herself to run some errands. She was going to go back to the hardware store and shake her head over their prices, Mercedes guessed. She unzipped her backpack and pulled out her homework for the week and the book of Frost poems. She slid the paper across the table toward Mr. Steadman.

"What have you got here?" He picked up the sheet. On the top she had written *A Report on Amelia Earhart, a Great American*. "Do you guys study anything other than aviators?" He was trying to be funny, after being crabby the time before. He didn't know she had picked Ms. Earhart to write on all by herself, after Mrs. Greene had explained in class the other day that she had crashed in the Pacific Ocean while trying to fly her plane around the world. That meant Amelia Earhart had died in water, like her momma's two brothers and her sister, coming over from Haiti and drowning in the ocean. When it was time for you to die, the water would come and get you. Even if you were on land, or up in the air, it would still come and carry you away.

The waitress with the long face came by and Walt asked for some coffee. Once again, Mercedes had nothing to point to; the hostess had forgotten to give them menus. But the woman asked if she wanted a strawberry milkshake as usual so all she had to do was nod. Then she watched Mr. Steadman read her essay.

He held his pen over the paper while he looked at it. She didn't like that; she thought he should put down the pen and pick it up only when he had to mark up something. But he didn't mark up much. He turned the essay over and read the second half, then flipped the paper over again and read the whole thing once more.

"This is so good, Mercedes," he said when he had finished. "You really tell a story here. Your essay has a beginning and a middle and an end. And it's interesting. This is great."

The waitress filled Mr. Steadman's cup with coffee and set a milkshake down on the table. Mercedes took the paper off her straw and had a sip. It was okay, this one. Not too powdery. All Sunday afternoon, she had worked hard on this assignment. She wrote the paper, then went through the checklist Mr. Steadman had given her. She made the corrections according to what his sheet said; then she rewrote the whole essay. So she ended up doing the assignment twice! It was the last essay she'd have to write on great Americans too. They were done with the unit after this week. She was tired of hearing about all these people and what they had done, but she was going to miss reading about Amelia Earhart. They were like each other, that was the thing. Amelia Earhart would go up in a plane and fly over water, all by herself, except when she had a navigator with her, but even then she was on her own, steering the plane, landing it, pushing all the buttons. She wasn't afraid of anything. She was a brave lady.

She was a rock. She wore goggles when she flew so her eyes wouldn't tear, so she could always see what was ahead of her.

Mr. Steadman circled one sentence, and then another. "Now you've got a couple of mistakes here and here. I'll let you figure out what they are." She set her eyes on him. "Or I can just tell you. This verb doesn't agree with this noun. You need to add an *s*. And this sentence needs to become two, like we've talked about before." She nodded. "There are some other, tiny things . . ." He began to scribble here and there. "But it's really good." He slid the essay back to her. "Great job, Mercedes. Hey, I've got something for you."

He handed her the book that he had brought in with him. It was a thin little thing, not big like *The Poetry of Robert Frost*. "This isn't a loan. You can have this." His mouth twisted, almost as if he had tasted something sour, but it couldn't have been from the coffee; he had yet to take a sip. "I'm sorry about that stuff I said the last time we met. You don't need to hear about my troubles. They're none of your concern. You've got enough to deal with, I realize that."

Mr. Steadman was giving her a present because he felt bad about telling her his momma was sick and some girl had paid for the room he lived in. She held the book in her hands. It was so light, like a pair of socks. She didn't like the cover: black with tiny white lettering. Who was Gwendolyn Brooks anyway? He had never mentioned her. She turned the book over. On the back cover, in the lower left-hand corner, was a picture of a black woman with big glasses. Is that why he was giving her this book, just because the lady who had written it was black? And why wasn't Mr. Steadman *loaning* her a copy? Maybe he hadn't read the book himself, or didn't think it was any good.

She set *The Selected Poems of Gwendolyn Brooks* on the table and slid it toward him. "I want to read what you read, Mr. Steadman. The important stuff."

She hadn't meant to talk; the words had just slipped out. She caught herself and looked down at the table.

"These poems are important, Mercedes." But Mr. Steadman didn't sound too convincing. His coffee cup clanked against the saucer. Hearing her voice had thrown him off, she guessed. "I haven't read them in a while, but that doesn't mean they aren't important. There's a lot of stuff I don't know that well that I should. But Gwendolyn Brooks is a serious—was a serious—poet. Actually I'm not sure if she's alive or dead. Anyway, she won the Pulitzer Prize. It says so right on the cover here. That's a big award they give to really good writers. She won that, just like Robert Frost did." He caught her looking over at his grandmother's old copy of *The Poetry of Robert Frost*. "You don't have to give that back to me," he said. "You can keep it as long as you want. I just thought, you know, it'd be easier to carry this around. And you might really like some of the poems. Then you'll have two poets you like reading, and in a little bit you'll have three, and then four, and then you'll be unfit for gainful employment. That's a joke."

She didn't get the joke; she just looked back and forth at the two books, then up at him. Whenever he said he was joking, Mr. Steadman was never funny; she wondered if he knew that.

The two of them sat there awkwardly. Mr. Steadman cleared his throat. "You know, you can be old and not know what you're doing. You can do stupid things, even at my age."

Mercedes said nothing. She wasn't following him, exactly. The waitress strolled over and asked if they needed anything else. Mr. Steadman said no and she dropped their check onto the table. As fast as she could, Mercedes fished her money out of the small pocket of her sweater. She placed the coins right next to the check, just like her grandmamma told her to: all the quarters on the bottom, and the nickels and dimes stacked on top of them like a little pyramid.

"No, no," Mr. Steadman waved his hands at her, "you don't have to pay . . ."

But she didn't take the money back. *When you put it on the table,* Grandmamma had said, pointing her finger at her so there would be no misunderstanding, *it stays on the table.*

Mr. Steadman looked at her. "I got it, really." But she didn't budge. "Okay," he said, kind of to himself. He took out his wallet, all thin and beat-up, and pulled out a couple of dollars. "Thanks," he said to her.

Her grandmamma was waiting for them at the door, so they wouldn't have time to read any poems today. Mercedes put the Frost book in her backpack, along with her essay on Amelia Earhart. Together the two of them walked through the restaurant.

"So you sure you don't want to try the book?" Mr. Steadman asked her just as her grandmamma stepped toward them.

Mercedes nodded.

"All right, how about I give it a read-through myself—just to refresh my memory—and tell you what I think?" She nodded again. Mr. Steadman looked at Mrs. Bittles. "We're trying to pick our next poet to read," he explained, yawning.

Mrs. Bittles squinted at him. "Mr. Steadman, you sound tired."

They stepped out onto the sidewalk.

"I've been over at Mount Auburn Hospital a lot the last few days," he said.

Mercedes tried to drop back so the two of them could have adult talk, but she couldn't drop back more than a few feet. There was a crowd of people walking around them and they just pushed her along.

"What are you doing there?"

"A friend of mine was assaulted in East Somerville. They fractured her skull, broke her nose—"

"What business did she have in East Somerville?"

"She's writing a book."

"She's writing a book about East Somerville?"

"Not exactly—"

"Who on God's green earth is going to want to read a book about East Somerville?"

"It's a book about Boston neighborhoods . . . women from different neighborhoods. What they do, that sort of thing. The hospital is releasing her today. I haven't been sleeping well; I guess I've been worrying about her."

Grandmamma looked back over her shoulder, just to check on her. When she spoke next she lowered her voice but Mercedes still heard her. "Mount Auburn's where they took Dontrelle Senior when he had his heart attack, but he was dead before they got him there. He was dead before the ambulance pulled up, they said afterwards."

The light changed and they crossed over to the brick sidewalk that ran outside of Harvard Yard.

"It's so scary, all of it," he said softly. Mercedes barely heard him. And suddenly he stopped walking. She almost bumped into him. He stopped walking just a few feet from the bus stop. And she figured it out right then. What was scary to him was the Early Bird Café. He had been there. When her momma and daddy had been killed, Mr. Steadman must have been there. That was what he had been hiding from her all along. That was why, that time the waitress dropped that tray, he dove right under the table. That was why he had taken the bus all the way out to Watertown to see her. And that was why he was tutoring her. He had seen them all die. He had been there, but he hadn't been shot. He had made it out okay. She wondered how.

"Oh, you can't be scared." Mrs. Bittles shook her head. And she reached back and grabbed Mercedes's hand. She was trying to give her strength, but Mercedes wasn't scared. She was a rock in the Jamaica Pond. Nothing scared her. But Mr. Steadman was scared of a lot of things. When dishes fell on the floor, he thought he was going to get shot. Her grandmamma should have taken ahold of *his* hand, not hers.

"You can be angry," Grandmamma said, just as their bus pulled up, looking back and forth at the two of them with her milky eyes. "You can live your life with anger in your heart, but you cannot live your life being afraid. That just doesn't work."

CHAPTER 37

Wednesday afternoon was clear and cold. Walt took the T over to the Back Bay to visit Ginger, who was recuperating now back in Blair Montgomery's apartment. The streets still brimmed with college girls and businessmen and shoppers, but Walt didn't feel himself to be moving among them so much as trudging alongside. His legs had forgotten the rhythm of his former neighborhood.

As he approached the steps of his old building, Ginger's mom stepped outside.

"Hi, Walt." As always, she seemed happy to see him.

"Hey, Mitzy."

Mrs. Newton wore a thick wool coat and black stockings, with a large pearl brooch on the lapel and a pair of pearl earrings. "I'm going over to Newbury Street to buy some clothes for my daughter. Harvard turns young people into slobs. It didn't use to be that way. Edward was a splendid dresser in college." She pulled a pair of leather gloves out of her purse but she didn't put them on.

"You two met in college?"

"We did, yes." She stepped back into the foyer and Walt followed her. "I came down one weekend from Smith with my roommate to visit her boyfriend. I met Edward at a party the first night we were in Cambridge. We were married a year later. Not an exciting story for the time, I'm afraid. Very quotidian."

The interior of the foyer had recently been painted, Walt noticed. The divot in the plaster from where the doorknob had knocked against the wall for years and years had been patched, and a doorstopper inserted on the baseboard. Just inside the door was a black mat. That was a good idea, putting something there where people could wipe their feet. Walt wished he had thought of that.

"How's our patient doing?"

"Resting at the moment. We returned from the dentist about an hour ago. Her mouth is still a little numb. If you see her jotting down notes, you tell her to cut it out."

"Will do."

"The last two days, she's been working absolutely feverishly on that book of hers. Even when she has something to eat, she keeps right on working." She looked him up and down, her eyes lingering on his battered pair of Doc Martens, or so Walt thought. "Her first . . . I don't know the appropriate term . . . well anyway, her first nervous collapse in college, when she had to withdraw in the middle of her first semester . . . has Ginger mentioned this to you? Perhaps I'm speaking out of turn."

"Not at all." Walt tried to maintain his languid pose, as if he were only half listening.

"Well, she took seven courses her first semester. Two of them she was auditing. She forged her advisor's signature in order to get permission from the registrar. This was when she decided that she wanted to be an Egyptologist. Don't mention the tomb of Ramesses II to her unless you want a mouthful. One night, Halloween in fact, she just passed out. Fell right out of her chair while she was studying. They found her on the first floor in that library . . . What's the one called that's entirely underground?"

"Pusey."

"Yes, *Pusey*." She lingered over the word. "I rushed up to get her, brought her back to New York, got her checked out, and then took her to our little place in the Hamptons. I nursed her back to health. Oh, she'd kill me if she heard me put it like that but a mother is allowed certain descriptive rights, I think. At the time, I swore, just having me dote on her would be enough for her to decide to take better care of herself. Ginger *hates* being doted on, in case you haven't noticed. But of course I was being silly. This is just how she is. So tough on herself—so, so tough. This is the only way she knows how to be."

In the face of such maternal concern, Walt suddenly found himself playing the role of the optimist. "I really think she'll feel better once *Girls I Know* is done."

Mitzy smiled at him. "Oh, Walt, I hope you're right. But you'd be surprised at how quickly she can be consumed by something new. My goodness, she declared philosophy as her major just after this last Thanksgiving! At first, I thought Peter Lombard was a classmate, she talked about him so much. But I should have known." Mitzy squeezed her fingers, bejeweled rings and all, into her gloves while Walt opened the door for her. "You don't have to wait for me to return; she's fine by herself."

"Oh, I don't mind, I really don't."

She tried to offer a good-natured wave but Walt saw right through it. She was worried about her daughter: worried and worn out. He watched her descend the stairs, then march across Beacon Street, assuming — correctly — that the cars would just stop for her. After she had disappeared around the corner, he turned and walked down the hallway to the elevator, which he took up to the third floor.

"It's open," she cried out meekly when he knocked, the words slightly slurred.

He stepped inside. The apartment had been transformed. There were no clothes on the floor. Ginger's belongings — her duffel bags, her books — were nowhere to be seen. The mattress on which she had slept, the mattress on which they had had sex that one time, had been propped on its side and set against the near wall. Only Sid's tank, with its heat lamps pointing down from above, remained as it had been before.

"I'm in here."

Walt stepped through the bedroom door, to the right of the fireplace, into the full splendor of Ginger's slovenliness. On the floor were books and clothes and more books and her photocopies of articles on MS-13: dozens and dozens of them, some of them with photos of kids showing off their 13 tattoos on their necks and faces and stomachs and wrists.

"I think maybe I like this thing after all," Ginger said. She was sitting in the middle of Blair Montgomery's waterbed. Her cheeks were puffy, her chin now with more of a green than fuchsia tint. The scrapes on her right cheek had begun to scab over and her nose, still puffy and red, had a discernible curve to it, like a tiny banana.

Walt sat down on the corner of the rubbery mattress. The two of them bobbed up and down for a moment.

"Do my new teeth make me look horsey? I feel like they're too big."

"No, they look great."

"Sorry, I'm slobbering a little. I can't feel my tongue." Her knees were propped up and she held a pen in her hand.

"What are you doing?"

"Writing the introduction to my book longhand. My mom hid my laptop. If she doesn't watch it there's going to be a chapter all about her." She set her journal down next to her. "You know something? You never talk about your dissertation. How's it going?"

"It's not." He felt a need to make some kind of excuse, which he resented but responded to anyway. "You know, the tutoring has been a little time-consuming—not just the meetings, but I've been trying to think about how to do a better job explaining things like grammar rules to her . . ."

Ginger yawned. "Sorry, I'm a little loopy from the local anesthesia." But Walt didn't believe her. He thought that just this brief mention of his work with Mercedes had—in a matter of seconds—bored her thoroughly. Even if she admired what he was doing, which was an open question, she didn't want to hear about it.

"So tell me more about *Girls I Know*. Do you have any interviews coming up?"

Really he was testing her to see whether or not she could resist the temptation to return once more to this tired subject.

"Actually, I think I'm done with the interviews. I'm flying back to New York with my mom on Friday. My dad put me in touch with a guy he went to school with who's a literary agent. I'm going to run the whole concept by him and see what he thinks. We're meeting at the Palm Court in the Plaza for lunch. You'd know how funny that was, if you were a New Yorker."

"I'll take your word for it. When are you getting back from New York?"

"It depends. If he thinks he can sell my book, I might stick around for a few days. Otherwise I'll be back early next week. Keep your fingers crossed for me, Walt."

"I thought you didn't care whether or not editors liked your book?"

"I care about getting the hell out of school, and if a publisher offers me a contract my parents are going to let me drop out. I have it in writing from them. Well, officially drop out. I'm already on medical leave. Getting hit in the head with a pipe does have its benefits. If only it didn't hurt so fucking much."

Walt wondered if Ginger really didn't want anything to do with Harvard. She had always claimed as much, but he had never believed her until right then.

"I'm feeling groggy, Walt."

"Can I get you anything?"

"No."

They both sat still. "Remember, Ginger, the other day, in the hospital, when you bounced that theory off me, about Ramon killing Flora to spare her?"

"Yeah. Have you been thinking about it?"

"I have, yes. And I have my own theory I'd like to ask you about."

"Okay."

He tried to collect his thoughts. "When you were poking around Boston, looking for members of MS-13 to interview for your book, I wonder if maybe that wasn't all you were doing. I wonder if maybe you were also trying, or at least some part of you was trying, to get hurt."

"You think I wanted this?" She pointed at her own face.

"Not *that*, exactly, but I do think you were taking the risks you were very deliberately."

"No, I get you." She stared down at her hands, at her long fingers. "I didn't want to get my skull fractured," she said. "But sure, I wanted to experience something . . . something real. I wanted to make a connection that wasn't just hypothetical, like so many connections are in philosophy. So I did some stupid things, clearly."

They both sat there. It was perfectly still in the apartment; the city seemed far away.

"We are pretty different," Walt observed. "I'm a poet. I mean, I see the world like a poet does. I make rhythms in my life, routines. I have rituals. I'm sentimental, idealistic. You're a philosopher. You want to understand stuff. Explain the world: get to the root of things. I guess we aren't very compatible."

"Oh, but compatibility is so overrated. Who wants to *share interests*? That sounds awful to me."

Walt reached over and took her hand. "I know you're going to hate hearing this, but I do feel sorry for you, Ginger. I'm sorry you were hurt like this."

"I don't hate hearing that. But you don't have to feel sorry for me, Walt. If this hadn't happened to me," once more she pointed at her face, "I wouldn't have figured out what was wrong with *Girls I Know*. I'm not saying the attack was a good thing. I'm not going to go that far, but I definitely learned from it, and maybe something good will come of that. If a better book is a good thing." She smiled at him thinly, her lips pressed together. Then she yawned again. "I'm so tired. Would you mind sitting here while I fall asleep? I'm afraid to sleep without anyone around."

"Sure."

Carefully, she shifted onto her side. Walt got up, drew the curtains, and then sat back down. Ginger reached her hand behind her hip. He held it. The two of them rocked softly on the waterbed. In just a few minutes, she had fallen asleep. An hour later, Mitzy Newton returned, her arms filled with shopping bags, and Walt slipped out of Ginger's room as quietly as he could, whispered goodbye to her mother, and headed back across the river.

CHAPTER 38

It rained all day Monday. Sitting at her tiny desk in Mrs. Greene's classroom, looking out the window, Mercedes pictured her grandmamma back at her house, pouring herself a cup of coffee, worrying about their trip over to Harvard Square later that afternoon: maybe her wig getting wet, maybe the two of them getting splashed walking down Dewey Street. Whenever it poured, the gutters clogged up and when the teenagers drove by, they'd swerve toward the puddles to try to kick up water. If they got you, you'd sometimes hear them laughing as they drove off.

She thought the rain was just going to keep on coming down into the night, but by the time Mercedes climbed onto the school bus at the end of the day, the sun had peeked out from behind the clouds. She took her seat way in back but she didn't take out the Frost book. She just stared out the window as they rattled along, at the pools of water in the street, thinking of all the people in the world who had died: enough to fill all the oceans and ponds with spirits. She pictured her momma waiting for her when she stepped off the bus. She imagined the two of them taking the T over to the Early Bird, picking up her daddy, and going bowling over in Telegraph Hill, like they did that one time. Her daddy was so strong, when his ball hit the pins they flipped around and made all kinds of racket. That was one place Mr. Steadman shouldn't go, on account of how loud noises scared him: a bowling alley.

Grandmamma was waiting for her just inside the door: her tan raincoat on, wearing those awful brown shoes of hers, the ones with the rubber soles and the Velcro bands that wrapped over their tops. Mercedes used the bathroom and then they stepped outside and her grandmamma locked the door and pulled against the knob a couple of times to make sure it wouldn't budge. She held her big old umbrella in her hand, the one that had the crack in the handle, but she didn't open it up because there was no rain. Instead, each time she took a step, she set down the metal tip of the umbrella on the sidewalk, so it went *click click click* as they walked along.

They didn't have to wait more than a minute for the bus. It pulled right up and they stepped on. Before, when she lived in Jamaica Plain, Mercedes never took the bus anywhere. Now she did all the time. She didn't like buses—didn't like the way they smelled, how they bounced up and down, and how people had to pull on that string to make the driver stop. The only thing she didn't mind on the bus was being able to look out the window. The sun was back behind the clouds again but no rain was falling, although you could smell the drops up there, waiting to tumble down.

In Harvard Square there were puddles everywhere, especially where the bricks in the sidewalk were sunk down. People all walked with their heads down, stepping around the water, lifting up their pant legs and skirts so they wouldn't get wet. She never saw anyone in a car try to drive through the puddles in this part of town. That was one difference between Watertown and Cambridge.

Inside the Greenhouse Coffee Shop, Grandmamma asked for a table for three. "You order that milkshake of yours when we sit down," she instructed Mercedes as they followed the hostess through the restaurant to a table in the far corner. "And drink it nice and slow. I need a glass of water."

The hostess set three menus on the table and Mercedes looked around for a waitress, but none of them seemed to notice them. They just kept on walking by, until Grandmamma tapped one on the arm. "I'd like a glass of water," she said to her. The waitress nodded, then glanced over at Mercedes, who pointed at the menu where *strawberry milkshake* was listed. The waitress took the menus and walked off.

"Are they this rude to you when Mr. Steadman is here?" Mercedes nodded and Grandmamma shook her head. "How a place like this stays open is a mystery to me." She pulled the money out of her purse that her granddaughter would need to pay for the milkshake and handed it to Mercedes, who placed it on the table.

Mr. Steadman came in right then, huffing and puffing. He saw them over in the corner and waved before stepping around the crowded tables and sitting down across from her, next to her grandmamma.

"You got your hair beaded." He pointed at the top of Mercedes's head.

"Her Aunt Denise did it for her. I can't, on account of my arthritis." Grandmamma tapped the table with her fingers just as the waitress set down the milkshake and glass of water and Mr. Steadman asked for some coffee. "Mercedes spent the weekend with her cousins," she added, after taking a long drink.

"Did you have fun?"

Mercedes shrugged. Why did adults ask questions like that? And suddenly she just missed everything so much. She missed the café. She missed her best friend, Kiki. She missed her bedroom in their old apartment: the way her sheets smelled, the purple walls. She wanted her daddy to pick her up and hold her. She wanted to put her head in her momma's lap and cry. She wanted her momma to be here so she could cry about her momma being gone. Without her nearby, Mercedes thought that if she started crying she'd never stop.

Grandmamma leaned hard against the table and stood up. "I'll leave you two," she said.

Where was she going now? She could barely stand. Mercedes handed her the umbrella. She and Mr. Steadman both watched her make her way slowly to the front of the restaurant. When she reached the door, one of the ladies walked around from behind the counter and opened it for her.

"She's tired, huh?"

Mercedes nodded. She pulled the Frost book out of her backpack. Her grandmamma's diabetes made her blood bad. That was why, on the weekends, they didn't do more. It wasn't because Grandmamma didn't want to be out and about; it was because her blood was bad.

"Where's your homework?" He eyed her, not like he was mad so much as like he was hoping maybe she'd let him in on a secret. She didn't say anything. "No homework this week?" She shook her head. "Really?" She nodded. They just had a long division worksheet to do. The schedule for the week was all different because this Friday they didn't have school.

"Let's talk about Robert Frost then. Do you have a favorite poem?"

She stared at the table. There was that one she liked so much. She wondered if he'd explain some of it to her. Her momma would want her to ask him questions if they were about poems, wouldn't she? Because she'd be learning, by asking and listening to what he had to say. Her momma would want the two of them to talk if their words weren't just filling the air for no reason. She would want that.

"I like the one about the trees. About the boy swinging from the branches."

Her voice was all scratchy. He leaned across the table to hear her better. "'Birches'?" She nodded. "I like that poem too," he said.

She opened the book and had to flip just a couple of pages to find "Birches." When she read a poem, if she didn't understand something, she'd pretend to write a question in the margin. Now she ran her finger along the edge of the paper, collecting her questions. "Mr. Steadman, what does it mean when he says he *subdued his father's trees?*"

"That means . . . well, he's bending them in the poem. The branches. *Subdue* means *bending*, more or less. He's making the trees his own, in a way."

The waitress brought Mr. Steadman a cup of coffee. When he took a sip, his face cringed.

"How do the trees belong to his daddy? They're too big for him to have planted."

"Maybe they're just on his land? I'm not sure—"

"What's a birch tree look like?"

"It's got these branches," he spread his fingers, "and, you know, leaves. How do you describe a tree? It's got branches, leaves, and a trunk."

He laughed. She laughed too, only without making a sound. It was maybe the first thing he had ever said that was actually funny: saying a tree had branches and leaves and a trunk. Why was that so funny? Maybe things were only funny when you couldn't say exactly why they were.

"My grandfather loved trees," Mr. Steadman said. "He knew all the different kinds. He taught me their names and how to identify them, but I've forgotten most of what he said. I was never any good at remembering that stuff. I wish I had written down everything he told me. But I still love trees, even though I don't know much about them."

She felt like that about her daddy's cooking. He had showed her how to make eggs, but whenever she had tried on her own, with just her momma there, they had never tasted right. She didn't want to make anything in her grandmamma's kitchen. There were hardly any spices in the cupboards and the stovetop had the kind of dirt on it that you couldn't wipe off and the counter had bubbles in it. You couldn't make anything in that kitchen that would taste decent; there was no way.

"Do you like trees?"

She tilted her head at him. That was a funny question. Didn't everyone like trees? She tried to think of why someone might hate them. Maybe if you had a little brother who was real sweet and one day a tree fell on him, then after that you would hate trees. But the tree would have to fall over on its own. If someone cut it down then you wouldn't hate the tree for falling, you'd hate the person for cutting it down.

Mercedes looked over the poem, not to read it, just to have something to look at while she thought. And she realized that she didn't just like trees; she loved trees. It was hard for her to think of anything on the ground that she loved more than trees, especially now that her momma and daddy were in water. She thought about it some more. Maybe she didn't hate Watertown just because her grandmamma's house was small and the floors were all tilted; maybe she also hated Watertown because there weren't many trees there. There were trees all around the school, big ones, but there weren't any nice trees on Dewey Street: just gutters that clogged up when it rained and cars missing hubcaps.

"I love trees," Mr. Steadman said to her. "I love the trees along the Charles, and in the Common. Maybe those are the best trees in Boston, the ones in the Common. Oh, and around Jamaica Pond. Those are great trees too."

She wasn't expecting him to mention the pond. No one had mentioned the pond to her since it had all happened. No one at school, no one in her family. But he just said it like there was nothing to it, like it was just a pond. She put her hand over her mouth. She didn't want the water to come out of her eyes, but it was hard to keep it in because he had caught her unawares, mentioning the pond like he had. She tried to breathe in dry air through her mouth to make the water inside of her stop churning.

"Oh, I'm sorry, Mercedes. I didn't mean to ..." Mr. Steadman pulled some napkins out of the dispenser. He pulled about twenty napkins out of it. They were the tiny napkins her momma didn't like. *You either give your customer a real napkin or you don't give them a napkin at all,* she used to say.

That helped, hearing her momma's voice in her head. She kept on breathing into the palm of her hand. She kept her eyes shut and thought of her momma when she just talked about nothing special: how nice her voice was to listen to, going up and down like a raft in water. She told herself she was a rock on the edge of Jamaica Pond. Did rocks cry? No, they did not. She blew her nose into one of the napkins. She told herself she was a tree, growing up next to her parents, drinking from them. Trees didn't cry neither.

She pulled the paper off the straw and took a sip of her milkshake. It didn't taste right. She was worried now that if she wasn't careful, the water would start to come out of her. She was worried it would get Mr. Steadman's grandmamma's book wet. Wouldn't that be something, after carrying it through the rain over and over again, if it got wet on account of her crying on it? That would really be something.

They sat there, the two of them, sharing the silence. They sat for a good little bit, until the waitress came by and asked if they wanted anything to eat. Mr. Steadman shook his head and she left the check for them.

"This might be the worst coffee shop in the world. What do you think?"

Mercedes nodded in agreement.

"I think it's about the worst." He pushed some of the napkins back into the dispenser. "Have you been back to the pond, since the winter?"

She shook her head.

He was thinking something. He opened his mouth but no words came out. He thought some more. "Would you like to go? I could take you. We could ask your grandmother. Would you like that?"

Every weekend, pretty much all year round, they had spent at least one afternoon at the pond. Sometimes she'd just walk around it with her daddy while her momma took pictures. Sometimes, in the warm months, she and her daddy would throw little rocks into the water, just to hear them go *plop!* They'd try to skip rocks along the water too, but neither one of them could do it very well.

She nodded.

"Maybe some weekend—"

"We don't have school on Friday."

"You don't? Why not?"

"Teacher workday. Then they have parent conferences. Grandparents can go to the conferences."

"Well, of course they can! *Parents* can mean grandparents too."

She believed him, since he knew all about words, but what he said surprised her. Parents were so different from grandparents. Grandparents were old and got tired so easily. And they dressed funny. She looked over just as her grandmamma stepped back through the doorway. She must not have felt up to walking around. Mr. Steadman saw her too. He left a few dollars on the table, next to her money, and they went over to meet her.

She waved them away. "Don't mind me. I'm back early. I didn't feel like doing any shopping. You just keep on working."

"Oh, no, we're done," Mr. Steadman said.

Her grandmamma looked at her. "Are you now?" Mercedes nodded. "Did you learn something, girl?" She nodded again.

"Let me walk outside with you," Mr. Steadman said. He held the door for them. They all crossed Mass Ave together and slowly made their way to the bus stop. They'd have a little wait now and there was nowhere nearby for her grandmamma to sit. Sometimes she'd try to lean against the big gate that opened into Harvard, but that didn't help her much. Mercedes wondered why they couldn't put a bench there for older people who got tired and had bad blood. That would have been the right thing to do.

"Mrs. Bittles, may I take Mercedes over to the Jamaica Pond this Friday, just for a little bit? She said she doesn't have school that day."

Grandmamma looked at him. "To the pond? You want to take her over to JP?" Her eyes narrowed. She was thinking hard. Mercedes watched her think. She was worrying about her, she could tell. *Don't worry about me,* she wanted to say to her grandmamma. *I'm a strong girl. I'm like a rock. Don't you worry about me.*

"It was my idea," Mr. Steadman explained.

Her grandmamma kept right on thinking. "Would you like to do that, Sweetness?"

Mercedes nodded.

"I can come by and pick her up—I mean, I can come out to your place on the bus. Say around ten in the morning?" He tapped the toe of his shoe against the sidewalk.

"No, I'll bring her into the square. That way you two can just get right on the T." Her grandmamma looked hard at her again. "You sure you want to go there? You don't have to. You can go there with your cousins in a few weeks, when it's a little warmer. You can go in the summer: all of us, Aunt Denise and Aunt Chantal, Uncle Dontrelle, all your cousins. We can all go together. You don't have to go right now. Do you want to wait?"

She shook her head. Grandmamma looked at Mr. Steadman. "You know what you're doing?"

He bit at his lip and glanced over at her, his chin bobbing up and down. "I think it might be good," he mumbled.

She squinted at him. "All right, then. I trust your judgment. You're a good teacher, Mr. Steadman." Grandmamma nodded for emphasis, kind of like she had just made up her mind on the subject right then.

Mr. Steadman seemed a little surprised. "Thanks," he stammered.

Their bus rounded the curve and made its way toward them.

"See you on Friday," he said to them both.

"We will see you on Friday," her grandmamma replied.

The bus door wheezed open and the two of them got on. Grandmamma paid their fares and they sat down right behind the driver, in the seats reserved for the elderly and handicapped. Mercedes could see Mr. Steadman through the window as he walked off. What did he do now? He couldn't have any family in Boston; if he did, then he wouldn't have spent all that time at the Early Bird Café. Did he make himself dinner? He couldn't cook, no way. Maybe he just read poems over and over again. She hoped he didn't. They made you sad, poems, if you read them without taking a break. She hoped he wasn't all alone. He didn't seem strong enough to be by himself all the time. He didn't even know how to make a fist. But he liked books a lot and they could keep you company, at least for a while. Still, she hoped he wasn't all alone. It was all so hard. Even if you were strong as could be, it was some kind of hard.

Walt walked back to his dorm room and sat down at his desk. He tried to read his *Norton Anthology*, but he was distracted by the liver spot on his left hand. It seemed more pronounced than when he had last looked at it. He wasn't getting any younger. What if Mrs. Bittles was right? What if he actually *was* a good teacher? Not in the sense that he could teach anyone, like his grandparents, but maybe in the sense that he could teach elementary school kids. Isn't that what she meant? Maybe that wasn't so crazy. Because he had helped Mercedes: that essay on Amelia Earhart was so much better than that thing she had first shown him, the paper on Paul Revere. It was just so much better. And he had come up with that worksheet . . .

He dragged the phone over from the side of his bed. The Post-it on which he had written Principal Reynolds's phone number was still stuck on his desk, right next to another Post-it reminding him to call the English Department to find out when Professor O'Shea had office hours. He dialed the principal's phone number. It was a little after five now; he assumed an answering machine would pick up, but instead he heard Mrs. Reynolds's voice, identifying herself cheerfully.

"Hello," he said. "This is Walt Steadman. You probably don't remember me; I'm tutoring Mercedes Bittles."

"Of course. Hi, Walt!"

"Hi. Listen, do you remember by chance . . ." he wrapped the phone cord around his finger. "You said . . . about Greater Boston." He was so nervous, his voice kept cutting out. He started over. "When we met that day, I think you mentioned being able to put me in touch with some teacher accreditation programs?"

"I sure did. Just a second, Walt." He heard the wheels of her chair squeak, then papers rustling in her hands. "Do you have a pen handy?"

CHAPTER 39

Wednesday morning, Walt woke up at almost eight. He showered, dressed, and grabbed the Gwendolyn Brooks collection he had tried to give Mercedes the other day, the book pointed out to him by the wide-eyed clerk at the Grolier Poetry Book Shop over on Plympton Street when he had asked for a recommendation of a racially or ethnically diverse poet. He headed off to Harvard Square. His plan was to sit in Au Bon Pain and try to reread Brooks's work for the first time since college, all while worrying about being shot in the head by someone with a *13* tattooed on his neck. Passing Out of Town News, he glanced down at the row of newspapers, none of which he ever intended to read again for the rest of his life, not after the Early Bird and Foss Park.

He stopped walking when he saw Ginger on the cover of that day's *Crimson*. It was the same student ID photo they had run after she had been attacked. But this story wasn't about her being attacked. A publisher had made an offer for *Girls I Know*. Ginger was on the cusp of signing what was described in the headline as a "six-figure book deal."

He paid for the paper and stepped away from the newsstand. Standing still in a stream of pedestrians, he tried to read the article from beginning to end, but all the sentences rushed together. He stepped over to the familiar bank of payphones and dialed Ginger's cell phone number. She picked up on the first ring.

"Hey, Walt."

"How did you know it was me?"

"You're *out of area*. Caller ID. We've been through this before."

"I just saw the *Crimson*. I'm holding it in my hand."

"God, can you believe those dweebs at the school paper got wind of it? Actually, I'm a little impressed."

"I can't believe—"

"The deal's not done yet."

"But it's going to be?"

"Apparently. Hey, it turns out selling a book is really easy. If I had known, I would have tried something harder."

Walt looked out on the square. For a moment, everything moving— the pedestrians, the cars—seemed to slow down, but then they sped up again. At first he had thought the whole concept was so stupid. A book comprising interviews with girls. For the longest time, he hadn't gotten it. He wasn't even sure now if he did.

"The confessional stuff I added was key. The bit I put in about getting the shit beaten out of me. All the editors liked that angle . . ." Ginger's voice trailed off.

"You sound so quiet," he said.

"That's because I'm not chomping on any gum. I can't chew gum anymore; it gives me a headache." She sighed. "No, it's just . . . Well, I guess I had mystified the whole publishing thing. I had expected a lot of rejections, so for everything to come together so quickly . . . I guess it's a little bit of a letdown."

Walt was tempted to point out that—among the general population—she might want to keep such lamentations about her quick success to herself, but he bit his tongue. A homeless man walked up to him and held out a Styrofoam cup. Walt opened his palm up toward the sky. "Come into Cambridge today, to celebrate. We can go walk around the Fogg Museum. I'll buy you a cup of coffee."

"Oh shoot, I'm still in New York. But I'm coming up to Boston tomorrow to clear my stuff out of Blair's apartment. Let's have brunch then, before I head back."

"You're moving away!"

"Yeah, back to New York."

"Just like that? In one day?"

"I don't have that much stuff to move."

"I wasn't thinking about your stuff."

There was a pause on the other end. "Don't get misty-eyed, Walt. New York and Boston are so close."

Who was she kidding? He would never visit her in the Big Apple. He'd get lost on the subway up to her apartment. No, he wouldn't even make it that far; he'd board the wrong train out of South Station and end up somewhere deep in Connecticut.

"My book's just bigger than Boston; that's what my editor says."

"He's probably right."

"It's a she."

"Of course." He felt a lump in his throat. Setting aside that she seemed to have every intention of leaving him behind, she was also content to turn her back on Boston, and he hated that. He hated that, as a city she had gotten to know as intimately as she did, the place didn't matter to her at all.

"How about we meet at the Charles Hotel?" she proposed.

"Okay, brunch at the Charles."

"None of this is a big deal, Walt. People move around."

"Right, I know. No big deal. Congrats again, on the book."

"Thanks."

He looked out across Mass Ave, at the redbrick buildings in the Yard, turned with their backs facing the square. "You're on your way," he said. "You're twenty and you're already on your way."

"Everyone's always on her or his way. It can't be helped."

She hung up on him. Walt no longer felt like drinking coffee and reading. He took a seat on the low concrete wall that wrapped halfway around the Harvard Square T Stop. He had been telling himself that he'd have to wait for her on the other side of her book; maybe this just meant his wait wouldn't be as long as he had imagined. He watched the Harvard undergraduates make their way up from the River Houses to the Yard: a steady stream, some chatting away in groups but just as many walking alone, staring ahead—grimly determined to go off and conquer the world. He stood up and began to walk, where he had no idea. He told himself to be happy for her, that what was good for Ginger would probably end up being good for him, too. She said her moving wasn't a big deal; he should believe her. Because they were connected, right? When she couldn't fall asleep by herself, he had held her hand. And pretty soon her book would be out of the way. There would just be the two of them; no more *Girls*

I Know. He walked past the bus stop where, just two days before, he had stood with Mercedes and Mrs. Bittles. *Of course I am happy for her,* he whispered to himself. *I am very happy for her. I am very, very happy.*

CHAPTER 40

"I'm going to kill myself," Javier said the next morning, when Walt returned from his shower. He was waiting for him in the hallway, a copy of the *Crimson* from the day before held in his hand. "I mean, six figures! What the hell! She's a child!"

Walt stepped around him, into his room. He went through his dirty clothes in search of garments that carried their dirtiness in the least obtrusive of ways. Javier watched from the doorway.

"You should tell her that a guy who lives in your hallway is on the cusp of committing suicide because of her book deal. Tell her I could have become an investment banker—that it isn't right that the kids whose papers I'm grading are selling books for six figures. Please tell her that."

"I'm not going to tell her that." Walt put on a pair of cords and a shirt with a collar. He ruffled his hair so it looked messy but not too messy. He stepped into his shoes. Since dinner the night before, Javier had been going on and on about Ginger's deal. Months before, when Walt had first spoken of her, Javier had summed her up as just another precocious Harvard undergraduate. Then, after the assault in East Somerville, he had reclassified her as a more-reckless-than-normal undergraduate. Now she was someone whose success required him to reassess his own life.

"She's got connections. She must have connections. You don't just write a book and have someone snap it up like that, not unless you know someone."

Walt ignored him. He knew, from his own experience, that nothing beneficial came from dwelling on Ginger Newton's Yankee peerage: that while her background explained her in a sense, this sense also missed who she really was. "I think I'm going to tell her that I don't want her to move to New York."

"You're going to tell her you like her?" Javier sounded disappointed. "Seriously, can someone give this girl some bad news?"

"I'm not the one for that mission. But, yeah, I'm going to say something about how I feel about her. She's tricky, though. I need to tell her I like her without making it sound like, you know, I *like* her."

"Right." He set his hands on the top of his belly, which had extended over the last month, and sighed contentedly. He was working the problem, which—as an economist—he couldn't help but enjoy. "Maybe you can point out that she's proven she can make a book work, but now she needs to prove that she can make a relationship work. Something like that, you know? Give her a challenge. She seems to like challenges."

"That she does." Walt plucked his parka off the floor.

"You've got to be confident too." Javier puttered back toward his room. "You have to exude confidence, but in a laid-back way."

"Right." Walt followed him into the hallway.

He leaned against his doorframe. "Remember, you've been there for her. All the time you spent in that hospital; you should bring that up, somehow."

Walt nodded as he shut the door to his room behind him.

"Hey, can I bounce something off you?" Javier grinned wryly. "It's an idea for a book. It'll be called *Graduate Students I Know* and will be made up of interviews . . ."

Walt headed for the stairwell.

Although the Charles Hotel sat in the middle of Cambridge, Walt had never been inside of it before. He had never been inside any of the hotels in Cambridge or Boston, since he had never had any out-of-town visitors. He passed through the low-ceilinged lobby and up the stairs to the main restaurant, Henrietta's Table, where brunch was served each day. Ginger was waiting for him at a table in front of the enormous windows that looked out onto the restaurant's patio, but she wasn't looking out the windows; she had opted to face the interior, where the people were.

"Hey, Walt!"

"Hi, Ginger."

She rose from her chair and circled the table. She had cut her hair in an oval to frame her face, the ends lingering just above her shoulders. She was wearing a camel-colored suede skirt and a black sweater. Her chin was still a little discolored from the attack and her nose, with its new curve, made her look older. When they embraced, he could smell her shampoo and body wash; he could feel her small, firm breasts, her right leg square up against his left thigh, and the smooth skin on the back of her neck where he had placed his hand.

"You smell like mold and sweat," she whispered, "like some nasty old graduate dormitory."

"You don't smell at all like your snake," he replied, his eyes closed.

"Oh, poor Sid. He's been neglected for so long now. I'm not the mother I once thought I was."

She pulled back from him. He lifted his hands off her body. He let her go. They sat down.

"Congratulations again on *Girls I Know*. That's amazing."

"It is, isn't it?" But she didn't sound very amazed. "Yeah, it's cool." She eyed the table. She didn't want to talk about her book deal, that was clear. It would be her curse, Walt decided, not to need any money and therefore to have it thrown her way again and again.

A busboy circled by with a pot of coffee. He filled Walt's cup. Ginger had been sitting there for a little bit; Walt could see her black leather journal, filled with scribbles, and a half-empty glass of orange juice.

"Is your editor asking you to change much?"

"She wants me to add some stuff. You know, interview New York girls, Jersey girls, make it more of an Eastern Seaboard thing. My editor thinks the category of the male is no longer interesting. She thinks we're done with it as a culture. She's all about the idea of *girls*. So, naturally, now I have my doubts. Well, I had them before, but I have more doubts now."

Walt took a sip of his coffee, which was nutty and piping hot and incredibly smooth. It was the best cup of coffee he had had since the Early Bird Café. A woman set a basket of bread on their table: wheat, rye, raisin, anadama. Heat billowed out of the basket, all the smells mixing together. Walt took a piece of rye. He sipped his coffee until he had finished it. As soon as he placed the empty cup on its saucer, the busboy glided back over and poured him another cup.

"Okay, enough about me. Have you made any progress on your dissertation?"

Walt added some cream and real sugar to his fresh cup of coffee. "Actually, I've decided that I don't want to be an academic."

"What do you mean?"

He felt nervous. "I love poems. I've always loved poems. But I don't want to write about poems. I just want to read them, maybe give the ones I like to other people to read. That's the kind of relationship I want to have with poetry. I don't want to be a critic."

She pushed against the edge of the table, extending her arms, so that the legs of her chair squeaked on the floor. "But in the Early Bird, when Ramon pointed the gun at you, you thought of your dissertation, bound on a shelf in Widener. You told me that!"

"I thought of what it would feel like to accomplish something. My dissertation was just a symbol of that." He fidgeted with the sugar packets on the table. "I just signed up for the Teacher Residency Program at UMass Boston. Classes start this summer. In the fall, I'll be working with a mentor. Then I'll get my own students the following year. There's a salary. It isn't much but it's something."

"Wait a second. You're going to teach elementary school?"

"I'm going to try." He took a bite of his bread; it melted in his mouth.

"In the Boston public school system?"

"That's the idea."

She leaned back in her chair, soaking it all up. Then she exhaled, scooted back toward the table, and took a sip of her juice. "All because of tutoring Mercedes Bittles?"

"No. Well, kind of. Because of a lot of things."

"So you two have connected after all?"

"I don't know if *connection* is the right word. We understand each other better. You were right and wrong about America: about class, about race. I was right and wrong as well."

"Well, I'm glad we've clarified all of that." She strummed the table with her fingers. He had fully expected her resistance to the idea of him becoming a teacher. It would never seem ambitious enough for someone like her. It would always sound too limiting, too small. She shifted uncomfortably in her chair. "Teachers get so ground down, Walt. You can pick them out on the street. They wear those polyester blends. They're all pasty. They have a dazed look in their eyes. I hate to think of you looking dazed."

They both sat still.

"Oh, I'm doing it again." Ginger shook her head. "I don't know what I'm talking about but I think I do. You know, ever since we met, you've listened to me way too closely. You've given me much more credit than I ever deserved. The truth is, I have no right to weigh in on your decision. I've never even been in a public school. What I'm thinking of isn't what that kind of work would be like, but what representations of it have looked like to me. I'm thinking of that Michelle Pfeiffer movie *Dangerous Minds*. I really hated that movie. I hate that kind of movie, about a teacher who goes into a classroom and changes lives. Yuck."

"I know what you mean." He opened the enormous leather menu and surveyed all of his options. He hadn't had a good meal in so long, he didn't know where to start. And they had everything at Henrietta's Table. It made him a little melancholic. He shut the menu. "You know, my grandparents were both teachers. They were *real* teachers. They knew what they were doing. They had the steadiness of good teachers. They were dogged. They made you listen to them without raising their voices. They let you know that what they were talking about was important without having to try to convince you. And it's not necessarily that I want to be *that* kind of teacher, but it's work that speaks to me. I get the stakes."

She nodded. "When you put it that way, I see what you mean."

"I should pay you back for the dorm room, since you thought you were funding an academic career. I mean, I should pay you back anyway—"

"Oh, I don't give a shit about that." And she smiled, dimples and all. "So that means we're both dropping out of Harvard. You for the second time! What a pair of losers we ended up being."

She lifted her water glass and they toasted their shared status as losers. Then, still staring into her eyes, Walt reached for her hand across the table.

"Hey, listen, don't move back to New York. Live with me. I'm going to rent a truly awful apartment somewhere. Rent it with me. We'll go fifty/fifty."

"A truly awful apartment, that's tempting."

"You'll learn to economize. It'll be fun for you."

"I'm sure it would be—"

"You'll finish up this book and the churning in your brain will die down some. No more Aquinas."

"No more Aquinas."

"I'll educate the young while you buy frozen rats for Sid. On the weekends, we'll go to your family's nearest vacation home."

"That'd be in Mattapoisett, but I'm warning you, it's a real dump—"

"And I'll teach you all about jazz. We'll listen to each of my records, one after the other. We won't play any of them more than once until we've listened to them all."

Ginger let his hand go. She ran her fingers through her hair. "All of that sounds lovely, Walt. The shitty apartment, the records. But wait a second . . . I thought you said we weren't compatible!"

"I thought you said compatibility was overrated!" He tried to maintain eye contact with her but he couldn't. She was looking askance now, at the floor.

"I'm sorry, Walt. I'm so sorry, but I have to go back to New York. I can't stay in Boston; I have to move on." She peered at him apologetically. It clearly pained her to hurt him, which hurt him all the more.

"You need someone to be around you," he said, trying his hardest not to sound as if he were pleading. "We all do. It's not a sign of weakness; it's a trait of our species."

"You sound like my mother."

Their server came by. Ginger ordered the fruit plate. Walt chose a cheese omelet with toast and hash browns. He chose something bland on purpose because he had a feeling he wouldn't be coming back to the Charles Hotel anytime soon and he didn't want to have to remember a great meal, along with everything else.

"I didn't say you needed someone to *take care* of you," Walt explained after they were alone again. "You should just have someone lingering around. And I have experience on that front, from my days as a superintendent. I'm a good lingerer."

She laughed loudly at that. "Oh, shit, Walt, believe me, if there was one person I'd choose for that thankless duty, it'd be you. But honestly, it would be thankless duty. You'd hate me after one month, or you'd go barking mad."

"Let me worry about that."

She looked down at the table. "It's just, there are so many things I want to do, and—you know—I'm not the best at pacing myself, which I think means I wouldn't make a very good *girlfriend*, not that I'm really comfortable with that term—"

"You don't have to explain." He felt tremendous sadness. He liked the idea of making his way through life with her. He didn't care anymore that her family had money, or that she had been given opportunities that someone like Flora, in her all too brief life, never had. The fundamental unfairness of life still pained Walt, but not in such a way that prompted him to point his finger at Ginger. That had been, he thought in hindsight now, more a strategy to unburden himself from any responsibility to remake the world that surrounded him than an expression of moral outrage.

"You want to hear about my next book?"

She wasn't kidding. These ideas of hers, they just excited her so much. She couldn't control herself. "I think it's going to be about birds, about how they migrate. I need to be done with humans for a while and birds are so interesting. Did you know the Bar-tailed Godwit can fly six thousand miles without stopping? Six thousand miles! And some birds can sleep in flight. Whinchats leave Europe in the fall to winter in the tropics . . ."

Their waitress brought out their food. In between her observations on avian navigation and the energy conserved by Canada Geese flying in V-formations rather than by themselves—upwards of twenty percent, according to a recent study—Ginger ate quickly. When she glanced down at the tiny watch on her wrist, Walt followed her gaze and noticed the manicured nails of her right hand: how the cuticles were—for the moment—unmauled, the fingers thin and delicate and refined. After they had both finished eating, she called over to the waitress and asked for their check, which the woman took out of her apron and placed on the table. When she did so, Walt realized that he hadn't felt anxious once during their meal, at least not about being shot. Even with his back to the entrance, it hadn't occurred to him until now how easily someone could have walked in with a gun and laid waste to all of them.

"I'm sorry, Walt, but I've got to meet my movers over at the apartment in twenty minutes."

"That's okay. Can I get it? Please."

But she had already pulled a credit card out of her purse. "Next time I'm in town, you can start to pay me back for all your mooching." She grinned at him.

The waitress scooped up Ginger's card and zipped off. She was back in a flash. And suddenly the scene that Walt had conjured and mulled over in anticipation began to slip away. Ginger signed the receipt, tossed her card into her purse, and stood up. They walked out of the restaurant, descended the carpeted steps, and passed through the lobby, onto the brick courtyard that wrapped around the front of the hotel. Now awash in sunlight, Ginger waved at a taxi idling about thirty yards from them. When it pulled up, Walt opened the door for her. She stepped into the taxi and rolled down her window.

"You'll make a great elementary school teacher."

"Do you think so?"

"I do. You'll look good, standing in front of a chalkboard."

"And I won't have the guts to give anyone a bad grade."

"Right. You'll be the ultimate pushover. They'll love you."

She smiled at him, her eyes squinting in the sun. He stepped back from the car. Not right away, but a few months down the road, he would really worry about her. He would think of her, obsessing about her latest project, and there would be so little he would be able to do. But she wanted it that way. That was why she had moved out of her dorm; that was why she was leaving Boston. When things felt easy, she moved on.

"Just call if you ever want to talk," she hollered. "No biggie." The taxi lurched into traffic as Ginger waved out the window. "I'm going to miss you!"

He watched the cab tear down Eliot Street, then turn onto JFK and disappear. And he couldn't help it: he wondered—really wondered— if he'd ever see her again.

Javier was sitting in the hallway, reading, while he waited for him to return. "What'd she say?" he asked when Walt appeared.

Walt opened the door to his room and threw his parka inside. "She said she has to move on. Her next book is going to be about birds. She said she cares about me, but she has to move on."

"She said no to being with you because she's going to write a book about birds?"

"Basically."

"She chose birds over you!"

"If you want to look at it that way."

Javier stood up. "I'm so sorry, man," he mumbled.

"No, it's okay. It could be much worse, all things considered."

"Yeah." He tilted his head at him. "You're a good-looking guy, you know? You'll be okay."

"Being a good-looking guy hasn't seemed to help me much up to this point in my life."

"You've got to use it more to your advantage."

"How do I do that?"

"Look at me! Obviously I have no idea." He drifted into his room and reappeared a moment later, his book bag slung over his shoulder. "Want to meet for dinner? Say around seven?"

"Okay."

The two of them exchanged an awkward high-five. Then Javier headed off to the library and Walt reentered the silence of his tiny room.

He walked over to the window. Outside, a few guys were throwing a football around. He watched them run lazy patterns, their passes skidding off the grass, bouncing against trees. He could do that, he realized. He could go out and buy a football somewhere and call up

Max and Scott, his old grad school friends, to see if they wanted to run around some. He'd have some explaining to do—he had disappeared for some time now—but they had disappeared themselves in the past. He didn't think he'd ever tell either one of them about witnessing the shootings at the Early Bird. He'd blame his disappearance on *The Poetics of Yankee Peerage*. That way, they would be able to keep their immaculate versions of Boston, or at least he wouldn't be responsible for their desecrations.

He grabbed his *Norton Anthology* and plopped down on his bed. So what if he was about to turn thirty and had just gotten his heart broken by a twenty-year-old girl from New York? At least, for the first time in a really long time, imagining his future didn't fill him with dread. After a long winter, Walt didn't feel quite so afraid anymore.

JAMAICA POND

CHAPTER 41

Mr. Steadman was waiting for them right at the bus stop in Harvard Square. He had parted his hair, which made him look older and kind of funny. And he was wearing a nice shirt, not one of those sweaters of his. Still, he needed some new clothes; the jeans he always wore had seen better days, and his shoes were all dirty and scuffed up.

Her grandmamma had made her bring along a jacket, in case it rained, but Mercedes wasn't the slightest bit cold, so on the bus she had taken it off and tied its sleeves around her waist. She was wearing a pair of jeans herself, along with a purple and white argyle sweater her momma had given her for Christmas. It was Mercedes's favorite sweater, but she hadn't worn it once since moving to Watertown. It was too nice to wear to school. So she put it on this morning, for her trip out to Jamaica Pond.

"Looks like the weather's cooperating," Mr. Steadman said to them as they stepped off the bus.

"It does. Am I meeting you back here?" Grandmamma asked.

"No, I can bring her home to you."

She nodded, then pulled three dollars out of her handbag, only vMr. Steadman waved it away. "No, no, this is on me. I insist. It was my idea."

She looked right at him to make sure there was no misunderstanding. Then she turned and put both her hands on Mercedes's shoulders, like her daddy used to do to get her attention. "If you don't feel like being there, you tell Mr. Steadman and he'll bring you right home. Do you understand?" Mercedes nodded. Her grandmamma raised her eyebrows at Mr. Steadman. "Understood," he said. "All right then." And she shook his hand.

They left her standing at the bus stop and walked down the street to the T entrance in the square. From there they rode the Red Line into Boston, standing between all sorts of people: some of them dressed real nice, others wearing dirty clothes and smelling bad. Mr. Steadman tried hard the whole time not to bump into anybody. He seemed a little nervous. Mercedes wasn't; she loved riding the subway. She loved the feeling of moving underground, of the city being up there above her, not knowing where she was, but waiting for her to come back. At Downtown Crossing they got on the Orange Line. There were plenty of seats open all around them and they sat down. Having the car pretty much to themselves seemed to calm Mr. Steadman down. He stared out the window while Mercedes tried to pay attention to everything: to how the train rocked on its tracks, to how, whenever they pulled out of a station, the people walking on the platform looked like they were moving in slow motion. She wanted to take it all in because she didn't know how long it'd be until she was on the T again.

"So your grandparents raised you?" The train came up above ground right before the Mass Ave Stop. Mr. Steadman shifted in his seat when she spoke. She didn't know much about him, just what he had told her that day in the coffee shop. And he had been a regular at the café. But that was about all she knew. Now she was trying to figure him out a little. He wasn't like anyone she had ever known: young and old at the same time. And he spent Monday afternoons with her, trying to help her learn, even though he didn't have any money.

He nodded.

"Growing up, did you have cable TV?"

Mr. Steadman shook his head. "No. Well, no one had cable back then. But we had a terrible TV situation. We only got a couple of stations." He paused. "Your grandmother doesn't have cable, does she?"

Mercedes shook her head.

"No big deal. Look at me; I grew up without it and I turned out fine."

"But you don't have a job, Mr. Steadman."

"That's true. Not at the moment. But I'm starting one here in a little bit. I'm going to be a teacher. What do you think of that?"

"Aren't you already kind of a teacher?"

"Yeah, I'm just going to make it official."

They pulled into and out of Roxbury Crossing. This was her Aunt Denise's stop. "How old are you, Mr. Steadman?"

"I'm twenty-nine." Her mouth opened a little; she couldn't help it. Weren't you supposed to be married at twenty-nine? Weren't you supposed to have kids? "Actually it's pretty young," he said. "Frost didn't publish *Mountain Interval* until he was in his forties. Some people get started later than others, but it doesn't matter when or where you get started, it just matters where you end up, right?"

She nodded, mostly because it seemed like he really wanted her to agree with him.

"My grandmother would read to me all the time when I was your age," he added. "She would read poems to my mother and me at night. She has a great reading voice. Slow but not too slow, and melodic."

The train bounced on the tracks.

"Where does your family live, Mr. Steadman?"

"Burlington, Vermont."

"Do you miss them?"

"Yeah, I do. I never used to, and I told myself that was because of how they were. You know, my grandmother's pretty old and my mom is sick. But now I think I didn't miss them because for a while I didn't know what to do with myself. I was kind of floating there for a little bit. I think it can be hard—when you're older—to be around your family when you don't know what you're doing with your life."

Her Uncle Randy was in jail because her grandmamma said he had never known what to do with himself. So it must be awfully important, when you got older, to always know what you should be doing. No wonder adults never looked like they were having much fun.

They rode the rest of the way without saying anything. When they stepped off the train, onto the platform at the Green Street Station, Mercedes felt all shaky inside. Even though she had eaten a big breakfast, she felt like she did when she was real hungry. The station smelled like it always had; it looked the exact same. That didn't seem right. Outside there was the playground where she had always played, and the fountain she used to run in, only it was turned off. Still, there were kids playing, and their parents watching them, all tired looking. That was the other thing about adults: lots of the time they looked so tired.

She turned away from the playground. She didn't want to see anyone who might recognize her. She didn't want to hear anyone call out her name. She didn't want to have to introduce Mr. Steadman. What if they asked what the two of them were doing there? What would she say?

They walked down Green Street, past the homes her momma had liked so much. *Any of these would do just fine, John,* she'd say when they'd walk around on the weekends, looking at houses. *I don't need a mansion, just something we can call our own.* And her daddy would shake his head while she led them around the neighborhood. *How come your hip never bothers you when we're looking at homes we can't afford?* he'd ask her, and they'd all laugh.

As they neared the end of Green Street, Mercedes realized that they weren't just headed toward the Jamaica Pond; they were walking toward the café too. She wanted to see the pond, but she didn't want to see the café. What if, somehow, people were still eating breakfast there? What if people she didn't know were running her momma and daddy's restaurant?

Mr. Steadman slowed down a little. He must not have thought about seeing the café either. They crossed over to the other side of Green Street. There was the dog grooming store and the bakery. There was the post office. She didn't let her eyes wander across the street. But then they were standing at the corner and there was no way to avoid looking. So she did; she looked across Centre Street.

The café wasn't there. The building was still there; she knew that because the second story looked the same. But the Early Bird Café was gone. There was no yellow awning. And the door wasn't blue anymore; it had been painted white.

Mercedes stared at the door. Had someone thought that her momma had been trying to be special, *putting on airs,* as her grandmamma

called it? Is that why they had painted it white? They must not have
known that, in Haiti, when her momma was a little girl there, people
had always painted their doors, because it was a big deal, having a
door. Besides, in Voodoo, that was one way you welcomed the good
spirits, by painting your door a bright color. Her momma hadn't had a
door to her house there because it wasn't a house where she had lived;
it was a little hut. So when her momma and daddy were at the bank,
borrowing the money to open the restaurant, right after they signed
the papers, her momma told the man who was helping them that the
first thing she was going to do was paint the door to their café blue,
because blue was the color of the water that had taken away her sister
and her two brothers. Her daddy had told her this story a hundred
times. And the man at the bank had said, *I hope you do paint the door
blue, Mrs. Bittles.* He had thought it was a good idea. That was like the
bank giving its permission for her to do it. Wainwright Bank: that was
the name of the bank. If anyone needed to check, they could go over
there and ask them.

"They painted the door," she said. She didn't mean to say it; the
words slipped out. Mr. Steadman just stood real still. "Why did they
have to paint the door?"

"Well," he stared along with her, "I suppose a new store is going
to open there, and maybe the people who are opening that store want
a white door."

"But everyone has a white door."

"That's true."

He looked away. He seemed nervous. Maybe it scared him, seeing
the café, even though the café was gone. Maybe it scared him, seeing
where it once was.

"I don't know why things have to change," he said. "I've never
understood that."

It wasn't right, making the café disappear like they had done. It
was like saying nothing her momma and daddy had touched was
allowed to stay in the world. Like with the dead. They were in water,
like her momma said, but why couldn't they still be in their bodies?
Why did the living have to be on the ground and the dead in water?
She didn't understand why the rules had to be so strict.

"Come on," Mr. Steadman said. And he took her by the elbow and together they walked over to Burroughs Street. This was the way she and her daddy had always gone to the pond, right past the really big, really beautiful homes: so beautiful, her momma had never liked walking by them, because—she said—working hard wasn't enough to get one of these places. You needed more than that.

She and Mr. Steadman crossed Jamaicaway and walked toward the pond. There were people jogging, some of them even in shorts, and couples holding hands. There were babies being pushed in strollers and a dad trying to get a kite in the air with his kids and dogs, lots of dogs, pulling on their leashes. The two of them sat down on one of the benches that faced the water. Out in the distance, she counted five white sails and even more canoes and kayaks. And there was the water itself, light blue, and the trees hanging over the pond on the far side, with trunks and buds and branches: the wind sweeping through them. It was a real pretty day.

They both looked out at the pond for a while. Mercedes could hear the wind blowing but she couldn't hear the water lapping against the rocks. The joggers on the path behind them hardly made any sound, just their shoes scraping and their breathing. When the paddles from the canoes and kayaks hit the water, she could see the sunlight flash, but she couldn't hear any splashes. She wanted to push against the silence. It was strange; at the moment, she didn't want to be the quiet's only friend.

"Do you know how to swim?" she asked Mr. Steadman abruptly.

"I do, yes."

"I do too."

She gazed at the pond. It hadn't changed at all. It was just like she remembered it. It wouldn't ever change, would it? They wouldn't let the pond change, the people who ran the city, not like they had let the café change. They wouldn't let that happen to the pond because it wasn't a place you could say belonged to one person more than another, so it would always be the same, wouldn't it?

"I miss your dad's omelets," Mr. Steadman said out of nowhere. "He'd put paprika in the Spanish one, wouldn't he?"

She nodded. He had shown her how to make a Spanish omelet

once, on the griddle at the café. He had let her beat the eggs. He had handed her the ingredients, one after the other. She made the whole omelet, from beginning to end. Her daddy said it was good enough to serve out front, but they didn't serve it. They shared it between them. All along, she had always thought she loved food, but really she had just loved her daddy's food.

"I loved his cooking. And your mom, she was so fun to talk to." His voice was way back in his throat. She glanced over at him. He had put his hand up to block his face from her view. He was hiding behind his soft hand.

She stared at the water. She told herself her momma and daddy were right there, out in the middle of the pond, where the water was deepest and clearest. They would always be right there. And now she was sad. Now it didn't help her to see her parents as water. It helped sometimes in Watertown but it didn't help here. She wanted her parents to be sitting next to her. She wanted her daddy to squeeze her tight, his hands smelling of eggs and syrup. She wanted her momma to chase after her on her bad hip, telling her she was in some kind of trouble. And then she wanted to feel folded into her arms. She wanted her momma and daddy to be as close as they could be.

"How come you aren't dead, Mr. Steadman?"

"What's that?"

All morning, when she had asked him other questions, this was the question she was really thinking of, and now it just came out of her on its own.

"That day, when Ramon shot everyone . . . you were there, weren't you? So why didn't he shoot you too?"

Mr. Steadman puckered his lips. He ran his fingers through his hair. "I got very lucky. He tried to shoot me, but his gun jammed. I know that doesn't make any sense, and I wish I could explain it better, but that's just what happened. I was really lucky. I was the only one who was lucky."

How could the gun go off when he pointed it at her momma and daddy and Flora but not when he pointed it at Mr. Steadman? He was right; it didn't make any sense.

"I'm sorry," he added.

"Don't be sorry. I'm glad you're not dead, Mr. Steadman."

"Thanks, Mercedes," he said.

She looked out over the water. She tried to keep her mind blank and just stare at the pond. That way, she could be a rock. But it wasn't the same when you were in Watertown and said you were a rock by the Jamaica Pond and when you were actually sitting there, looking at the pond yourself. She could feel the tears, building up behind her eyes, so she started breathing through her mouth to dry them out, but they were just building and building and before she could help it they started trickling out. It wasn't her fault; the pond was pulling the tears out of her, taking her water for itself. She had been so strong; her momma had to be proud of her. She hadn't cried at the funeral. She hadn't cried the first day at school, when everyone was looking at her and whispering. She had never cried on the bus once. She had never cried in front of her grandmamma. She had been real strong. But now she wasn't feeling very strong.

"Oh, geez, I'm so sorry, Mercedes." Mr. Steadman put his hand on her shoulder. His breath was catching and his nose was running. He kept on sniffling. "I'm so sorry. I shouldn't have brought you here. I thought it might be nice, to see the pond again, but I didn't think it through. I'm so sorry."

She shook her head. This was where she wanted to be, that was the thing. It was just hard to be here.

"We can go right now if you want. I'm real sorry." He stood up but she shook her head again and he sat back down.

She started to cry real hard now: so hard, her shoulders bent in, her elbows digging into her sides. She felt her throat tighten and ache. There were tears running down the back of her mouth while other tears ran down her cheeks. Tears on the inside and outside of her all at once. She set her head down on her forearms so that the tears fell onto the ground between her knees. She cried like this for a long time. She made the dirt between her feet turn dark with her water. And then she began to cry less. She sniffled a few times, wiping her nose on the sleeve of her sweater. When she looked out at the pond again, it was the same as before, only the light had changed because the sun had gone behind a cloud. And she had stopped crying, even without feeling her momma's hands patting her head. She had stopped crying on her own.

The minutes went by. She could hear Mr. Steadman sniffle a few times but she didn't look over at him so she wasn't sure if he was crying or not. It was okay if he was; she wouldn't think any less of him. Mr. Steadman wasn't like other grown men; she knew that. She had pretty much always known that. But she hadn't been fair to him before. He was a good person, Mr. Steadman. He was his own kind of something.

The two of them just sat on the bench in the silence, looking out at the water, until Mr. Steadman spoke. "I reread those Gwendolyn Brooks poems," he said, his voice all cracked and unsure of itself. "She wrote one about Robert Frost that I had completely forgotten; isn't that something? I was thinking we could read them along with some other poems I have in this big book called an anthology. Do you know what an anthology is?" He glanced over at her. "An anthology is a bunch of poems all put together, written by a whole lot of different people."

She didn't say anything. There weren't any words in her right then. She was empty inside.

They sat there for a good long time, looking at the pond. And then Mr. Steadman stood up. "I guess we should be getting you home," he said.

Mercedes didn't want to go. It didn't feel right. But staying all day wouldn't make a difference. She'd have to leave at some point. Still, it didn't feel right, just walking away. It felt like she should do something, so she held out her hand and waved goodbye to the pond. She waved at the water, and then they walked off.

It took a long time for them to make it all the way back to Harvard Square on the T, and even longer for the bus to come to take them out to Watertown. The whole time, neither one of them said anything. She had worried that the quiet wouldn't take her back if she cried, but she was wrong. The quiet had been waiting for her the whole while.

Her grandmamma had put on one of her old aprons and was arranging two small flowerpots on the stoop when they walked up to her house.

"I hope it's not too early for these geraniums," she said to Mr. Steadman, before looking over at Mercedes. "Probably is, but we need to brighten things up a little bit, don't you think?"

Mr. Steadman nodded while her grandmamma looked her over, her eyes squinting so hard, it was a wonder if she could see out from behind her eyelids.

"How was the pond?"

Mercedes nodded. Grandmamma gave Mr. Steadman a look as well.

"It was good," he said. Then he turned to her. "So this coming Monday, we'll start our new poets. I'll bring along my *Norton Anthology*. You'll like that book; it's huge."

Mercedes nodded. "Thank you, Mr. Steadman," she said.

"Yes, thank you, Mr. Steadman." Mrs. Bittles wiped her hands on the front of her apron and extended them both toward him.

"You're welcome," he said to both of them, and then, just to her: "I'll see you on Monday, Mercedes. Don't forget your homework."

They watched him step off the stoop and then walk down the sidewalk, his head bobbing as he moved along. Mercedes wondered what was going on in his mind. Maybe he was wishing that he owned a car, or thinking about that girl who had paid for his room, or one of the poems he liked a lot, or her daddy's cooking. The thing was, you never really knew what other people were thinking. There was no way to be sure.

They stepped inside. Her grandmamma locked the door behind them. Mercedes hated the sound the bolt made when it went into the doorframe. She walked back into her bedroom. She was going to read on her bed like she always did, but then she decided to bring the Frost book out with her into the living room: keep her grandmamma company a little, since she had been gone all morning.

Grandmamma was sitting in the ugly yellow chair, reading a *Reader's Digest*. There were cartoons in those magazines, Mercedes had looked at them, but they were cartoons for adults; there was nothing funny about them.

"This woman, her car went into a ravine and they pulled her out with something called the *Jaws of Life*. Pulled her right out of the roof of her car! How about that!"

Mercedes lay down on the couch and put her feet out over the end. She opened the book right to "Birches."

Her grandmamma set down her magazine.

"Whatcha doin' over there, girl?"

"Reading."

"Are you now? Whatcha reading?"

"Robert Frost."

"My my. Reading Robert Frost. Always reading Robert Frost."

She could feel her grandmamma's eyes on her, watching her read. Maybe grandparents were like parents, at least in the way they could just watch you without doing anything.

"I do love you, Sweetness." She sounded tired, the way she said it: not like she was trying to be nice so much as just admitting the truth. There were the two of them in this little house. That was it. There were just the two of them.

Mercedes finished the poem and turned the page. "I love you too, Grandmamma."

CHAPTER 42

Walt stood at the bus stop, but after waiting a few minutes, he realized that he didn't need a ride back to campus; it was a beautiful spring day, after all. So he began to head down Mount Auburn Street, past the small apartments and storefronts pressed up against the sidewalk. He passed the Mount Auburn Cemetery on his right while cars barreled beside him. On his own two feet, he entered Cambridge from the west, from Watertown.

He walked very slowly. He felt oddly calm. He had wanted to see the pond for the same reason that his favorite poets liked to write about the spring: because when the trees began to bud and the grass started to turn green it felt as if there was no such thing as death — that what had seemed to die had really just gone underground, to reappear a few months later. When he had imagined their trip across the town, he hadn't even thought of the Early Bird Café, at least he hadn't thought of the restaurant itself. But then he realized, looking at its whitewashed door, that the city was like the pond. It too was always making itself anew, always covering up its losses, always trying to start over.

Mount Auburn forked to the right but Walt walked straight ahead, onto Brattle Street. On either side of him these massive, beautiful homes loomed, with their enormous porches, green shutters, and flagpoles. They were houses but at the same time they were old residents of Cambridge themselves: imperturbable and aloof. Even though they were contained within the city, they were somehow insusceptible to change. They didn't cover up their losses. Rather, they looked out on their surroundings with a combination of sympathy and disdain.

As he neared Harvard Yard, Walt decided that he wasn't ready to go back to Perkins Hall. It had been so long since he had just gone on a walk, with no particular destination in mind. So instead of heading left, toward the Science Center, he turned right and walked in the direction of Harvard Square, toward the Charles River.

He passed through the square, by Out of Town News. He thought of Mercedes, how she had dressed so nicely to visit the pond, the place her mother had photographed all those times. There was something heartbreaking about seeing children in nice clothes. He wondered what Ginger was doing right then: probably hunkered over her laptop somewhere in New York, working on her book. He thought of his family. It was lunchtime. That meant his grandmother was feeding his mother at their kitchen table: spoonfuls of applesauce and mashed potatoes and vanilla pudding. Baby food. Stuff she could swallow easily. Sometime in the near future, he would take the Vermont Transit bus up through Fitchburg and Keene, through Rutland and Middlebury, all the way to Burlington, just to tell them in person that he wasn't going to finish his PhD. And while they would be proud of his decision to become an elementary school teacher, the announcement would crush them both a little; they would so hate to let Harvard go. And Walt thought of meeting Mrs. Reynolds at the Lowell Elementary School, and her suggestion that led him to look into becoming a teacher, none of which would have happened if he hadn't gotten involved in Mercedes's life. And he thought of Ginger, sitting in her hospital bed with her face broken apart, and Flora, shot in the head. And then he thought of Mercedes once more, now weeping at the pond, and then Ginger again, and then his mother and grandmother, and then Natalie Bittles and Flora. He pictured the living and the dead. He thought of all the girls he knew.

The flow of pedestrians carried him along, past Tower Records and Urban Outfitters and the coffee shop on the corner that changed hands all the time. On his left, he passed Kirkland and Eliot House, those beautiful, majestic dormitories where the Harvard undergraduates lived, and then the John F. Kennedy Park opened up on his right. Walt crossed Memorial Drive and took a left so that he could walk along the banks of the Charles. The wind whipped through the sycamore trees, scattering their buds like mist. As the joggers and the rollerbladers and the couples holding hands passed him on this early spring day, he walked slower and slower, until he stepped off the path, sat down in the grass, and looked out across the river, toward Boston.

An eight-man shell passed him in the water. He could hear a woman on the path behind him, on her cell phone, making dinner plans. He could hear a girl saying to her boyfriend, "Get out of here!" while the boyfriend laughed loudly. They were students. They would live here for a time and then they would move away. But he wouldn't move away. Even if he needed one day to take care of his mother, he would take care of her here. Walt would stay in Boston until he died. And he listened to these students behind him laughing, these kids on the cusp of becoming adults, and next—quite naturally, or so it seemed to him—he thought of his sperm, frozen in test tubes across the river, waiting to be parceled out, waiting to be put to some use. How funny that he, of all people, cast such a web through Boston: that he, of all people, was linked to so many. Years would go by and Walt would still never be *from* here; he knew that. He would never be the mayor of Boston. He would always be an interloper. But nonetheless, he would also be a city father. Over time, his bloodline would flow and branch like a river, out into the compassionate and cruel corners of this city that he would nourish so. This city he did not hope to understand. This beautiful, this melancholic metropolis. This patchwork of townships and enclaves where he would grow old teaching the young.

Acknowledgments

My deepest thanks go to my agent, Miriam Altshuler, who was a supporter of this project from its earliest incarnation, and a tireless, levelheaded friend. At SixOneSeven Books, Andrew Goldstein and Michelle Toth acquired, edited, and published this work, improving it immeasurably along the way. Forming friendships with both of them was an unexpected windfall to writing this book for which I am very grateful. My colleague and confidante Eileen Pollack went through *Girls I Know* more than once, each time with great intelligence and ruthlessness. Over the years, Nicholas Delbanco has shared with me his considerable wisdom and advice, about writing specifically and life more generally, and I am indebted to him in more ways than I can record here. C. Dale Young, a gifted poet and doctor, generously offered his medical expertise for crucial scenes in this story. My dear friend Kevin Kopelson was a sounding board for me throughout the writing process, and a shrewd reader at its conclusion, as were Danny Hack and John Whittier-Ferguson. The Ucross Foundation provided me with an incredible studio space in which to work as a writer-in-residence. My parents, Ben and Libby Trevor, have been unfailingly supportive of me my entire life. This book is dedicated to my children, William and Cecelia, and in memory of my sister, Jolee.

Portions of chapter seven first appeared as a short story, also entitled "Girls I Know," that Michael Koch was kind enough to edit and publish in *Epoch* (vol. 53, no. 2, 2004). I am also grateful to Dave Eggers and Laura Furman for anthologizing the story in *The Best American Nonrequired Reading 2005* and *The O. Henry Prize Stories 2006* respectively, and encouraging me in my work on this book.

Some events in the recent history of Boston have been resituated in time and altered slightly to suit the narrative of this story and the needs of the characters, none of whom are drawn from real people.

If you live in the Boston area and are interested in supporting tutoring, reading, and writing programs for under-resourced youth, please consider donating to—or volunteering at—Grub Street or 826 Boston. Outside of Boston, if there is no 826 chapter close to where you live, a list of allied nonprofit organizations can be found online at http://www.826national.org/.

About the Author

Douglas Trevor is the author of *The Thin Tear in the Fabric of Space* (University of Iowa Press, 2005), which won the Iowa Short Fiction Award and was a finalist for the Hemingway Foundation/PEN Award for First Fiction. His short fiction has appeared in *The Paris Review, Glimmer Train, Epoch, Black Warrior Review, Ontario Review, The New England Review,* and about a dozen other literary magazines. His stories have also been anthologized in *The O. Henry Prize Stories* and *The Best American Nonrequired Reading.* He lives in Ann Arbor, where he is an Associate Professor of Renaissance Literature and Creative Writing in the English Department at the University of Michigan. This is his first novel.

CPSIA information can be obtained at www.ICGtesting.com
Printed in the USA
BVOW071459070413

317477BV00001B/4/P